MUSICAL DIMENSIONS

A Festschrift for Doreen Bridges

*Edited by
Martin Comte*

MUSICAL DIMENSIONS

A Festschrift for Doreen Bridges

*Edited by
Martin Comte*

Australian Scholarly Publishing

© Martin Comte 2009

First published 2009
Australian Scholarly Publishing Pty Ltd
7 Lt Lothian St Nth, North Melbourne, Vic 3051
TEL: 03 9329 6963 FAX: 03 9329 5452
EMAIL: aspic@ozemail.com.au
WEB: scholarly.info

in association with

Australian Society for Music Education Incorporated
ASME Monograph No. 8
PO Box 5
Parkville
Victoria 3052
Australia
www.asme.edu.au

ISBN 978 1 921509 41 4

All Rights Reserved

Copyediting by Martin Comte
Design and typesetting by Sarah Anderson
Cover Photograph and Paper Engineering by Sarah Anderson

CONTENTS

Editor's Note		ix
Contributors		xi
Introduction Margaret Whitlam AO		xxv

1	The Many Facets of Music Martin Comte	1
2	The Australian Test for Advanced Music Studies: A Watershed in the Assessment of Musical Ability Jennifer Bryce	16
3	Studio Music Teachers and Teaching: Roles and Responsibilities Amanda Watson	28
4	Establishing Dalcroze Teacher Education in Australia: A Task for Sisyphus Joan Pope and Sandra Nash	37
5	The Developmental Music Program Deanna Hoermann	57
6	Principles and Practices and Musical Truths Richard Gill	67

7	A More Comprehensive Approach to Music Teaching	
	Robert J. Werner	71
8	The Melbourne UNESCO Seminar, 1956:	
	A Watershed in Australian Music Education Jane Southcott	80
9	Arts and Academies: The Australian Musical Experience	
	David Tunley	99
10	That Everyone May 'Gather His Quota' Jamie C. Kassler	110
11	Music Education in the 21st Century:	
	Challenges and Predictions David G. Woods	121
12	Informing Practice in Early Childhood	
	Music Education Sheila C. Woodward	133
13	Research into Self-concept Development, Academic Achievement	
	and Musical Participation of Adolescents Jennifer C. Rosevear	147
14	Singing Locally; Thinking Globally: Why Community	
	Choirs Matter Tom Bridges	159
15	Learning to be a Composer George Palmer	169
16	Two Spells Ross Edwards	176
17	Music for Children and Young People David Forrest	178

18	Schumann and the English Critics: A Study in Nineteenth Century Musical Reception Janet Ritterman	192
19	Georg Benda's Keyboard Sonatas Warren Bourne	212
20	Musicianarchy Michael Kieran Harvey	229
21	A Case for Multiculturalism in the General Music Classroom Marvelene C. Moore	235
22	Western Musical Identity and Practice in Contemporary South Africa: Lessons from Doreen Bridges Caroline van Niekerk	241
23	We Sing Now: A Rirratjingu Song Session Jill Stubington	257
24	What does it mean to be a good teacher? Stephen Hough	287

Editor's Note

I thought it important that the Australian Society for Music Education should use the occasion of Doreen Bridges' 90th birthday to celebrate her broad contribution to music in its many dimensions. At the same time, I hasten to add, Doreen has not stopped contributing! She continues to be active in many facets of music: as a writer, researcher, performer and mentor. I am delighted that David Forrest, on behalf of the Australian Society for Music Education, took-up my suggestion that the society pay tribute to Doreen in this way. The book complements *Doreen Bridges: Music Educator*, a collection of her writings published by the society in 1992.

Contributors were given free reign in terms of the nature of their contribution. The articles, which represent the broad gamut of music, were subject to a blind review process by the Editorial Board of the *Australian Journal of Music Education*. Whilst referencing systems are consistent within articles, there has been no attempt to aim for uniformity across the publication.

I want to record my gratitude firstly to ASME and its National Council – under the leadership of Dr Jennifer Rosevear, the National President – for supporting this project. Secondly, to Doreen Bridges for her ongoing advice and wisdom. Thirdly, to all of the contributors who have freely and generously become involved in this endeavour. Finally, I want to record my deep appreciation to Margaret Whitlam

AO for graciously agreeing to write the *Introduction*, to Ross Watson who kindly allowed me to reproduce one of his paintings, and to David Forrest who provided incalculable assistance with the editing and publication of this *Festschrift*.

Martin Comte
Melbourne, June, 2009

Contributors

Warren Bourne studied Music and English literature at the Victoria University of Wellington, New Zealand, and began exploring eighteenth century music on a beautiful Kirckman harpsichord. He specialized in Musicology and keyboard performance in his academic studies and completed his PhD in early twentieth century music. He was appointed as a Lecturer in Music at the old Adelaide Teachers' College in 1971 and alongside a strong commitment to Music Education continued to study seventeenth and eighteenth century music and its performance practice on clavichord, harpsichord and organ. He has held numerous organ appointments and given regular recitals. Since his retirement as a Senior Lecturer in Musicology at the University of Adelaide he has held the position of Choral Director at Bethlehem Lutheran Church in Adelaide City and plays a John Barnes copy of Franz Josef Haydn's last clavichord of 1794, a Johann Bohak of Vienna.

From 1983 he was National Secretary of the Australian Society for Music Education and in 1986 he was elected National President of the Society, a position he held until 1990. Subsequently he was made an Honorary Life Member of the Society. Presently he is National Secretary and Treasurer of the Royal School of Church Music Australia.

Tom Bridges (b. 1953) has played the violin as 'a good amateur', written satirical scripts and directed music for the theatre, written about music for *Soundscapes* magazine (now defunct), sung bass in choirs of all descriptions, and is currently a member of The Spooky Men's Chorale. Since 1991, when he was the founding conductor of the Sydney Trade Union Choir, he has directed community choirs of one sort or another. Currently he conducts a choir at Warrimoo in the Blue Mountains (NSW) not far from where he lives at Hazelbrook. He has been active in the Australian folk music scene for the past fifteen years, particularly as a performer and arranger with groups using vocal harmonies. He lists his three most influential experiences as those gained (1) from his time studying music at UNSW 1996–8, (2) from attending a Pete Seeger concert in Sydney in 1963, and (3) in infancy from his music-education-savvy mother [Doreen Bridges].

Jennifer Bryce is a Senior Research Fellow at the Australian Council for Educational Research (ACER) where she leads the Humanities, Arts and Social Sciences team in the Assessment and Reporting Research Program. Dr Bryce's current work includes test construction, analysis and interpretation, research and policy advice in arts/humanities curriculum, and educational assessment within Australia and internationally (including programs in Jordan, Botswana and Colombia). Jennifer has been employed by ACER on two occasions. Her current employment started in 1992. She was also a staff member from 1970 to 1977 when she worked as a research assistant to Dr Doreen Bridges on the development of the Australian Test for Advanced Music Studies and later, with Max Cooke, on the development of a Music Evaluation Kit. Jennifer has been a secondary school teacher of humanities, classroom music and careers education. She has also been a studio music teacher of the oboe and a free-lance performer. She worked for 10 years in the Educational Resources Department of Lincoln School of Health Sciences, La Trobe University. Jennifer studied at the University of Melbourne (BA, BEd), at the Victorian College of the Arts (Diploma of Arts, Music Performance), and the title of her PhD from RMIT University is 'Constructing Intra and Interpersonal Competencies in a Context of Lifelong Learning'.

Martin Comte graduated from The University of Melbourne with BMus and BEd degrees. He has an MEd from La Trobe University and a PhD from The University of Michigan. Prior to retiring from RMIT University in 1999, he had held positions of Dean and Associate Dean (Research) in the Faculty of Education & Training, and Associate Dean (Cultural Development) for the wider university. Since leaving the university he has continued to work as a Music and Education Consultant in Australia and overseas. He was the first person to be appointed to a Chair in Music Education by an Australian university. His board/council membership has included the Australian Ballet School, the Chamber Strings of Melbourne, and Musica Viva Australia. He is a Past President of ASME, a Past Chair of the ISME Commission for Music in Schools and Teacher Education, and a former Editor of the *Australian Journal of Music Education*. He is an Honorary Life Member of ASME and a Fellow of the Australian College of Educators. In 2009 he was awarded an Order of Australia Medal for services to music and arts education. His publications include *Doreen Bridges: Music Educator*, *Music Education: International Viewpoints*, and *Giving Children a Voice*.

Ross Edwards is one of Australia's best known composers who has created a unique sound world by which he seeks to help reconnect music with elemental forces and restore such qualities as ritual, spontaneity and the impulse to dance. Intensely aware of his vocation as a composer since childhood, he has largely followed his own direction, shunning sensible career moves and trusting that the music will speak for itself. He takes very seriously what he believes to be his responsibility to make the most effective use of one of the planet's most powerful forces to communicate at the highest possible artistic level. His music, universal in that it is concerned with the age-old mysteries surrounding humanity, is at the same time deeply connected to its roots in Australia, whose cultural diversity it celebrates, and from whose natural environment it draws its ethos – as well as many of its shapes and patterns – from such sources as birdsong and the mysterious drones of summer insects. Edwards' belief in the healing power of music is reflected in a body of contemplative works inspired by sounds of the Australian landscape.

Ross Edwards' compositions, which are performed worldwide, include five symphonies, concertos, orchestral, chamber and vocal music, children's music, film scores, opera and music for dance. Works designed for the concert hall sometimes require special lighting, movement, costume and visual accompaniment – notable examples are his Fourth Symphony, 'Star Chant', and his oboe concerto 'Bird Spirit Dreaming'. Based in Sydney and the Blue Mountains, he is married with two grown-up children. Doreen Bridges was one of his lecturers when he was an undergraduate music student at The University of Sydney in the 1960s.

David Forrest is Associate Professor of Music Education in the School of Education at RMIT University. His research interests include curriculum development and policy, music for children, and the life and educational philosophy of DB Kabalevsky. He is the National Publications Editor for the Australian Society for Music Education, and Editor of the *Australian Journal of Music Education* and the *Victorian Journal of Music Education*. He is a Board Member of Victoria's Arts Management Advisory Group, the International Society for Music Education, and the International Council of Music and Arts Education (Russian Academy of Education, Moscow). His PhD is from the University of Melbourne. He is the first person to have been elected a Fellow of the Australian Society for Music Education.

Richard Gill is one of Australia's pre-eminent conductors and music educators. He regularly conducts for Opera Australia, the major Australian orchestras and the State opera companies. He is Music Director of Victorian Opera and Artistic Director of the Sydney Symphony's Education Program. He has been Artistic Director of OzOpera, Artistic Director and Chief Conductor of the Canberra Symphony Orchestra, and the Adviser for the Musica Viva In Schools program. He has held several important posts, including Dean of the West Australian Conservatorium of Music and Director of Chorus at the Australian Opera. He has received the country's most prestigious awards, including the Order of Australia Medal, the Bernard Heinze Award for

Services to music in Australia, an Honorary Doctorate from Edith Cowan University in Western Australia, and the Australia Council's Don Banks Award 2006.

Richard's 2009 conducting engagements include Meet the Music, Discovery and Sinfonietta concerts for Sydney Symphony; the world premiere of Grandison's violin concerto with The Queensland Orchestra; Faure Requiem and Ears Wide Open with the Melbourne Symphony Orchestra; and for Victorian Opera, Don Giovanni, Rembrandt's Wife, and Ariadne auf Naxos.

Michael Kieran Harvey is an Australian-based pianist who was born in Sydney and studied in Canberra with Alan Jenkins, at the Sydney Conservatorium with Gordon Watson, and at the Liszt Academy, Budapest, under the Director, Professor Sandor Falvai. His career has been notable for its diversity and wide repertoire encompassing concertos, chamber music, traditional through to contemporary classical solos, and experimental and original works. Renowned for his performances of new music, he has dedicated much of his career to promoting the works of Australian composers.

Michael has recorded more than 30 solo CDs and has been awarded numerous international prizes, including the Grand Prix in the Ivo Pogorelich Piano Competition (Pasadena), the Debussy Medal (Paris), four consecutive Australian "Mo" awards for best classical artist, the Australian Government's Centenary Medal for services to Australian music, and most recently he has been nominated three times for the Helpmann Award. His recordings are regularly nominated in the ARIAs and APRAs.

In 2005 the estate of the late Susan Remington established the Michael Kieran Harvey Scholarship in honour of his contribution to Australian music, and to encourage future directions in keyboard art music. He is currently on staff at the Australian National Academy of Music.

Deanna Hoermann has combined a career in music education with educational research and administration. She taught music and languages in secondary schools before being appointed Director of the Developmental Music Research Program that looked at the appropriateness of the Kodaly approach to music education for primary schools in NSW. This led to her engagement as a lecturer and consultant both nationally and internationally. Her involvement in curriculum and policy development preceded her appointment as an Inspector of Schools, Director of Schools, Secondary High School Principal, and Manager of the School Leadership and Executive Learning Unit in the NSW Department of Education and Training. She is currently involved with consultancy work.

Deanna was a member of the foundation committee of the International Kodaly Society and served as its President for eight years. She founded the Kodaly Music Education Institute of Australia. Deanna has been a member of a number of state and national Boards and Advisory Councils in the Performing Arts. She was a driving force behind the development of Newtown High School for the Performing Arts. Deanna has published widely in the area of music education. Her doctorate, from the University of New South Wales, in the area of Change Management, used the development of Cherrybrook Technology High School as its case study.

Stephen Hough is widely regarded as one of the most important and distinctive pianists of his generation. He appears regularly with most of the major American and European orchestras under the finest conductors, and gives recitals at major venues and festivals across the world. He has a catalogue of over 40 CDs that have won many prizes, including seven Gramophone Awards and three Grammy nominations. He is also a writer and composer, and recent performances of his compositions include the world premiere of his cello concerto with Steven Isserlis, two Masses for Westminster Abbey and Westminster Cathedral, and a trio for members of the Berlin Philharmonic.

Jamie C. Kassler was elected a fellow (1991) of the Australian Academy of the Humanities for contributions to musicological theory and was a recipient of the Centenary Medal (2003) for service to Australian society and the humanities in the study of philosophy. She is author of a number of books, including *Inner Music* (London: Athlone, 1995) and *The Beginnings of the Modern Philosophy of Music* (Aldershot: Ashgate, 2004).

Marvelene C. Moore is a James A. Cox Endowed Chair and Professor of Music Education at the University of Tennessee, USA. She specializes in vocal music pedagogy and research with an emphasis in general music education and choral music for students grades 3–8. She holds an AB degree from Talladega College, Alabama; MME and EdS degrees, George Peabody College for Teachers; and the PhD degree from the University of Michigan. She did post-graduate study at the Jaques-Dalcroze Institute-Geneva, Switzerland; Kodaly Institute-Esztergom, Hungary; and the Orff Schulwerk Institute-Salzburg. Marvelene recently received the Dr Martin Luther King Junior Commission Arts Award and the Tennessee (USA) Hall of Fame Award for recognition of her outstanding accomplishments in the advancement of music education in Tennessee schools and the United States. She currently serves on the Executive Board of the International Society of Music Education (ISME) and is president of the Tennessee Alliance for Arts Education. Over the past thirty years she has acquired a national and international reputation. In 1995 she founded of the National Symposium on Multicultural Music at the University of Tennessee, an event that brings national and international educators, artists, and researchers together to present sessions and concerts on music of different genres. Dr Moore has published extensively, including *Making Music*, a textbook series, K-8 (2001, 2005).

Sandra Nash, as Director of Studies for Dalcroze Australia, has run Summer Schools in this country since 1994 and coordinated visits by overseas Dalcroze specialists. An experienced classroom and studio teacher, she has taught in universities in Sydney and Quebec, Canada, and given workshops in East Asia, Japan, Europe and North America. Sandra is the Australian delegate to the International Federation of Eurhythmics Teachers (FIER) and in 2003 was invited to become a member of the Collège of the Institut

Jaques-Dalcroze, Geneva. Sandra has a BMus (Sydney), Dalcroze Licentiate (London), and Dalcroze Diplôme Supérieur (Geneva). She is currently undertaking doctoral studies at the Sydney Conservatorium of Music.

George Palmer was born in 1947. He has been a Judge of the New South Wales Supreme Court since 2001. In 2003 his music came to the attention of the ABC, resulting in a feature story on ABC TV, a live national broadcast of a concert of his orchestral music and the release by ABC Classics of 2 CDs of his music, *The Attraction of Opposites* and *Exaltate Dominum*.

In 2007 his string quintet, 'Not Going Quietly', was premiered by the Sydney Omega Ensemble. Many other works have been performed by the Adelaide Symphony Orchestra, West Australian Youth Orchestra, chamber groups and ensembles. George Palmer was commissioned to write the Papal Mass for World Youth Day 2008 in Sydney. The Mass, 'Benedictus Qui Venit', for large orchestra, choir and soloists, was performed in the presence of Pope Benedict XVI and 350,000 people. In November 2008, the Sydney Omega Ensemble premiered his Concerto for Two Clarinets and the internationally acclaimed Seraphim Trio performed his piano quartet, 'The Way It Is', in Sydney, Melbourne and Adelaide. In July 2009 The Queensland Orchestra will premiere his Concertino for Two Guitars, with virtuoso soloists Slava and Leonard Grigoryan and in September The Christchurch Symphony Orchestra will perform a new work, Starting from Now.

George Palmer is married with three children and lives in Sydney.

Joan Pope OAM PhD is President of Dalcroze Australia and, as one of the few practising Dalcroze Eurhythmics teachers in Australia, is regularly invited to conduct courses in South East Asia. She is well-known for her creative approaches and voluntary service to community arts with pre-schoolers and seniors, and has served on education and arts boards nationally and internationally. Her PhD thesis (Monash University) was on the teaching of Dalcroze in Australasia, from 1918. She has an MEd, BEd (Edith

Cowan University); BA, DipEd (University of Western Australia); Dalcroze Licentiate (Sydney), and Dalcroze Diplôme Supérieur (Geneva). Joan is an ACHPER Fellow and Honorary Life Member of AUSDANCE, ASME and Dalcroze Australia.

Janet Ritterman (née Palmer) was born in Sydney, where she studied at the Conservatorium and at Sydney Teachers' College. She completed her studies in London, gaining a Masters degree and a doctorate of the University of London. Since 1970 she has lived in the UK. As a pianist, she has specialised in chamber music performance and in the training of gifted performers. Her research interests relate principally to European concert life, performance practice, instrumental pedagogy and the development of the conservatoire.

Much of Janet's career has been in higher education. She worked at Middlesex Polytechnic, then at Goldsmiths (University of London) and at Dartington College of Arts, initially as Head of Music, latterly as Principal. From 1993 to 2005 she was Director of the Royal College of Music London and Visiting Professor of the University of Plymouth. Now a Vice-President of the RCM, she continues to act as an adviser on the arts and higher education. In this capacity, she serves as a member of the Austrian Wissenschaftsrat, chairs the Board responsible for the funding of arts-based research for the Austrian Research Council and is a member of the Conseil de Fondation of the Haute École de Musique de Genève.

A Fellow of the British Higher Education Academy, Janet was appointed Dame Commander of the British Empire (DBE) in 2002 for services to music.

Jennifer Rosevear completed a Bachelor of Music, with a major in Music Education, at the University of Adelaide's Elder Conservatorium of Music, followed by Honours in Music Education and a Graduate Diploma in Education. She taught music at Thorndon High School for one year and at Woodville High School for six years from 1977 when its Special Interest Music Centre began operating. She was a Music Curriculum Writer for the Education Department, 1983–1984, before her appointment as a lecturer in Music Education in 1985 at the former City Campus of the South Australian College of Advanced Education. In 1991 this campus amalgamated with the University of Adelaide and Jennifer continued her work in Music Education at the Elder Conservatorium of Music where she is currently Head of Music Education and Head of Undergraduate Music Programs.

Jennifer completed a Master of Music Education through the University of Western Australia in 1995, and in 2008 she completed her PhD on the topic of Engaging adolescents in high school music. Her research interests include the role of playing by ear and improvisation in music education, and relationships between academic achievement and musical involvement. She is currently the National President of the Australian Society for Music Education. She was a member of the Senior Secondary Assesment Board of South Australia Music Subject Advisory Committee from 1984–2008.

Jane Southcott is a Senior Lecturer in the Faculty of Education, Monash University (Clayton Campus). She teaches pre-service teacher education students in music education and educational sociology. Jane is the program director for the Masters coursework programs. She supervises research students at honours, masters and doctoral levels, and publishes widely in Australian and international journals. She is also a regular presenter at conferences and on the editorial boards of national and international journals. Currently Dr Southcott is researching experiential education, performance anxiety, music and positive ageing, and continuing her work on the history of music education in Australia, England, Europe and America.

Jill Stubington completed her first degree at the University of Queensland and then moved to Melbourne to become Research Assistant to Dr Alice Moyle. She visited north-east Arnhem Land in 1973, 1974 and 1975 making extensive recordings of senior singers. Having completed her PhD at Monash University, she moved to Sydney in 1985 to take up a position in the School of Music at the University of New South

Wales. There she taught courses in Australian Aboriginal music, Australian traditional music and other musicological subjects for 20 years. Her book *Singing the Land: The power of performance in Aboriginal life* was published by Currency House in 2007. Now retired from full-time teaching, she remains a Visiting Research Fellow at the University of New South Wales.

David Tunley is best known internationally for his research and publications on 18th and 19th century French music; he has also contributed to studies of Australian music and music education. As well as articles in the *Australian Journal of Music Education* and *Studies in Music*, with Frank Callaway he co-edited and contributed to *Australian Composition in the Twentieth Century* (Melbourne, OUP, 1980) and has recently published a monograph, *William James and the Beginnings of Modern Musical Australia* (Sydney, Australian Music Centre, 2007). He has served on various national Boards, including chairmanship of the AMEB and Music Board of the Australia Council. He is an Emeritus Professor and Honorary Research Fellow at the University of Western Australia, a Fellow of the Australian Academy of the Humanities and was made a Chevalier in the Napoleonic Ordre des Palmes Académiques for his work on French music and was made a Member of the Order of Australia for his contribution to music in his own country.

Caroline van Niekerk is full Professor of Music Education at the University of Pretoria. Her undergraduate degree in Music and English plus a teacher's diploma were followed by two licentiates – one in School Music and one in the Theory of Music – her MMus and PhD. She also holds qualifications in fields as diverse as translating, editing, television presentation, leadership and negotiating skills.

Caroline returned to the University of Pretoria in 1996 from her post as Director in the South African National Department of Education. Prior to five years spent in national government she lectured at a variety of tertiary institutions. The author/editor of many publications, she has been involved in the supervision of over 100 masters and doctoral theses, examines nationally and internationally and has been fortunate to travel extensively and speak at conferences throughout the world.

From 1992–1996 Caroline was a member of the ISME Board of Directors and in 1998 responsible for all the arrangements for the programme of the ISME world conference in Pretoria. From 2000/2001 she was the first President of the Pan-African Society for Music Education, and re-elected as Secretary General of the Society for the biennium 2001–2003 and again until she resigned in December 2005.

Amanda Watson is an Instrumental Music Teacher with the Department of Education and Early Childhood Development, Victoria, Australia. Dr Watson has taught Classroom Music at primary and secondary levels and initially trained as an Early Childhood Educator. Her research interests include values education, music and arts curriculum development in schools, and developing professional standards for music teachers. She has given considerable voluntary service to professional teaching associations, serving in both office-bearer and committee positions. Amanda was the Australian Society for Music Education (ASME) Victorian Chapter Secretary for 13 years and Public Officer for 10 years and has served continuously on the ASME Victorian Chapter Council since 1983. She has been a member of the ASME National Executive and the National Secretary for nine years. Since 1999 she has acted as an assistant for the ASME National Publications Editor, editing *ASME Update*. Amanda is currently serving her second term as President of the Council of Professional Teaching Associations of Victoria (CPTAV) and has served two terms as Vice President. She has been the CPTAV representative for ASME Victoria since 1992 and a Board Member of the Australian Joint Council of Professional Teaching Associations representing CPTAV. Amanda is a member of the Victorian Institute of Teaching Accreditation Committee, representing Victorian Government secondary schools.

Robert J. Werner holds BME, MM and PhD degrees from Northwestern University. He began his teaching career as the Director of Instrumental Music for ten years in a public high school in Evanston, Illinois. In 1966 he became an Associate Professor of Music at the State University of New York at Binghamton and went on to be the Director of the Ford Foundation funded Contemporary Music Project from 1968–73. In 1973 he became the Director of the School of Music at the University of Arizona until 1985 when he was appointed the Dean of the College–Conservatory of Music at the University of Cincinnati until 2000.

Robert Werner has been President of the College Music Society (1977–78), the National Association of Music Schools (1989–91) and the International Society for Music Education (1984–86), which he also served as Treasurer (1987–2000). He also served as Vice President of the American Classical Music Hall of Fame (1996–2000) and Co-Chair of its National Artistic Directorate (1996–2007). He has been a conductor, clinician and speaker at numerous national and international music societies and associations. He has been a consultant and accreditation reviewer for over 100 institutions in the United States and internationally.

David G. Woods was appointed Dean of the School of Fine Arts at the University of Connecticut in 2000. He was Dean of the School of Music at Indiana University from 1997 to 1999. He served as Dean of the College of Fine Arts at the University of Oklahoma from 1991 to 1997. He was Director of the School of Music at the University of Arizona from 1985 to 1991. From 1974 to 1984 he was Chair of the Division of Music Education at Iowa State University. He was Director of Music at Colorado Academy from 1966 to 1974. He received a Bachelor of Music degree from Washburn University and a Master of Music and Doctor of Philosophy degrees from Northwestern University in Evanston, Illinois. He has also studied at the Copenhagen Conservatory of Music and at the Aspen Institute.

Dr Woods has written numerous books and articles on music education and has presented workshops, lectures and clinics throughout the United States, Europe, Australia and China. He was a Senior Fulbright Scholar in Iceland in 1981 and completed an extensive research study of the langspiel, an Icelandic folk instrument.

In 1987 he was a Senior Fulbright Scholar in Australia, where he lectured and initiated research studies in curriculum development in music at the University of Sydney. Dr Woods is known for his writing, research, and study of early childhood music education. In 1981, he was named Outstanding Teacher of the Year at Iowa State University and in 1992 he was named Outstanding Alumni Fellow by Washburn University. In 1993 he was named Outstanding Administrator of the Year at The University of Oklahoma and in 1995 he received the Governor's Arts Award from Oklahoma. Dr Woods is the Chairman of the Publications Committee for the College Music Society and serves as a member of the International Advisory Panel for the Frank Callaway Resource Center for Music Education at the University of Western Australia.

Sheila C. Woodward is Chair of Music Education at the University of Southern California. She is a native of South Africa and earned her PhD in music education from the University of Cape Town in 1993 and a Performer's Licentiate in Organ from the London Royal School of Music. Dr Woodward served two terms on the Board of Directors of the International Society for Music Education (ISME) from 2004–2008. She served on the ISME Early Childhood Music Education Commission from 1996–1998, four of those years as the chair, and on numerous other professional boards in both the USA and South Africa. Dr Woodward's research focus is Music and Wellbeing. She explores this from before birth to adulthood, with studies on the fetus and neonate, the premature infant, the young child, at risk youth, the juvenile offender and the adult musician. She has published numerous articles, in addition to chapters in David J. Elliott's *Praxial Music Education: Reflections and Dialogues* (Oxford, 2005) and in S. Malloch and C. Trevarthen's *Communicative musicality: Narratives of expressive gesture and being human* (Oxford, 2009). She has won grants to bring numerous South African musicians to the USA to work alongside American students and faculty.

Introduction

It gives me great joy to introduce these songs of praise for Doreen Bridges. She and I are of an age (mature) and over many years we have shared some exciting moves in music education. The NSW Conservatorium of Music was the scene of my own piano exams, of choir and verse speaking competitions for schools. She, of course, was always a teacher and became both boss and administrator of many sections of that institution – while I was a fundraiser and delighted audience member. There will be so many tales well told and we will all appreciate the telling.

Good on you, Doreen!

Margaret Whitlam AO

1: THE MANY FACETS OF MUSIC

Martin Comte

This volume is a tribute to Doreen Bridges AM, the doyenne of Australian music education, and has been undertaken to mark the occasion of her 90th birthday in 2008. Through her research, writings, teaching and mentoring she has probably had a greater influence on music education in Australia than anyone else. This is not the first time that the Australian Society for Music Education (ASME) has paid tribute to her. Some years ago the society published *Doreen Bridges: Music Educator* (Comte, 1992), a collection of her writings on a wide range of topics to coincide with its twenty-fifth anniversary celebrations.

Dr Bridges obtained the first Australian PhD in music education (*The role of universities in the development of music education in Australia 1885–1970*, University of Sydney, 1970). She has been member of Council of the Canberra School of Music and a member and Chair of the Board of Governors of the NSW (now Sydney) Conservatorium of Music, where she also taught. In addition, she taught for many years in the Music Department of Sydney University and was in charge of music at the Nursery School Teachers' College. In the 1970s Doreen worked with the Australian Council for Educational Research under a government grant to produce the Australian Test for Advanced Music Studies (1978), for which she wrote the Report and Handbook. Other publications include *A Developmental Music Program, Stages 1, 2 & 3* (1984, 1987, 1991) (with Deanna Hoermann), *Catch a Song* (1985), *Music, Young Children & You* (1994a), and *More than a Musician: A Life of E. Harold*

Davies (2006). For several years Doreen was a member of the International Society for Music Education's Research Commission and also very involved in the society's Early Childhood Commission. She received an Order of Australia in 1984 for services to music education. Other honours include Honorary Life Membership of the Australian Society for Music Education, the Australian and New Zealand Association for Research in Music Education, and the Kodaly Music Education Institute of Australia; the Australian College of Educators paid tribute to her by electing her a Fellow.

Doreen's incisive PhD was an examination of the hold the universities in Australia had on music education, including studio music teaching, principally through the music examination system and in particular the Australian Music Examinations Board (AMEB) and its antecedents – a system that is peculiar to Australia and other countries that are or have been part of the British Empire. Such an examination system does not exist, for example, in the USA or continental Europe. In her thesis she recommends the re-education of music teachers and the transformation of the AMEB system into an *advisory* service for teachers, parents and students. There are those who lament the fact that even now the AMEB – despite undergoing considerable change – remains, principally, an examination and not an advisory organization. Indeed, it might be argued that this external examination system is the most flourishing facet of music education in Australia today – much more so than general classroom music in schools. This in itself gives some indication of many Australian music teachers' and parents' questionable 'need' to send children for external music examinations; unfortunately, it is strongly embedded in our music teaching psyche that if you learn an instrument you must sit for music exams. Even at that time Doreen was not alone in her criticisms of the AMEB. Just a few years earlier an eminent Australian academic and musicologist, Roger Covell (1967, p. 285) wrote:

> It is possible for a student to reach advanced grades and even attain the awesome state of having 'letters' after his or her name without having any but the most constricted horizons of musical awareness.

Some would argue that the situation today is not radically different and that there is a sense in which the criticisms of Doreen Bridges and Roger Covell still have currency. Certainly, 25 years after her PhD study Doreen was still lamenting the situation:

> I regret the voluntary subservience of studio music teachers as well as parents to an Australia-wide music examination system derived from similar British systems developed towards the end of the nineteenth century, and basically little has changed except for an expansion of the repertoire and the subjects examined. (Bridges, 1994a, p. 54)

This and other concerns underscored Doreen's development (1973–1976) of the Australian Test for Advanced Music Studies in conjunction with the Australian Council for Educational Research.

Doreen (or Dee, as she prefers to be called) is still active in music making, writing and research and continues to inspire and mentor others. She has said, 'I have been very fortunate in that I have had such a variety of educational experiences. These have enabled me to function over a very wide spectrum, and to become involved in many facets of music education ranging from infancy to post-graduate levels' (Comte, 1992, p. vi).

Whilst most of the contributors to this volume know Doreen personally, some know her through her writing or other areas of involvement in music and music education. Still others have been invited to contribute because they are people whom Dee herself particularly admires. One of the younger contributors, when invited to participate, initially responded that he did not know Doreen; I mentioned some of her areas of involvement in music and music education and received the following response: 'You mean THAT Doreen! Of course I'll contribute.'

The contributions represent the breadth and diversity of Dee's interest and involvement in many facets of music. Contributors represent the fields of performance, musicology, ethnomusicology and, of course, music education in its many manifestations. This breadth and diversity spans many hundreds of years – indeed thousands of years – in the history of music. It also represents incredible change (some would say *development* or *evolution*).

When considering this I keep thinking of the accompanying image which has fascinated me for some time. It is a painting by the Australian artist Ross Watson, inspired by Ter Borch (*Untitled #3/2003. After Ter Borch, 1662*[1]). Ter Borch (1617–1681), a contemporary of Vermeer, was one of the finest Dutch portrait painters of his time. His portraits were distinctive for their psychological intensity and his ability to express with subtlety the interactions between figures. Typically, his characters are writing letters or making music.

In some respects, it seems to me, Ross Watson's painting can be seen as a metaphor for this collection of writings. Indeed it might be a metaphor for developments in music and music education over the centuries. Equally, it may be viewed as a metaphor for developments in the field during Dee's professional life.

Looked at simply the painting depicts a woman in a pose and costume similar to one used by a number of artists of the period. The man, by contrast, is pure 21st century. He belongs to the mobile phone generation where things are instantaneous and readily 'disposable'; he is living in an era of inbuilt obsolescence, a time in history when a notion of permanence is increasingly giving way to one of transience (have we gone the full circle?). For him the written word is almost as instantaneous as the spoken word. He does not need to wait for months for a letter to arrive or his response to be received. Today, communication is 'instant' – and often very brief: a few words (heavily abbreviated), often interspersed with images. I am one of the unfortunates who needs to consult a reference chart in order to understand some of the characters :-) lol.

Of course, the woman in the painting represents but one relatively finite point in the evolution of music (and painting) whereas some of the contributions in this volume refer to much earlier times. A letter, it must be acknowledged, is a sophisticated way of communicating. But this is not to deny that earlier – and,

to some extent, continuing – forms of communication, including drumming and smoke signals, also represent sophisticated communication systems.

Unlike some of the works by Ter Borch, Ross Watson has chosen not to portray any interaction between the two people in his painting; nor is there any psychological intensity between them. One figure is juxtaposed against the other. Whilst they share a canvas, they do not share their worlds. Unlike her world, I conjecture that, to some extent at least, the man inhabits a virtual world. They are not interacting; the man has his back turned away from the woman. This, for me, only serves to highlight how far we've come in music and what scant regard we sometimes have for the past. I think it is a criticism of music today – and, indeed, education – that we often ignore the past and our heritage and in so doing fail to acknowledge that we and our artefacts are essentially a product of it. But more than this, the image of the man with his back turned to the woman suggests to me the 'typical' home today where individual members sit in front of their respective computers or the television screen engaging in various activities to the detriment of conversation within the family. There is a sense in which experience – lived daily experience – is becoming an increasingly solitary pursuit. No wonder many young people no longer see the need for 'congregating' in order to experience music or the theatre. The implications of this for music making, music sharing and music teaching are enormous.

I wonder how much thought went into the writing of the letter being read by the woman. To what extent was every word that appears on the paper considered? To what extent did the writer search for the 'right' word? How many times was the letter drafted before the final version? Equally, and in contrast, I wonder what thought went into the young man's text message. Was it simply part of a series of text messages that he would exchange with the same recipient during the course of the day – a kind of ongoing, instant dialogue? A 'If I don't get the message across with this text message I can just as easily send another one' attitude.

In my imagination I wonder too how many times the woman read that letter. Did it contain any ambiguity that might have taken months to clarify by return mail?

By contrast, if the young man's text is unclear it is a simple matter to send or receive another one for instant clarification (or, conceivably, more confusion).

Sadly, so much of the music that young people are surrounded with today is transient in much the same way that text messages are. Whereas letters have been a great source of information to historians and others, it is unlikely that text messages will be saved for posterity in the way that letters have been. But does this matter? I can't imagine the average text message being savoured, re-read many times in the same way that we read letters (although I did once receive a message saying 'The goldfish just died.' I read it over and over, quite incredulous, for it had looked quite healthy in its tank that morning!). I suspect even emails tend to be trashed more than they are saved.

To some extent the image of these two people represents a major issue in music education today. There is a glut of music. Much of it is disposable and transient. There is so much of it that young people often adopt the attitude that there is no need to listen to it a second time: rather, they simply move on to the next piece they have downloaded. Music is just a commodity. It is approached by some in the same way as we approach a Kleenex tissue: we tend to use it once only; when we need the next 'fix' we simply pull another one out of the box. For others music is nothing more than 'wallpaper': there merely to avoid silence.

But why, to be fair, should I expect young people to listen, re-listen and listen again to the same thing when there is so much other music to devour – or at least surround themselves with? This, I suggest, has implications for reflection, analysis, and informed evaluation that getting on the 'inside' of a work involves. The obvious question thus becomes: what does 'listening' entail for many young people today? An important element of much music experienced by them is volume; there's even a sense in which if it's loud it's good and if it's soft it's not. (We've all pulled-up at traffic lights and been bombarded by the deafening noise from the car alongside – or two across!) Nuance is not a subtlety of much of the music that today's youth listen to. I can't help thinking how much easier it might have been to teach music to the woman in the paining who lived in an era that was not one where noise and piercing volume were prized. Through my rose-coloured glasses I also envisage that music teachers in those days did not have to fight the need for instant gratification that they do today; it was an era when it was not so easy to push the 'eject' button. But, of course, I must remind myself that at the time in which this woman lived an education in and through music was limited to a certain class and was not available to the masses.

So much for my own ponderings as I contemplate Ross Watson's painting. Indeed, so much for my ponderings when I read each of the contributions to this volume, all of which have caused me to let my mind wander and go down paths that I have not explored. I hope that you, too, will find these articles not only informative and entertaining in themselves – but also a springboard for your own thinking.

At the outset I wish to acknowledge Margaret Whitlam AO for graciously agreeing to write an Introduction to this volume. A contemporary of Dee's, Margaret has a great love of music and the arts and was extremely supportive when I approached her to undertake this task.

Jennifer Bryce outlines one of Dee's major undertakings: the Australian Test for Advanced Music studies (ATAMS), which Jennifer appropriately describes as 'a watershed in the assessment of musical ability' that came about in part because of 'general dissatisfaction with music examinations in Australia'. Jennifer rightly asserts that even by today's standards it is a robust test. There is strong reason to regret that the test has not been updated and embraced more widely. This essay might be seen alongside Amanda Watson's contribution which looks at the role of studio teachers of music in Australia: those charged with developing children's 'musicality' and performance skills – and determining to some extent how these should be assessed.

The contributions by Joan Pope and Sandra Nash, Deanna Hoermann, and Richard Gill provide perspectives and insights on three music educators and their theories and practices that had a profound influence on music teaching throughout the 20th century, continuing into this century. Joan Pope and Sandra Nash discuss the introduction of Dalcroze Eurhythmics into Australia and attempts to establish a credentialed training system of teacher education. It is a story of determination by people deeply committed to spreading Jaques-Dalcroze's philosophy and teaching. Deanna Hoermann details how she introduced the Developmental Music Program – based on the work of Zoltan Kodaly – into schools in New South Wales and beyond. In this she was supported by Dee Bridges and together they published seminal books that adapted the work of Kodaly to Australian schools. Richard Gill, who has done more to popularize the work of Orff in Australia than anyone else, kindly allowed us to reprint an address he gave a few years ago at the opening of an Orff conference.

Robert Werner has revisited the ground-breaking Contemporary Music Project that he directed in the USA, commencing in the 1960s. It was this and the associated concept of 'Comprehensive Musicianship' that Dee acknowledges had a profound effect on her own thinking. Jane Southcott examines developments in music education in Australia in the 1950s that led to the establishment of ASME in 1967. She points out however that despite all of the activity that has occurred in the intervening years, many of the issues in music education that were current in the 1950s and 1960s are still the subject of concern today; one wonders how far we've really travelled. In his essay, David Tunley considers the contribution of the *academy* – 'established' musical institutions or organizations – to radical musical techniques and styles when they have been introduced in Australia. He points out that 'Those in the vanguard of artistic innovation are not necessarily welcome in places where the main purpose is to conserve tradition'. In an essay spanning centuries, Jamie Kassler examines long held attitudes about Western music that, she maintains, even today are unexamined or unrecognized. In the process she reminds us that for Doreen and others who came before her, creativity is a potential of the many and not merely the few.

Writing from a North American perspective, David Woods presents challenges and predictions for music educators in the 21st century. In doing so he identifies considerations for moving ahead in the development of teacher preparation programs. Sheila Woodward, also from the USA, argues cogently from a multidisciplinary perspective for the importance of music in early childhood education. In Australia, Jennifer Rosevear draws our attention to the benefits of music education to young people at the other end of the spectrum – adolescents – with respect to self-concept, academic achievement and musical participation.

An education in music is not limited to the teaching that occurs in the studio, the school, or the university, as Tom Bridges argues. Tom, Dee's son, extols the musical, social and global benefits of community choirs. In arguing that music-making is necessary for human survival he speaks of music's transformative powers when it is made – and shared – actively with others.

George Palmer gives us a unique perspective on combining the life of a lawyer and Supreme Court Judge with that of composer; he shares with us his attempt to attain a fulfilling work/life balance. It is the story of his journey in music through various stages of his personal and professional life. In the process he pays tribute to the Australian composer Ross Edwards, another contributor to this volume. Ross Edwards has graciously dedicated two of his children's pieces – *Two Spells* – to Dee. 'Spell 1 (Healing)' and 'Spell 2 (Wishing)', with accompanying performance notes, are reproduced in this volume from the composer's original manuscript. Children's pieces are also represented from another perspective by David Forrest who gives us an insight into the music that Kabalevsky, the Russian composer and music educator, wrote for young people.

Janet Ritterman discusses attempts to establish Schumann as a 'respectable' composer in Britain, initially through the attempts of his wife, the concert pianist, Clara Schumann. It took some years before the composer gained public favour in that country, unlike his earlier acceptance in continental Europe. Warren Bourne introduces us to the keyboard sonatas of a lesser known composer born almost 100 years before Schumann: Georg Benda. It won't surprise me if Dee, who is still playing Bach and discovering new insights into his music, won't be tempted to start exploring Benda – if, of course, she hasn't done this already!

The Australian pianist, Michael Kieran Harvey, who has established a national and international reputation for his insightful and virtuosic performances, provides interesting viewpoints in response to a number of questions that were presented to him. In an email to me, Dee wrote of his recent performance of a work by the Australian composer Larry Sitsky, especially written for him, 'I've never heard such playing, nor such a difficult work.' Stephen Hough, the eminent British concert pianist, invites us to ponder what it means to be a good teacher. Those of us who know Dee have in her the ideal model of teacher, mentor and friend.

Marvelene Moore from the USA argues strongly for a multicultural approach to music education in the general music classroom. In the process she outlines musical benefits that can be derived from this approach as well as social and personal gains. Caroline van Niekerk from Pretoria describes how Black South Africans have embraced Western music despite a recent history in which this music has been derogated. She stresses that this is not happening through coercion or manipulation; nor is it being achieved through a lack of support for indigenous and traditional African musical styles and idioms. Jill Stubington introduces us to music associated with Australia's aborigines in north-east Arnhem Land; she undertook three field trips there in the mid-1970s to investigate the musical structures of clan songs within their social and ceremonial contexts. This is an appropriate reminder that we in Australia have a long heritage of music that extends back for several thousands of years – long before the 'establishment' of the Western music tradition that is principally taught in schools and universities; and certainly several thousands of years before letter writing (or notation) as evidenced in Ross Watson's painting was practised.

To return to Ross Watson's painting: it serves to remind us of the inevitable evolutionary nature of civilization. Equally, it might be seen to indicate that skill and artistry have been forsaken in some endeavours for speed or the 'immediate' and what is expendable. The implications of this for the experience and teaching of music – and dance and theatre – are tremendous.

Despite the obvious benefits, I think we're missing something today with the ready accessibility of CDs, DVDs, film and television. How important is it that we physically attend a live performance as distinct from hearing it on a CD or watching a DVD? Why go to the theatre and be a member of an audience when one can see it on a DVD or just download it? Why go to an art gallery when one can download as many images as one wants? And am I being excessively sentimental in seeing something special in the 'feel' of a letter, the paper on which it is written, its scent, and knowing it has been touched by the writer? I was heartened recently to read the Australian journalist and broadcaster, Phillip Adams (2009, p. 38) bemoaning the changing face of newspapers: "There's something about the feel, the smell, the rustle of a newspaper that cannot be replaced or replicated." Surely the same applies to the letter!

But, if Ross Watson's painting can be viewed as a metaphor for development, or at least change, what of a positive nature can we extrapolate as far and music and music education are concerned? Surely it is that human beings still have an insatiable desire to communicate. This, of course, is what every artist, regardless of the medium, has attempted to do throughout history. Costumes may change, the medium may change, societal norms may change, but the desire to communicate – and be understood – is a universal phenomenon in the history of human beings. Music, like the letter or the mobile phone, is concerned with communication or the transmission of a 'message'; although our ways of doing this have undergone radical transformations over time as composers have adapted to – and been at the forefront of – new technologies, our need to communicate remains as strong today as it ever was. Our communication palate today is broader and more technologically advanced: but is it richer? The painting serves to remind us that new technologies must not become an end in themselves: they must not dictate the nature of the message but merely transfer it. Whilst it is true that new technologies can change our ways of thinking, we need to reassure ourselves that this is for the better.

The painting highlights the fact that human beings have been recording their thoughts and achievements for millennia, although not always in written form. An ongoing quest on the part of historians, ethnologists, anthropologists and others is to decipher or give meaning to that which is recorded or documented in some way. At the same time, we know that in the history of music, notation is but one way of recording music; it is however a relatively accurate one – certainly with respect to

Western music up to at least the beginning of the 20th century. Where music is not so recorded it presents its own body of problems for researchers. This also underscores the fact that some music has never been 'documented', let alone notated.

I have no doubt that, with time and perspective, the dominant communication systems of today, as represented by the mobile phone in the painting, will not seem such 'abhorrent' instruments as I might be seen to be suggesting. Of course they have a place. One only has to have a car break down in the middle of nowhere to realize this; and then hope, of course, that one's phone is not out of range! For the mobile phone does allow us to record instant thoughts (just as composers, historically, have done through notation or electronic recording devices). Indeed, the modern mobile phone allows us to capture pictures as well; and, of course, it allows us to record sounds. Maybe I've been too harsh on this modern-day substitute for a letter ...

Jacques Attali (2009), in his recently published book, *A Brief History of the Future*, predicts some changes that will occur with respect to the arts in the next twenty years:

> By 2030, new artworks will mingle all media and all means of distribution. It will no longer be possible to distinguish between what is owed to painting, to sculpture, to film, or to literature. Books will tell stories with three-dimensional images. Sculptures will dance with the spectators to new kinds of music. Games will more and more become ways of creating, imagining, informing, teaching, and surveillance, of raising self-esteem and the sense of community awareness. Movies past and future will be viewable in three dimensions, completed by sensorial stimulators and virtual smells. It will also become possible to ... broadcast three-dimensional concerts, plays, sports events, lectures, and classes. (pp. 126–127)

Despite these predictions, it was a sobering thought for me to read a book published this year on Aboriginal art entitled, *Painting the Song*. This presents Kaltjiti art and the art of the Pitjantjatjara and Yankunytjatjara lands encompassing South Australia, the Northern Territory and Western Australia. The book presents art of peoples for whom culture and art are not separate: they are one. Aboriginal people are artists, dancers and singers of the Tjukurpa – the Dreaming, their traditional Law. *Painting the Song* reminded me that Attali is incorrect if he believes that we will have to wait for the future before it becomes impossible to distinguish what is owed to individual art forms: for this is not uncommon in Aboriginal culture in the past and present. At the same time, Attali does highlight new possibilities for experiencing the arts in twenty years time.

I wonder, when a similar book to this *Festschrift* is undertaken in twenty-plus years, what new dimensions of music will be written about. I wonder how 'the letter' will fare. Will it, in fact, prove to be a more permanent tool of communication than the mobile phone or email? Or will the mobile phone be displaced by something that even a familiarity with the iPhone has not yet prepared us for? Will the piano indeed still be favoured – despite its antiquity – as a preferred means of communication in music?

But let the argument not simply be seen as one of new technology versus retention of the old. For there are ethical and social reasons for questioning the new, as Attali (2009, p. 81) has identified:

> In 1947, the electric battery and the transistor (two key inventions) make radio and record players portable. This is a major revolution, for it allows the young to dance outside the ballrooms and therefore be free of parental supervision – liberating sexuality, opening them to all kinds of music, from jazz to rock, and thus announcing youth's entry into the world of consumption, of desire, and of rebellion.

For the truth is that for many young people today, music is not simply something that one listens to for the sake of listening: the experience is often seen to be heightened by the taking of drugs. Listening to music is not merely an aural experience: it is a chemical experience. Has civilization brought us to this? What a twist it is on the development of listening skills as I knew them in my teaching days!

Despite a 'fear' or negativity – some might say skepticism – on my part, I derive great consolation in my belief that all of the contributors to this volume recognize the importance of interacting and communicating with people 'face-to-face'. Doreen Bridges herself has commented:

> more and more the intimate physical contact between performer and instrument is being eroded – it is so easy to press buttons to produce at least some desired effects. But even the most sophisticated digital electronic instruments cannot completely substitute for the subtle nuances over which a performer has control through touch or breath. (Bridges, 1994a, p. 55)

On a personal level I hope, as a teacher and performer, that we will never be reduced to being the invisible person in the room. I also hope that it will never be the case that what we have to offer will only be accepted if the audience has been chemically 'prepped' beforehand.

I have thoroughly enjoyed pondering Ross Watson's painting and contemplating Attali's look into the future. What Attali and others – including government and educational bureaucrats – don't acknowledge nearly enough, it seems to me, is that music and the other arts have a pivotal role to play in the future of humanity: aesthetically, ethically, socially and spiritually. There is a danger at the present time of putting all of our concerns into global warming and climate change: let us not forget our basic needs as human beings – needs that only the arts can satisfy. And let us hope that whatever happens we never completely turn our backs on the merits of the letter. At the same time I acknowledge what Robert Werner has reminded us in this volume: that our role is to prepare children for their future – not ours. And equally I concur with Michael Kieran Harvey's criticism that training in music is largely predicated on the past.

Dee Bridges has spanned a considerable period of change in the history of music and music education. She has managed to keep abreast of this change and, indeed, to initiate and give direction to some of it herself. Underscoring her deep and enduring involvement in this quest has been her ability to reflect, interpret, assess and give meaning to what has been occurring in the many faceted world of music. And for this we all have reason to be grateful.

References

Adams, P. (2009). Phillip Adams. In *The Weekend Australian Magazine,* June 6–7.
Attali, J. (2009). *A Brief History of the Future.* Crows Nest, NSW: Allen & Unwin.
Bridges, D. (2006). *More than a Musician: A Life of E. Harold Davies.* Melbourne: Australian Scholarly Publishing.
Bridges, D. (1994a). *Music, Young Children & You.* Sydney: Hale & Iremonger.
Bridges, D. (1994b). An Australian Perspective. In M. Comte (Ed.) *Music Education: International Viewpoints. A Symposium in Honour of Emeritus Professor Sir Frank Callaway.* Perth: ASME/CIRCME.
Bridges, D. (1978). *Australian Test for Advanced Music Studies Report and Handbook.* Hawthorn: Australian Council for educational Research.
Bridges, D. (1970). The role of universities in the development of music education in Australia 1885–1970. Unpublished Ph.D thesis, University of Sydney.
Comte, M. (1994). *Music Education: International Viewpoints. A Symposium in Honour of Emeritus Professor Sir Frank Callaway.* Perth: ASME/CIRCME.
Comte, M. (1992). *Doreen Bridges: Music Educator,* ASME Monograph No.2. Melbourne: ASME.
Covell, R. (1967). *Australia's music: Themes of a new society.* Melbourne: Sun Books.
Hoermann, D. & Bridges, D. (1984, 1987, 1991). *A Developmental Music Program,* Revised Edition, Teachers Manual (incorporating Student books), Stages 1–3. Brookvale, NSW: Educational Supplies.
James, D. (2009). *Painting the Song: Kaltjiti artists of the sand dune country.* Melbourne: McCulloch & McCulloch Australian Art Books.

Notes

[1] Untitled #3/2003. After Ter Borch, 1662. Oil on board 122 x 94 cm has been reproduced with permission from Ross Watson, www.rosswatson.com, enquiries@rosswatson.com

2: The Australian Test for Advanced Music Studies: A Watershed in the Assessment of Musical Ability

Jennifer Bryce

Introduction

It was probably 1973. Dr Doreen Bridges was in the passenger seat as we puttered out to Tullamarine airport in my little Volkswagen Beetle. She was still totally engrossed in the test items we had been discussing all day, whereas I was concentrating on the traffic and anxious that she might miss her flight home to Sydney. I tried to take in the instructions she shouted over the noise of the rattling engine. I remember her throwing pieces of paper onto the back seat but I can't remember now whether they were items she wanted to discard, or tasks I was to carry out over the next few days – I was her research assistant. Early on she said I was to call her 'Dee'. She doesn't like 'Doreen', maybe because of the C. J. Dennis association: 'Er name's Doreen … Well, spare me bloomin' days!' I was so in awe of this focused dynamo of a woman, it was hard enough to dispense with the 'Dr', let alone use a diminutive. But that was at least 35 years ago. She is now a dear friend and mentor, and will be 'Dee' throughout this piece.

Reasons for developing the Australian Test for Advanced Music Studies (ATAMS)

Music continues to be one of the most challenging areas to assess in an authentic and reliable manner (McPherson & Thompson, 1998). Either authenticity and validity are compromised by the testing of discrete elements of music (such as pitch discrimination or meter) rather than the whole or, where a whole performance is considered, the assessment is often open to subjectivity and reduced reliability with a decision made by one or two people, because it is too costly for institutions (such as the Australian Music Examinations Board) to employ and fully train a team of judges and examinees.

In 1969, general dissatisfaction with music examinations in Australia was voiced at the First General Assembly of the Australian Society for Music Education (ASME). This led to a research project undertaken by Dee through the Australian Council for Educational Research (ACER) and funded by a grant from the Australian Advisory Committee for Research and Development in Education (AACRDE) (Bridges, 1978).

At the time Dee had articulated many of the problems and challenges of assessing music education. She had been critical of the stultifying effect of a system such as the AMEB, which imposed an outmoded and British-oriented approach on most aspects of music education (Bridges, 1970, p. 124). She also criticised the examinations of the time as not highly valid or authentic. For example, scales and exercises were evaluated for their own sake, in isolation from musical works, rather than being seen as a means to overcoming technical problems in those pieces. Dee has pointed out that although there were pieces by Debussy on the AMEB syllabus from 1921 onwards, the technical work did not include the whole-tone scale (Bridges, 1970, pp. 130–1). Likewise, theory was treated mainly as 'a mathematical exercise divorced from musical context'. Dee has asserted that students could complete theory exercises without having any idea of what the music actually sounded like (Bridges, 1970,

p. 146) and that there was 'an extraordinary contradiction' between the richness of music available to young people in Australia and the 'impoverished diet' that formed the basis of music examinations up to the 1970s. She argued that a likely reason for this situation was a lack of any coherent philosophy of music education and hence a lack of clarity as to why particular skills or competencies were being tested (Bridges, 1978, pp. 13–14).

At the 1969 ASME conference, Dee presented a paper that summarised her views on measurement and assessment in music education at that time. She underlined the importance of good assessment to help teachers understand whether their objectives are being achieved, whether students are making progress and whether students need extra help in certain areas. She distinguished between tests of ability, achievement and aptitude, using definitions from a recent International Seminar on Experimental Research in Music Education: ability was defined as 'present functioning level', achievement as 'measurable progress towards clearly-defined goals' and aptitude as 'innate capacity' (Bridges, 1969).

Tests that purport to measure musical ability, achievement and aptitude have been available since the publication of Seashore's measures of 'musical talents' in 1919 (Seashore, 1919). But, as Dee points out in the handbook to ATAMS, such tests have various limitations. These include being divorced from a genuine musical context, or being drawn from a limited range of music, sometimes being delivered only by piano or by contrived aural stimuli and sometimes requiring value judgments of an aesthetic nature (Bridges, 1978, pp. 10–11).

Dee has pointed out the importance of testing 'musical perception' and memory where the 'inner hearing' involved is an essential component of musicality. She suggests that tests which are divorced from a musical context (such as those using contrived aural stimuli, not using musical phrases etc.) are testing only 'aural acuity', not the real substance of music (Bridges, 2008).

With direction from the Research Committee of ASME, it was decided that the problems articulated at the 1969 ASME General Assembly could be addressed by developing a test for use at the point of entry to tertiary music courses. Year 12 level was selected because there appeared to be a clear need for a reliable measure for entry to music courses. At the time, Dee states, 'staff in many tertiary institutions offering music apparently found the examination results so uninformative that they were conducting auditions and administering their own *ad hoc* tests … of aural perception and musical literacy' (Bridges, 1978, p. 3). The Research Committee also advised that the research should be confined to assessment of 'those musical abilities that could be evaluated objectively' (Bridges, 1978, p. 4). Thus the development funded by the AACRDE was for an objectively scored test of generalised musical abilities at the tertiary entrance level.

The proposal to develop ATAMS seems to have been viewed as the starting-point for a general review of the provision of music education in Australia by ASME. This is endorsed by an ACER newsletter of the time that entitled a lead article describing the development of ATAMS as 'A Test for Music Studies, Opus 1' (ACER, 1972). Although there have been government sponsored reviews of music education provision since that time (Pascoe et al., 2005) there seems to have been no systematic extension of the substantial research that ensued from the ASME 1969 General Assembly.

The test development process

A logical starting-point for developing any test is to define clearly what is to be tested – in the form of a test construct. Dee undertook an extensive review of published music tests and the literature on music testing. This involved a thorough exploration of concepts such as 'musicality', 'aural-visual discrimination', and 'musical cognition'. It was decided that ATAMS should incorporate the most useful features of existing tests and examinations whilst avoiding their disadvantages and limitations. It had been agreed that the test would exclude assessment of students' musical performance and composition in order to produce a measure that could be objectively scored. The kernel of the test construct was the ability to 'make sense' of music by being able 'to hold in the mind certain musical patterns while at the same time receiving other aural impressions as the music continues' (Bridges, 1978, p. 18).

Following an analysis of all Australian syllabuses that pertained to the population who might undertake ATAMS, a list of minimum competencies and items of musical knowledge common to examinations specified as prerequisites for Australian tertiary music courses was sent to the heads of all conservatories and departments of music in universities for criticisms, comments and suggestions (Bridges, 1978). Lists of competencies and skills are, by their nature, cryptic and although there was agreement about the basic elements to be tested, it was still necessary to consider in depth what is involved, for example, in writing a rhythmic or melodic pattern from dictation (Bridges, 1978, p. 20) in order to tease out these processes and develop multiple-choice (objective) questions to test them. Dee was concerned to use a very wide range of musical examples. Whilst the examples should be unfamiliar to candidates, they were to come from actual pieces of music (to try to ensure, for example, that ATAMS was testing *musical* perception rather than aural acuity). In the selection of examples Dee was influenced by the work of Werner who stated that 'musicianship in our pluralist society should focus on the development of concepts and skills to enable students to perceive, comprehend and manipulate the elements common to all musics' (Werner, 1969, pp. 15–26).

After extensive investigation and consultation it was decided that the test should be presented in three separate books:

1. tonal and rhythm memory and musical perception (this would assume no prior learned musical knowledge);
2. aural/visual discrimination, score reading and understanding of notation; and
3. comprehension and application of learned musical material

(Bridges & Rechter, 1974)

Book 1 could be used in isolation for courses where no prior musical knowledge was expected.

Table 1 below provides a very general outline of the main elements of the test construct and the section of the test where they are measured. This is discussed by Dee in much greater detail in the ATAMS Handbook and represented in a more detailed table (Bridges 1978, p. 39).

Table 1: Content of ATAMS

Proposed content	ATAMS book
aural imagery and memory	Book 1
ability to read music, to understand the printed score, and to correlate heard sounds with their notation	Book 2
aural recognition of musical elements including intervals, scales, basic chords, tonality and durational aspects such as meter, note values, tempo etc.	Book 3
ability to comprehend and apply terminology in common use	Book 3
aural recognition of: instruments, mode of performance, sound sources, instrumental combinations, principles of organisation, stylistic characteristics of well-known composers, same/different styles of unfamiliar music	Book3/Book 1

Test construction followed a rigorous process outlined in Figure 1 below. The progression shown in diagrammatic form looks deceptively straightforward, but this was not the case; the search for appropriate musical examples was painstaking, some panel members had difficulty adjusting to the notion of a music test that was strikingly

```
┌─────────────────────────────────────────────────────────────────────────┐
│  Development of draft test items (including selection of appropriate    │
│  musical stimulus)                                                      │
└─────────────────────────────────────────────────────────────────────────┘
                                    ▼
┌─────────────────────────────────────────────────────────────────────────┐
│  Panelling of draft items with experts from conservatories,             │
│  universities, teachers' colleges and schools                           │
└─────────────────────────────────────────────────────────────────────────┘
                                    ▼
┌─────────────────────────────────────────────────────────────────────────┐
│  Piloting of panelled items with 1st year music students and            │
│  discussions with students and their teachers                           │
└─────────────────────────────────────────────────────────────────────────┘
                                    ▼
┌─────────────────────────────────────────────────────────────────────────┐
│  Redrafting, editing, further panelling                                 │
└─────────────────────────────────────────────────────────────────────────┘
                                    ▼
┌─────────────────────────────────────────────────────────────────────────┐
│  Trial testing of 3 forms of the test with Year 12 music students,      │
│  teachers' college music electives students and 1st year university     │
│  music students                                                         │
└─────────────────────────────────────────────────────────────────────────┘
                                    ▼
┌─────────────────────────────────────────────────────────────────────────┐
│  Psychometric analysis, interpretation                                  │
└─────────────────────────────────────────────────────────────────────────┘
                                    ▼
┌─────────────────────────────────────────────────────────────────────────┐
│  Revision and editing                                                   │
└─────────────────────────────────────────────────────────────────────────┘
                                    ▼
┌─────────────────────────────────────────────────────────────────────────┐
│  Testing of a provisional final form of ATAMS                           │
└─────────────────────────────────────────────────────────────────────────┘
                                    ▼
┌─────────────────────────────────────────────────────────────────────────┐
│  Psychometric analysis, interpretation                                  │
└─────────────────────────────────────────────────────────────────────────┘
                                    ▼
┌─────────────────────────────────────────────────────────────────────────┐
│  Revision and editing                                                   │
└─────────────────────────────────────────────────────────────────────────┘
                                    ▼
┌─────────────────────────────────────────────────────────────────────────┐
│  Publication of the final form of ATAMS                                 │
└─────────────────────────────────────────────────────────────────────────┘
```

Figure 1: Process of development of ATAMS

different from the familiar AMEB examinations or the published music tests of the time and there were no similar measures to indicate whether students could handle the test requirements, hence extensive pilot testing was necessary.

The process outlined above took place over almost three years of intensive work. There was much re-thinking, re-wording and some changing of musical examples. One difficulty was posed by the nature of music itself – it exists over time. This affected the length of the test. In addition to the time taken to listen to musical examples, time had to be allowed for reading each question and answering it. For reliability it is necessary to have several questions testing a particular skill. The final test takes three hours to administer – this includes a mandatory rest period. Three hours was found to be the minimum time to provide a valid and reliable test that covered the breadth of skills and competencies required.

I was privileged to work as research assistant on the development of ATAMS and I remember the intensity of the work. I had been working at ACER for a couple of years on humanities tests, so I was familiar with the testing procedures of drafting, panelling, trial testing and analysing. But doing this with musical examples was especially challenging. There was the issue of having a piece of recorded music for every question – people scrutinising the test questions in panels, for example, had to be supplied with good quality recordings, and in the 1970s this was difficult. ATAMS was developed before the ready availability of cassette tapes – the tests were first produced on reel-to-reel. Dee seemed to be completely engrossed in the test. She made frequent visits to ACER, which in those days had just one office in Melbourne. I sometimes went to Sydney, where I stayed and worked at her home in Lindfield. I must have taken my oboe, as I remember one time playing chamber music with Dee at the piano and her son, Tom, who was still at school, playing violin. It was on occasions such as these that Dee provided me with a model (which I've never been able to live up to) of a woman who managed to weed the garden, make her own yoghurt and prepare dinner whilst simultaneously making decisions about appropriate musical examples for measuring a particular kind of chord progression.

It was fascinating to supervise some of the trial testing – we had to ensure that the test was undertaken in conditions as similar as possible in all testing sites. It was particularly difficult to ensure that equipment for playing the tapes was of sufficiently high quality. On one occasion the Director of ACER, Dr Radford, came out to Monash University with me to help supervise the test. This was most unusual for a person in such a senior position, and indicates his high level of interest in this novel enterprise. As a very junior staff member I was quite anxious about spending more than three hours in his company – what would we talk about? My anxiety was unfounded – he was kindly and generous. My most amusing experience was when I took the trial tests to Tasmania. I went over on the ferry, the bundles of tests and the precious tapes locked carefully in my car. I was worried about being sea-sick, but an eccentric missionary befriended me and insisted that the remedy was double gins and tonics, which she ministered and charged to the Anglican Church of Australia. I don't remember much of the voyage, but I certainly wasn't sea-sick!

ATAMS and the future

Even by today's standards, ATAMS is a robust test. A consideration of the psychometric data reported in the Handbook (Bridges, 1978) suggests that it stands up to the requirements set for good published tests. Taking the final 1975 version of the test, the facilities range from 92% (very easy) to 25% (very difficult – only 25% of candidates answered correctly) for Book 1, 90% to a very low 18% for Book 2, and 87% to 25% for Book 3 (Bridges, 1978, p. 49). In Book 1 there are six out of 30 items that would not 'pass' rigorous standards of item discrimination (indicating whether candidates who do well on that component of the test get the particular question correct), one out of 30 items for Book 2, and two out of 30 items for Book 3 (Bridges, 1978, p. 55). There may well be good explanations for these outcomes. It would be very interesting to compare these with data gathered today. The 1975 reliability coefficient for the test as a whole is high: 0.91 (KR20) and for each of the separate books (i.e. considering a smaller number of items) it is higher than 0.80 (Bridges, 1978, p. 68).

There was a range of validation studies undertaken. For example, an investigation of criterion-related validity compared scores on ATAMS with scores on similar existing standardised tests (acknowledging that such tests are not exactly the same as ATAMS). Components of the *Aliferis Music Achievement Test* were found to be similar to Book 2 of ATAMS (Bridges, 1978, p. 72) and, although a large sample could not be obtained, there was a significant result, suggesting predictive validity, when the results of advanced (3rd and 4th year or post graduate) students were compared with a group of high-scoring students at entrance level (Bridges, 1978, p. 73). Some other interesting data emerged from studies at the time. For example, it was shown that a group classified as having high practical ability (results in high level AMEB exams, and/or Year 12 practical music exams) in music achieved significantly higher on ATAMS than a group classified as having low practical ability. There were similar results for students classified as having high results in theoretical exams. It is unfortunate that some of these studies were not pursued over a longer time-frame in Australia or replicated some years later.

A substantial piece of research was undertaken between 1980 and 1990 in Warsaw with a sample of 3000 students, which indicated that ATAMS measured relevant abilities and predicted success in music studies (Meyer-Borysewicz, 1990). ATAMS appears to have proved a useful tool in the investigation of musical giftedness in Poland (Manturzewska, 1992). It has also been used in Australian studies, such as research by Weidenbach (1994), where Book 1 was used with university students who had diverse musical backgrounds.

ATAMS was reviewed in the Eighth Mental Measurements Year Book (Phelps, 1978). Professor Phelps sees the use of actual music of diverse periods and styles as 'a strong feature' and he sums up the test very favourably saying it is 'undoubtedly the best and most up-to-date test developed to measure the prior achievement of entering college music students' and he finds the musical examples 'interesting and tastefully presented'. He considers the test to be better than the two Aliferis tests used at the time in the US for a similar purpose. His only criticisms are brushed over as insignificant; sometimes too much time is allowed on the tape for answering questions and too many aspects of 'music achievement' are covered. At the time of review the final handbook wasn't available where the test construct is fully outlined and the need for these examples explained.

Coda

Today I was driving to the airport in my silent six-cylinder saloon (the Volkswagen was abandoned 20 years ago). The radio was tuned to ABC FM and a successful Australian opera singer was interviewed. She mentioned the importance of having a 'solid' music education. She had attended the Sydney Conservatorium in the mid 1970s. I realised that she had probably taken ATAMS. I wonder whether she obtained high scores? It set me thinking about the various avenues of research that have not yet been explored in Australia and the relatively minor adjustments that could make ATAMS a valuable assessment tool for 21st century music educators. When Dee started work on the test in 1972, did she have any idea that such a claim might be made 37 years later?

References

Australian Council for Educational Research, *Newsletter*, No. 15, December 1972.
Bridges, D. (1970). *The Role of Universities in the Development of Music Education in Australia 1885–1970*. Doctoral Thesis, University of Sydney.
Bridges, D. (1978). *Australian Test for Advanced Music Studies Report and Handbook*. Hawthorn: Australian Council for Educational Research.
Bridges, D. (1969). Measurement and Assessment in Music Education, *ASME Conference Report, 1969*. Reprinted in M. Comte (Ed.) (1992). *Doreen Bridges: Music Educator*. ASME Monograph Series No. 2, Parkville: Australian Society for Music Education Inc.
Bridges, D. (2008). *Evaluating Musical Intelligence*. Unpublished paper.
Bridges, D. & Rechter, B. (1974). *Australian Test for Advanced Music Studies*. Hawthorn: Australian Council for Educational Research.
McPherson, G. & Thompson, W. (1998). Assessing Music Performance: Issues and Influences, *Research Studies in Music Education*, 10, June 1998.

Manturzewska, M. (1992). Identification and Promotion of Musical Talent, *High Ability Studies*, 3, 1, 15–27.
Meyer-Borysewicz, M. (1990). Candidates for the Chopin Academy of Music as tested with the Australian Test for Advanced Music Studies by Doreen Bridges, *Psychology of Music Today*, 212–219. Cited in Bridges, D. 2008.
Pascoe, R. et al. (2005). *National Review of School Music Education: Augmenting the Diminished*. Canberra: Australian Government.
Phelps, R. (1978). [Review of Australian Test for Advanced Music Studies]. In O. Buros (Ed.), *The Eighth Mental Measurements Yearbook*, 1, 174–175. Highland Park, NJ: The Gryphon Press.
Seashore, C. (1919). *The Psychology of Musical Talent*. Boston: Silver Burdett.
Weidenbach, V. (1994). Keyboard Instructional Praxis in a Computer-Based Learning Environment, *Research Studies in Music Education*, 3, December 1994.
Werner, R. (1969). Music in General Education, *Report of the First National Conference of the Australian Society for Music Education*. Cited in Bridges, 2008.

3: Studio Music Teachers and Teaching: Roles and Responsibilities

Amanda Watson

A significant and valuable part of music education for pre-school, school and tertiary-aged students and adult learners is the private music lesson. This activity normally occurs outside formal education institutions and is variously referred to as private or studio music teaching, private music lessons or private music instruction. The teaching of music at home or in a private studio is a cottage industry and unregulated in Australia. Anyone can set themselves up as a studio music teacher regardless of their personal training and competence. Consequently the quality of work is variable, across the full spectrum from outstanding to very poor. Many have music qualifications and broad experience as professional musicians. A lesser number have a recognised teaching qualification, while others, including senior secondary and tertiary students, have no music or teaching qualifications. Some providers earn a living from studio teaching and the associated business of running a private studio. Teacher registration through a statutory board of teacher registration is not necessary, although in Australia studio teachers may obtain a police record check. However, without regulation, no official inspection of this documentation can be made. There is no compulsory or lawful requirement for the provider of a studio music teaching service to register a business or company name, to have their qualifications certified or accredited, to have their teaching activities assessed or for the teaching venue to be inspected by an outside agency.

Some private music studios run as a commercial business and have a close link with the music industry; however the settings in which they operate are diverse. The music studio in a private home may be purposefully designed or easily adapted for this type of work, using a study, office or spare room in the house or detached building in the garden. In some cases the family living room is the teaching venue because there is no other space and this choice is often not the best environment for learning and teaching. Some teachers rent a shop front or teach in a room of a retail music store. Others may teach in a larger music school, often a converted house or rented premises from a regular day school and commence their teaching when the day students have departed. Some are self-employed and own their studio premises and equipment, others work for wages. Often on a weekday, they begin work about 3.00pm and teach until approximately 9.00pm. They teach all day Saturday as well. In very large music schools that may employ 20 or more specialists, lessons are available during the day. Studio teachers are also represented in the conservatoires in tertiary education and in regular day schools where they are employed as specialists. Private lessons in many schools attract a fee.

Studio music teachers offer a variety of services including solo lessons, group lessons, theory and musicianship, preparation for examinations administered by external bodies, concerts, performances, auditions for professional employment, eisteddfods and competitions and accompaniment services. It is recommended that owners of studios have written policies outlining their services and details about payment, missed lessons and teaching times.

Studio music teachers need additional skills other than those associated with the services they offer. They need coaching and mentoring, counselling and career guidance skills. They need communication skills with parents and the school music teachers of their students. Studio teachers teach the instrumental music aspects of senior school certificates and need to understand the required syllabus and cooperate with the student's school. They need business and management skills, as the private studio no matter how small or the actual venue where the teaching takes place involves receiving lesson payments, paying tax, insurance, employees and complying with many other business transactions. Contrary to the wide-ranging acknowledged skills of the studio teacher, there are providers of this type of service who demonstrate little or no ethical or business skills and remain insular.

Studio teachers work with students at different levels of achievement. Some will teach from beginner to advanced standard, others beginner to intermediate standard, or advanced standard only. Similarly some have a preference for the age group they teach, for example, young children though to adults, no adults, primary and/or secondary age, or tertiary-enrolled students.

Studio teachers teach for economic reasons and/or professional reasons. Some teach instrumental music or classroom music all day in a school and go home to teach regular private students for financial security. Some teach other disciplines in schools and as amateur musicians impart their knowledge to private students. Others teach for the professional challenge or take a few private students often by request. These people may or may not have music and/or teaching qualifications and may work in occupations outside teaching and music. Some tertiary students who play an instrument, and who are studying in a wide range of disciplines (not necessarily teaching and/or music) teach for financial survival during their studies at university, and likewise professional musicians not in ongoing professional employment also teach for a large percentage of their time. A comprehensive doctoral thesis investigating what musicians do for a living by Bennett (2005) highlights the significance of teaching in this career choice.

In Australia as an example, professional musicians who have full-time employment in a professional capacity, for example, the Melbourne Symphony Orchestra or with the Australian Defence Force music ensembles or State Police Force ensembles, teach in conservatories, specialist music schools such as the Victorian College of the Arts Secondary School and privately as part of their professional responsibility to impart their knowledge, experience and skills.

As well as the undergraduate and postgraduate courses offered by universities with a specific purpose on preparing instrumental and vocal music teachers for employment in schools and to a lesser extent the private studio, a number of organisations provide suitable short courses. Musicians and teachers can enrol in teaching courses provided by examination bodies and many are offered at the award level. In Australia, these qualifications are recognised by the studio music teacher associations for the purposes of membership and inclusion in their own lists of registered teachers. The Australian Music Examinations Board (AMEB) offers the diploma Teacher of Music Australia at three levels: certificate, associate and licentiate. The Australian and New Zealand Cultural Arts (ANZCA) offers three levels of diplomas – associate, licentiate and fellowship – with a focus on performing, teaching, theory, composition and history and literature. The St. Cecilia School of Music offers professional teaching diplomas in music for Australian candidates at advanced, diploma and fellowship levels. The Australian Guild of Music Education System is a registered training provider and provides vocational training for performers and teachers. The Trinity Guildhall's teaching diplomas are available to candidates in many countries with the Specialist Music Teaching and the Instrumental/Vocal Teaching diplomas offered at the associate and licentiate levels. The Suzuki Music Association in Australia offers structured courses in instrumental teaching at the primary, intermediate and advanced levels tailored to its specific teaching philosophy and similarly in other countries.

Although information about the training of instrumental and vocal teachers is readily available in Australia, a project undertaken by the Association of European Conservatories (AEC)[1] highlighted other issues. In March 2008 the Erasmus Network for Music under the auspices of the AEC hosted a conference to explore the education of instrumental and vocal teachers in Europe in the conservatoire setting. As part of the Erasmus Network, the *International Network for Vocal and Instrumental Teacher Education (INVITE)* was formed. Kaarlo Hildren remarked:

INVITE has been created because of the lack of mobility and collaboration in the field of instrumental teacher education and the fact that the different national systems and educational traditions led to a lack of comprehensibility. Furthermore, rapidly changing work contexts and professional roles of instrumental teachers are an important development that needs to be faced. (p. 3)

With a focus on conservatoire education, the conference identified that INVITE had a role to play from the perspectives of the student, the teacher and the institution. Some of the issues discussed that are particularly relevant to studio teaching are:

From a students' perspective:
Students have difficulties in studying pedagogical subjects abroad. It is hard to find information about the content and structure of institutions' pedagogical studies.

From a teachers' perspective:
Sharing and reflecting needs to be done on an international level, because the specialist know-how is fragmented and scattered.
The competence and qualification requirements of instrumental and vocal teachers are different in all countries. Therefore it is difficult for teachers to find employment abroad. (p. 3)

Although teacher registration may not be required to teach in the studio setting, there are many professional teaching associations that studio music teachers may join that provide a credentialing service. Some of the music teacher associations in Australia, specifically representing piano teachers, offer accreditation for their members based on the qualifications and experience that potential members record on a membership form. The Western Australia Music Teachers' Association (WAMTA) offers courses exclusively for their own members in rudiments and harmony, history of music, aural training and teaching principles that are recognised by WAMTA for accreditation as a studio teacher. Similar certification of qualifications[2] are offered by the music teacher associations in America, for example, California, Florida and North Dakota, and in Canada where a studio teacher must first join a provincial group and automatically becomes a member of the national association. Interestingly the Saskatchewan Registered Music Teachers' Association has *The Registered Music Teachers Act (2002)*. In Australia, teachers who join groups such as Suzuki Music or the Yamaha Music Foundation can only remain accredited by completing a set amount of professional learning each year provided by the organisation, with a focus on their particular philosophy.

Guidelines or advice for practice are only available to members as part of the membership services provided by music associations. Many have a code of ethics and other services offered include professional learning opportunities, for example, conferences, master classes and short courses and aspects associated with establishing a maintaining a private studio (e.g., business practices, templates for communications and tax advice). Websites now provide access to this type of material for members and as an example the Incorporated Society of Musicians (UK) has developed a number of Information Sheets containing professional material that can be purchased by non-members.

People who are teaching music privately and are not members of a professional association and do not have a connection with a school may not have access to appropriate resources, information and professional guidelines to inform their practice. Similarly parents seeking a teacher for their child may find it difficult to access any appropriate documentation. As a colleague said, "Your parents are your employers, if they don't like your work they move their child to another teacher". Although as already mentioned in this paper, resources are provided as part of membership services of a professional association, the provision of professional teaching standards or guidelines are lacking. One prominent exception is the Professional Certification program managed by the Music Teachers National Association (MTNA) in America. The program exists for teachers who teach music to students of any age level in private or group settings and is based upon a set of five standards defining what a competent music teacher should know and be able to do:

Standard I: Professional Preparation
Standard II: Professional Teaching Practices
Standard III: Professional Business Management
Standard IV: Professionalism and Partnerships
Standard V: Professional and Personal Renewal (MTNA, 2009)

A person who wishes to participate in this program completes a portfolio demonstrating the requirements of the professional standards and upon fulfillment of the standards, is granted the MTNA Professional Certification credential with the designation, Nationally Certified Teacher of Music (NCTM). To maintain this designation the applicant must continue to fulfill the standards through the renewal process (MTNA, 2009).

In recent years concerns have been expressed by individual Australian studio music teachers and through the Music Council of Australia[3] for the development of professional standards designed for the specialist work environments occupied by studio music teachers who may have little or no access to similar material available to teachers who work as instrumental teachers in schools. The writing of professional teaching standards for Australian educators commenced in 1999 with the awarding of three Australian Research Council grants. Four professional teaching associations representing English and Literacy, Mathematics and Science, each working in conjunction with Monash University in Melbourne was funded to develop professional standards for accomplished teachers of these disciplines. This activity inspired many other professional teaching associations to write standards for their own disciplines. The author of this paper has developed professional standards for studio teachers[4]. The specialist teaching of studio music teachers and their unique work environments are not specifically covered by professional standards for school teachers. The author aims is to develop a document taking a national overview that is non-specific to any Australian State or Territory and accessible to anyone who is a studio music teacher. The draft guidelines are based on the *ASME National Framework for Music Teaching Standards* (ASME, 2005) and use the headings Professional Knowledge, Professional Practice, Professional Learning and Professional Values.

Despite the lack of regulation in this part of the education environment, the studio music teacher makes a very large contribution to the instrumental music education of students of all ages. In this very brief overview of studio teaching in Australia, America, Canada and Europe it is evident that there are varying degrees of cohesion within and between the many organisations representing music teacher associations, specific instruments, voice, philosophies of teaching and institutions awarding qualifications. A significant factor is the lack of established professional standards administered on a country level that studio music teachers can use to demonstrate what they know and are able to do.

Notes

1. More information can be found at the Association of European Conservatories websites: www.aecinfo.org, www.polifonia-tn.org, www.bologna-and-music.org
2. Web references: California, www.mtac.org; Florida, www.fmta.org; North Dakota, www.ndmta.org; Canada, www.cfmta.org
3. Music Council of Australia, http://www.mca.org.au/web/component/option,com_kb/task,article/article,48/
4. The document Studio Music Teaching in Australia including draft Code of Ethics and Guidelines for Studio Music Teaching Practice is available from the author.

References

Australian and New Zealand Cultural Arts Limited (2009). *Diploma Examinations*. Retrieved 1 March 2009 from http://www.anzca.com.au/files/XL4DS1XSIE/Diploma_Exams_Supplement.pdf

Australian Guild of Music Education System. (2009). *Industry and Tertiary Courses.* Retrieved 1 March 2009 from http://www.guildmusic.edu.au/Pages/AGMED%20Pages/AGMED.html

Australian Music Examinations Board. (2009). *Teaching Awards.* Retrieved 1 March 2009 from http://www.ameb.edu.au/site/index.cfm?display=121807

Australian Society for Music Education (2005). *ASME National Framework for Music Teaching Standards.* (www.asme.edu.au/projects.htm)

Bennett, D. E. (2005). *Classical instrumental musicians: Educating for sustainable professional practice.* Unpublished Ph.D. thesis, University of Western Australia, Perth.

Erasmus Thematic Network for Music (2008). *The education of Instrumental and Vocal teachers in Europe – Changing professional roles and contexts.* Retrieved 8 January 2009 from http://www.aecinfo.org

Incorporated Society of Musicians. (2009). *Information Sheets.* Retrieved 20 January 2009 from http://www.ism.org/publications/info

Music Teachers National Association (2009). *MTNA Certification.* Retrieved 5 January 2009 from http://www.mtnacertification.org

Saskatchewan Registered Music Teachers' Association. (2009). *The Registered Music Teachers Act (2002).* Retrieved 7 January 2009 from http://www.srmta.org

St. Cecilia School of Music. (2009). *Diplomas.* Retrieved 1 March 2009 from http://www.st-cecilia.com.au/index.php?option=com_content&task=view&id=20&Itemid=35#diplomas

Suzuki Talent Education Association of Association. (2009). *Teacher Training.* Retrieved 1 March 2009 from www.suzukimusic.org.au/training.htm

Sydney Conservatorium Open Access Program. (2009). *Summer School.* Retrieved 1 March 2009 from http://www.music.usyd.edu.au/community/summer_school.shtml

Trinity Guildhall. (2009). *Teaching Diplomas.* Retrieved 1 March 2009 from http://www.trinitycollege.co.uk/site/?id=1588

Yamaha Music Foundation. (2009). *Yamaha Music Education Centre.* Retrieved 1 March 2009 from http://www.yamahamusic.com.au/education/musicfoundation.asp

Western Australia Music Teachers' Association (Inc). (2009). *Courses.* Retrieved 12 January 2009 from http://www.musicteacherswa.org.au

4: Establishing Dalcroze Teacher Education in Australia: A Task for Sisyphus[1]

Joan Pope and Sandra Nash

Prelude

Dr Doreen Bridges acknowledges the benefits of well-taught Dalcroze Eurhythmics as part of an intelligent music education and has for many years been a sympathetic supporter.[2] This chapter traces the efforts made to establish Dalcroze Eurhythmics teacher education in Australia. Whilst the very existence of the method depends on having properly trained teachers the number of qualified Dalcroze teachers in Australia has always been minimal. Prior to the mid-1950s, training courses could be undertaken in London, Geneva, several centres in America, but not in Australia. The prospect of it being an integral element of musical education in Australia remains elusive.

Emile Jaques-Dalcroze (1865–1950), a Swiss composer and teacher, saw the need in the late 1890s to reform music teaching because the emphasis on technical virtuosity was at the expense of musical understanding. He created a tripartite approach encompassing rhythmic movement, ear-training (solfege), and improvisation. His aim was to unite mind (intellect and emotion) and body (senses, actions, instincts) and thereby develop the whole person as a creative, balanced, adaptable and autonomous individual with the capacity for musical experience and expression through physical movement of the whole body (Greenhead, 2007, pp. 78–81). Jaques-Dalcroze conducted his first teacher training course in 1907 in Geneva and later, following four dynamic years at Hellerau, near Dresden, he established the Institut in Geneva in 1915 (Tingey, 1943). This is the institution from which the highest qualification, the Diplôme Supérieur is granted and the recipients have 'the rights and responsibilities' to maintain standards, in the name of Jaques-Dalcroze, and to prepare and examine trainee teachers of the method.

Dalcroze principles were soon embraced by the Music Appreciation movement in England, led by Stewart Macpherson and Ernest Read. As teachers at the Royal Academy of Music, their mission was to educate the wider public by carefully structured lessons in aural culture. Read was Director of Music at the London School of Dalcroze Eurhythmics (LSDE) from 1919 and Australians who pursued Dalcroze training in London adopted his ear-training methods. It was the LSDE, founded in 1913, which encouraged the spread of Dalcroze Eurhythmics ideas to Australia (Tingey, 1974). The excellent teaching staff at the LSDE were inspired by the innovative approach developed by 'M'sieur Jaques', as he was affectionately known. The course included anatomy, art history, choral singing, fencing, gymnastics, keyboard harmony, harmony and counterpoint, psychology, teaching methods and score-reading, in addition to Rhythmics, Improvisation, Solfege, and *Plastique animé,* in which the body is used to express, 'in real time', the form of a composition.[3] Peer teaching was an important component and essays were required on musical subjects such as anacrusis, accent, unequal bar-times and phrasing, accompanied by exercises demonstrating these as physical experiences. The training emphasised effective planning of classes for children and entailed practice-teaching with different age groups in London schools where students were observed by staff who engaged them in critical discussion. The Dalcroze students participated in the demonstrations conducted by Jaques-Dalcroze during his regular tours to England and patterned future public displays on his formats. This comprehensive course became the model for later developments in Australia.

First efforts in the antipodes
Seven Australian women completed the rigorous three-year course at the LSDE between 1917 and 1927, but only two became involved with training future Dalcroze

teachers, Heather Gell (1896–1988) in Australia and Cecilia John (1877–1955) in England.[4] Five of the Australians returned to their home State and commenced teaching, typically at independent girls' schools and in private classes. It was difficult for them to replicate the range of subjects they had themselves experienced, nonetheless, several added ear-training, singing and piano lessons to their rhythmic movement classes for children and adult amateurs. The participants were engaged in demonstrations, which served as powerful advertisements of the work. These teachers imparted their knowledge with great enthusiasm despite little organizational support, and few opportunities to visit each other.

Several obtained positions at Kindergarten Training Colleges in their home States. Irene Wittenoom commenced a five year involvement with the WAKTC in 1918 which thus became the first tertiary institution in Australasia to offer Dalcroze Eurhythmics. In 1920, Adelaide kindergartener, Heather Gell, on the advice of Agnes Sterry, spent six weeks with Wittenoom being coached on LSDE course requirements (Pope, 2008, p. 125). Sterry, a well-qualified English music teacher familiar with the new Aural Culture and Music Appreciation system, had come to Adelaide around 1915 where she became Gell's mentor. Gell graduated from Adelaide KTC in 1916 when Lillian de Lissa was Principal. De Lissa had made an extensive visit to Europe and England in 1914, taken a course in Italy with Maria Montessori, observed the teaching at the Hellerau College of Jaques-Dalcroze and been impressed by the new Dalcroze Eurhythmics School in London (de Lissa, 1915, p. 3). Gell determined to study at the LSDE and left Adelaide in late 1921. This was costly and there is some evidence that her mother, the young second wife of elderly H. D. Gell, secretly pawned some of the family silver to assist her financially! Gell missed the first term of the English academic year, but was permitted to take the course in shorter time, and passed in July 1923, with excellent results. She returned to Adelaide and began classes for children and adults in 1924. Like Wittenoom in Perth, she soon added kindergarten teacher-training to her weekly commitments.

Cecilia John, from Tasmania, was already at the LSDE.[5] After attending the International Womens' Peace Conference in Switzerland in 1919, John commenced studies at the LSDE the following year and joined the Executive Committee of the Dalcroze Society in 1923. She made two trips to Australia in connection with Dalcroze demonstrations and the awarding of scholarships sponsored by the LSDE, but returned to work in England. She became Warden of the LSDE in 1930, and Principal in 1932, a position she retained until her death in 1955. Both John and Gell have been described as domineering, forceful, forthright, even brusque in manner, with John likened to a bulldozer and Gell to a great galleon in full sail.[6]

Jaques-Dalcroze had stipulated that a teacher-training course in his method required at least three members of staff to possess the Diplôme. This was to prove an almost insuperable difficulty for countries distant from Europe and none of the Australian graduates held this qualification. A first step towards possible Dalcroze teacher training in Australia occurred in 1924 when Ethel Driver, Mistress of Method at the LSDE, presented a lecture-demonstration in Melbourne as part of a six-month promotional tour of Australasia. It followed a successful two week Summer School conducted by Driver, John and Gell at Carlton Teachers' College. Amidst the enthusiasm, a proposal to include Dalcroze Eurhythmics at Melbourne University was seriously considered by both the Committee of the Conservatorium and Percy Ingham, Director of the LSDE, but the proposal lapsed several years later. Bernard Heinze, the newly appointed Director of the Conservatorium had other priorities and the economic depression inhibited progress.[7]

The uphill battle begins

Gell wanted promising students to train in London and to this end the newly formed SA Dalcroze Society fund-raised, and in late 1925, Marjorie Bonnin was able to commence the course.[8] She completed the Certificate, and was the first Australian to gain the Licentiate of the Royal Academy of Music (LRAM) in Aural Culture. Bonnin returned to Adelaide in 1927, and joined Gell's thriving private practice. Several years later Bonnin again visited London and was on the staff of the Summer School conducted by Jaques-Dalcroze. By the mid-1930s however, she had withdrawn from the arrangement with Gell in Adelaide, and taught private piano students only. Margaret Scales, another of Gell's students, also received a scholarship to the LSDE in 1928, but left to pursue a nursing career.[9]

These were personal setbacks for Gell in her desire to establish a group of Dalcroze teachers in Adelaide, but Dalcroze Eurhythmics in other States also suffered. In WA, Wittenoom had moved to Singapore, so the KTC, the WA Dalcroze Society and the LSDE arranged for Elly Hinrichs, a London teacher with the Diplôme, to come to Perth in 1926. She had the qualification required to conduct Dalcroze Eurhythmics teacher-training and hopes were high. Regrettably, her prickly personality made her unpopular and after four years she returned to England without establishing a training course (Pope, 2008, pp. 237–241).[10] English-born Nancy Rosenhain, LSDE graduate of 1928, was offered a position at Carlton Teachers' College in 1929, but a change of government in Victoria, put a stop to engagement of new staff, and led to cutbacks in music in education (Kirsner, 1973, pp. 44–45).[11] Meanwhile in NSW, English Dalcroze teachers Mary Whidborne, Phyllis Crawhall-Wilson and Kitty Webster, taught privately and at independent schools but are not recorded as being involved with Dalcroze teacher-training. No documentation has been found of Dalcroze teachers in Tasmania or Queensland at this time, and although teachers of physical culture offered 'rhythmics', it was more akin to expressive dance than to the music-centred Dalcroze approach (Pope, 2008, p. 246).

Gell had returned to England in the early 1930s and gained the LRAM in Aural Culture which enhanced her musical standing in Adelaide and especially with Dr E. Harold Davies, Director of the Conservatorium. During the 1920s and 1930s, Davies played a leading role on the Australian Music Examinations Board and in 1924, with the help of Agnes Sterry and Ivy Ayers, prepared a syllabus for Musical Perception (Bridges, 1971, pp. 87–93). The AMEB also saw itself as an advocate for music as a subject in schools. Gell replaced Ayers at the Conservatorium in 1934 and in the same year, Davies proposed a Teachers' Licentiate Syllabus in Musical Perception with a view to providing music teachers in schools, and enlisted the help of Gell. Besides demonstrating ability in performance, theory, aural perception, musicianship and improvisation, candidates were to submit a digest of lessons. They would teach a class in front of the examiners, and undergo a *viva voce* on aspects of class management, teaching and psychology (AMEB *Manual* 1936, pp. 99–104). The two-year course began in 1936, but the numbers taking the examination were small and the syllabus only lasted seven years.

Strangely, after all the groundwork, Gell had designed a course which few could deliver, and which she herself taught only for a year. Gell gave the course from February 1936, but was away in England in 1937 and one of her eurhythmics students, music graduate Mary Jolley replaced her. Jolley continued to teach the course till 1943. In 1940, Doreen Jacobs was one of the candidates and, strongly influenced by Davies, she has always been an advocate of ear-training and the development of the whole musician. While this was not a Dalcroze teachers' course and did not involve body movement, it embraced other elements of the Dalcroze work, notably ear-training and improvisation. Perhaps Gell saw an opening here for training Dalcroze teachers in the future for, apart from her work in Adelaide, Dalcroze Eurhythmics had nearly disappeared in Australia and there was no immediate prospect of establishing a course in the country.

New opportunities and another push for courses for teachers

Gell was engaged by the Australian Broadcasting Commission to present broadcasts to schools of a *Music through Movement* program modelled on that of the BBC, and in late 1938, she moved to Sydney, where the ABC's federal office was located.[12] During the war years Gell and the ABC, in conjunction with the Education Departments of several States, arranged demonstrations and short courses for teachers taking these broadcasts. In this way, Gell became a household name in the Eastern States, though not all were taken with her 'assumed BBC voice'. The *Teachers' Booklets* which Gell wrote to accompany the broadcasts provided an incentive for her book, *Music, Movement and the Young Child*, which would become a text for trainee-teachers. The manuscript was completed by the mid-1940s, and had a supportive foreword by E. Harold Davies, but due to war-time paper shortages, it was not published until 1949, sadly after the death of Davies.

In the 1930s the LSDE had gained the approval of Jaques-Dalcroze to implement a one-year part-time Dalcroze Elementary Course. Gell exploited this opening and encouraged primary school teacher, Eileen Williams, to travel to England in the late 1930s to gain this qualification. Williams duly returned and assisted Gell with monitoring teachers' responses to the broadcasts and developing classes for school teachers. Lesley Cox, from Adelaide, moved to Sydney in 1944–45 to 'learn the ropes' and joined NSW teacher Nancy Wright (later Mrs. Robison), and others, under Gell's tuition in this initiative.[13] Elizabeth Wade commenced a weekly session for music education students within the Melbourne University Conservatorium in 1943, which proved to be the forerunner of those conducted for many years by Nancy Kirsner at this institution and at Monash University.[14]

Gell continued to encourage people to attend the LSDE and Wright took up the challenge, graduated and returned in 1949. Lady Mary Champion de Crespigny (née Jolley) completed part of the LSDE course in the early 1950s but returned to Adelaide before qualifying, however Merle Walkington, an Adelaide kindergarten director, graduated in 1954. It was impossible for Cox (Mrs. R. Cuthbertson) to attend the LSDE at this time, and her 'unqualified' status was one which Gell sought to address in her resolve to 'one day' establish a training course in Australia. Not only were the few Dalcroze specialists geographically scattered in Australia, but it was still the case that not one of them possessed the Diplôme, as required by Jaques-Dalcroze, to conduct teacher-education in his method.

Now or never: the toil begins in earnest, 1950–1957
Jaques-Dalcroze died in 1950 and Gell regretted that circumstances had not permitted her to gain the all-important Diplôme from him personally. Now in her mid-fifties, Gell realized that unless she did something about the situation herself, and quickly, the possibility of establishing a training course in Australia would become even less likely. She heard that Elinor Finley (née Archer), an English woman with the Diplôme, was living in Australia. This was fortuitous for Gell's plans.[15] Gell travelled to England to 'brush up' her Dalcroze skills, determined to gain the Diplôme. She spent time with both the LSDE staff at Milland Place in the country, and the new Dalcroze Training Centre in London. In Geneva she held discussions with the son of Jaques-Dalcroze, a lawyer and member of the foundation responsible for the protection of the method, regarding the legal authority to establish a training course. Gell's book was accepted as her thesis and she gained the Diplôme and was authorised to commence Dalcroze teacher-training.

On returning to Australia, Gell travelled to most States during 1955, promoting her intentions and auditioning prospective students. She offered a half-scholarship in each State and one full scholarship, which would cover fees for the entire course. The latter was awarded to Joan Gray (now Pope and one of the writers of this article) of Perth. The news that this young woman had, in the meantime, married and was bringing her husband with her to Sydney, completely flabbergasted Gell. For several decades she had suffered when her chosen students either changed direction, or got married and discontinued studies. She was prepared to dedicate her life to wearing the symbolic mantle of Jaques-Dalcroze and his method, and it seemed incomprehensible to her that not everyone else shared her enthusiasm. It was no doubt a relief that her 'scholarship girl' not only came to Sydney, but completed the course.

A solitary struggle
The entire operation of 'The Australian School of Music and Movement' was undertaken by Gell; there was no committee, no funding, no institutional assistance

or oversight other than Gell's endeavour to fulfil her obligations to the Institut Jaques-Dalcroze. She could not offer her students the range of subjects given in the 1920s in London, and was sad that they would never experience the inspirational presence of Jaques-Dalcroze.[16] However, she was able to call on specialist teachers to complement her course. Edith Lanser conducted classes integrating art, design and music concepts, with practical art-craft techniques including puppets and class room aids. Doreen Jacobs (now Bridges) taught harmony, counterpoint and piano. Weekly ballet technique lessons were given by Elizabeth Mackerras.[17] All the Dalcroze subjects and teaching methods, rhythmics, keyboard improvisation, ear-training and creative group expression were taken by Gell. Teaching practice was arranged at several challenging schools, and detailed observation was required of Gell's own Saturday morning children's classes. There were five full-time students, two from WA and three from NSW. Both WA students had previous qualifications; one, Phillipa Orr, a recent kindergarten graduate, the other, Joan Pope (née Gray) who had spent several terms at the London Dalcroze Training Centre, was part way through a UWA Arts degree.[18] They were joined twice a week by five teachers completing the Elementary Certificate. A larger group formed an evening class for adults, some of whom had been attending Gell's classes for many years. There were three mature-age teachers in Adelaide, Lesley Cox, Patricia Holmes and Mary de Crespigny, completing their written work by correspondence and awaiting the opportunity to take examinations scheduled for 1957.

Gell continued her own teaching, lecturing at the Nursery School Training College (NSTC), sometimes visiting three schools before commencing lessons with the Dalcroze students in the afternoons and evenings. Students from all these locations were incorporated in her original, but somewhat frantic, annual theatre productions.[19] Gell still had weekly *Music through Movement* broadcast programs to plan and record, and *Teachers' Notes* to prepare for publication. The ABC was preparing for television in 1956 and Gell was heavily involved in script preparation, and practical trials for a proposed series of programs for young children entitled *Time to Play*. Her Dalcroze training students were dragooned into scripting ideas, manipulating puppets, and appearing in costume 'on-camera'.[20] Working with Gell was arduous but rewarding.

Gell and her mother had lived together for many years and, sadly, Mrs. Gell died during the early part of 1956. Although it put considerable strain on her health, Gell was determined to present a session at the inaugural UNESCO Conference on Music Education planned for late May in Melbourne. A draft copy of her lecture indicates she was keen to emphasise that Dalcroze work was not simply for young children, but had a place in musicians' studies.[21] Some months later Gell conducted an intensive course for music teachers and adult music students in Melbourne, in conjunction with Elizabeth Wade. Her trainees from Sydney participated, because Gell wanted them to experience the approach of a different Dalcroze teacher. She generously paid their rail fares.

The year ended with the news that in 1957 Gell could use the Nursery School Training College (NSTC) Hall and piano rooms when available. Joan Fry, the Principal, had long been an ardent supporter of Gell's work and her encouragement meant a great deal to Gell. The two-storied building behind the College, a former bakery with stables, had been purchased by the College and, when renovated, would be available, at nominal rent, as a permanent centre for the 'Dalcroze Music and Movement School'. Such hopes prompted the development of a local committee and Gell invited significant interstate musicians to become patrons. She sought funds to furnish the centre, and to raise the air-fare needed to bring Mme. Monica Jaquet, from Geneva's Institut Jaques-Dalcroze, to Australia to conduct examinations, present demonstrations and courses.[22] Unfortunately three students had withdrawn from the training course for personal reasons, so once again Gell faced difficulties of recruitment and finance. A promotional trip to Adelaide in May 1957, gave Gell, assisted by Walkington, the opportunity to coach the candidates there prior to their practical examinations and present demonstrations showing the creative aspects of the training course and its potential to offer 'new careers' in music studies.

Jaquet's visit was both a triumph and an ordeal for Gell. A triumph in that she had the 'genuine article' from Geneva, for Jaquet presented very well indeed, but exhausting in both travel demands and the continual concern about finances. Gell was even making and selling jars of marmalade at her classes to raise funds. She had the moral support of various professors of music, but the practical organization relied on Gell and her few Dalcroze colleagues. Vincent (née Wilson) in WA, Wade, Kirsner and Finley in Victoria, and the Adelaide group, all gave their services and hospitality. Gell called upon old school friends, such as Mary Scales, and former associates in the pre-school world for assistance.[23]

The article by Jaquet in *Le Rythme* summarises the journey from her viewpoint, and she noted wryly that 'to teach eurhythmics in Australia the teacher should have a private plane!'(Jaquet, 1957, pp. 27–31). Memorable classes were taken alone by Jaquet in Perth, whilst for the Adelaide, Melbourne, Canberra and Sydney sessions she was accompanied by Gell and the trainee students. It was a physically demanding schedule for all concerned with several demonstrations each day and attendance at related conferences. Jaquet conducted an intensive course for the trainees in Sydney and observed their teaching. She was the senior member of the jury of five required for the Licentiate examination.[24] Gell gained dispensation from M. Gaby Jaques-Dalcroze to have only three instead of all five members holding the Dalcroze Diplôme, as long as she provided documentation for a senior musician-educator and another suitable person to join the jury. Doreen Bridges was called on and, with the inclusion of Williams (LSDE Elem. Cert.), it was agreed the Sydney jury of three Diplômees – Jaquet, Finley and Gell – with Bridges and Williams, could proceed.

Cox and Holmes from Adelaide passed immediately. The same jury, without Jaquet, re-convened in November to examine Pope and de Crespigny. Lady Melville graciously awarded the Licentiates and praised the apparently untiring energy of Heather Gell. The past two years of the first Australian Dalcroze Training Course had been a huge strain on Gell's health, and she worried about how many more Dalcroze teachers she would be able to train.

An endless striving to achieve: consolidation 1958–1970

The newly qualified teachers from Gell's course spread into various related fields: the South Australians, Cox and de Crespigny returned to their studios and private schools, and Holmes, to the Education Department's music advisory staff. Pope freelanced in Tasmania, teaching kindergarten college trainees, in schools, and gave two terms of the ABC *Music through Movement* sessions from Hobart. Back in Perth in 1959 she delivered eurhythmics classes at the University of WA, and at the KTC to students in all three years, a situation which continued till 1974, when the college became part of the Western Australian Institute of Technology (WAIT), later Curtin University. Pope's part-time work was constant there until 1999. One of her students, Robyn Ewing was inspired to discover more about Dalcroze Eurhythmics and drove to Sydney to study with Gell in the late 1970s. She gained her Licentiate, returned to Perth, directed Kindergartens and played an active role in the Early Childhood Association in WA.[25]

The 1960s saw further expansion of awareness of Dalcroze through demonstrations given for the newly formed Australian Society for Music Education (ASME) in 1967, and articles in its journals. In Sydney, Gell continued her teaching at the NSTC, and used its premises for the Dalcroze Elementary Certificate. From 1940 to 1980 Gell delivered these courses in Sydney and Adelaide with the help of Cox and de Crespigny; and similar courses were conducted in Melbourne (Kirsner) and Hobart (Wade) which Gell examined. Approximately 100 teachers graduated during that period.

Finley and Gell formed an Australian Dalcroze Teachers Union (ADTU) in 1968 to support the widely scattered teachers and the first *Newsletter* issued in that year, reveals the extent of Dalcroze courses for teacher development in Australia. Wade described her classes with second year students at the Tasmanian Conservatorium of Music and Nancy Kirsner reported on Dalcroze classes at Melbourne University, with first year B. Mus. students, and at Monash University with first and second year music education students.[26] From Adelaide, Cox gave an account of her studio classes and demonstrations and reported on the Australian Pre-school Conference in

Sydney at which Gell presented sessions. Walkington was engaged by the Adelaide KTC to visit schools, supervise music work and give demonstration lessons and lectures for teachers.[27]

Gell and Cox travelled to Geneva in 1965 for the Dalcroze Centennial Congress and Gell's travel diary provides a lively account. She showed a film of her work with children, gave a presentation on 'Music and the pre-school child' and renewed contact with international colleagues. She visited radio and television studios in Paris and London and discussed TV programs for children on BBC television with Rolf Harris (Gell, 1965).[28] In Japan, Mr. Itano, a graduate of the New York Dalcroze School, was teaching up to 300 students at the Kunitachi College of Music and, impressed with Gell's work in Geneva, he invited her to Tokyo on her way home. She accepted and taught college students and children from a nearby kindergarten. A recent visit to Japan by Nash showed that Gell had made a marked impression, and Itano's subsequent translation of Gell's book, published in 1973, became widely used (Nash, 2006).

Re-forming a Dalcroze Society of Australia in 1971

By 1970, Gell was 74 and there was still an urgent need to expand Dalcroze Eurhythmics in tertiary music institutions, and attract musically qualified students to become Dalcroze teachers. A meeting to re-form a Dalcroze Society was called and Doreen Bridges became president. Gell had always been good at using social connections to further her endeavours and her list of vice-presidents reads like a Who's Who of Australian music.[29] The first annual report of the Society provides a description of the preparations and execution of a most ambitious project to bring a distinguished teacher to Australia. Most of what follows is taken from Bridges' report (Bridges, 1972).

After lengthy negotiations with Robert Abrahams of New York, the Society, supported by the Queensland Orff Society, applied to the then Australian Council for the Arts for a grant. This was approved, but Abrahams became unable to tour, and Elizabeth Vanderspar, a Dalcroze teacher at the Royal College of Music in London, replaced him.

Gell coordinated arrangements with Dalcroze representatives in all States and over six weeks in Australia, Vanderspar visited six States. The tour was a resounding success. Through imaginative use of examples by Messiaen, Bartok and Stravinsky, Vanderspar showed that Dalcroze Eurhythmics had an important role in music education in the twentieth century. Advanced musicians were attracted by the improvisation aspects of her demonstrations and this was important because gaining their understanding was necessary for the work to be accepted at tertiary level. Vanderspar worked with children and adult students in classes already established by Dalcroze teachers in Sydney, Melbourne, Adelaide and Perth. She gave lecture-demonstrations in four states for the Australian Society for Music Education (ASME), including an in-service course for teachers arranged jointly in Adelaide by ASME and the Education Department. Public demonstrations were held in Adelaide and at the Sydney Conservatorium.

Vanderspar's visit prompted Daphne Isaacson (Mrs. J. Proietto) from Melbourne and Sandra Nash from Sydney, to go to London to take Vanderspar's Dalcroze Teachers' course. Robert Pritchett from Melbourne followed later and all gained the Dalcroze Licentiate.[30] Nash was invited to Geneva and completed the Diplôme during 1975–76. Nash's first contact with Gell had occurred as a student (1968–71) at the Music Department, University of Sydney. She stated that

> Dee Bridges arranged for our music education seminar to attend Gell's evening class in Newtown. After some initial uncertainty about an elderly, rotund woman wielding a drum, the overwhelming impression was of an ingenious teacher who, through her improvisation and listening 'games,' could trigger movement and sharpen one's ears in an unprecedented way. As a pianist, it was the physical experience of rhythm which struck home: a 'third dimension' which aided clarity and rhythmic security in performance. [31]

A summer school at the University of New England followed and Nash began Dalcroze training with Gell in 1972. Her decision to study with Vanderspar in London produced a mixed reaction in Gell whose pride was wounded. Her student was free to choose, and Gell understood the lure of travel, but was afraid to lose yet another.

By the late 1970s the Dalcroze Licentiates in Australia also included Micheal Giddens and Robert Bilsborough (Melbourne) and Margaret Smith (Sydney).[32] Other teachers invited by the Dalcroze Society of Australia were Helen Erberveld, Rotterdam (1973), Marta Sanchez, Pittsburgh (1979), Lisa Parker, Boston (1984), Hettie van Maanen, The Hague, president of FIER, the International Federation of Eurhythmics Teachers (1986), and Malou Hatt-Arnold, Geneva (1989 and 1991). The latter two assisted yet another endeavour to create qualified teachers in Australia. Some eight people were examined in Adelaide and passed as 'Associate teachers' who could work under the direction of a Licentiate. This allowed Cox, in particular, to establish an 'umbrella' connection for six such teachers. Sadly, when she was no longer active, the link vanished.

Rex Hobcroft's directorship of the Sydney Conservatorium (1972–1982) coincided with a period of innovation and expansion in music education and also with the first year of full-time responsibility for the training of almost half the NSW State's music education students at the Conservatorium.[33] Gell wasted no time in approaching Hobcroft about the inclusion of Dalcroze Eurhythmics in the then Diploma in Music Education (DME) four-year course. Having seen Wade's work in Hobart, he needed no further convincing (Cox et al., 1995, p.121). The Dalcroze Specialist Certificate had been created for students at the Royal College of Music, London, to allow them to incorporate Dalcroze principles within their professional careers. Gell instituted the same qualification in Australia and students from the Sydney Conservatorium could take an external exam and submit written work. Gell took these classes for a few years but by 1976, due to her age, they were handed over to Ruth Caldwell who had gained her Licentiate with Gell in 1968. Caldwell continued to give an elective class to students in all years well into the 1980s. Twenty-eight such graduates have incorporated Dalcroze ideas into their work in schools, universities, research, community arts organisations, theatre and therapy.

In 1973, after 30 years of service, Gell retired from the NSTC, but continued to teach privately. The College had only recently moved into a new building in Burren Street, Newtown, where Gell had designed a purpose-built room for movement on the top floor and raised money to buy a grand piano. Her successor as Director of Music was Doreen Bridges. She upheld Gell's ideals on the importance of music and movement in early childhood, but shifted the emphasis away from the use of the piano, instead encouraging unaccompanied singing and song-writing. The ISME Conference in Perth, 1974, which Gell was unable to attend, included a number of presentations on Dalcroze work co-ordinated by Pope.

Postlude

In 1981, Gell returned to Adelaide and died in 1988. She left money to support Dalcroze teacher education in Australia and Alethea Eddy, president of the Dalcroze Council of Australia, organized an appropriate Deed, and Trustees were appointed. The Heather Gell Dalcroze Foundation has supported annual Summer Schools since 1994, funded overseas teachers, publications, scholarships and travel, a role which continues to the present day. Although many people from Australia and neighbouring countries have participated in the Australian Summer Schools, the aim of producing more qualified Dalcroze teachers has not been fulfilled. Dalcroze lessons require space and teachers with a high level of improvisational skill, and classroom teachers find other approaches such as Orff and Kodaly easier to implement with large classes. While studio teachers and choral conductors are drawn to Dalcroze for the challenging ear-training possibilities, the intriguing use of physical dissociations[34] and all-round musicianship, their lack of formal teacher education is a hindrance. These are structural problems with no obvious solution in Australia.

The changes in tertiary education mean that the old networks of shared ideology and personal support no longer work in the same way. While the Dalcroze philosophy offers so much across different fields of art and education, it is too broad in a world of specialization; the training is long and requires more hours of practical work than universities are prepared to provide. Although the few Dalcroze teachers in Australia today face an uncertain future, there are encouraging signs. Interest in Dalcroze throughout East Asian countries has grown over the last ten years. Dalcroze leaders are being invited to work in teacher development in Thailand, Hong Kong, Singapore, Taiwan and Japan, and many students are prepared to travel seeking Dalcroze classes. The face of Dalcroze today is indeed changing and it is becoming more international and less Euro-centric. More innovative ways to deliver courses are being created and dedicated efforts continue in Australia and around the world.

Notes

1. Sisyphus was condemned, for eternity, to push a rock uphill, but at the moment of triumph and achievement it rolled back and the toil commenced once again. This theme was put to music by Ann Driver, teacher of improvisation at the LSDE and was portrayed vividly, as a Movement Study, by Cecilia John on the Australian tour in 1923–24.
2. Dr Bridges accepted the position of Patron of Dalcroze Australia (Inc.) in 2008.
3. LSDE notebooks of Gell (1921–23) and Wilson (1924–27) held by Pope.
4. The seven were Irene Wittenoom (WA) 1917, Heather Gell (SA) 1923, Cecilia John (Tas-Vic) 1923, Marjorie Bonnin (SA) 1927, Thelma St John George (Vic) 1927, Dorothea Michel (NSW) 1927, Jean Wilson (WA) 1927. Michel married in London and did not return to Australia.
5. John, an experienced singer and singing teacher, was well-known in Melbourne as a suffragette and anti-conscription campaigner and associated with the *Woman Voter*. She was the first secretary of the Save the Children Fund in Australia, and later, from London, the Overseas Director of the organisation.
6. Tingey, N. (1974). Personal comment from a student at NSTC, Sydney 1960s. Pope, J. (2005).
7. Minutes of Conservatorium University of Melbourne Archives. Acc 97/160.1903–1927; 1927–1930. Minutes of Dalcroze Society of Great Britain, 1915–1939, held at National Resource Centre for Dance, University of Surrey.
8. Bonnin had been Sterry's student as a child in Adelaide and was a talented pianist, sensitive improviser and gifted in composition. She had been in Gell's rhythmic classes for several years as a young adult.
9. Dr D. Bridges, personal conversation, April 2006. Doreen Jacobs attended Sterry's classes in Adelaide. When Sterry returned to London, Heather Gell took over the classes. Jacobs recalls receiving a prize from Gell for an inventive instrument of tuned bottles. Jacobs also took piano lessons from Miss Scales and thought, as a young child surely would, that it was a wonderful name for a music teacher.

10 Jean Wilson (Mrs R. H. Vincent) took the WAKTC classes following Hinrichs' return to England, and later, in the early 1940s, played an important part in the development of *Kindergarten of the Air, Let's Join In* and other ABC music programs broadcast to schools. She continued broadcasting until 1969. (Pope, 1994). Stella O'Keefe, a WA school teacher, studied at the LSDE 1933–1936, then stayed in England for many years and did not pursue a career in Australia.

11 Nancy Rosenhain was 'not unconnected'. Her uncle was Sir John Monash. She taught privately from his home in Toorak and followed Thelma St John George at Preshil School in Melbourne. She married pharmacist Marcus Kirsner, an *aide-de-camp* to Sir John, in 1932.

12 Gell commenced teaching in Sydney at the KTC in 1939, and the Nursery School Training College in 1943. She ensured that her 'School of Music and Movement' in Adelaide continued through assistant teachers under her guidance, knowing they were not yet qualified Dalcroze teachers.

13 The one year part-time course included movement, keyboard improvisation, ear-training, creative use of percussion instruments, practical classroom projects and written work. It was approximately 100 hours of tuition.

14 Wade had initial lessons from Thelma St John George in Melbourne, 1936; attended the Paris Dalcroze School in 1937, and graduated from the LSDE in 1941, which had evacuated to the country, after the threat of London bombings.

15 Finley (Elinor Archer) gained her LSDE Certificate in 1929 and her Diplôme shortly after. She, her husband and young family had been living in India but during the war moved to the safety of Australia. In Melbourne, Finley was glad to renew friendship with Kirsner (née Rosenhain) with whom she had shared training in London.

16 Gell possessed a great sense of fun and playfulness and regularly each July on the birthday of Jaques-Dalcroze, dressed-up as M'sieur Jaques with a man's suit, old fashioned waistcoat and fob watch, theatrical moustache and goatee beard. She then gave a rhythmics class in hilarious French, breathtaking piano improvisation and recounted amusing anecdotes she had collected or experienced with him and his students.

17 Elizabeth was the sister of conductor Charles. He had made orchestral arrangements for Gell's rhythmic dramas in past years, played in and conducted several of her theatre productions.

18 Both Phillippa Orr and Joan Gray had been in the same class at St. Hilda's School. Gray was the first Arts student to enrol in the new Music unit conducted by Frank Callaway, Reader in Music at UWA in 1954. She had gained LRAM (Speech and Drama) and LRAM (Mime) in London during 1953, and met Gell that year in London.

19 An aspect of these productions was Gell's alarming custom of distributing lengths of material (often flimsy georgette) and expecting them to be turned into perfect costumes without providing patterns. For those of us who could not sew this was particularly worrying for, at the first sight of the dodgy ill-draped or poorly pleated costumes, Gell would let everyone know about one's incompetence in no uncertain terms. The hand dyeing of these objects was conducted in Gell's laundry-wash-house. These were the years when tights could not be obtained unless hand knitted or reconstructed from lisle stockings, and leotards were non-existent in the shops. One 'adapted' a Bonds singlet!

20   Pope recalls being a vocal Magpie whilst scrambling to operate a glove puppet beneath a low table; another calling magpie was required to fly in on a rod and fishing line from the side of the studio a few seconds later.

21   Pope was involved in this demonstration at Melba Hall, with a student of Elizabeth Wade. Gell spoke to the various heads of music departments and professors who attended this conference. They were soon 'enlisted' in her desire to resurrect the short-lived Dalcroze Societies which had been formed in four States in 1923–1924.

22   The letters went to friends and parents of her students. When 'Miss Gell' button-holed you it was difficult not to acquiesce to her requests; it was simpler to agree. She was persistent and persuasive.

23   Mary Scales, a friend from Gell's school days as a boarder at Tormore House in Adelaide, married Sir Leslie Melville (ANU Canberra) and both were helpful to Gell. Many figures in early childhood education, such as Gladys Pendred, well understood Gell's endeavours. Gell had enjoyed, since Adelaide in the 1930s, the support of the wife of a former Governor-General, Lady Zara Gowrie, who ensured that Gell had a role in the music and movement policy of the Commonwealth-sponsored child research centres in each State.

24   The Licence was known in the 1920s and 1930s as the Teaching Certificate.

25   After her untimely death in 2003, it was revealed that Ewing left $10,000 to the Heather Gell Dalcroze Foundation, a sign of her enduring support for the work.

26   Kirsner gave many demonstrations and acknowledged the active support of Professor George Loughlin at the University of Melbourne and Professor Trevor Jones at Monash.

27   While neither Holmes nor de Crespigny are mentioned in the 1968 DTU report, the former was lecturing trainee- and in-service teachers in Adelaide and incorporating Orff and Dalcroze methodologies into her courses, and the latter was teaching at Presbyterian Girls School, Adelaide.

28   Gell produced and delivered TV programs in Adelaide and Sydney in the late 1950s and 60s. Bruce Gyngell, who met Gell at Channel 9 in the 1960s described her as 'one of the more memorable people that I have met in my time in broadcasting' (Cox et al., 1995, p. 99).

29   Professors George Loughlin & Trevor Jones (Victoria); Patricia Holmes & Dr. Malcolm John (South Australia); Don Kay (Tasmania); Professor Frank Callaway, OBE, Georg Tintner & Harry Bluck (Western Australia); Lady Melville and Ernest Llewellyn, CBE (ACT); Roger Covell, Terence Hunt, Joan Fry and Rex Hobcroft (NSW).

30   Isaacson also qualified as a music therapist.

31   Personal comment, Nash to Pope, March, 2009.

32   As a leading figure in Kodaly Music Education, Smith has enriched those teachers' course with aspects of Dalcroze. Studies by Giddens (1983, 1994) have added significantly to research about Dalcroze and have contributed to a wider understanding of the work in Australia.

33   Before 1972 this training had been shared with Alexander Mackie Teachers' College in Sydney.

34   Jaques-Dalcroze devised numerous exercises of dissociation for mental and muscular agility, rather like the 'pat your head while rubbing your tummy' variety. In his case one might be gesturing in legato with one hand whilst making staccato movements in space with the other; or conducting three-time with the left arm and four-time with the right, simultaneously, then at a signal change over without missing a beat.

References

Australian Dalcroze Teachers' Union. (n. d.). *Newsletter No.1*. (The content suggests it is 1968).
Australian Music Examinations Board. (1936). *Manual 1936*.
Bridges, D. (1972). *First Annual Report of the Dalcroze Society of Australia*, 27 Sept.
Bridges, D. (1971). *The Role of Universities in the Development of Music Education in Australia. 1885–1970*. Unpublished PhD thesis, University of Sydney.
Cox, L., Holmes, P., & Pope, J. (1995). *Recollections – one hundred tributes to the life and work of Heather D. Gell*. Eden Hills SA: Lesley Cox Publications.
de Lissa, L. (1915). *Education in Certain European Countries; report by Miss L de Lissa*. South Australian Government Paper, No.75. House of Assembly, September, 1915.
Gell. H. Personal cuttings scrapbook, beginning in 1920. State Library of South Australia. Gell papers.
Gell, H. (1949). *Music, Movement and the Young Child*. Sydney: Australasian Publishing.
Gell, H. (1965). Handwritten travel diary, State Library of South Australia, Gell papers.
Gell, H. (1968). Movement – a necessary element in Music Education, *Australia Journal of Music Education*, No 3, October.
Giddens, M. (1983). *Freedom Through Rhythm: the Eurhythmics of Emile Jaques-Dalcroze*. Unpublished M.Ed. thesis, University of Melbourne.
Giddens, M. (1994). *A Unity of Vision: the ideas of Dalcroze, Kodaly and Orff and their historical development*. Unpublished PhD thesis, University of Melbourne.
Greenhead, K. (2007). The ideas and practice of Dalcroze Eurhythmics in the contemporary world. In J. Southcott (Ed.). *Dalcroze from a Distance; a miscellany of current research*. Turramurra: Heather Gell Dalcroze Foundation.
Jaquet, M. (1957). Voyage en Australie. In *Le Rythme* (Geneve). Oct.–Dec.
Kirsner, N. (1973). Rhythm: the essence of life and music, *Australian Journal of Music Education*, Oct.
Nash, S. (2006). Bridges between Australia and Japan. *Mouvements – Journal of the Institut Jaques-Dalcroze*, Geneva.
Pope, J. (1994). *ABC School Broadcasts in Western Australia 1938–1946: an investigation into radio programmes for early childhood featuring music and movement, dance and drama*. Unpublished M.Ed. thesis, Edith Cowan University.
Pope, J. (2005). High hopes and hindsight: promoting Dalcroze Eurhythmics in Australia 1923–24. In D. Forrest (Ed.), *A Celebration of voices*. ASME National Conference Proceedings, Melbourne.
Pope, J. (2008). *Dalcroze Eurhythmics in Australasia; the first generation, from 1918*.Unpublished Ph.D thesis, Monash University.
Tingey, N. (1943) *The record of thirty years: the London School of Dalcroze Eurhythmics 1913–1943*. London: Dalcroze Society of Great Britain.
Tingey, N. (1974). *A record of the London School of Dalcroze Eurhythmics and it graduates at home and overseas*. London: Dalcroze Society of Great Britain.

5: The Developmental Music Program

Deanna Hoermann

The story of the Developmental Music Program begins in 1969. I was a Secondary Music Specialist at Northmead High School and was very discontented with the Higher School Certificate aural results of my students. The students' difficulties and frustrations convinced me that I needed to learn a great deal more about how to develop a student's aural abilities. My quest led me to Debrecen, Hungary at the end of 1969 and I was astounded when I attended a national solfege competition and heard what the students from Kindergarten to the tertiary level were doing. It was at this time that Marta Nemesszeghy invited me to visit her school in Kecskemet. This experience was overwhelming and I was convinced that I needed to test the musical ideas of Kodaly within the Australian context. It was Marta who convinced me that to do this I had to begin with Kindergarten children.

This was not an easy task, particularly with the bureaucratic regulations that surrounded both primary and secondary schools at the time. Good fortune smiled as the Principal of Northmead High School had a deep love of music and agreed that I could visit a nearby primary school and experiment during two of my preparation periods per week. I negotiated with the Infant Mistress of a nearby school to gain access to a kindergarten class and identify a teacher who was willing to work with me. I worked with a kindergarten class in Baulkham Hills Primary School for 10 weeks before I became aware that I needed permission from the Infant Inspector before I could work in one of her schools.

My experience in the early childhood area at this time was limited to private piano teaching, I had the Hungarian model and musical sounds swirling in my head but no predetermined expectations within the NSW context. I believed at this point that I needed to work with teachers who had some musical knowledge. However, this belief quickly changed as I worked in Kindergarten classes and recognised:

- the children's spontaneous delight with the singing games, finger plays and rhymes.
- this delight generated constant requests from the children for their favourite singing games to be repeated between my visits. It was the children's joy and enthusiasm that drew many reluctant classroom teachers into participating in the music activities with the children. Their initial reticence was slowly overtaken by curiosity then a growing interest in this music learning process.
- the class teacher used the singing games in ways that related to the children's other learning processes, such as literacy and numeracy.
- word of the program spread though the surrounding schools and generated an increasing number of requests from other teachers to visit and see what was happening for themselves.

However, during this short period I had the chance to start gathering material, apply my limited knowledge of the Kodaly approach to young children and observe the impact of singing games, rhymes and finger plays on the young children. Simultaneously I began experimenting and adapting aural activities for my secondary level students with quite appreciable success.

News of this 'unofficial' experiment reached the Infant Inspector and caused more than a few ripples. It should be acknowledged however, that it was through the efforts of Hilary Jackson, the Infant Inspector, that a limited experiment was established with official sanction. As a first step three infant departments were selected in schools that were in close proximity to Northmead High School and a greater amount of release time was made available for me to visit these neighbouring infant departments. I started the program on the basis of a demonstration model. Infant teachers at Kindergarten, Grade 1 and Grade 2 were nominated to participate and I visited once a week to teach these particular classes while the classroom teacher observed and participated in the singing games with the children. Momentum grew and a number of these teachers wanted to learn more about the methodology and the singing games in order to be a little ahead of their children. This led to voluntary professional development sessions that were conducted after school or on weekends and the number of voluntary unpaid attendees grew.

The professional learning model of a classroom teacher working with a music specialist on a regular basis, in step-by-step progression with the children, was modelled to some extent on the teacher training program used in demonstration schools. It made sense to build musical skills simultaneously in the children and the teacher. As the weeks passed by it became obvious that:

- the power of fun in learning had stimulated and driven teachers' interest
- the music specialist / teacher relationship provided a safety net for inhibitions and uncertainties
- the instant analysis and feedback about the children's responses to the material and the musical challenges facilitated the connections between musical learning and general learning
- the integration of music into the daily learning experience had an impact on teaching in other learning areas
- the program stimulated the ingenuity and creativity of many classroom teachers.

The reaction to the work was very positive and after twelve months experimentation the response of educators encouraged the Director-General of Education to establish a program to test the appropriateness of the Developmental

Music Program for NSW Primary Education in 10 schools in the Metropolitan West Area of Sydney. This program was funded through Commonwealth money and I was released from my Secondary position to take up full time direction of the program. There was one proviso that was embedded in the conditions for the continuance of the project and that was the involvement of primary-trained classroom teachers, not music specialists. In many instances this presented a double challenge, the development of musical skills, often in unwilling teachers, and the development of knowledge and skills in the area of music methodology while still progressing the students' musical learning. Many teachers were astonished and often intimidated by the children's seemingly effortless acquisition of musical skills.

The program grew from my involvement in one kindergarten class to Kindergarten, Grade 1 and Grade 2 classes on a weekly basis in three schools to a pilot program in ten schools. Successful outcomes resulted in an increase to two consultants to cover this work commitment. The number of consultants built to five as the program spread from the ten pilot schools to over two hundred primary schools in the Metropolitan West Region.

The curriculum and teaching materials were being developed, trialled and tested simultaneously on a week by week basis. By the beginning of 1972, through a chain of unbelievable events, I had the chance to work with Marta Nemesseghy, the Director of the Kecskemet Primary School in Hungary. She had been selected by Zoltan Kodaly to develop the curriculum for the music primary schools in Hungary. Although many Americans were eager to gain the rights to her work she chose to work with me to develop the first stage of the music curriculum for NSW schools. We worked together for 2 – 3 hours every day for 6 weeks in a Budapest Hospital as she struggled with a tumour on the brain. For me this was a traumatic experience but her grace, brilliance and passion for the work was inspirational. At the time I did not fully understand the enormity of the privilege that I had been given. We could only communicate in German and my experimentation in the Australian kindergartens provided the material and ideas that we captured and built upon in the *Teachers Manual for Marta Nemesseghy's Children's Song Book*.[1]

The opportunity to work with such outstanding proponents of the early childhood area continued in Australia with the visit of Dr Doreen Bridges to the Kodaly-based Developmental Music Program that I was introducing into 10 primary schools in the Western suburbs of Sydney in the early 1970s. She was a lecturer at the Nursery School Teachers' College and was excited by what she saw. Dr Bridges recognised that the program was not only filling a void for her teacher trainees but was clearly demonstrating the beginnings of the music learning process. Not only was Dr Bridges supportive of the work but was very clear about the challenges that I was facing and the extraordinary opportunity I had been given. Her intellectual incisiveness, strength of conviction and depth of knowledge about early childhood music education were a great source of inspiration. In truth she provided a compass for the musical journey that I was beginning – *testing the appropriateness of a Kodaly-based program for NSW Primary Schools.*

Gwynneth Herbert[2], a psychologist with the Department of Education, had responsibility for the testing of students in the basic skills of literacy and numeracy in the schools in which I was working. She recognised that the music program was meeting the needs of students and was convinced that its impact on the children's literacy and numeracy scores could be measured and compared with the results of students in schools where the music program did not exist. She was indeed correct. The introduction of children's songs and singing games, as an essential part of the daily curriculum, was not only assisting teachers to capitalise on the beginning of the music learning process but also significantly effecting the students' general learning. It is interesting to note that after all these years, this research was cited a number of times in the recent National Review of School Music Education.[3]

The Developmental Music Program afforded me the opportunity to test the ideas presented in *Marta Nemesseghy's Children's Song Book* and to change and enrich the learning program accordingly. It was at this time that multiculturalism was having a significant impact on teaching and learning in our schools. I had to gather nursery rhymes, songs and games that developed a musical learning sequence, capture the underpinning principles as proposed by Kodaly and apply the unique features of the English speaking context. The provision of a professional music learning program for teachers that simultaneously developed a level of musical skills as well as an understanding of the methodology was indeed challenging. Although I did not fully realise it at the beginning of the project, the Director-General of the NSW Department of Education afforded me the opportunity to undertake a longitudinal study that covered a period of 15 years.

The history of the musical and methodological development of the project can be traced through the publications associated with the program. It began with the publication of *The Teachers Manual for Marta Nemesszeghy's Children's Song Book*, *The Developmental Music Program's* Teachers Manuals and Children's Books–Stages 1 & 2. I was privileged to be able to revise these publications in partnership with Dr Bridges. We worked well as a team, learning from each other and being inspired by the task. In addition we published *The Developmental Music Program*[4]–Stage 3 and *Catch a Song*[5]. These publications represent the practical application of song material, concepts and ideas delivered by five consultants in 200 different types of schools. What the books illustrate is the continuous experimentation and improvement of the introduction and delivery of musical concepts as well as a broadening of the source of musical materials. The books trace the development of iconic representations built on the children's non-verbal perceptions, for example, representations of the simple or compound beat holding their rhythms and notes and the ringing of doorbells on the staff to lay the foundations for the concept of major and minor seconds and the building of modal systems. Each of these creative modifications grew from practical application and clearly illustrates the importance of the pre-symbolisation steps in the music learning process. What the books do not capture is the extraordinary choral sounds of normal children in normal schools. The allocation of a grant in 1979 from the Australia Council led to the documentary film *Are You Listening*[6] directed and produced by Bill Fitzwater. This captured segments of normal children in the Western suburbs schools, teachers and consultants doing extraordinary musical things. The combination of general learning practices with specific musical concepts provided a glimpse of the rich pool of ideas, creativity and experimentation upon which the program was built.

Teachers provided children with listening and moving experiences that were embedded in the singing games and rhymes. For example, through movement the children represented their aural perceptions of particular musical characteristics and along with their teachers gradually developed, from Kindergarten on, their vocabulary of musical capabilities and understandings.

The introduction of the Musica Viva Program into schools was a result of my belief that professional expertise should be used not only to enrich the learning experiences of the students, but also to train and develop the skills of staff within a musical performance context.

Teachers were able to identify their existing strengths and recognise their existing gaps. Access to the learning resources, professional support and demonstration lessons provided powerful evidence of the program as a successful model of professional learning. It was also clearly demonstrating that it is the quality of the interaction between a teacher and the students that makes the difference. It was not only the interaction between the music specialist and the classroom teacher but also the frank and critical interaction of teachers with their 'fellow travellers' within the project that greatly enriched the learning process and formed a very powerful network of professional learning practitioners.

By this time the project had gained national and international recognition. Consultants and music educators from every state of Australia as well as from Singapore, Hong Kong, Germany, England, Canada and America visited music demonstration lessons given by classroom teachers and were inspired by the results that they were witnessing. After a world-wide search the Singaporean Government developed their music education system based on the Developmental Music Program. The Queensland Department of Education under the leadership of Ann Carroll used the program as a basis for their state-wide primary classroom music and instrumental programs. Such recognition had its positive and negative aspects and set in train political forces that caused angst within the hierarchical, bureaucratic NSW system.

Around 1980 the Minister for Education, Mr Paul Landa, initiated a review into Primary Music Education.[7] The work of this committee was led by Mr Rex Hobcroft, Director of the Sydney Conservatorium of Music. Dr Bridges was a significant member of this committee who fought strongly for recognition of music as a central and most important part of the primary curriculum, particularly in her correspondence with influential political and departmental officers. An outcome of the Review was a recommendation that the plan that had been developed by the Review Committee for primary music education be implemented throughout the state of NSW. This plan had been based upon the model of the Developmental Music Program and was costed in detail. The report was submitted to the Minister and then the hand of fate intervened with his sudden death. Nothing more was ever heard of this report.

Soon afterwards the NSW Department of Education undertook a revision of the primary music curriculum. The 'involvement model' of curriculum development was adopted and involved many people with no musical or curriculum development knowledge. As the process of wider involvement progressed unfortunate divisions within the musical fraternity began to emerge. An in-depth study of the strengths or difficulties of different approaches or their attendant research studies was not undertaken. The musical activities that were having a positive impact on the students at both primary and secondary level were not critically evaluated or creatively developed. Sequencing of the music learning activities was not a matter for serious discussion. Indeed the process of curriculum development was not informed by empirical research data or solid evidence of what constituted an effective classroom music program. Self-interest and factionalism relegated this unique opportunity for strategic musical thinking and planning to a golden moment lost. The result was the glossy production of a music curriculum that paid lip-service to aspects of the Developmental Music Program, made little sense to the unsupported and musically untrained early childhood and primary classroom teacher and as a result was not translated into general practice.

After this experience I believed that I needed to understand more about the nature of the bureaucratic and political systems and how one might be able to influence the decision-making process. Slowly I came to the realisation that if the system was to change then I had to understand a great deal more about the change process. Dr Bridges was now a most important mentor and for some time had strongly encouraged me to undertake Doctoral Studies. Following my work with the Curriculum Development Directorate I was offered the opportunity to become the professional assistant to the Deputy Director-General of Education. This position opened up other opportunities such as the planning and development of Newtown Performing Arts High School and my appointment as Director to the Cherrybrook Cluster of Schools with general responsibility for twenty nine primary and secondary schools and specific responsibility for the continued planning, development and implementation of Cherrybrook Technology High School.

It was Professor Geoff Scott who suggested that I should use the development of Cherrybrook Technology High School to trace the forces that accompany planned systemic change as the theme for my Doctorate. It was Dr Bridges who encouraged and supported this decision and who took the time to read and provide critical advice on the progress of my thesis *The Dynamics of Implementing a Planned Change in a Public Education System*.[8] My gratitude to her for her level and quality of advice as a mentor is constant.

Through my work in the Developmental Music Program I learned about the importance of leadership and change. This experience highlighted for me the importance of the role of the Principal and the executive staff and the role of those fulfilling informal leadership roles, in instituting any long-term change into practice. Therefore my movement into these areas seemed to be a natural career progression. I also understood the importance of sound models of professional development for teachers and leaders and this was perhaps one of the most effective and long lasting outcomes of the Developmental Music Program.

There were many aspects of the Developmental Music Program that were ahead of its time, particularly in the areas of whole school planning, classroom observation, the mode of demonstration teaching and the level of collegial support. There is still a great deal to learn and in times of such fiscal restraints I believe that we have to mine the successful experiences of the past, adapt them for the current context and conditions and continuously strive to improve our students' opportunities to access quality musical learning. My thanks go to all those who participated in the success of the project and very special thanks to my mentor, colleague and special friend of so many years Dr Doreen Bridges.

References

1. Hoermann, D. (1973). The Teachers Manual for Marta Nemesseghy's Children's Song Book. Brookvale: Owen Martin Publications.
2. Hoermann, D. & Herbert, G. (1979). *Report and Evaluation: A Developmental Music Programme of Music Education for Primary School* (Kodaly -based). Brookvale, NSW: Educational Supplies.
3. Department of Education, Science and Training. (2005). National Review of School Music Education. Canberra: Department of Education, Science and Training
4. Hoermann, D. (1979). A Developmental Music Program – Stage 1 Student Book. Brookvale, NSW: Educational Supplies.
   Hoermann, D. & Bridges, D. (1984). A Developmental Music Program – Stage 1 Teachers Book. Brookvale, NSW: Educational Supplies.
   Hoermann, D. & Bridges, D. (1987). A Developmental Music Program – Stage 2 Teachers Book. Brookvale, NSW: Educational Supplies.
   Hoermann, D. & Bridges, D. (1987). A Developmental Music Program – Stage 2 Student Book. Brookvale, NSW: Educational Supplies.
   Hoermann, D. & Bridges, D. (1991). A Developmental Music Program – Stage 3 Teachers Book. Brookvale, NSW: Educational Supplies.
   Hoermann, D. & Bridges, D. (1991). A Developmental Music Program – Stage 3 Student Book. Brookvale, NSW: Educational Supplies.
5. Hoermann, D. & Bridges, D. (1985). Catch a Song. Brookvale, NSW: Educational Supplies.
6. Australia Council. (1979). Are You Listening. Film release.
7. NSW Ministry of Education. (1981). The Ministerial Task Force Enquiry into Primary Music Education. Sydney: NSW Ministry of Education.
8. Hoermann, D. (1998). The Dynamics of Implementing a Planned Change in a Public Education System. Unpublished Doctoral Thesis, University of New South Wales, 1998.

6: Principles and practices and musical truths[1]

Richard Gill

When Carl Orff and Gunild Keetman began their epic journey in the field of music education during the latter part of the twentieth century they could not possibly have known that a group of individuals in January 2006 would congregate in the Antipodes to continue the basic tenets of the Schulwerk, bringing to this unique approach to music education their own musical ideas, their own ways of implementing these ideas enshrouded in their own philosophies of music education.

One can imagine that Carl Orff and Gunild Keetman would have been thrilled at the unbridled enthusiasm for music education these people have, founded strongly in the belief that a child understands music best when that child makes its own music; that is, goes through the motions of being a composer. Orff and Keetman would also have been genuinely astounded that their ideas had undergone such extensive transformations yet still preserving the same fundamental principles.

The Orff Schulwerk approach admits and encourages all those who have an interest in the teaching of music, movement and related activities, irrespective of the level of musical attainment of the practitioner. This is not meant to say that music can be taught by anyone regardless of training; far from it: but it is at conferences such as this one and through courses held throughout the year all over the country that practitioners can hone skills, sharpen musical wits, learn new techniques, practise and develop old techniques in the quest to become ever better and ever stronger as teachers of music.

At a conference such as this, the musical emphasis is placed on doing, making, experimenting, testing, and improvising. Through improvisation and exploration of musical ideas children, under the guidance and instruction of music teachers, can be led to discover the ways in which sound behaves, the ways in which that sound can be organised to make musical forms and the ways in which those forms can be presented to listeners so that the forms can be comprehended.

These activities are done, or should be done, for their own sake; that is for the sake of music, because music is quintessentially good and worth teaching for its own sake.

Music is an essential part of a child's education because it has the capacity, different from the other art forms, to take the child into the realms of the abstract, to stimulate the imagination uniquely by virtue of its abstract nature, to evoke, suggest, imply and stimulate a variety of responses because it deals with sound which is perceived at its highest level, aurally: that is the nature of music.

At Orff Schulwerk conferences there is always an air of high expectation from the presenters and the participants. Participants are hungry for new ideas, presenters are keen to demonstrate their techniques and involve all participants in the business of making music. There is an expectation that at morning teas, lunches and the like, participants and presenters will meet, exchange ideas, compare teaching circumstances, evaluate what is learned, consider ways of implementing what is learned, complain about how little time is devoted to music generally in the curriculum and discuss ways in which things can be made generally better.

Those music teachers involved in the Orff Schulwerk movement are by nature resourceful, imaginative, indefatigable, thirsty for knowledge and ever keen to explore new territories. Schulwerk conferences, therefore, are fertile grounds for these teachers with the conference developing into something of a music-frenzy at each session, particularly where there is a bass xylophone involved and where participants might be killed in the rush to play the only bass xylophone in the room.

Throughout this week and indeed all the time we are teaching music, we need to remind ourselves that we teach music for music's sake, notwithstanding all the extrinsic benefits music can bring such as enhancement in other learning areas and the like. It is imperative that we stand up as a force of musicians and teachers and speak up about music education as something that is worth doing for its own sake. We are not in the classroom to enhance the work of the mathematics teacher or the science teachers and quite frankly I don't see them going out of their way to relate all their curriculum areas to music.

We are in danger of losing the distinctiveness of our subject once we start to relate too loosely and too freely to other disciplines. While me might seek to make obvious parallels within and to other disciplines, our main job is to teach music as music, to give children an opportunity to appreciate the uniqueness of music through making their own music, to provide children with a rich array of musical experiences reflecting the breadth and depth of music's vast and comprehensive repertoire, subsequently providing opportunities to react to this repertoire in their own ways. Orff Schulwerk practitioners are uniquely placed to offer this type of experience.

In 1963, the New South Wales Department of Education issued a Primary School Music curriculum. From this document come the following quotes:

1. Music is a significant part of the cultural heritage of every nation and race. Not only has each country its own traditional music reflecting the habits and customs of its people, but many nations have added to the common store of music. As part of the culture of man, music can make its own contributions to enrich the life of the home, the school and the community. For this reason alone its place is justified in the school curriculum.
2. While the syllabus makes provision for variations of ability in class teachers, this is in no way inconsistent with the right of every child to sing, listen, play, compose and move to music according to the child's individual interests and abilities.

How enlightened are these remarks! How pertinent they are today! How well they fall in line with the principles and practices of Orff Schulwerk!

...

Orff and Keetman would endorse your work a hundred times over, not that it needs their benediction or validation or indeed anyone's benediction.

You as a teacher are unique with your special strengths, special qualities and special paths to the musical minds of children.

Let no one deflect you from your path but rather seek from others how your path can be made more musical and lead you closer and closer to the musical truths which deal with goodness and beauty....

Note

1   This paper is an edited version of a speech given at an Orff Conference in Sydney on January 8th, 2006. It is reprinted with permisssion of the author and the Editor, *Musicworks*, Journal of Australian National Council of Orff Schulwerk.

7: A More Comprehensive Approach to Music Teaching

Robert J. Werner

It is a privilege to contribute to a volume honoring Doreen Bridges. We met at the first national conference of the Australian Society for Music Education, in Brisbane, in 1969. It was evident that she was interested in everything pertaining to music education including the latest learning theories. We shared our thoughts on the new, at that time, book by Jerome Bruner *The Process of Education*. Through the years I would find out that this interest had served her well as she became a significant force in developing the field of music education, at all levels, in her country.

Doreen seemed open to all music and particularly interested in the integration of music study, as represented by the concept of "Comprehensive Musicianship" (CM) which had been developed by the Contemporary Music Project in the United States during the 1960s and continuing into the 1970s. I had the opportunity of introducing this concept at the Brisbane conference. From that time on she investigated and promoted this in her work as a more comprehensive approach to the teaching of music.

The sixties and seventies were a time of great interest in the applied theory and philosophy of music education and the implication this has on the training of the musician and musician teacher. Whether in a school general music class, a studio, or a graduate seminar, an education in music is what happens between the teacher and the student in a given learning situation. This is where the theory and principles are applied based on the teacher's personal philosophy, which is primarily formed through their professional training.

Thus, I feel it would be appropriate to take this opportunity to reintroduce the concept of comprehensive musicianship to another generation of teachers of music. The genesis of this curricular reform began in 1959 when the Ford Foundation funded a project to place 12 young composers a year in-residence in public schools. They were to write for the school's music resources and be advocates for contemporary music to the students and teachers. Soon it became apparent that neither the professional curricula for music educators nor composers provided a common understanding of music. Hence, an investigation of college music curricula was begun. The original Young Composers Project was renamed the Contemporary Music Project (CMP), and with continued funding the Project's mission was expanded to continue placing composers in-residence while also reviewing and transforming professional music curricula.

Some of the concerns that began to become evident and be discussed were: the effect of separate curricular tracks for the various sub-disciplines, the fragmented content of the curricula, and an avoidance or delaying of instruction in contemporary music as well as often ignoring the music of other cultures. It was acknowledged that the graduate curricula held an important place in any revision of undergraduate study, since this is where the future college faculty is educated and probably acquire their perception of and approaches to college teaching. The college music curriculum begets the college teacher who then continues the cycle. Often specialization was being taught to such an extent and with such authority that a broad historical perspective became difficult. At the same time, students were seeking a more meaningful relationship between the content of their education and the careers they expected to pursue.

With this as background CMP organized a national invitational seminar in 1965 at which the concept of 'comprehensive musicianship' was identified as the foundation for a college education in music for all disciplines be they composer, teacher, performer, or scholar. The Project took on the task of developing and promoting this concept and its implementation as it applied primarily to college baccalaureate education and also its application for pre-college to graduate curricula. To do this it established the Institutes for Music in Contemporary Education (IMCE) in over thirty university music programs throughout the United States.

After four years the IMCE initiative produced several recommendations for the most effective means of realizing a more comprehensive curriculum. As a result, during its final five years, 1968–1973, the Project supported extensive efforts for promoting such a curriculum through workshops, institutes, publications and presentations while at the same time now placing more mature composers in-residence in larger contexts, such as cities and states, across the country.

This more comprehensive education in music emphasized the synthesis of the various components of musicianship rather than the perpetuation of the compartmentalization of instruction that was so often found to be the norm in most college programs. It was based on the premise that the major components of the curriculum should be listening and analysis, performance, and an understanding of the compositional process through personal writing skills.

To better understand the basis for this new curricular reform it might be helpful to review the national seminar's essential statements and recommendations.

1. The content and orientation of musicianship training should serve all music degree students, regardless of their eventual specialization.
2. Training in the practice of composition is an essential element in the development of comprehensive musicianship and it should be part of the required subject matter in college music programs. Compositional experience should equip future musicians to better understand the compositional principles underlying any work so that they may be imparted to students and applied in performance or the study of music theory or history.

3. The goal of aural and analytical training should be to achieve a more discerning insight into musical structure, which is a necessary condition for the highest degree of aesthetic response.
4. Music history should be interpreted as a body of material useful for illuminating the study and performance of music, and not merely as subject matter in itself.
5. The curriculum should emphasize the inherent connection between historical and theoretical studies and the relationship of these studies to performance.
6. The basis for musical learning is the same at all stages of instruction, only differing in the degree of detail. This educational process should move from the obvious and concrete to the more subtle and abstract.
7. A comprehensive musicianship curriculum requires eventual experience in each of the three categories of musical learning: being introduced to a concept, being taught a skill, and being exposed to a musical work. Their interrelatedness allows the student to enter this cycle through any of the three categories.
8. Comprehensive musicianship training should incorporate conceptual knowledge with technical skills so as to develop the capacity to experience fully, and achieve the ability to communicate the content of, a musical work.
9. Courses in musicianship should be designed to synthesize knowledge acquired in all musical studies. Continuity should develop between a course on one level with those preceding or following it.
10. Musicianship studies should relate contemporary thought and practice to a more expanded repertoire of previous and current times by viewing the present as the repository of all that has preceded it.
11. Courses in musicianship should be considered an open-ended and evolving discipline, which provides the student with the means to seek and deal with material outside and beyond their formal education in music, as the basis for a lifetime of experiences with music of all kinds.

These recommendations became the foundation for a more complete education in music as it was applied at all levels of instruction through curricula based on a broad perspective of what was considered to be 'music'. CMP's activities had shown that for musicians to be able to deal competently and creatively with contemporary music the required 'theory' courses should be concerned with <u>all</u> aspects of music and that pedagogical approaches should make possible the synthesis of technical skills and conceptual knowledge so that the student would have a strong and broad base for their specialized studies. Thus, such a more comprehensive approach to the development of musicianship should be applicable to all music.

It also was evident that teachers of comprehensive musicianship courses were not dependent upon the guidelines of only one textbook, but drew extensively upon examples from a wide variety of music literature contained in scores and anthologies. Often several textbooks were used mainly for reference. The historical range of these courses encompassed music from the Renaissance, or earlier, through the most contemporary. Teachers of CM used the examination of the musical score as the point of departure for the understanding of concepts, the development of skills, the attainment of historical perspective, and as a means for the students to attain the capacity to make their own technical and aesthetic judgments. The comprehensive musicianship courses often combined the more traditional courses of introductory music history, sight singing, ear training, keyboard harmony and some basic study of form and analysis and orchestration. Many observed that this combining of courses provided a more satisfactory structure for the integration of musical understanding.

This increased scope and expansion of course content was indeed challenging to the teacher but it showed that students developed greater awareness and a depth of comprehension of many styles and periods of music far beyond the traditional compartmentalized approach. Students were more analytical, could express themselves more clearly and had a greater perspective of a variety of music early in their professional education.

CMP then sponsored workshops and courses specifically for both school music teachers and college professors to provide opportunities for them to apply these concepts as a means for developing their own personal approach to a more comprehensive teaching of music. It was emphasized that this was basically a new attitude or approach to a musical education that offered a solid, yet flexible, framework which could be adapted to the strengths and weaknesses of both the faculty and the students.

This approach might be thought of as providing experiences in three essential components of musicianship: creation, performance, and analysis (that is listening, either through visual or aural perception). In a comprehensive program of study, these components are based on an ability to use the elements common to music of all times and places. These "common elements", as they were known as, were defined on the basis that music consists of:

A. Sound, divisible into
    a. Pitch
        i.   Horizontal ('melody')
        ii. Vertical ('harmony')
    b. Duration (rhythm)
    c. Quality
        i.   Timbre
        ii. Dynamics
        iii. Texture
A. These sound elements are used to articulate shape, or form (including the possibility of a lack of defined form).
B. Every musical work must be viewed in its own context including stylistic, historical, cultural and other considerations.

These elements were identified not as a part of a rigid methodology, but rather as the basis of a relatively flexible model that would give continuity and cohesion to a more comprehensive consideration of the many expressions of 'music' that man has devised. Obviously the application of such a methodology requires an open and inquisitive attitude seeking to find more effective ways of providing students with the ability to deal with an expanding repertoire and applied musicianship. It is not expected that every student will be as competent in each area of study as a specialist in that area but it is intended to give each student a broader perspective of their area of specialization and the background to make more mature independent musical judgments.

Over the ensuing years the concept of comprehensive musicianship has continued to be used by a number of teachers as the foundation of music instruction and the basis for textbooks, including the elementary basic series editions. Today it would seem that it is even more applicable, in our ever-changing society, as we seek to define music's purpose and place.

Over the last four or five decades one of the most significant changes that has occurred in music programs in higher education in the United State has been the number that have shifted their focus from their traditional role of training school music teachers, because of the original teacher training mission of their colleges, to having more of a conservatory focus and encouraging more students to become performers. This has happened at the same time as the number of opportunities for professional positions has become more limited. Therefore, it could be argued that the comprehensive approach is even more relevant to the training of performers so as to better prepare them to function more successfully in today's highly competitive music environment.

When the entering professional students begin the study of music they come with an extensive and eclectic background derived from their web driven popular culture. Many will already have a developing sense of musicianship and will probably have been involved in a variety of music making activities. The technology that the professional and general student is immersed in has certainly changed the way they participate in and understand 'music'.

Students in pre-collegiate music study share in this ever-expanding universe of cultural and musical experiences. The technology that they are so familiar with and use constantly will probably have brought them into contact with a variety of world cultures and their music. This technology has also significantly changed the way people engage with and come to internalize music. No longer can western European art music be the sole focus of music instruction in any curriculum. Because for some the traditional study of music can seem almost irrelevant as they sense a dichotomy between 'their music' and 'classical music', which they view as 'school music'.

Music education in today's environment requires a highly competent musician-educator who demonstrates, by example and practice, the concept of comprehensive musicianship as it relates to teaching. The professional curriculum for teacher training should be as rigorous and comprehensive as for any other music specialty. These programs must strive to recruit the most competent student musicians into the field and instill in all professional music students the need for them to be supporters, through out their careers, of quality music programs in the schools.

There is no doubt that the need to examine the efficacy of our curricula is as important now, if not more so, than it was fifty years ago. What started as an attempt to create greater understanding of contemporary music through a composer-in-residence program eventually expanded into an examination of professional curricula and then into developing the means of providing more comprehensive music curricula. This initiative to provide more relevant means for training future professionals could certainly be a model for consideration today. Professional musicians should be prepared to meet the needs of today's culture and the place of music within it. As a result, we are again seeing composer-in-residence programs being developed for all types of professional music students, which are intended to provide meaningful musical experiences for both students and the general public.

The changes that have occurred during these past few decades seem to suggest that we should view the place of classical music within the larger context of the increasing variety of music available in our worldwide cultures. Technology's pervasive influence has made this a universal concern and opportunity.

By promoting the concept of comprehensive musicianship, as it can be applied to the study of music from elementary schools through the university, the Contemporary Music Project took on the role of a catalyst for the reassessment of the nature of music and the use of musical processes in teaching and learning. Any such undertaking demands an expansion of attitudes and knowledge about music and music learning. But as with any reform, this requires considerable risk-taking and perhaps failure at times, which can be intimidating to teachers at all levels of instruction.

It is hoped that this discussion of the work of CMP, and in particular the concept of comprehensive musicianship, might prompt some of today's teachers to consider how it might be used to more effectively teach music in this constantly changing world. Certainly music is a field that requires a more comprehensively educated professional if that individual is to experience success in any of its many facets. The future place of classical music in society could perhaps depend on this method of preparing tomorrow's professionals.

Thus, a professional education in music that sees the present as giving meaning to the past and purpose to the future can provide a more encouraging perspective for the profession. For it must always be remembered that we are preparing students for their futures – not our past.

References

Music Educators National Conference. (1965). *Comprehensive Musicianship, The Foundation for College Education in Music*, A Report of the Seminar sponsored by the Contemporary Music Project at Northwestern University, April 1962. Washington: Music Educators National Conference.

8: The Melbourne UNESCO Seminar, 1956: A watershed in Australian music education

Jane Southcott

Introduction

In 1956 Australian music educators met in Melbourne at a Seminar run under the auspices of the United Nations Education, Scientific and Cultural Organisation (UNESCO). John Bishop (1957) stated that, 'the occasion was wholly significant and important in the history of music in Australia, for never before had Australian and New Zealand musicians in the several and different fields of Music Education been brought together to discuss their work and examine it alongside the work of their colleagues' (p. 2). This august group met, conferred, networked, and made a number of resolutions about what needed to occur in Australian music education. Recently we have, in part, repeated this process in the preparation of the *National Review of School Music Education* (Department of Education, Science and Training, 2005). Resonances occur between the resolutions passed fifty years ago and those made in the first decade of the twenty-first century. This discussion will focus on some of those confluences. Of the 250 people who attended the 1956 seminar, three have been interviewed and their perspectives add to our understanding of what was said and done. Oral history interviews have been undertaken with Patricia L. Holmes who represented the Supervisor of Music from South Australia, Joan Pope who demonstrated the Dalcroze approach under the tutelage of Heather Gell, and Doreen Bridges (née Jacobs) who was invited to attend by John Bishop to expound on her ideas concerning the teaching of musical theory. In 2006

Bridges referred to the Melbourne UNESCO Seminar in 1956 as an 'absolute watershed ... it was a great meeting of all the aspects of music education, school, everything... it was from there that the seed was sown of ASME.' This discussion will not explore every issue raised at the Melbourne Seminar but will focus on those that addressed the teaching of music in schools. It seems that many of the issues raised in 1956 remain unresolved and in need of attention.

UNESCO Music education conferences, 1953 and 1956

In 1949 UNESCO began a programme to improve the teaching of visual art which expanded to include music education, with an International Conference on the role of music in the education of youth and adults in Brussels, 29 June to 9 July 1953. A Preparatory Commission was established by the International Music Council (IMC) and co-chaired by Bernard Shore, United Kingdom. This conference set the organizational pattern that was to be replicated three years later in Australia. Representing Australia at the international conference was Bernard Heinze who was to be instrumental in the organization of the subsequent Melbourne conference. Heinze was elected as one of the Vice-Presidents of the interim body created in the wake of the Brussels conference, later to become the International Society for Music Education. The final recommendations of the Brussels conference included 'To organize a seminar or pilot project on music education in a Member State of Unesco [sic]' (Walters, 1953, p. 8). The Brussels conference also emphasised the importance of 'folk music ... as a social binding force' (Walters, 1953, p. 7) reflecting a contemporary interest. They also discussed the formation of dedicated music libraries to support the work of educators and musicologists. The 1953 conference ended with an 'atmosphere of enthusiasm' (Walters, 1953, p. 4).

The Australian National Advisory Committee for UNESCO considered itself fortunate that Heinze, their Chairman, had attended the Brussels conference. On his return to Australia, Heinze proposed that a seminar on the Role of Music in Education should be held. This seminar was planned by a working party chaired by

Heinze and comprising John Bishop, Dorothy Helmrich, and Margaret Sutherland. Like the Brussels conference, the Melbourne event was organized into three Working Commissions. Both conferences included trade displays, exhibitions and concerts. At least 250 'distinguished educators and musicians from all parts of Australia and also from the Dominion of New Zealand' attended the Melbourne conference. In addition, two overseas visitors were present, both of whom had attended the earlier conference in Brussels – Bernard Shore and Jack Bornoff (Weeden, 1957, Foreword). Shore (1896–1985) was, at that time, Her Majesty's Chief Inspector of Music in Schools and his attendance was supported by the British Council. Shore was also a notable composer and performer. Included in the programme was a 'lovely' viola recital given by Shore on the Friday evening (Pope, 1956). Bishop (1957) described Shore as 'a most human and refreshing ambassador. Always a lively and spirited speaker, his practical experience and realistic approach to the day-to-day problems of the teacher were warmly received' (p. 3). Bornoff was the Executive Secretary of the IMC (UNESCO) based in Paris and it was UNESCO that supported his trip to Australia. Bishop (1903–1964), the Elder Professor of music and director of the Elder Conservatorium (Adelaide), was a well-respected conductor and music educator. He had, in 1943, been one of the founders of the National Music Camp Association and was very influential in Australian musical life (Southcott, 1997). Helmrich (1889–1984) had been instrumental in the founding of the Arts Council of Australia and was, at this time, teaching singing at the New South Wales State Conservatorium (Bourne, 1997). Sutherland (1897–1984), an established composer, teacher and performer, was also associated with a number of music organizations, including the Australian Music Advisory Committee for UNESCO (Symons, 1997).

The General Committee of the 1956 Melbourne conference was chaired by Heinze while Bishop was the Director of the Seminar. As in Brussels, the Melbourne conference was organized into three Working Commissions, known as Committees A, B. and C, chaired respectively by Frank Callaway (Perth), Percy Jones (Melbourne) (1914–1992), and Dorothy Helmrich (Sydney). H.J. Russell, secretary to the Australian National Advisory Committee for UNESCO, was the Rapporteur-General to the Seminar. In the published report, introduced by W.J. Weeden, the Chair of the Australian National Advisory Committee for UNESCO, and presumably prepared by Russell, the nominated members of each Committee were identified as well as the speakers on a range of topics, twenty-two of whose presentations were included in the final report (Weeden, 1957).[1] However, as 250 attended, there were many additional music educators in attendance, not all of whom were named in the official report.

The Committees

Committee A considered 'Music in Schools' and Callaway was joined by Ruth Flockart (Melbourne), Terence Hunt (Sydney), Doris Irwin (Melbourne), and Wilfred King (Hobart). Edgar Nottage (1919–2008) acted as Committee Rapporteur. Four of the members of Committee A held positions of some responsibility in their state education systems. Callaway (1919–2003) was a reader in music at the University of Western Australia. He was to become the foundation professor there in 1959 (Stowasser, 1997). Terence Hunt (1936–2007), Irwin (1905–1994), and King (dates not known) were the Supervisors of Music in New South Wales, Victoria, and Tasmania respectively. Nottage, as Principal Advisory Teacher in Music, held the equivalent position in West Australia. Flockart (1891–1985) was a respected teacher of music at Methodist Ladies' College, Melbourne. Patricia Holmes (1925–1998) was in Melbourne both to attend the Seminar and consult with Irwin about the new South Australian primary music programme (Holmes, 1991). As with most such conferences, the opportunities for conversation and networking are often as significant as the formal proceedings although rarely are such interactions recorded.

Committee B focused on 'The training of the practising musician' and Jones was joined by Jack V. Peters (Adelaide), Hugh Brandon (Brisbane), and Frank Hutchens (Sydney). Peter Platt was their Rapporteur. Understandably, all the members of this committee were academics, employed at tertiary institutions that prepared future professional musicians. The Chair, Jones (1914–1992) was the Vice-Director of the University Conservatorium of Music, Melbourne. Platt (1924–2000) was a Lecturer in Music, University of Sydney, Peters (1920–1973) was a Lecturer in Music, University of Adelaide, and Brandon (1906–1984) was a Lecturer at the University of Queensland. Hutchens (1892–1965) was a Professor, at the NSW State Conservatorium of Music.

Committee C discussed 'The Enjoyment of Music' and the Chair, Helmrich, was assisted by Charles R. Bull (Sydney), Lindley Evans (Sydney), John Horner (Adelaide), and William G. James (Sydney). The Rapporteur for this committee was Kenneth Hunt (Melbourne) (Bishop, 1956, p. 1). Sensibly, for a committee that considered the development of music audiences, two federal Programme Directors from the Australian Broadcasting Commission were included – Charles R. Bull, responsible for Education and James, responsible for Music, both of whom were based in Sydney. In addition the members were Evans (1895–1982) a well-known composer and Lecturer at the NSW State Conservatorium of Music, Kenneth Hunt (1920–2002) a Senior Lecturer in the Faculty of Music, University of Melbourne, and Horner (1899–1973) a Lecturer at the Elder Conservatorium, University of Adelaide, who was shortly to become the South Australian delegate to UNESCO.

The Seminar
Bishop and the leaders of the discussions were congratulated for 'providing for the members of the Seminar fullest opportunities to examine and discuss all important aspects of music in education' (Weeden, 1957, Foreword). It is clear that those in positions of responsibility were chosen to represent various interests and geographic locations. Understandably, there were allegiances formed between representatives from particular interests or locations. Pope (1956) wrote that she soon found Callaway and Nottage, after which she changed the designation on her name badge, putting WA before NSW. She 'noted a colossal and growing feeling of unity amongst the West Australians.' Originally from Perth, Pope had been Callaway's student in 1954–1955.

Additional presenters identified in the Report were selected to represent an even wider range of interests and locations. The 'discussions were led by a team of forty musicians representing each State of the Commonwealth and New Zealand. The success of the Seminar was greatly due to the brilliance of their leadership, their resourcefulness, charm and ready humour' (Bishop, 1957, p. 4). Unfortunately, the report does not list all who attended nor all the concerts and gatherings that occurred. Luckily, a first hand description of the Seminar exists in the letters that Joan Pope wrote home to her parents in Western Australia. She described the opening reception hosted by Heinze

> at the Gallery Recital Room at the Art Gallery.... There is a very comprehensive display room showing music books, scores texts, etc. The reception was fabulous. The French tapestries were hanging and a group of fine Melbourne artists, Juri Tancibudek (1st Oboe) [Melbourne Symphony Orchestra], John Glickman and his wife Sybil Copeland ('leaders' of viola and violins) and Muriel Luyk (soprano) gave a glorious recital of fascinating works by Margaret Sutherland who played the piano parts. Bernard welcomed everyone at the door and introduced his wife. I went in with Tussy Fraenkel and as we were walking away Heinz said: "That girl reminds me of someone ... I know! Joanne Priest!" Well, while the queue of handshakers grew he kept me talking about her and ballet, and said he had noticed me this morning and wondered who I was. Gosh! I sort of floated to my seat. Rex [Hobcroft] sat next to me and his friend the composer Dorian le Gallienne sat behind. (Pope, 1956)

The Seminar was organized in a manner that has become familiar to conference attendees. Following the opening session there were 'ten days of a tightly packed programme of addresses, discussions and music' (Symons, 1989, p. 226). The Plenary sessions began at '9.15 on the dot' (Pope, 1956). There was 'a fine exhibition of Australian, English and American books, music and materials ... arranged through the help of Publishers and Music Warehouses' (Bishop, 1957, p. 4), and both large and small concerts. Schools in and around Melbourne provided young performers to begin each session with a short programme of music. Students who had been attending the May Music Camp also performed. There were more formal evening concerts. Pope described the Saturday evening concert, 'at the town Hall – "King David" a modern oratorio by Honegger; it was most exciting and very well done. I was seated between Callaway and Mr. Terry Hunt (Sup. of NSW School Music) and had good opportunity of both listening and exchanging remarks' (Pope, 1956).

Heinze (1957) set the scene for the conference, giving the inaugural address on 'Music and education' in which he argued for the importance of music in human education as offering balance, mental training, and life-long interest, through engagement with 'best music' of all periods (p. 7). Bornoff (1957) followed this, discussing 'Music and international understanding' in which he listed the seven main aims of the ICM that 'exists to promote a real international understanding and the interchange of musical culture throughout the world' (p. 8). Bornoff (1957) stated that, 'music is by no means an international language in the sense that some people would have us believe … [there were] many fascinating differences between the musical traditions of various countries' (p. 8). Shore (1957), offered a 'Survey of school music development in Great Britain' in which he suggested that he had 'gained a strong impression that the vitality and spontaneity so noticeable in Australian education and music derives from the fact that Australia is not trammelled by too much tradition' (p. 20). However, until this point music education in Australian schools had largely followed British models.

This discussion will focus on one aspect of this Seminar, the work of the Music in Schools Committee A and comparisons will be drawn with some of the recommendations of the recent *National Review of School Music Education* (*NRSME*) (Department of Education, Science and Training, 2005). It is beyond the scope of this discussion to address the findings of Committees B and C or to consider the individual papers. Bishop (1957) acknowledged that the division of the Seminar into three topics was, to some degree, impossible, stating that, 'it was quickly realized that teaching – its philosophy, planning and practice – does not fall readily into such strictly ordered grouping. Certain basic problems are fundamental to us all. For this reason, at the daily Plenary Session the subject for discussion was one in which the majority of members of all groups found both interest and application, such as, "A new approach to basic musicianship", or "The development of an active interest in music through radio broadcasting to schools"' (p. 4). It was concerning the first of these that Doreen Jacobs (1957) (now Bridges) presented a paper of the same name, 'A New Approach to Basic Musicianship' (pp. 51–54). Jacobs was invited by Bishop, who somehow knew about her interest in changing the way theory was taught,[2] to give this paper in which she 'spoke about joining the theory and the musical perception syllabi together' (Bridges, 1991). This was slow to occur. At a subsequent UNESCO conference in 1965 Bridges proposed and Alison Holder seconded, 'to unite the theory and the then musical perception syllabuses [AMEB] which became musicianship, to unite them into one syllabus and Heinze then got me to prepare a joint syllabus' (Bridges, 2006). In her presentation, Jacobs decried much of the contemporary practice of teaching basic musicianship. She argued that students who can read music may 'nevertheless be musically illiterate … [unable] to hear mentally a note they write' (Jacobs, 1957, p. 53).

In his introduction, Bishop stated that the sharing of ideas was not only stimulating but also most revealing as, 'many lessons were learned again, and above all, the important one that, as educationists, we cannot afford to be uninformed … repeatedly throughout the discussions it was demonstrated that the teaching and achievements of an earlier period of music experience and training had a direct and vital effect on the development gained at a later stage of study' (Bishop, 1957, p. 2). Some of these demonstrations of methods and ideas did not make it into the published conference papers. For example, Heather Gell (1896–1988) came from Sydney to give a demonstration lecture on Dalcroze Eurhythmics. Gell was determined to attend. Pope (2006) thought that Gell saw this as her 'opportunity to tell the big boys' about the method and her demonstration was directed to the adult level to correct the misapprehension that Dalcroze Eurhythmics was only applicable to the teaching of younger children. Gell had only short notice about the conference as there had been "a slight bungle in the NSW distribution of notices" and not many people knew about it (Pope, 1956). Gell was doubly determined to be there as she heard that the less qualified Mary de Crespigny had been invited to present a demonstration. Writing at that time to Priscilla Barclay, Secretary of the Dalcroze Teachers' Union, London, Gell made her determination clear. She wrote, 'I forced myself to respond to The Dalcroze Call in that a UNESCO Music Education Seminar was being held in Melbourne ... I flew to Melbourne and my scholarship girl (Joan Pope) was there too. I prepared a paper and gave a demonstration on the three main branches and I was told by teachers it was one of the best things in the seminar' (Gell, 1956). Pope had already decided to attend the conference. She told her parents that, 'Doreen Jacobs my Harmony teacher mentioned that she was taking one of the discussions at a UNESCO Music in Education conference-seminar in Melbourne from the 24 May to 2 June. Well I started thinking about this, and thought "well, that is what I am DOING" and it might be jolly interesting' (Pope, 1956). It is unfortunate that Gell's attendance and presentation were not mentioned in the official report. At that time, Pope was training in the Dalcroze approach under Gell in Sydney. Pope recalled the demonstration that she was part of in the Melba Hall at the Conservatorium of Music. Gell spoke and played the piano and Elizabeth Wade moved with Pope (Pope, 2006).

The findings of Committee A: Music in Schools

Committee A covered a wide range of issues and the members were well aware of the problems faced by school music in Australia. The group members found a sense of camaraderie, developing in constructive conversations 'an appreciation of common tasks, common goals and aspirations and in the tackling of them a sense of "aloneness" was dissipated and a sense of "companionship" established' (Weeden, 1957, p. 10). All the topics discussed are still under discussion today. Fifty years ago the group stressed the importance of a sequential music education from 'the pupil's first day in the kindergarten to his last day in the secondary school' which should 'carry over into the musical, social and home life of the community' (p. 10). The representatives of each state had brought their curricula to share, many of these were new and marked the culmination of the previous half century of music in schools. Various aspects of school music were discussed, often informed by individual presentations. Music reading was discussed. It was generally agreed that the 'techniques being perfected in the general reading programme of the young child should be applied ... to the problems of music reading' which would prepare the child for 'simple creative work in "basic musicianship" ... both in the classroom and the private studio' (p. 10). Vocal music was recognized as the basis of school music and the issues of supporting the developing adolescent voice with suitable repertoire were acknowledged (p. 10). The playing of musical instruments was recommended. Percussion bands were 'now firmly established in Junior schools, although rarely found at other levels of education' (p. 11). The delegates were aware that the percussion band did not allow for pitch development and would benefit from the addition of pitched instruments. Mention was made of the 'recent work of leading European educationists' (p. 11). This oblique reference was presumably to the Orff *Schulwerk* methodology. Holmes recalled that she had transcribed some of the Orff pieces from recordings but, at that time, the first English translation of the Orff *Schulwerk* had not been published (Holmes, 1991). Recorder playing was established as a class activity in many schools. It was described as 'not merely a "teaching aid"; it is a genuine instrument' (p. 11). Under the heading, 'The school orchestra and band', it was acknowledged that there had been remarkable progress in some countries both here and overseas that 'has proved class tuition methods to be most effective that they can form the basis for school orchestras which should not be "something special" but should be the norm in every school' (p. 11). At this time, school orchestras were not common in Australian schools. The Seminar participants considered that part of the problem was that there were still import tariffs on musical instruments and one of their recommendations was that these be lifted.

The Seminar recognized that the training of teachers was problematic. The supply of music specialists was deemed inadequate for the needs of schools. It was suggested that all primary 'teacher trainees be given instrumental and musicianship training' to develop 'greater musical proficiency among student teachers, which, strengthened by adequate teacher training and subsequent "in-service" courses, would enable those entering the primary school service to deal more adequately with music in the classroom' (Weeden, 1957, p. 12). Those training to be school music specialists should have 'a comprehensive training ... [which] should include courses in harmony, counterpoint and those kindred subjects' necessary to be a musician. This should include a 'mature performing ability ... sufficient keyboard technique ... [the ability to] sing intelligently ... be a competent conductor ... basic technique [on] various orchestral instruments ... side knowledge of the repertory of school vocal and orchestral music ... experience in teaching method, preferably acquired by regular, supervised and discussed teaching periods in the schools themselves' (p. 12). While recognizing that teacher education was not always ideal, Committee A recognized that in-service courses were of vital importance and that there should be more school orchestral concerts and school music broadcasts 'to stimulate and direct an active interest in music' (p. 13). The group also discussed the equipment necessary for school music, recommending that 'every secondary school should have a well constructed and equipped music room containing all the classroom aids necessary for a modern and realistic approach to the teaching of music... radiogram, records ... music books and strip films' (p. 13). While the technology may have changed, the need for a well equipped, dedicated facility for school music has not. In 1956 the new state-of-the-art visual aid for classroom music was the film strip. Holmes presented a paper on this. She explained that it involved 'having a film strip and the score up in front of Kindergarten, Grades Ones and Twos and the teachers being provided with accompaniments in staff notation; they tinged the Indian Bell and they [the teachers] turned the strip film on for the children'. The series of films she presented were linked with a series of radio broadcasts which provided the musical examples (Holmes, 1992).

In their conclusion, Committee A were optimistic that 'educational authorities will be courageous enough to face and solve' the administrative problems in finding the proper place for music in schools. They asked for 'the wholehearted co-operation and support of political leaders' (Weeden, 1957, p. 13). Committee A felt that in primary and even more in secondary schools, attention had been 'placed on the "economic man" rather than on man as a whole, complete personality.... We believe that only in the latter is the child given full opportunity for attaining the best of which he is capable as an individual. The contribution of music under such child-centred experience is vital and should be indispensable to his complete growth' (p. 13). To attain this, effective music teacher education was essential. The Committee stated that, 'the quality of music in schools will always depend on the quality and efficiency of the teachers. In view of the limited pre-college music experience of many trainees for primary school teaching and the brevity of their college training, more in-service training is needed' (pp. 13–14). The need for more comprehensive teacher education was the first major issue. The second was the need to integrate music throughout the various levels of education in which 'the curriculum, the teacher and the pupil interact to give the total school experience' (p. 14). The Committee stressed that it was the education of the whole child that was important, particularly in the primary school where the teacher is usually a generalist. They asserted that,

> It must always be remembered that teachers of music are first of all teachers of the children and then of a subject. It is what music does for the child that really matters, not what the child does for music. The widest possible connotation of the term 'music in education' requires the singing of music, the playing of music, the creation of music, the listening to music, the relating of music to the total curriculum of the school... All we ask is that in school music should be accorded equal opportunity with all other activities of the mind and spirit, thereby showing to the child and to the adult a better way of life and living. (pp. 14–15)

The other Committees produced findings as comprehensive and perceptive as these. The Seminar eventually wound to a close. By the end of the conference, Pope was tired, as 'so much has happened, so many people have talked, expressed views, promoted controversial discussions etc., we have heard so much music that frankly I am overwhelmed and am feeling tired and exhausted!' Despite this, Pope found the Seminar most stimulating and 'exhilarating mentally if not physically. At the moment I feel very mixed up as my mind can hardly cope with the assimilation of all the varied topics, situations, backgrounds and futures of Music Education. It has been a most marvellous opportunity to find out about, and size up several education policies, training facilities and so on' (Pope, 1956). Bishop also noted that, 'by the end many may have been tired, but there was no indication of exhaustion either of ideas or language' (Symons, 1989, p. 228). The seminar finished on a 'Saturday morning with the final meeting and reports of various committees, resolutions to be brought forward to AMEB, Education departments etc on many subjects ... We all wonder what will happen now, but coming from a UNESCO body, someone influential may take notice of these Australia wide problems' (Pope, 1956). Bishop (1957) stated that, 'the most important step taken was left to the final ten minutes of the Seminar when a suggested plan for the establishment of an "Australia – New Zealand society of Music Education", which should become linked with the International body, was endorsed by members' (p. 4).

The Resolutions concerning Music in Schools – 1956 and 2005

Of the numerous resolutions passed by the UNESCO Seminar in 1956, four directly addressed music in schools:

1. This seminar emphasizes to Educational Authorities that no post-primary school is complete without a properly designed music room and equipment. Just as science cannot be handled successfully without special facilities so music also has special needs;

2. This Seminar considers that, in common with educational practices in other parts of the British Commonwealth, music in Australasian schools should be recognized as a basic subject at all levels, demanding at the post-primary state (as a non-examinable subject) a minimum of two periods a week until the final two years of the secondary school and one period per week thereafter;
3. This Seminar directs the attention of the Ministers of Education to the inadequate supply of school musicians and the lack of adequate numbers of students in training as school music teachers and requests them to take steps to see that this serious gap in music in schools is rectified;
4. Because the pre-service musical experience of primary school teachers is usually inadequate, this Seminar asks Departments of Education to consider: (a) the provision of more extensive facilities for in-service training for such teachers; and (b) the provision of a course in essential musicianship, including practical skills, for secondary pupils contemplating teaching as a career. (Weeden, 1957, p. 71)

These are prefaced by the same assertions made by Committee A concerning the recognition of the importance of school music and the necessity for adequate teacher education and provision of facilities and resources. Nearly fifty years later, the *NRSME* (Department of Education, Science and Training, 2005) began by asserting the 'value of music education for all Australian students', the necessity to 'place immediate priority on improving and sustaining the quality and status of music education' and the need to 'provide sufficient funding to support effective, quality music education that is accessible for all Australian children' (p. xiv). The *NRSME* stressed the importance of providing 'sequential, developmental music education programmes' and to 'improve the standard of pre-service music education for all generalist classroom teachers' (p. xv). The *NRSME* addressed specialist music teacher education programmes with a desire to improve the quality and expand the provision of current offerings to ensure that 'primary and secondary specialist music teachers can develop and maintain their knowledge, understandings, skills and values about teaching music' (p. xvii). As in 1956, the recent *NRSME* identified the importance of the voice in school music and the intention that every Australian student should participate in initial instrumental music programmes. The *NRSME* also addressed school music facilities, recommending that all schools have adequate facilities and provisions to support engagement in 'continuous, sequential, developmental music education programmes' (p. xxi). These provisions should include music technology, hopefully as 'state-of-the-art' as the film strip was in 1956. The *NRSME* made further recommendations which did not echo quite so exactly the recommendations of 1956. In 2005, the *Review* also recognized the crucial role of school leadership, the desire for all primary school students to have access to music specialist teachers, the importance of effective liaison with music organizations, and that effective programmes should demonstrate their quality through appropriate accountability measures. Other than the last few, the *NRSME* covers almost identical ground to the 1956 Seminar. It is disheartening to recognize how much time and effort has gone into what is, in some repects, little progress in the recognition and support of school music.

Bridges (1979) listed reviews of school music that were undertaken after the first UNESCO Seminar. She included

> Graham Bartle's *Music in Australian Schools* (1968) and the joint study of the Schools Commission and the Australia Council on Education and the Arts (1977) … the Unisearch Report by Roger Covell, *Music in Australia: Needs and Prospects* (1970), *The Arts in Schools* report by the interdepartmental committee appointed to enquire into the education of school children in New South Wales (1974), the joint ASME–ACE inquiry in *Music in Kindergarten, Infant and Primary Schools* (1975), the *Curriculum Services Inquiry* of the Victorian Education Department in 1976, and similar inquiries in other states. (p. 7)

Bridges pointed out that,

in all these reports there is a consensus that, despite pockets of excellence, the classroom teaching of music is inadequate and ineffective, particularly during the critical learning periods of early and middle childhood. The reports stress the lack of confidence and competence in music teaching and comment on the fact that large numbers of teachers have little or no commitment to music as part of the educative process. Most see it mainly as entertainment. Insufficient professional support for non-specialist teachers and inadequate teacher preparation emerge in the reports as key factors in the low standards and status of music in primary and pre-primary education. Institutions concerned with the pre-service education of teachers are urged to devote more time to music, to see that course content is relevant, and to ensue that students undergoing practice teaching are advised by music specialists when giving music lessons. (p. 7)

Conclusion

The UNESCO Seminar in Melbourne in 1956 was in many ways a watershed. The gathering of music educators from across the country was unprecedented and set the pattern for many future seminars and conferences. New curricula and methods were shared. Music educators gained strength from both the informal and formal aspects of these conferences. Formally, wide ranging presentations addressed issues and offered ideas about new and exciting ways of teaching and learning music. Informally, networks were established that could be maintained both locally and nationally after the event. The enthusiasm and optimism in the post-war 1956 deliberations is evident. Recommendations addressed many topics and it was hoped that action would follow. One of the positive outcomes of the conference was the eventual establishment of the Australian Society for Music Education in 1967 that has continued to provide opportunities for sharing ideas and expertise. A less happy acknowledgement must be made – that, despite all this activity, we continue to have the same conversation. Music in schools still needs advocacy. Teacher education, both pre-service and in-service, still needs improvement. Resources and facilities are often not what they could or should be. Despite this, music educators continue to strive to deliver effective, sequential, engaging music education in schools as they did in 1956.

Acknowledgements

I wish to thank Dr Doreen Bridges and Dr Joan Pope for allowing me to interview them, and Sandra Nash for sharing her transcription of Heather Gell's letter.

Notes

1   Mary Kennedy, Keith Newson, Joan Bazeley 'A critical appraisal of the Australasian school music scene'; Keith Newson, Terence A. Hunt, G.R. D'Ombrain, Joan Bazeley 'The training of the teacher (school music)'; Doris M. Irwin 'Curriculum planning for the primary school'; Joan R. Webb 'Curriculum planning for the secondary school'; Wilfrid King 'Curriculum planning for the area school'; Patricia L. Holmes 'The strip film as a means of music education'; G.J. Reid, Barbara Carroll, Joan Easterbrook-Smith 'The development of an active interest in music through radio broadcasting to schools'; Ida Robson 'The place of singing games and folk song dramatization in musical activities; Frank Callaway 'The school orchestra and band'; Keith Newson 'Musical development through the use of percussion'; Barbara Carroll 'The value of recorder playing'; Edgar Nottage 'Class singing with special reference to the adolescent voice'; Terence A. Hunt 'Classroom equipment and its use'; Ida Robson 'The development of the creative mind'; Doreen Jacobs 'A new approach to basic musicianship'; Nancy Martin 'The teaching of music reading'; J.V. Peters 'Harmony and its teaching'; Peter Platt and Mary Martin 'Music in the Faculty of Arts'; Federal Music Department, A.B.C. and Barbara Mettam "The enlarging of musical horizon and experience through orchestral concerts for children, youth, adults'; Professor D.R. Peart 'Music and its place in everyday life'; Joan Hammet 'The therapeutic value of music'; Nancy Martin and Kenneth Hunt 'The majority of young people cease music-making in their after-school years. Why?'

2   Bridges (2006) recalled, "now, that is very interesting because he somehow knew about my interest in changing the theory type of thing and he and John Horner was in Adelaide and I don't know how John Bishop knew that … when he was first appointed he wanted me to teach – he wanted me to take teacher education classes at the Conservatorium but I didn't want to come back to Adelaide … at that stage I was in charge of the Commonwealth Reconstruction Training Scheme as far as music went and I had to visit all of the states that had music at tertiary training to do a review of it … I was probably still at the Universities Commission in 1949 … He invited me and John Horner each to prepare – we were to share

the session and we were each to prepare a paper on a new approach to basic musicianship because my whole thing was that it should be much more real and have an aural component ... so I gave my paper and John Horner gave a paper ... Heinze was the chairman of this and he actually organized this through UNESCO".

References

Bishop, J. (1957). Introduction. In W. J. Weeden, (Rapporteur). *Music in Education Report of the Australian Unesco Seminar* held in Melbourne May – June, 1956. Australia: Australian National Advisory Committee for Unesco, 2–4.

Bishop, J., Jones, P., Helmrich, D., Callaway, F. & Russell, H. J. (1957). *Music in Education Report of the Australian Unesco Seminar* held in Melbourne May – June, 1956. Australia: Australian National Advisory Committee for Unesco.

Bourne, W. (1997). Helmrich, Dorothy Jane Adele. In Bebbington, W. (ed.) *The Oxford Companion to Australian Music*, Melbourne: Oxford University Press, 263–264.

Bridges, D. (1979). Music Teacher Education: Problems, Perspectives, Prospects and Proposals. Proceedings of National Conference Association of Music Education Lecturers and Australian Society for Music Education, Melbourne, 7–11.

Bridges, D. (1991). Interview, 1 December.

Bridges, D. (2006). Interview, 20 December.

Department of Education, Science and Training (2005). *National Review of School Music Education: Augmenting the diminished*. ACT: Department of Education, Science and Training, Australian Government.

Gell, H. (1956). Correspondence with Priscilla Barclay, 9 June.

Heinze, B. (1957). "Music and Education" An Address given at the Inaugural Session of the Seminar. *Music in Education Report of the Australian Unesco Seminar* held in Melbourne May – June, 1956. Australia: Australian National Advisory Committee for Unesco, 5–7.

Holmes, P. L. (1991). Interview, 15 July.

Holmes, P. L. (1992). Interview, 18 December.

Jacobs, D. (1956). A New Approach to Basic Musicianship. *Music in Education Report of the Australian Unesco Seminar* held in Melbourne May – June, 1956. Australia: Australian National Advisory Committee for Unesco, 51–54.

Pope, J. (1956). Private correspondence.

Pope, J. (2006). Interview, 4 October.

Southcott, J.E. (1997). Bishop, John (Lionel Albert Jack). In W. Bebbington (Ed.), *The Oxford Companion to Australian Music* (p. 59). Melbourne: Oxford University Press.

Stowasser, H. (1997). Callaway, Sir Frank Adams. In W. Bebbington (Ed.), *The Oxford Companion to Australian Music* (pp. 93–94). Melbourne: Oxford University Press.

Symons, C. (1989). *John Bishop: A life for music*. Melbourne: Hyland House.

Symons, D. (1997). Sutherland, Margaret Ada. In W. Bebbington (Ed.), *The Oxford Companion to Australian Music* (pp. 535–537). Melbourne: Oxford University Press.

Walter, A. (1953). *United Nations Educational Scientific and Cultural Organization Report on the International conference on the role and place of music in the education of youth and adults,* Brussels, 29 June – 9 July 1953. Retrieved 1 April, 2009 from unesdoc.unesco.org/images/0012/001272/127234EB.pdf

Weeden, W. J. (1957). Foreword. *Music in Education Report of the Australian Unesco Seminar* held in Melbourne May – June, 1956. Australia: Australian National Advisory Committee for Unesco.

9: Arts and Academies – the Australian musical experience

David Tunley

The relationship between artistic activities and those institutions set up to support and maintain them has not always been an easy one. Those in the vanguard of artistic innovation are not necessarily welcome in places where the main purpose is to conserve tradition, the institutions then running the risk of looking foolish when – eventually – the *avant-garde* becomes the *arrière-garde*. One has only to think of the French Impressionists who in the 1860s were refused exhibition space in the annual Salon de Paris of the Académie des Beaux Arts, only to become the world's most-loved painters. Some thirty years before this Berlioz's first three submissions for the Prix de Rome (judged by the Music Section of the same Académie) were failed because of their 'modernity', his fourth achieving success simply because he gritted his teeth and forced himself to compose in a more traditional style. The list of academies rejecting originality is probably endless, if for no other reason than the unfolding of the arts in Europe (to which we are heir) is the result of a restless search for innovation and change, leading to one generation reacting against the style of the previous one. Australian music has not been immune from these changes, even if they took longer to reach our shores and take root here.

Of this time-lag Roger Covell has suggested that, in addition to the geographical remoteness from the major European centres that limited the musical experiences of budding composers in Australia in late colonial times and the early 20th century, there was also the sense of cultural inferiority that accompanied our then provincial society. He wrote:

> It became one of the first tasks of able musicians to demonstrate that they could write fluent and grammatically acceptable music in established idioms. It was necessary that the idioms be established in order that the demonstration could be convincing to their fellow-countrymen. A radical style would have been interpreted in Australia in the earlier years of this [20th] century merely as a confession of incompetence.[1]

The present essay considers what has been the reaction of the 'academy' to radical musical techniques and styles when they began to be introduced here. The term 'academy' is widely` interpreted in this essay as meaning our permanent – or at least, long-lived – musical institutions or organisations (such as universities, conservatoria, opera companies, symphony orchestras and the over-arching national broadcaster), most of them established from the late 19th century to the middle of the 20th century. I would like to consider the part played by three of them. The first is the Australian Opera – now called Opera Australia.

From the mid-19th century onwards Sydney and Melbourne, in particular, presented a scene of extraordinary vitality in performances of opera presented by a host of visiting companies – all the more remarkable considering the distance they had to travel from the world centres. Harold Love places the achievements of W. S. Lyster's opera companies in the late 19th century – which he claims were unmatched until 100 years later - in the wider context of

> a huge westward moving theatrical tide that swept ambitious young performers from England and Ireland onto the talent-hungry stages of New York, Boston and Philadelphia and then just as surely launched them towards the frontier in search of a public that would be prepared to allow them unquestioned stardom. For the Lyster singers this happy situation was reached in Melbourne and Sydney.[2]

The firm place that opera held in those two major cities is further reflected in the elegant theatres that were built there – in Sydney, the Prince of Wales Theatre, in Melbourne, the Princess's Theatre and the Theatre Royal. Nevertheless, these colourful performances in colonial times (often with great international stars in the leading roles) were – like the solo performances from celebrated visiting pianists, violinists and singers – essentially ephemeral events. There was no permanent institution to sustain their momentum or establish a local tradition. The rise and decline of organisations such as J. C. Williamson and J. & N. Tait, whose powerful entrepreneurial empires eventually merged, suggests that in Australia commercial institutions have lacked the financial staying power (and the artistic vision) needed for permanent support of the performing arts. (Even Sir Thomas Beecham, lacking neither vision nor – at the beginning – financial resources, was temporarily bankrupted by his own opera company). Unlike in the USA where private benevolence on a grand scale has created long-lasting cultural institutions, in Australia these have needed federal and state government funds if they are to reach permanent status. In opera, this was to come in financial aid to the various opera companies in the major cities and, eventually to the Australian Opera in 1970, which had its roots in the Elizabethan Theatre Trust. Despite those crises inevitably associated with opera companies the world over, the Australian Opera – now called Opera Australia – has survived to a point where it may hopefully be described as a permanent cultural institution in our country. In that sense it comes under my heading of 'academy'. That it has maintained and sustained operatic activities in Australia for nearly forty years (often in association with state opera companies) is in no dispute;[3] what is less known is its encouragement to innovative Australian composers, who were certainly not shown the institutional door like the Impressionist painters of the 19th century.

While only a handful of Australian operas have been mounted in full production (Larry Sitsky's *Lenz* (1974) and *The Golen* (1993), Anne Boyd's *The Little Mermaid* (1985), Brian Howard's *Metamorphosis* (1985), Richard Meale's *Voss* (1986 & 1990) and

Mer de Glace (1991), Brian Howard's *Whitsunday* (1988), Richard Mill's *Summer of the 17th Doll* (1999), and *Batavia* 2001)), on the other hand, a number of them have been given workshop productions. One of the first innovations of the artistic director Moffatt Oxenbould (appointed to that position in 1984) was the establishment of the National Opera Workshop. He described it as

> engaging with selected composers in workshopping sections of completed operas or works in progress, giving the creators access to the resources and expertise of the national company. We would feel reasonably content if at the end of ten years our audience, and also our artists, regarded the presentation of contemporary Australian opera as a normal function of the company, just as they would expect each year's repertoire to include works by Mozart, Rossini, Verdi, Puccini, Wagner and other proven composers of the past 300 years.[4]

Although the National Opera Workshop no longer operates, in the five years that it did thirteen mainly short operas by contemporary Australian composers were either commissioned and/or work-shopped. These were by Michael Barnes, Andrew Ford, Michael Whitiker (two operas), Ross Fiddes, Donald Hollier, Colin Brumby, Gillian Whitehead, Felix Meagher, David Stanhope, Douglas Knehans, Stephen Lalor and Allan John. The touring arm of the Australian Opera – OzOpera (established 1996) – has also performed operas by Graeme Koehne and Jonathan Mills. The performance or workshopping of 26 contemporary Australian operas in its forty-year history is a notable achievement and speaks well of the first institution mentioned in this essay. A comparative study of this situation with major opera companies elsewhere has yet to appear.

We'll now consider the second of our 'academies' made up of different university music departments or faculties and conservatoria. It was through private funds that the study of music at university level was made possible in Australia: at the Universities of Adelaide (1884) and Melbourne (1890) – through endowments from the pastoralist

Thomas Elder and the grazier Frances Ormond respectively. More in common than just through generosity of each of these two landed gentlemen, the two first faculties of music in Australia took a step virtually unknown in UK and Europe: the decision to create conservatoria *within* Faculties of Music – a pattern not followed when music eventually came into other leading tertiary institutions in various states in the second half of the 20th century. Looking back we can see it as perhaps fortunate that the early chairs of music in Adelaide and Melbourne were filled by men of vision – such as the third Elder Professor, E. Harold Davies (whose biography by Doreen Bridges gives us a fine glimpse into the man and his period[5]), and the colourful Foundation Ormond Professor W. G. L. Marshall Hall.[6] Perhaps it is not surprising that with such unusual beginnings university music in Australia has not been quite so hidebound as has often been the case in other countries. Indeed, some later professors of music of those two universities, and later elsewhere, have displayed marked entrepreneurial or performance skills rather than academic achievements. The creation of independent conservatoria or practical schools of music have added to the mix of our permanent musical institutions. Particularly from the mid-1960s onwards the influence of these institutions on innovative trends in composition, as well as pedagogy and performance was impressive. Inevitably, this was bound up in the musical proclivities of the heads of the faculties or schools. But it would be difficult to make out a case that tertiary musical institutions were generally averse to appointing progressive musicians to lead them. The regeneration of the Australian university scene in the 1960s (following the implementation of recommendations in the Murray Report) was so powerful that tertiary institutions in many parts began to flourish in a sustained way, many universities and conservatoria now becoming powerful focal points in musical developments in Australia – in many cases, in the very vanguard of innovation and experimentation. In this context, the words 'institutionalised' and 'academic' seem to have taken on a new and unexpected meaning!

Through national seminars and workshops in the 1960s Australian universities took the lead in encouraging young Australian composers to catch up with their counterparts overseas. The first of these was a Seminar for Composers hosted by Adelaide University and sponsored by UNESCO in 1960, followed a few years later by two similar events at the University of Tasmania. From 1968 to 1975 The University of Western Australia, largely in conjunction with the ABC and the West Australian Symphony Orchestra, hosted eight Composers Workshops at which 168 works were performed (and some recorded). Although some of the programmes included a few works from the older generation of Australian composers, most others (including first performances) were by emerging contemporary composers who were to become well-known in later years, such as Nigel Butterly, Colin Brumby, Larry Sitsky, Richard Meale, Ross Edwards, Ann Boyd, Don Banks, Jennifer Fowler, Barry Conyngham, Carl Vine, George Dreyfus and others.[7] Such seminars were a catalyst, and led to a number of gifted and experienced overseas composers invited to visit or to settle in Australia. An even more significant step was the appointment of forward-looking Australian composers to campuses around the country.

First of these was the appointment of Peter Sculthorpe in 1963 to Sydney University by the Foundation Professor there – Donald Peart. Eschewing the extremes of musical modernism Sculthorpe developed his own distinctive style and was to influence many composers who came to study with him in the multi-faceted ambience of the Department of Music established in 1947 by Donald Peart. Its Foundation Professor was a man of remarkably diverse interests – unique in Australia at the time – encompassing scholarship and performance of music from early to modern times. He resuscitated the Australian Branch of the International Society for Contemporary Music, and the universality of his musical vision was to inspire many students. Three years after Sculthorpe's appointment to Sydney the Cambridge-educated John Exton, who had studied with Dallapiccola in Italy, was appointed to the University of Western Australia, where, amongst other activities, he set up one of the early electronic music studios in the country. These, of course, proliferated and were soon to be found in almost every university or conservatorium. That at UWA was one of the attractions for the British-born composer Roger Smalley who arrived in 1976 as a Visiting Fellow, later becoming a permanent member of staff. He had been an associate with Stockhausen and in London had gained the reputation as a musical *enfant terrible*, overshadowing for a time his extraordinarily wide interests and musical sympathies. Smalley arrived in Australia at a time when a number of highly-gifted composers, having left Australia to study overseas, were returning, bringing with them a refreshing cosmopolitan outlook and an enthusiasm to share their experiences with the younger generation of composers coming into universities and conservatoria. This was the decade when composers like Nigel Butterley, who had studied with Priaulx Rainier in London, was appointed to Newcastle, and Barry Conyingham to Melbourne. In that same period Keith Humble was appointed Foundation Professor at La Trobe University. Other appointments such as composer-in-residence or visiting musician quickly followed, bringing to campuses around Australia musicians of experience and expertise like Don Banks and Larry Sitsky, to mention just two. Such appointments were often made possible through grants from the then newly-established Australian Council for the Arts (1973), later re-named The Australia Council, and which has become one the major 'permanent institutions' in our country. It is easy to see that in the development of a more contemporary Australian musical style the universities and conservatoria played a vital role. Far from holding back innovation and experimentation they were in its vanguard, and these developments gave a momentum that is still felt today. Seen from our present day vantage-point these were indeed halcyon times.

Our third institution is undoubtedly one of the most important and far-reaching of all: the ABC. Here is not the place to outline the history of the national broadcaster in relation to music – this has been done elsewhere, most recently by Martin Buzacott[8] whose main focus in his splendid book is the development of ABC orchestras in each state. It is worth noting, however, that when the Australian Broadcasting Commission began its transmissions on 1 July 1932, it followed the same spirit of encouragement to Australian performers and composers as evident in the Australian Broadcasting Company, which had been set up earlier for a period of three years while the Commonwealth Government decided upon the future of a permanent national broadcaster. This same spirit of encouragement to Australian music in both organisations is hardly surprising, for Bernard Heinze was deeply involved in both, first as part-time Director-General of Music in the Company and then as Music Advisor to the Commission. In both organisations his trusty associate was the composer/pianist William James.[9] In Heinze's words when reporting on the place of music in the Company '... It is the desire of the broadcasting authorities to give performance to new and sincere work, and to give the public at large an opportunity to hear it.'[10] A programme devoted to compositions by Australian composers had been broadcast by the Company comprising: *Jenolan* (Rex Shaw), *Divertissement* for four violins (Frederick Hall), a string quartet (George English), *Omar* (Frederick Hall) and an arrangement for male quartet of *Australian Bush Songs* (presumably by William James). Yet this was a mere trickle of Australian works in comparison to the second year of its operation (1933), when the Commission conducted a competition for Australian composers attracting some 800 original works. Some of the winners were to become well known in later years: Fritz Hart, Lindley Evans and Clive Douglas. One of the winning works was by Margaret Sutherland who had recently returned to Australia after studying in England with Arnold Bax. Unfortunately that work – Suite for String Orchestra – has been lost. More's the pity, for it would be interesting to compare it with an earlier work, her Violin Sonata (1925), which David Symons has described as 'a ground-breaking work in the history of Australian music.'[11] The following year the ABC organised a second competition (the English composer John Ireland as adjudicator), the winners including some of the same names as before with the addition of Alex Burnard. Perhaps more important than competitions was the decision in 1939 to broadcast a monthly programme of Australian compositions, some of those hitherto unpublished.

Such encouragement to Australian composition was dramatically underlined when the newly-arrived Eugene Goossens was shown a copy of an orchestral score by an extremely shy composer, leading to a brilliant performance of John Antill's *Corroboree* by the ABC's Sydney Symphony Orchestra in 1946. Welcomed in all quarters, this work was seen as a new dawn for contemporary Australian composition, and Raymond Hansons's brilliant Trumpet Concerto was soon to be performed – also through the personal encouragement of Goossens. But the bright day took much longer to arrive. Certainly there were a number of Australian works given studio performances (particularly of works by Clive Douglas, Robert Hughes and Dorian Le Gallienne and others), but most of the recordings from these were not for commercial use, and the works rarely appeared in mainstream subscription concerts. But this was to change dramatically with the appointment of the conductor John Hopkins as the ABC's third Federal Director of Music in 1963. With this appointment music in the national broadcaster – and as a result – in the nation itself was to enter a new era. One of his first acts was to appoint three young forward-looking composers to the programming staff: Nigel Butterley, Richard Meale and Ian Farr, bringing to the ears of radio and concert audiences European and Australian works of uncompromising originality. These were often heard in the ABC's Prom Concerts, initiated and usually conducted by Hopkins, and which reached such a pitch of excitement as to suggest that that the younger generation felt that here was hardly time enough to catch up with the modern world. The momentum generated in those years is still felt today and contributed to a totally unprecedented respect for and recognition of the great wealth of musical talent found in this country.

A recent development in the ABC's encouragement and support for serious Australian composition has been the emergence of the country's most important recording company: ABC Classics. This has brought to the ears of countless people works that would have otherwise remained unknown to most people. Since its inception in 1987 ABC Classics has issued the works of some 40 contemporary Australian composers in CD recordings of a quality that earlier Australian composers could have only dreamt of.[12]

Conclusion

It would be idle to suggest that the enthusiasm towards encouraging musical innovation described above has been consistently maintained in the three institutions chosen for this essay. After all, institutions largely reflect the personal persuasion and commitment of their directors and the constraints of the bureaucracies that administer government-funded organisations. And it would be fair to point out that the highest intensity of support occurred around the same time within each of these institutions, i.e. during that remarkable period starting in the 1960s when, for a complex of reasons, Australian cultural life threw off much of its sense of inferiority and new, strong winds of change blew over the country. It was therefore to be expected that the 'academies' would respond to this and take leadership in it. Indeed, the Australian Opera was born during this very time.

But neither should we ignore the fact that visionary leadership had been much in evidence in the history of the two institutions created in the late 19th and early 20th centuries, overturning the long-held popular belief that institutions hold back the tide of innovation. In the Australian experience, for the most part, the reverse has held. The oldest of these two are, of course, the universities and, as has been mentioned, Music was introduced into them in a way that was distinctly different from traditional universities overseas. Moreover, the early professors were men of vision whose influence was still felt many years later, even up to the second half of the 20th century. In the 1960s, for example, chairs of music were held by what might excusably be called the 'grand professors' – Bernard Heinze, Frank Callaway and John Bishop – all of whom saw music in universities as stretching well beyond campus and classroom and encouraging an international outlook that was to influence not only musical composition, but also to a very great extent the practice and professionalism of musicology and music education. In this latter activity the work of Doreen Bridges deserves a most honourable mention. The national broadcaster was equally fortunate in its choice of musical leadership in Bernard Heinze and William James. Both men, with the encouragement of Charles Moses (the first general manager of the ABC) saw the way by which Australian music could be inspired by overseas practice and yet retain its individual voice. The youngest of the three institutions, the Australian Opera, grew up in the heady days of the 1970s[13] when Australian cultural life was catching up with international trends, particularly with the assistance of another powerful organisation created at that time: The Australian Council for the Arts, later renamed the Australia Council. In the long view, far from acting as deterrents to musical originality, the three 'academies' described in this essay have given long-lasting encouragement and support to it, and we owe much to them.

Notes

1. Roger Covell, Australia's Music: Themes of a New Society (Sun Books, Melbourne, 1967), 146.
2. Harold Love, The Golden Age of Australian Opera (Currency Press, Sydney, 1981), 3.
3. For a richly documented account of The Australian Opera and its beginnings, see Moffatt Oxenbould, Timing is everything – a life backstage at the opera (ABC Books, Sydney, 2005) from which some of the details of commissions, workshops etc have been taken.
4. Oxenbould, 425.
5. See, Doreen Bridges, More Than a Musician – a life of E. Harold Davies (Australian Scholarly Publishing, Melbourne).
6. For a concise account see Peter Tregear, The Conservatorium of Music University of Melbourne – An Historical Essay to Mark Its Centenary 1995–1995 (Centre for Studies in Australian Music, The University of Melbourne, 1997).
7. For a full list of works performed at these workshops see John A Meyer, Touches of Sweet Harmony – Music in The University of Western Australia (CIRCME, The University of Western Australia, 1999, 156–162).
8. Martin Buzacott, The Rite of Spring: 75 Years of ABC Music Making (ABC Books,. Sydney, 2008).
9. See David Tunley, William James and the Beginnings of Modern Musical Australia (Australian Music Centre, Sydney, 2007).
10. The Australian Broadcasting Company Limited Year Book 1930 (Sydney, 1931), 38.
11. David Symons, The Music of Margaret Sutherland (Currency Press, Sydney, 1997), 15.
12. I am grateful to Natalie Shea for documentation concerning composers and their works recorded by ABC Classics.
13. For a detailed account of the period, see David Tunley, 'A Decade of Musical Composition in Australia 1960–1970', Studies in Music, vol. 5, 1971, and 'Australian Composition in the Twentieth Century – A Background', Australian Composition in the Twentieth Century (ed. Frank Callaway and David Tunley, OUP, Melbourne, 1980).

10: That Everyone May 'Gather His Quota'

Jamie C. Kassler

During her long and fruitful career, Doreen Bridges acted on her belief that children have a natural capacity for singing (and, hence, for music) and that, *under proper conditions and by appropriate means*, this capacity emerges concurrently with a child's other capacities for naming and counting. She therefore became an advocate of early (pre-school) music education, during the course of which she faced numerous obstacles to its implementation—for example, entrenched public policy, inert bureaucracies, vested interests and, no doubt also, long-lived and tenacious attitudes about music that today remain unexamined and, perhaps, even unrecognised. As a way of celebrating Doreen's contributions as a music educator and scholar, this essay will examine, very briefly, the last-named obstacle in order to suggest some future lines of scholarly inquiry that might help to explain, at least in part, why music is such an inessential part of education in Australia.

I shall begin with Roger North,[1] who in 1728 pointed out:

> It is certein that aptitude is not found alike in all persons, for the respective organs may be differently capacitated; and education, together with a peculiar attention as well as favour [i.e., inclination] to musick, in divers persons will exceedingly vary; but except the naturally incapables (if there are any such) no person duely assisted hath reason to despair, as many are apt to doe; but every one that will apply and persevere may gather his quota....[2]

North's democratic assumption—that with due assistance *everyone* 'may gather his quota' in music—was not usual in his time (or indeed, in ours). For the educational theory of his day followed the ancient Greek distinction between 'liberal' and 'mechanical' studies, the former suited to the 'free' man, the latter to the slave. The so-called 'free' man had no need to work and could give time to subjects of cultural value, whereas special skill was the province of the 'unfree' man, who was required to work.[3]

Early in the seventeenth century, this ancient distinction re-appeared in England in the guise of two competing educational ideals. One ideal, the humanist, was concerned with the upper classes, whose education was to produce a well-rounded, cultured person. Since music was regarded as part of culture, it was included in the ordinary education of the upper classes. But because 'mechanical' studies were not esteemed, excessive skill in music—professionalism—was to be avoided as time misspent, especially in the case of 'men of business', that is, courtiers, statesmen and others involved in public affairs. By contrast, the puritan ideal of education was concerned with the needs of the lower and the (then rising) middle classes, who, in different ways, needed to earn a living. Hence, stress was on technical and vocational training, so that music, unless pursued as a vocation, was regarded as a waste of time and associated with 'odd' company.[4] Although learning to sing hymns was encouraged for both lower and middle classes and although (eventually) other musical skills were deemed appropriate for the latter class, children were discouraged from learning music if the type in question was considered inappropriate for one or the other sex[5] or if it was deemed to have evil effects because it was associated with immoral behaviour.[6]

You will note that each of the two educational ideals placed certain restrictions on the extent to which a person could 'gather his quota' in music. In the educational ideal for the upper classes, music was to be cultivated not as a vocation but as a genteel accomplishment, either theoretical (by men) or practical (by both men and women), whereas in the educational ideal for the lower and middle classes, music study was rudimentary unless chosen as a vocation. But, as one educational writer pointed out, those who practice music 'for Bread are in but small Repute', and the 'Grave and Rigid of all Ages have look'd upon Music as of *no public Utility*'. Hence, unless a youth was 'not resolv'd to turn Musician entirely, or has not an independent Fortune', he should avoid 'Improvement' in singing, because 'if he is oblig'd to follow any Business that requires Application, this Amusement certainly takes him off his Business, exposes him to Company and Temptations to which he would otherwise have been a Stranger'.[7]

That music has evil effects is an idea with a long and complicated history, only parts of which have been systematically studied. In order to tell a short version of the story, it will be useful to begin with mythology and the cult of Dionysus, the rites of which were intended to lead to a final state of ecstasy and divine possession (*enthousiasmos*). The most characteristic parts of the Dionysian *orgia* were music and dancing as aids to ecstasy, to the sense of union with the godhead and to the power of seeing visions.[8] As a means to this end, musicians used the aulos, the cacaphonous sounds of which were produced, like the bagpipe, by air pressure and, hence, required tempered systems of tuning based on irrational numbers. Here, in a nutshell, is a source for two strands of the idea that music has evil effects: on the one hand, its use to arouse sensuous appetites; on the other hand, its association with 'irrationality'.

The first strand appears in the writings of the Fathers of the early Christian church, who associated certain musical instruments with the sexual morality of the players (apparently failing to recognise that one should never confuse the manner with the matter). And they acted on their denunciations of instrumental music by legislating penalties.[9] Then, when a systematic doctrine of opposition to instruments developed in the third and fourth centuries, it was accompanied by a rise of asceticism, the neoplatonic strands of which extended the restrictions from instruments to singing. Augustine, for example, was inclined 'to approve the custom of singing in the church'; but he did not wish to commit himself 'to an irrevocable opinion', because 'when I find the singing itself more moving than the truth which it conveys, I confess that this is a grievous sin, and at those times I would prefer not to hear the singer'.[10]

The issues involved in these patristic polemics against music were still alive in North's day (and even afterwards), as exemplified in the many debates concerning the inclusion of music, instrumental or vocal, in the church of one or another religious denomination.[11] Some, for example, objected to singing, whereas others countenanced singing but scrupled about metre. Some condemned 'promiscuous' singing in which good and bad singers alike took part, whereas others objected to anyone being heard but the minister. And then there were those who doubted that women should break their silence in the church at all, a silence that was customary in a number of different religious traditions, Islamic, Jewish and Christian, in the last of which the moral authority for women's silence was the biblical text, I Corinthians xiv.4, 5:

> Let your women keep silence in the churches: for it is not permitted unto them to speak; but they are commanded to be under obedience, as also saith the law. And if they will learn any thing, let them ask their husbands at home: for it is a shame for women to speak in the church.

In response not only to that biblical text but also to the belief that singing in church is a 'light exercise' and, hence, of little value, Roger North gave reasons for including singing and instruments, at the same time pointing out how difficult it was to find enough voices to make a choir. Indeed,

> One might without a desperate solescism [i.e., breach of manners] maintain that if female quiristers were taken into quires instead of boys, it would be a vast improvement of chorall musick becaus they come to a judgment as well as voice, which the boys doe not arrive at before their voices perish, and small improvement of skill grows up in the room, till they come to man's estate.

But, he added, 'both [biblical] text and morallity are against it; and the Romish usage of castration is utterly unlawful, and is scandallous practice wherever it is used'.[12]

By morality North meant religious morality (i.e., the law referred to in the biblical text); but in other writings the beam of his critical reflections was focused on an ethical theory, then emerging from old roots.[13] That theory, which emphasised utility, was given specific content by Jeremy Bentham at the end of the eighteenth century. Afterwards known as utilitarianism, its chief maxim is, the greatest happiness of the greatest number, which requires not only that an individual should act to produce the greatest good but also that the distribution of goods to the public should maximise overall happiness. Note, however, that there are problems with each obligation. At the level of private morality, the problem is that people have their own particular lives and reason-giving commitments—they are not mere receptacles of happiness and instruments for producing it. At the level of public morality, the problem becomes, how to measure 'goods'; and the answer tends to be, 'on the basis of their utility'.[14] This answer, of course, causes difficulties for music, which many still think has little public utility other than to titillate or to raise money for charity.

Even though today Bentham is known as a social reformer, yet it is not widely known that he also sought to reform music by proposing the establishment of a national music 'seminary'.[15] That his proposal came to nought may be due to its content, which included a comparison between music and alcohol, both of which, he supposed, possessed the same property of furnishing 'sensation' for every waking moment. Hence, he dwelt at length on the use of specific kinds of music that produce either morality or immorality. For example, he asserted that vocal music could become an instrument of mischief, especially when singing takes place in convivial societies (e.g., taverns). It should not be surprising, therefore, that Bentham classed music under the category of 'hedonistics', by which he meant studies that affect the nervous system and cause intoxication.

Although intoxication implies immorality, it also implies irrationality; and this is the second strand of the idea that music has evil effects, a strand that may be illustrated from the dialogues of Plato. In several of these dialogues he treated art—spoken or sung eloquence or rhetoric—as a serious and dangerous rival to philosophy defined as rational thought—thought based on universal principles. For him, the task of philosophy was contemplation of the mathematical truth on which, he supposed, the material world is founded—the divinely-ordained 'harmony' (i.e., symmetry, proportion, order) that is intrinsic, absolute and inherent and, hence, resolvable into arithmetic, geometric and harmonic proportion.[16] But in one dialogue he devoted exclusive attention to the question of art, which he differentiated from philosophy by claiming that art is neither based on universally applicable principles (i.e., ratios) nor on an understanding of its subject matter (i.e., it has no conceptual content). These statements are primarily negative, showing what art is not. But Plato also offered some positive suggestions, showing what art is. According to him, art is a divine allotment, which the artist apprehends in a non-sober, non-cognitive, and, therefore, mad intuition. When so intoxicated, the artist, like an automaton, conveys this divine madness to the audience in the same way as iron rings transmit the power of a magnet.[17]

Note that Plato treated the processes of art as synonymous with creativity, which he defined pathologically as divinely-inspired intoxication. Note also that he made the processes of art and philosophy different and irreducible by conceiving the former process as irrational and the latter as rational. In 1979 Plato's treatment was given modern expression when the Ayatollah Ruhollah Khomeini declared:

> Music is no different from opium. If you want your country to be independent, you must turn radio and television into educational institutions and eliminate music. Music makes the brain inactive.[18]

Khomeini thus recognised the power of music and sought to ban it. And Plato, too, had recognised its power; but instead of banning it, he sought to control it by legislation.[19] The latter has been the approach of many subsequent governing bodies, including, nearer to our own time, those of the former Soviet Union and other authoritarian regimes.

For the purposes of this essay, however, the important point to note is this: that the Platonic conception of art cannot form the basis for a set of educational practices aimed at fostering creativity. For this reason Sharon Bailin (1988) sought to demythologise the Platonic conception of art by isolating and critically examining five widely-held, inter-related beliefs about creativity. The beliefs are as follows:

1. Creativity is intimately connected with originality understood in terms of the generation of novelty.
2. The value of creative products cannot be objectively determined, because creativity involves discontinuity.
3. The production of products is not central to creativity, because evaluation is not objective.
4. The creative process is necessarily free and unconstrained, because it involves breaking rules and established patterns.
5. The act of creation involves 'something more' than skill; namely, an imaginative element which is transcendent and irreducible (this belief closes the circle).

If creativity involves that which is new (Belief 1), then it is divergent and disconnected from the usual, the ordinary, the accepted. Consequently, it involves a radical break with the past and with existing traditions, as well as a fundamental change in conceptual frameworks. If creativity is characterised by a radical break with past traditions and their accompanying conceptual schemes (Belief 2), then there are no standards or criteria according to which creative works can be assessed. Consequently, evaluation must be entirely subjective. If creativity does not involve a product (Belief 3), then it must be a novel mode of thinking which is marked by leaps of imagination, irrational processes, rule-breaking, suspension of judgment and spontaneous generation of ideas. Consequently, ordinary thinking—the opposite of novel thinking—must be marked by logic, habit, rigidity, strict judgment and the adherence to previously established rules and patterns.[20] If the creative process does

Fenelon, François de Salignac de la Mothe. (1707). *Instructions for the Education of a Daughter* [1687] (trans. and revised by George Hickes). London: Jonah Bowyer.

Hayburn, R. F. (1979). *Papal Legislation on Sacred Music 95 A.D. to 1977 A.D.* Collegeville, Minnesota: The Liturgical Press.

Kassler, J. C. (2009). *The Honourable Roger North (1651–1734): On Life, Morality, Law and Tradition.* Farnham: Ashgate.

Kassler, J. C. (2002). Musicology and the Problem of Sonic Abuse. In L. Austern (ed.). *Music, Sensation and Sensuality.* New York: Routledge.

Kassler, J. C. (2001). *Music, Science, Philosophy: Models in the Universe of Thought.* Aldershot: Ashgate.

Kassler, J. C. (2000). Roger North. In S. Sadie & J. Tyrrell (eds). *The New Grove Dictionary of Music and Musicians* (2nd ed., pp. 53–6). Vol. 18. London: MacMillan.

Kassler, J. C. (1979). *The Science of Music in Britain, 1714–1830: A Catalogue of Writings, Lectures and Invention.* New York: Garland Publishing.

Kassler, J. C. (1976). Music made Easy to Infant Capacity 1714–1830: Some Facets of British Music Education. *Studies in Music*, 10: 67–78.

Locke, J. (1989). *Some Thoughts concerning Education* [3d ed., 1695] ed. with Introduction, Notes, and Critical Apparatus by J. W. & J. S. Yolton. Oxford: Clarendon Press.

Maddox, M. (1979). Music in Iran: The Ayatollah's less-than-perfect Pitch, *The Christian Science Monitor*, August 20, pp. 1, 10.

McKinnon, J. (1965). The Meaning of the Patristic Polemic against Musical Instruments, *Current Musicology*, Spring: 68–82.

North, R. (1990). *Roger North's The Musicall Grammarian 1728* ed. with Introductions and Notes by M. Chan & J. C. Kassler. Cambridge: Cambridge University Press (re-issued 2006).

Reynolds, Mr. [?Richard]. (1708). Objections consider'd against the Duty of Singing, *Practical Discourses of Singing in the Worship of God: Preach'd at the Friday Lecture in Eastcheap. By Several Ministers.* London: N. Cliff and J. Philips. pp. 100–45.

Stanhope, P. D., 4th earl of Chesterfield. (1775). *Letters ... to his Son....*[1774] (6th ed., 4 vols.). London: J. Dodsley.

17 See Dorter (1973). For the mindless automaton in some later writings, see, e.g., Edgeworth and Edgeworth (1801: vol. 3, 32–7): 'Mere artists are commonly as stupid as mere artificers, and these are little more than machines', for the 'length of time which is required to obtain practical skill and dexterity in certain accomplishments is one reason, why there are so few people who obtain anything more than mechanical excellence'. To prevent 'this species of intellectual degradation, we must in education be careful to rank mere mechanical talents below the exercise of the mental powers'. For one such a ranking, see Bain (1894: 564–67), who traced out 'a scale' of the arts, 'beginning at the most intellectual and ending with those that have this quality in the lowest degree'. According to him, music is the art most representative of 'the lowest degree' of intellect, for even 'great' musicians have 'often a very low order of intellect, as measured by the ordinary [psychological] tests'.

18 Maddox (1979: 1).

19 See Anderson (1966: 64–110, especially 84–91). According to the Jansenist divine, Fenelon (1707: 167), 'Plato ... severely rejects all the softer airs of the Asiatic music', i.e., the music of the Dionysian cult, and 'with much greater reason the Christians, who ought never to seek pleasure for pleasure's sake, ought surely to have an aversion for these poisoned allurements'.

20 i.e., Belief 3 conceives reason and emotion as polar opposites, rather than as closely intertwined. For example, reasoned assessments are at the basis of many emotions, and cognition is necessarily suffused with emotion, as in a desire to know, a love of truth, a repugnance of distortion, a respect for the arguments of others.

Augustine's version, number, weight and measure. Hence, North (1990: 229) was correct in his judgment that the tract was on 'any thing rather then musick, of which there is not the least discovery'.

References

Anderson, W. D. (1966). *Ethos and Education in Greek Music: The Evidence of Poetry and Philosophy*. Cambridge, Massachusetts: Harvard University Press.

Anon. (1698). *A Letter to a Friend in the Country, Concerning the Use of Instrumental Musick in the Worship of God: in Answer to Mr. Newte's Sermon preach'd at Tiverton in Devon, on the Occasion of an Organ being Erected in that Parish-Church*. London: A. Baldwin.

Augustine. (1961). *Confessions* tr. with an Introduction by R. S. Pine-Coffin. Harmondsworth, Middlesex: Penguin Classics.

Augustine. (1939). *St. Augustine on Music* (trans. R. C. Taliaferro). Annapolis: Maryland.

Bailin, S. (1988). *Achieving Extraordinary Ends: An Essay on Creativity*. Dordrecht: Kluwer Academic Publishers.

Bain, A. (1894). *The Senses and the Intellect* [1855] (4th ed.). London: Longman, Green and Co.

Dorter, K. J. (1973). The Ion: Plato's Characterization of Art, *Journal of Aesthetics and Art Criticism*, 32: 65–78.

Edgeworth, M. & Edgeworth, R. L. (1801). *Practical Education* (2nd ed.). London: J. Johnson.

Notes

1. For a brief biography, see Kassler (2000); see also Kassler (2009).
2. North (1990: 102, italics mine).
3. For details, see Kassler (1979: vol. 1, xxv–lxii).
4. According to Locke (1989: 252), who gave this notion its most influential expression: '*Musick* is thought to have some affinity with Dancing, and a good Hand, upon some Instruments, is by many People mightily valued. But it wastes so much of a young Man's time, to gain but a moderate Skill in it; and engages often in such odd Company, that many think it much better spared: And I have, amongst Men of Parts and Business, so seldom heard any one commended, or esteemed, for having an Excellency in *Musick*, that amongst all those things, that ever came into the List of Accomplishments, I think I may give it the last place.'
5. See Kassler (1976) and Kassler (1979), the last of which includes important sources for attitudes to music in education—conduct books published between 1714 and 1830. For an example of appropriateness (i.e., decorum), see North (1990: 100 and n.14).
6. See Locke (1989: 252) regarding not having 'your Son the Fiddle to every jovial Company, without whom the Sparks could not relish their Wine'. See also Stanhope (1775: vol. 1, 225, vol. 2, 178): 'a taste of fiddling and piping is unbecoming a man of fashion', because that kind of music-making conduces to 'illiberal' pleasures like drinking.
7. Campbell (1757: 89–93, italics mine).
8. See Kassler (2001: 1–20). For noise in our day, see Kassler (2002).
9. See McKinnon (1965) for some of the penalties (e.g., denial of baptism, excommunication) See also Hayburn (1979) not only for the penalties in later eras but also for evidence that music considered lascivious by a preceding moral theologian becomes acceptable to a succeeding one.
10. Augustine (1961: 239).
11. For the case against music, especially organ music, see, e.g., Anon (1698), who cited many authorities, including a number of the church Fathers. For the case in favour of singing in church, see, e.g., Reynolds (1708).
12. See North (1990: 211–12). See also Reynolds (1708: 128–29), who interpreted the biblical text as applying only to 'the Womens usurping an *Authority to prophesy*, and become *publick Instructors* in the Church', adding: 'This upon many Accounts would be very indecent'.
13. See Kassler (2009).
14. Bentham coined a new word ('deontology') for the science of obligation derived from utilitarianism.
15. For a description of, and brief comment on, Bentham's manuscript, see Kassler (1979: vol. 1, 84–6).
16. Proportion ('harmony') is thus Plato's preferred music—the silent music that Augustine considered in *De musica*, a tract in six books. The title, of course, is a misnomer, because the first five books are devoted to a technical discussion of *prosodia*, i.e., the metric proportions of poetry, whereas the sixth is a restatement of Plato's belief that the providential ordering of the material universe is founded on mathematical truth, i.e., the three kinds of proportion—in

not involve rules, skills and knowledge (Belief 4), then mastery of specific disciplines is constraining, locking one into the prevailing conceptual framework. Consequently, 'anything goes'. If the 'something more' in creativity is inexpressible (Belief 5), then it is unknowable. Consequently, it is impossible to be 'clear about creativity'.

As Bailin demonstrates, there are numerous problems with such beliefs and their consequences. For example, can novelty (Belief 1) be a complete definition of creativity, or is it only one mark on a scale of creative endeavours? If there are no objective criteria for judging creative products (Belief 2), how can teaching or criticism proceed? If creativity is a mode of irrational thinking (Belief 3), how do we know when creativity takes place? If discipline—i.e., mastery of a skill—constrains creativity (Belief 4), how do we proceed? And if the 'something more' of creativity is unknowable (Belief 5), how do we recognise it? Of all these problems, however, two are worth emphasising. First, if creativity is a pathological characteristic of individuals (Belief 3), it will be supposed, e.g., by those devising personality tests, that only a few people will be able to engage in the creative process. As a consequence, creative potential will be denied to humanity as a whole, irrespective of specific achievements. Second, if discipline constrains creativity (Belief 4), there will be no way to foster creativity. For discipline requires rules of performance that are internalised as skills (tacit knowledge). These skills are not a matter of blind and automatic performance but involve deliberation, flexibility and the constant possibility for revision. Indeed, it is mastery of skills that allows one the freedom to make significant and even original contributions within dynamic and evolving traditions.

Even though Bailin uses the term 'creativity' to include the gamut of human endeavour—personal and interpersonal, private as well as public, practical as well as theoretical, her critique has profound implications for educational practice in music. For like North and Doreen, she holds that creativity is a potential of the many, not merely the few, an assumption, of course, that does not deny the fact of differing aptitudes. And by being clear about creativity, she has opened the way to a further, perhaps even more difficult clarification: how to foster creativity so that in a democratic society *everyone* may 'gather his quota'.

11: Music Education in the 21st Century: Challenges and Predictions

David G. Woods

When pondering the future of music teaching and learning in the 21st century, the foundational influence of Doreen Bridges manifests itself in an international context. Doreen Bridges represents the broad based, comprehensive foundation of music learning that embodied every segment of pedagogy in the musical arts during the last half of the 20th century and influenced the beginnings of reform and curricular reconstruction in music education in the 21st century. This paper is dedicated to Doreen Bridges and her vision and insight and explores the current trends in music teaching and learning, the character of our students in the 21st century, and the enormous impact of new technologies on music teaching. This paper also explores public policy including the Voluntary National Standards for PreK–12 Music Instruction in the United States as well as President Obama's Call to the Arts. Reflecting the vision of Doreen Bridges, this paper outlines steps for forward movement in the field.

A number of years ago the great author Kurt Vonnegut was asked to give a commencement address at a well-known university in the United States. Mr Vonnegut was introduced and went to the podium in front of several hundred graduates and said, "Things are very, very, very bad and they are never going to get better again. Thank you." With that statement Kurt Vonnegut sat down and the audience, including the graduates, contemplated the grim and barren future of life.

There have been times in the history of music teacher training and music teaching and learning that it seemed that nothing would get better again and the challenges facing music teachers at times seemed insurmountable and back breaking. However, there are several trends today that indicate that things are going to get better again and that specific achievements and future plans are making a significant difference in higher education and specifically in teacher training in higher education.

First, is the changing character of students. The traditional college student 18–22, full time and living in residence now constitutes only 16% of all students in universities and colleges in the United States. The new majority in higher education in the United States is part-time female working adults over 25 years of age. Students today come to college in the United States largely because they want credentials. They have private lives outside of the campus and in some cases they have jobs, they have families, they have friendships and college is not the primary activity in their lives. This trend has permeated post-secondary education in other countries outside of the United States.

The second trend is the rise of new technologies. As a profession, we are moving to new materials that can be customized for the students in our classes. Soon there won't be any excuse for those professors who still use "yellowed" notes to teach classes year after year. The range of materials in music education and the scope of teacher training that will be possible are going to be incredible in terms of customizing and individualization. The environment facing teacher training in higher education must deal with the new technologies, computer software, instructional application, and distance learning. John Kratus has stated that, "Technology has forever changed the experience of music".[1] Certainly, as we reflect on the 20th century we can chart how the development of the radio and the phonograph made it possible for people to listen to music without being physically present. In the first decade of the 21st century the digital music revolution has been equally profound. Our students have mastered the use of MP3 players and have taken advantage of the more portable, more accessible and more individualistic musical environment. The internet with all its technological variations has not only changed the way music is disseminated, but it has changed the sociological environment that our students are in.[2] If we, as music educators in the 21st century, do not adapt to the emergence of technology in our teacher training programs, then the health of our effectiveness in teacher training will indeed be "very, very, bad."

In the United States, the musical and artistic-environments have significantly been modified. More than one-third of the nation's largest 100 radio markets have no classical music. A recent article by the Chair of the American Symphony Orchestra League notes, "The ground beneath us is shifting – has already shifted – in fundamental ways. We are seeing changes in the public perception of culture and taste."[3] Because of technology, our students today have the opportunity to individualize their cultural horizons, to select at a moment's notice music to listen to while walking down the street or to class and to select a diverse variety of styles and genres in music. Many of these styles are never a part of the music education experience in the classroom. In many regions of the United States there is an enormous gap between the individual musical environments and horizons and the music curriculum that is experienced in the public schools. Recent research suggests that adolescents in the United States listen to music an average of two to four hours per day.[4] Students create their musical tastes from a rich array of music from all cultures and all time periods. There is a remarkable disparity between the cultural development and the musical environment selected through technological devices by students as compared to the lockstep, traditional music teaching in today's schools. In this ever changing world of technological advances and music dissemination and distribution, opportunities exist to broaden, strengthen and improve the musical skills of students throughout the world.

In the late 20th century, I participated in an experiment in technology with Curtis Price, Director of the Royal Academy of Music in London. At the time, I was Dean of the School of Music at Indiana University and together Dr Price and I pioneered a project in the area of interactive video and distance learning, using a wide bandwidth and satellite link enabling us to reach, by instantaneous video, students at both the Royal Academy in London and students at the Indiana University School of Music. Immediate feedback was available in these sessions and some of the finest professors at Indiana University and at the Royal Academy of Music in London shared their ideas and thoughts while working personally with students in their studios. Not only were music fundamentals, skills, and techniques shared by musical leaders in two different parts of the world, but musical styles and genres were shared, compared, and performed. That experiment ten years ago at Indiana University and the Royal Academy of Music in London has now given way to many exemplary programs in instantaneous video linkages throughout the world. This technological advancement has made our world of music teaching and learning a more intimate one, a closer one, and a more accessible one for our students in many diverse environments and cultures.

It became apparent during the discussion at the Tanglewood II Symposium held at Williams College in late June 2007, that music teachers need to recognize that the nature of music in the world as compared to the nature of music in school curricula is quite different. In order to make music learning relevant and immediately applicable to our students in the 21st century we need to adapt our content to the ever changing and varied musical content experienced by our students. The profile of our students today has changed dramatically and the teaching environment has changed with a wide array of new technologies.

In 1994, the Music Educators National Conference in the United States endorsed a set of Voluntary National Standards for PreK-12 music instruction. These Standards in music, along with similar standards in the areas of theatre, visual arts, and dance were developed in a broad based and comprehensive context that had as its goal the emergence of a national consensus of artists, educators, and the public. In many ways during the last decade of the 20th century, the Voluntary National Standards became the major structure for many music programs across the United States. Paul Lehman, Professor Emeritus of Music at the University of Michigan–Ann Arbor, and former President of the Music Educators National Conference in the United States, played a central role in the development of the Standards. Professor Lehman stated several years ago that

> The individual states predictably have followed diverse paths in developing the Standards. Many of the State Standards are excellent and have served their purpose very well. Most of them are very good. A few however are disappointing in that they are too vague and too lacking in detail. The Standards should be specific enough to provide a basis for writing curricula, developing lesson plans and assessing learning.[5]

Although it is my opinion that the position of music in American education was affected dramatically the moment we began to work on the Standards, we need the resources and staff time to implement the Standards fully and we need the commitment necessary in our teacher training institutions to provide a world class education in music for all young people. This education in music must be realistic and must embrace the musical world that our students are exposed to everyday of their lives. In 2006, Paul Lehman chaired a taskforce to review the 1994 Standards and to consider whether they should be revised to reflect current conditions in music teaching and if so, how would this process take place? The task force under Lehman's leadership found that there were certain misunderstandings regarding the National Standards throughout the country. The taskforce also found that there was a definite misunderstanding about the role of the Standards in general. According to Lehman and his task force, "The single most frequently expressed concern regarding the National Standards in the surveys is that they are unrealistically high and simply cannot be achieved in the limited instructional time available to many music teachers."[6] This prevalent concern gets at the very heart of the purpose of the National Standards. The Standards were meant to provide a vision for the future of music learning and musical development. The Standards actually set forth long term goals for what music education should be in our culture and in our society, including the reform of methodologies and practices associated with the teaching and learning of music in the public schools in the United States. The structure of the Standards should allow for the emergence of new literature, new music, and indeed new sounds in our programs and in our curricula. The Standards should embrace the new technologies emerging in our society today and should incorporate those technologies within a comprehensive and spiral curriculum emphasizing the comprehensiveness of the musical art form. In addition, the Standards should allow us to contemplate new and expanding vehicles of learning beyond the traditional ensembles that are predominant in our secondary programs in the United States. The Standards summarize what our students should know and what they should be capable of doing as a result of the instruction. The curricula materials are up to the teacher and these materials must connect with the ever changing and ever evolving musical world that our children live in. Recent research has revealed that although the elementary music specialist does devote class time on all nine Standards, relatively, not much of this time is devoted to creative and artistic decision making skills. Indeed, related research clearly indicates that elementary specialists in the United States devote nearly 50% of their class time to singing and playing and not to analysis and creating.[7]

Clearly, the National Standards have given us a format in which to move forward. It is up to us not only in the United States, but all over the world to adapt curricular structures that will include what our students need to know today in order to enjoy and to love music making, music listening, and music creating in the future.

During the Bush Administration in the United States, the Arts were identified as basic and essential to the education of young people in the country. However, those of us in administrative roles in Music in the United States observed that the local interpretation of the Federal *No Child Left Behind* education law was seriously affecting access to music education for America's public school students. Although the law identified the arts as a core subject area, testing requirements in literacy, maths and science forced local school districts in the United States to divert resources and funding away from other subjects such as the Arts. The problem was that most districts became focused on those subject areas that were assessed and tested and that the districts disregarded the fact that literacy goes beyond reading and writing but also encompasses the more global perspective of how we make meaning in our world.

The current administration of President Barrack Obama has championed the arts and culture. In his two bestselling books, *Dreams From My Father* and *The Audacity of Hope*, President Obama clearly articulates the role and the value of creative expression. In his campaign, he developed a platform in support of the Arts. A platform that is relevant to a global music education movement. His platform embraces the importance of reinvigorating creativity and innovation as a part of the very fabric of life. President Obama has stated that, "We must nourish our children's creative skills. In addition to giving our children the science and math skills they need to compete in the new global context we should also encourage the ability to think creatively that comes from a meaningful arts education."[8]

President Obama's Arts Platform is the first ever presidential paradigm for the Arts in the United States. President Obama's Platform initially listed eight strategies, including increased funds for the National Endowment for the Arts (NEA). The three priorities relevant to this paper on the future of music education in the world include:

- The expansion of public and private partnerships between schools and art organizations.
- The creation of an artists corps.
- The initiation of a campaign that emphasizes the importance of an arts education.[9]

The new President's commitment to the Arts comes partially from his own experience. "When I was a kid," he told a crowd in Wallingford, Pennsylvania on April

2, 2008, "you always had an art teacher and a music teacher. Even in the poorest school district everyone had access to music and the other arts".[10] The recent financial stimulus packages presented to the Congress of the United States to boost the economy included many tools to help the Arts even though the economic realities loom as a challenge to museums, art organizations, and performance ensembles. The creative utilization of the stimulus monies may indeed advance the cause of arts education in this country to a greater extent than ever imagined during the *No Child Left Behind* years of the Bush Administration.

As teachers, music educators, and administrators in this ever changing world of music and culture, we have today an opportunity for effective action for initiating positive steps forward. I would like to suggest to you a strategic profile of moving ahead positively and productively in the development of teacher preparation programs during the new era of revitalization of Arts in education through the Obama Platform. Of course these recommended initiatives will not work in all universities and in all programs in higher education. They are suggestions that could make a significant impact in the teaching and learning of music in a global context.

First, I have long advocated that children should be the core of our teacher preparation programs. Those of us who teach pedagogy in higher education can demonstrate theoretical applications through practice. This is an active research approach. University laboratories can be developed that initiate new approaches and new understandings of the teaching of music. Laboratories for children can embrace the new music of our society and can focus on extensive analysis of the sequential approach of teaching and learning of music and can provide an outlet for the spontaneous creation of music. In 1987, I sat in such a laboratory in Sydney, Australia with Doreen Bridges, as we spent several hours with two, three, and four year old children sharing songs, movement, and creative explorations. It is this type of laboratory environment that I am proposing that will provide opportunities for the children at all ages in our communities to expand their knowledge base of the elements and the content of music.

The second positive step forward I would recommend for consideration, is the establishment of Music Education Centers in the schools themselves. I am suggesting that Music Education Departments in schools and conservatories actually teach their courses in methodology, psychology of musical learning, tests and measurements, and other subject areas within the environment of a local school. The close relationship with the music teacher and administrators in that particular school will help develop a positive environment for the practical application of learning theories, as well as methodologies and approaches. Taking musical content as the core of this initiative will help to demonstrate our resolve and dedication to the improvement of musical literacy.

Third, I suggest that we design courses not only in music education, but in other areas of the music curriculum in higher education for active community involvement by students.

Fourth, I suggest a partnership between Music Education Departments in higher education and the leadership in music education in public schools and in larger school systems. This partnership would include a carefully planned observation process or internship process early in the career of the university students. It would also bring the administrative leadership of the community schools into the university community itself to discuss issues and problems of education at an early point in the education of future teachers.

Five, I recommend the initiation of programs that would place exemplary university faculty, not always in music education, but in other areas of the department, school, conservatory or college, in regularly scheduled classes and rehearsals in the public school. These educational opportunities would provide observational possibilities for our students and would continue to develop the skills and abilities of the university teaching staff.

Six, I suggest that we initiate with every undergraduate music education student, an early research question about teaching, learning or technology. Such an assignment could occur in an introductory music education class or could be a part of any course, including music theory and music history at the undergraduate entry level. This research question or research project, if you will, would stay with the student throughout the first year of undergraduate studies and would be expanded in subsequent years.

Seven, I recommend, as a follow-up to item six, that the practical application of research occur as an outgrowth of the early establishment of research projects or research questions.

Eight, in institutions that have both the baccalaureate and the graduate levels of music education, graduate curricular structures could be developed that would include the mentoring of undergraduate students and the interaction of graduate students and undergraduate students in the practical application of research initiatives. It is proposed that these initiatives could, in fact, be located in the local community schools.

Nine, I suggest that practical assessment instruments be introduced early to undergraduates, including achievement testing and aptitude testing in music so that a thorough assessment of the educational process in music education can occur in all aspects of the teaching/learning process and in the development of teaching and learning skills and content.

Ten, I recommend that we provide opportunities for all teachers of music, from music theory classes to applied music, to participate in discussions and seminars regarding teaching/learning theory and pedagogy. This becomes an all encompassing model for undergraduate students as well as graduate students if all professors within a unit understand the process of education as well as the process of educational assessment.

Eleven, it is essential to embrace the magnitude of technological developments and advancements that enhance the musical culture of our students. Teachers today need to be relevant and they need that relevancy to emerge directly from the unique musical worlds that have been developed by our students.

Twelve, and finally, I recommend that significant emphasis be placed on the content of musical learning as *Music* and that we never lose sight of what *Music* is and its fundamental role in the lives of human beings. New technologies and new materials must have at the very core of their existence a solid musical content which will help initiate a new generation of approaches to musical literacy in our society.

In summary, those of us in music education today have an enormous opportunity in front of us to focus on music as content and to create an urgency for music to be "basic." The twelve initiatives that I have suggested in this paper may help as we create new opportunities and possibilities for establishing music as an irrevocable core enterprise of President Obama's Call to the Arts.

Musicians and teachers will find a way to implement these initiatives. We will find a way to integrate our studies with other subjects, to make an impact on professional musicians regarding the importance of the development of musical literacy in children, and we will find a way to utilize technology in our educational reforms in music teaching and music learning. We will find a way to integrate early an understanding of the basic musical characteristics of children in our students, and we will find a way for our students to actively implement and analyze those theories in the public schools.

This is a positive time, even though we are facing enormous economic challenges in almost all countries of the world. It is a time that is exciting as we are challenged by educational reforms in all areas and a time when we find the solutions to the issues presented in this paper within *Music* itself. Walt Whitman once wrote in the poem, *The Sleepers*, "I dream in my dream all the dreams of the other dreamers/and I become the other dreamers." Let us dream together with Doreen Bridges, of a time when the Arts will not be questioned as a core academic subject and the Arts become basic to education and to society all over the world. In the words of Maya Angelo, "We want to compose a good world. It is an honorable and noble profession."

Notes

1. John Kratus, "Music Education at the Tipping Point," *Music Educators Journal* 94, no. 2 (November 2007): 45.
2. Ibid, 45 – 46.
3. Lowell Noteboom, "A champion for Orchestras," *Symphony* (July/August 2006): 37–39.
4. Steven C. Martino, et al., "Exposure to Degrading Versus Nondegrading Music Lyrics and Sexual Behavior Among Youth," *Pediatrics* 118, no. 2 (August 2006): 430.
5. Paul R. Lehman, "National Assessment of Arts Education: A First Look," *Music Educators Journal* 85, no. 4 (January 1999): 34–37.
6. Paul R. Lehman, "A Vision for the Future: Looking at the Standards," *Music Educators Journal* 94, no. 4 (March 2008): 28.
7. Norma J. Kirkland, "South Carolina Schools and Goals 2000: National Standards in Music," Ph.D. dissertation, University of South Carolina, Columbia (1996).
8. Barack Obama, "A Platform in Support of the Arts," *Barack Obama and Joe Biden: Champions for Arts and Culture*, www.barackobama.com (2008).
9. Gloria Goodale, "Obama's Call to the Arts," *Christian Science Monitor* (January 16, 2009) 13. www.scmonitor.com/20009/0116/p13s03-algn.html.
10. Ibid, 13.

12: Informing practice in Early Childhood Music Education

Sheila C. Woodward

Introduction

Within the lifetime of prominent Australian educator, Doreen Bridges, Early Childhood Music Education has been established internationally as a professional field with a recognized body of research and evolving trends in theory and practice. It has been thrust from early assumptions that infants were incapable of complex cognitive skills (rendering any early experience of music so primitive that it could hardly be considered truly musical in nature) to a place of understanding that humans are born with inherent capacities for processing and learning music on highly intricate, multimodal levels. Not only do neonates naturally respond to music and "motherese" (the musically-rich, lyrical style of speaking in which mothers instinctively interact with their babies), but they possess a remarkable capacity for sharing music with others in communicable, empathetic ways (Fernald et al. 1985, 1989; Papousek & Pasousek, 1981; Malloch & Trevarthen, 2009).

Through the lenses of ethnology and anthropology, we have descriptons of musical activity being interactively shared between elders and infants in all cultures (Dissanayake, 2009). However, the past century has seen urbanized, technology-driven communities across the world undergo radical changes in daily musical lifestyles. Fortunately, an explosion of scientific research has provided a foundation for encouraging parents to maintain active musical interactions with their children.

Furthermore, it has guided the development of theories, curricular design, and pedagogical approaches that underpin formal early childhood music learning programs made available by professional music educators.

However, not all has gone well in our field, as the dissemination of scientific discoveries across a media-frenzied, global society has led to misinterpretations and unfortunate applications. We're still battling ripple effects of the Rauscher et al. (1993 and 1994) studies on spatial task in relationship to music, which somehow was interpreted to mean that 'music makes babies smarter'. The concept only succeeded because policy makers in many parts of the world had already duped parents into believing that our humanity is best served through concentrating on maths, language, and science. In these particular countries, virtually anything else is seen as immaterial in the quest for 'getting ahead' in life, and music has been widely sidelined in their formal education programs. Indeed, there are many parents prepared to invest time and money on broadening their children's education. However, in light of the hype about *music and the brain*, unfortunately they might not consider playing Mozart because it enriches the child's *soul*. And we can't help but recoil from some of the inappropriate commercial music products and educational programs parents lap up in good faith. As if these matters are not discouraging enough, we also have to contend with those parents who think that a recording of music or a music video can be a high-quality 'babysitter', allowing them free time to steal away and make phone calls, or tend to life's other concerns.

But we should not complain that some of the world's communities are devaluing music if, as early childhood music researchers and educators, we don't firstly offer quality musical experiences to young children that have parents bringing them back for more; and secondly, if we don't participate in the public debate, helping the community articulate values of music and interpret scientific research appropriately. For example, studies show that if a mother pays little attention to a musical sound introduced into the play environment, the infant's response is diminished compared with when the mother responds to the sound with expressive gesture and pleasure

(Hobson, 2004). Aren't we the ones who should be phoning the media houses to say '*this* is why we need to be actively engaged in sharing our love of music with our children?' Furthermore, we need to be constantly critical of our own work and vigilant in allowing rigorous research to inform our practice. Bridges (1989) was quick to reprimand us when she saw practice conflicting with our scientific knowledge of children and their musicianship. With our field having been partly hijacked by 'illegitimate' commercial enterprises, some of which don't even require any level of musicianship in their teachers, the importance of continuously informing our work is especially critical.

So, where do we go to find the research that informs our practice? Undoubtedly, the most remarkable factor has been the increasingly diverse representation of disciplines in our literature. Indeed, one of the great strengths that emerged in the late twentieth century was the trend towards interdisciplinary interaction of scholars. Our field is now bolstered by support from multiple areas of study, such as developmental psychology, neurology, linguistics, ethnomusicology, and sociology, to name just a few. The most fundamental issue lies in recognizing the multimodal nature of young children's musical experience, which lies at the heart of the critical need to view perspectives from diverse disciplines.

Multidisciplinary dimensions to early childhood musical experience and education
Education
At the turn of the 20th century, one of the greatest proponents of democratic ideologies, John Dewey (1900, 1937) offered surprisingly progressive theories of education that have, to a greater or lesser extent, influenced thinking in education in much of the Western world. Woodford (1995) describes Dewey's concept of students being given freedom 'to develop and pursue their own interests, enthusiasms, and convictions that they could become fully functioning members of democratic society, able to contribute intelligently to its continued development' (Woodford, 1995, p.

1). Teachers were challenged to strive for achieving individuality, the onus being on the teacher to provide the right kind of social environment to achieve this (Dewey & Tufts, 1932). However, it was pointed out that students should be willing participants in their education. Woodford (2005) describes the Deweyan concept that, 'no one was justified in managing others without their consent. And coercion only discouraged individual responsibility and creativity' (p. 2). In early childhood music education, we are especially sensitive to enticing children rather than enforcing behaviors, while nurturing the individual, creative spirit.

Psychology

Psychology has dominated educational thinking since the late nineteenth century. In particular, one of the many, but probably the most influential fields of psychology on education has been that of developmental psychology – itself covering a wide range of aspects, including perceptual/sensorial skills, sensorimotor skills, conceptual thinking, representational/symbolic thinking, communicative and linguistic processes, social/interactive skills, expression/emotion, and self-regulatory/coping processes (Fogel, 2001, pp. 13, 14). Just a few key areas of impact from psychology will be mentioned here, with no attempt being made to provide an overview (something that would outweigh the capacities of this limited literary endeavor). One is the focus on play (Frost et al., 2005) and, in particular free play, which is non-adult directed. Children's spontaneous music making during free play has come under particular spotlight and brought a new level of understanding to our field (Campbell 1998; Bannan & Woodward 2009). Identifying these spontaneous musical activities as a natural, inherent part of infants' capacities, we have been led to question what is it about formal schooling that causes most children to gradually stop improvising and composing musically? We have considered whether we should be particularly vigilant in promoting these creative musical tendencies when children first enter formal schooling, a time when these activities still occur as a natural part of their daily existence. As teachers, we also have been able to apply the concept of the psychologist

Mihalyi Csikszentmihalyi (1996) that, for creativity to take place, there needs to be an awareness of a problem: a tension that ignites creative energies. The challenge to teachers is to avoid formal education being constantly teacher-directed and to allow young children continued exposure to questions and tensions that will continue to drive their explorative instinct. As Wendy Sims (2004) explains:

> To young children, research is play, and play is research. Young children are the most inquisitive, active, energetic "researchers" that any of us could possibly hope to find. Investigating their environment is their work, their play, their research. The energy and creativity they bring to these efforts constantly amazes and inspires me. Young children continually identify problems, try out various solutions, and evaluate the results. Often they even include the dissemination component of research, although it may be through a proud exclamation, a gleam in the eye, a wide grin, or a tug on the hem of their mother's skirt, instead of a 20-page double-spaced manuscript. (p. 4)

In another major contribution to our field from the psychology literature, *enjoyment* is identified as central to the meaning of our existence (Csikszentmihalyi, 1998). Csikszentmihalyi describes achieving the deepest sense of enjoyment as something we experience when we are in 'flow'. This *flow* is said to occur in a moment of complete focus, the attention pulled away from the self and anything else, to the experience at hand, where there is immersion and transcendence. To achieve this level of enjoyment in the flow experience, Csikszentmihalyi maintains that there needs to be a perfect balance between challenge and skill. These ideas were echoed in musical terms by the philosopher, Elliott (1995), who sees enjoyment and self growth as the pinnacle of musical experience. He points out the role of the music teacher in ensuring this balance between challenge and skill in the student's musical endeavors. Early childhood music specialist, Lori Custodero (1997, 1998, 2000) directly sought out evidence of *flow* in early childhood musical activities, and demonstrated that children naturally adjust the balance of challenge with skill levels in their spontaneous musical activities.

Adult-directed activities were seen to interrupt flow until a level of familiarity with new material is achieved (sometimes taking a couple of weeks), when children become free to engage in more deliberate actions and thus transcend into a state of focus.

The development of instruments in the Psychology field for the testing of skills, achievement, and aptitude has had a major impact on testing in education, where we've seen trends in testing rise and fall. Admittedly, much of our research in early childhood music education has involved the testing of achievement in order to identify developmental stages, the nature of young children's musical experience, and the best approaches for teaching. As regards aptitude testing, the field garnered some major attempts at expansion from early in the twentieth century, when Carl Seashore (1919) published his first set of aptitude tests. Bridges (1969) pointed out how some of the tests, such as Wing's Tests of Musical Ability and Appreciation (Wing, 1948) and Gordon's Musical Aptitude Profile (Gordon, 1965), left us walking on thin ice. The growth of interest in humanistic education in the 1950s to 1970s led towards a rejection of testing in music. Thankfully, the idea of offering music instruction only to those considered *talented* was put to the grave by musicians and psychologists who brought it to the world's attention that all children are musical. Kabalevsky, Kodàly, Orff and Suzuki were amongst the strongest proponents for all children deserving and needing music education. Each of them developed approaches to education that were inclusive of all children and which had, by the end of the century, spread across continents to large parts of the world. Our profession has vigilantly followed this idea that all children are musical, and received a boost of confidence from the psychologist, Howard Gardner (1983) in his declaration that musicality is one of the inherent intelligences of humanity. However, during the later part of the century there was a resurgence of focus on standards and standardized testing in many parts of the world. This phenomenon assigns teachers to more of a managerial role than a creative one (Woodford, 2005). In some cases, *process* suffers at the expense of *product*. Not always convinced of their validity, Bridges (1969) cautioned us to take a hard look at methods of assessing musical abilities and achievements. In young children, for example, Bridges (1989) advocates testing children on skill in keeping a steady beat only when applied to pulses within the normal range of the children's walking speeds, not slower adult speeds. She observed that, when within their natural range, children have far less difficulty keeping a steady beat. Woodward (2002) detailed the need for testing to be appropriate to the child, especially considering developmental skills and cultural contexts.

Broadening our fields of influence

From the 1880s, the efforts of psychologists to determine how children learn have given us a basis for deducing how we should teach. An innovator in transforming thinking in music education, Roger Rideout, explains that this influence waned from the 1980s, as educators turned to biological evidence to justify practice (Rideout, 2006). In addition, neurological research has opened new windows to details on how the brain processes musical experience (Hodges, 2000). Furthermore, attention has shifted strongly towards sociological perspectives (Hargreaves & North, 1997). Rideout (2006) explains that sociology requires teachers to cease inward looking justifications for our profession, and redefines what we do as occurring within processes of social integration. The recent surge of interest in sociology has spawned music scholars who have 'begun to view the concept of childhood as a historical, critical, and aesthetic framework for analyzing repertoires traditionally associated with children' (Kok & Boynton, 2006, p. ix). And the expanding field of Children and Childhood Studies increasingly informs our work.

Ethnomusicology

Ethnomusicologist, John Blacking (1973) describes humans as inherently musical. He sees music as universal, being an activity that take place in all societies, yet as unique to each community, specific to each group. Green (2002) describes how early musical learning is steered in socially acceptable directions. She contrasts scenarios of a young child in London banging a spoon on the table, which might result in having it taken away, with a similar scenario in Venda, where family members might join in with polyrhythms. In his studies of the Venda in South Africa, where he observed a high level of musical skill in all members of the community, Blacking (1973) was led to believe that all human beings have musical potential and that it is social factors that lead to its realization or suppression. He proposes that societies communicate through ritualizations that infants acquire, rendering them more aware of themselves, and also of their existence, responsibilities and associations within the community. Ideas pertaining to the enculturation of young children (Sloboda, 1985) have been expanded with the idea of socialization that recognises the role of society in hindering, nourishing and directing musical potential.

Sociology

Avid proponent of transformation in music education, Paul Woodford (2005) explains that music should be taught with intellectual, social, moral, and political dimensions. As Suzuki told the mother of one of his students 'Your son plays the violin very well. We must try to make him splendid in mind and heart also' (Suzuki, 1969, p. 26). While some might argue that the study of music itself contributes towards the child acquiring a more noble nature, history has firmly taught us that music alone does not make a better human being (Brown & Volgsten, 2006). Many see music as a powerful unifier that brings social harmony and cooperation through the discipline, sensitivity, communication and respect required within the discipline of making music. The general public is probably well aware of the values and ethics being taught to young children through the lyrics of songs. However, this is, of course, just a small part of the many messages and meanings we convey to children, sometimes imparted through the simplest physical gesture, facial expression or vocal cue, in our shared musical experience. The social context of music is critical to how the child will experience it. Besides considering the dimensions in which we engage with children in music, we should also consider how children will naturally create their own meanings and representations in music. It is particularly in children's original, creative work that we should both welcome and 'listen to what they say through their music' (Woodward, 2007, p. 33). In an extreme example, it has been proposed that young children in violence–torn countries may be using their own adaptations of familiar music as a coping mechanism, singing of terrifying things they don't appear to openly discuss (Bannan & Woodward, 2009). Minks (2006) points out that, until recently, studies have mostly concentrated on how adults socialize children, while 'it is clear that children also socialize one another and they socialize their elders into new roles and activities, as any new parents can attest' (p. 211).

As Early Childhood Music educators, we need to be vocal in the public conversation about the nature and role of music in the life of the young child. We hear of schools scattered across the world that increasingly cut spending on music in public education, with even younger children not receiving as little as a one weekly music class. We cannot afford to allow the media to interpret our research and politicians to decide on the relevance of music to humanity. Woodford (2005) believes that we must engage in political and social debates, interacting with a cross-spectrum of individuals and groups. He states that achieving success in this requires familiarizing ourselves with social and political thinking and agendas pertaining to music and education, while developing our own sense of purpose and social vision, within frameworks of ethical practice, citizenship, and moral values.

Philosophy

Philosophical thinking came to the forefront of the music education intellectual debate from the 1970s, predominantly through the writings of Bennett Reimer (1970, 2003). Guiding students towards aesthetic appreciation of beauty and helping them to connect with their feelings in response to music were viewed as being amongst the principal roles of teachers. A former student of his, David Elliott (1995) expressed abhorrence at the thought that the former might be attempted exclusively through listening-based appreciation classes and lauded a practice-based philosophy of music education that would develop well-rounded musicianship. This idea was not new to education. Dewey (1934) had exhorted that even a crude experience, as long as it is authentic, is more appropriate in giving us understanding of the nature of aesthetic experience than the study of an object. While parents and teachers throughout the century have probably needed little provocation from intellectuals to persuade them to actively participate in music with young children, there is no doubt that social changes across much of the 20th century have impacted worldwide urbanization trends and the increasing prevalence of technology in day-to-day life. These have, of course, led to indelible modifications to 'modern world' family musical cultures where active music making appears to happen less and less. As educators, we've been engaged in encouraging parents to remember, value and pass on their cultural heritage to their children. Most importantly, we have made calls for listening to the voice of children through their songs – the music they create and the new musical cultures that they develop in their lifetimes (Woodward, 2009).

Culture

Some interesting trends have taken place over the twentieth century with regards to cultural issues in Early Childhood Music Education. With the expansive colonization of vast areas of the globe, and subsequent cultural oppression of one group over another, it's a wonder that many ethnic music cultures were not obliterated altogether. Perhaps some aspects have, indeed, been eradicated, while others will have suffered indelible alterations. The rebuilding of nations after two World Wars has also led to strong influences of certain cultures over others. This was especially prevalent in countries such as Japan and Korea, which adopted rigorous music training programs for children in Western Classical music. Decades later, music educationalists sounded the alarm, worried that traditional musics were being threatened by possible extinction if they were not firmly thrust back into formal schooling. But beyond a call for return to one's cultural roots, the professional music community has succeeded in calling for a wider sense of community and the deepening of intercultural tolerance and 'cross border' understanding through offering a multicultural music education to all children (Elliott, 1995, Woodford, 2005). As we've moved into a new century, the world has become a 'global village' with technology providing children and their communities with access to music of virtually any culture they desire. International commercial markets have generated global musical subcultures that extend beyond physical boundaries of race or nation. The recent impact of technology on the musical cultures of young children across much of the world has surely been irrefutable.

Conclusion

In drawing to a close our brief discussion regarding just a few of the many areas now informing our research and practice in music education, a couple of critical matters in applications might be briefly mentioned. How we approach research in early childhood is vital. Not only are the children our focus, but, as Sims (2004) declares, their natural, inquisitive nature in exploring their surroundings should be our model as researchers. A key component to our research, as Sims explains, is to involve what is natural to children. While this might involve objectively observing what children do when undirected by adults, Sims insists that, in adult-directed research, participation should not only be fun, but should also involve what makes sense from a child's perspective. For example, she says that her adult thinking in one particular study required the children to respond by drawing a cross on the picture of a face. The puzzled expressions of the children led her to quickly change that instruction to drawing a *nose* on the face, and she could not fail to recognize the immediate enthusiasm of the children and their ease in taking part when the activity made sense to them. Perhaps the key ingredient in both research and practice of music in early childhood should surely be respect, applied in every facet of our operation, but most of all, in respect for the child, who is at the center of what we do. As we have ventured into a new century, we now benefit from 'tip of the finger' accessibility to rich, diverse banks of literature that inform our teaching practice from multiple perspectives. And at the heart of our conversations we would do well to be increasingly aware of sharing with children the companionship of music, reminding ourselves of music's essential existence within social contexts and our roles in fostering inherent musicality. In facilitating environments where children have freedom to explore and we value their creations and contributions, we ensure that children's voices will be heard. For, it is in the communicative nature of early childhood musical experiences that meaning is truly energized.

References

Bannan, N. & Woodward, S. (2009). Spontaneous Musicality in Childhood Learning. In S. Malloch & C. Trevarthen (Eds.), *Communicative musicality: Narratives of expressive gesture and being human*. Oxford: Oxford University Press.
Blacking, J. (1973). *How musical is man?* Seattle: University of Washington Press.
Boynton, S. & Kok, R. (Eds.). (2006). *Musical Cultures and the Cultures of Youth*. Middletown: Wesleyan University Press.
Bridges, D. (1969). *Measurement and assessment in music education*. Paper presented at the First National Conference of the Australian Society for Music Education, Brisbane, 1969, and published in the Conference Report, Perth.
Bridges, D. (1989). Effective music lessons for young children: some problems and contradictions. *International Journal of Music Education*. 14.
Brown, S. & Volgsten, U. (2006). *Music and manipulation: On the social uses and social control of music*. New York: Berghahn Books.
Campbell, S. P. (1998). *Songs in their heads*. New York: Oxford University Press.
Clayton, M., Herbert, T., & Middleton, R. (2003). *The cultural study of music*. London: Routledge.
Csikszentmihalyi, M. (1996). *Creativity: Flow and the Psychology of Discovery and Invention*. New York: Harper Perennial.
Csíkszentmihályi, M. (1998). *Finding Flow: The Psychology of Engagement with Everyday Life*. New York: Basic Books.
Custodero, L. (1997). *An observational study of flow experience in young children's music learning*. Unpublished doctoral dissertation, University of South California, Los Angeles.
Custodero, L. (1998). Observing flow in young children's music learning. *General Music Today* 12(1): 21–27.
Custodero, L. A. (2000). Engagement and experience: a model for the study of children's musical cognition. In G. L. C. Woods, R. Brochard, F. Seddon, & J. A. Sloboda (Eds.), *Proceedings of the Sixth International Conference on Music Perception and Cognition*. Keele, UK: Keele University Department of Psychology.
Dewey, J. (1939). Democracy and Educational Administration. In J. Ratner (Ed.), *Intelligence in the Modern World: John Dewey's Philosophy* (pp. 400–401). New York: Modern Library.
Dewey, J. (1900). *The school and society*. Reprinted. Chicago: University of Chicago Press (1990).
Dewey J. & Tufts, J. H. (1939). Ethics. (Rev. ed.). Reprinted in J. Ratner (Ed.), *Intelligence in the modern world: John Dewey's Philosophy* (pp. 761–778). New York: Modern Library.
Dissanyake, E. (2009). Root, leaf, blossom, or bole: Concerning the origin and adaptive function of music. In S. Malloch & C. Trevarthen (Eds.), *Communicative musicality: Narratives of expressive gesture and being human*. Oxford: Oxford University Press.
Elliott, D. (1995). *Music Matters: A New Philosophy of Music Education*. New York: Oxford University Press.
Fernald A. (1985). Four-month-old infants prefer to listen to motherese. *Infant Behavior and Development*, *8*, 181–195.

Fernald, A. (1989). Intonation and communicative intent in mothers' speech to infants: Is the melody the message? *Child Development*, 60, 1497–1510.
Frost, J. L., Wortham, S. C. & Reifel, S. (2005). *Play and Child Development* (2nd ed.). New Jersey: Pearson.
Fogel, A. (2001). *Infancy: Infant, family, and society* (4th ed.). Belmont: Wadsworth/Thompson Learning.
Gardner, H. (1983). *Frames of Mind: The theory of multiple intelligences*. London: Heinemann.
Gordon, E. (1965). *Musical Aptitude Profile*. Boston: Houghton Mifflin Company.
Green, L. (2002). *How popular musicians learn*. Hampshire, UK: Ashgate.
Hargreaves, D. J. & North, A. C. (Eds.) (1997). The *social psychology of music*. Oxford: Oxford University Press.
Hobson, P. (2004). *The cradle of thought: Exploring the origins of thinking*. Oxford: Oxford University Press.
Hodges, D. A. (2000). Special focus: Music and the brain: Implications of music and brain research. *Music Educators Journal* 87:2, 17–22.
Kok R. M. & Boynton, S. (2006). Preface. In S. Boynton & R. Kok (Eds), *Musical Cultures and the Cultures of Youth*. Middletown: Wesleyan University Press.
Malloch, S. & Trevarthen, C. (2009). Musicality: Communicating the Vitality and interests of life. In S. Malloch & C. Trevarthen (Eds.), *Communicative musicality: Narratives of expressive gesture and being human*. Oxford: Oxford University Press.
Minks, A. (2006). *Afterword*. In S. Boynton & R. Kok (Eds.), *Musical Cultures and the Cultures of Youth*. Middletown: Wesleyan University Press.
Papousek, M. & Pasousek, H. (1981). Musical laments in the infant's vocalization: Their significance for communication, cognition, and creativity. In L. P. Lipsitt & C. K. Rovee-Collier (Eds.), *Advances in infancy research. Vol 1*, 163–224. Norwood: Ablex.
Rauscher, F. H., Shaw, G. L., Levine L. J., & Ky, K. N. (1994). Music and Spacial task performance: A causal relationship. Presented at the American Psychological Association 102th Annual Convention. LA, CA. August 12 – 16.
Reimer, B. (1970). *A Philosophy of Music Education*. New Jersey: Prentice Hall.
Reimer, B. (2003). *A Philosophy of Music Education. Advancing the Vision* (3rd Ed.). New Jersey: Prentice Hall.
Rideout, R. R. (2006). What would a Sociology of Knowledge Mean in Music Education? A paper for the Social Science Special Research Interest Group Meeting. Music Educators National Conference, Salt Lake City, Utah.
Seashore, C. E. (1919). *Seashore Measures of Musical Talent*. New York: The Psychological Corporation.
Sims, W. L. (2004). What I've Learned about Research from Young Children. *Applications of Research in Music Education*. 23, No. 1, 4–13.
Sloboda J. A. (1985). *The musical mind*. Oxford: Clarendon Press.
Suzuki, S. (1969). *Nurtured by Love*. New York: Exposition Press.
Wing, H. (1948). Tests of Musical Ability and Appreciation. *British Journal of Psychology* Monograph Supplement No. 27.
Woodford, P. G. (2005). *Democracy and music education: Liberalism, ethics and the politics of practice*. Bloomington: Indiana University Press.

Woodward, S. C. (2002). Assessing young children's musical understanding. *Music Education International.* ISME Issue 40: 112–121.
Woodward, S. C. (2005). Critical matters in early childhood music education. In D. J. Elliott (Ed.), *Praxial music education: Reflections and dialogues* (pp. 249–266). New York: Oxford University Press.
Woodward, S. C. (2007). Nation Building — One Child at a Time: Early Childhood Music Education in South Africa. *Arts Education Policy Review*, November/December *109* (2), 43–53.

13: Research into self-concept development, academic achievement and musical participation of adolescents

Jennifer C. Rosevear

Introduction

The importance of music in early childhood education is widely recognised (for example, Bridges, 1994; Kalandyk, 1996; Kazimierczak, 2004; Mills, 2005). Doreen Bridges has been most influential in not only advocating for the crucial role that music plays in babyhood and early childhood, but in producing books and other resources which continue to provide practical support to parents, teachers and pre-service teachers. In these early childhood years, music plays a central part in everyday life and contributes to children's overall development, such as in

> their thinking processes, language development, control and co-ordination of body movements, orientation to the space around them, their ability to relate to others, and development of self-control and self-esteem. In addition, music provides children with the emotional satisfaction that comes from aesthetic experiences (no matter how simple) and with opportunities for self-expression. Probably no other single pursuit has the potential to do so much for a child. (Bridges, 1994, p. 14)

Throughout childhood and adolescence, music continues to contribute to many facets of the intellectual, social and emotional development of individuals. This paper will briefly explore some of the research into self-concept development, academic achievement and musical participation during adolescence.

Self-concept

Self-concept development is a complex process, and Dweck's (2000) entity and incremental theory of intelligence provides a basis for considering how self-beliefs can influence motivation and learning. If people hold an entity belief about their intelligence, they believe that their capabilities are predetermined and there is little that will change these (Dweck, 1986; Dweck, 2000; Hargreaves & Marshall, 2003). Those who hold entity beliefs are more likely to 'show low persistence and performance deterioration in the face of failure' (O'Neill, 2002, p. 81), and to 'develop an overconcern with proving their competence, avoid challenges, and show an inability to cope with failure or difficulty' (O'Neill & McPherson, 2002, p. 39). In the incremental theory, capabilities are viewed as being susceptible to development through learning and as being improved through increased efforts (Dweck, 2000). Such beliefs are more likely to promote attitudes which draw on 'learning goals, effort and strategy attributions for setbacks, and the belief that effort increases ability' (Dweck & Molden, 2005, p. 137). Therefore, individuals who have incremental beliefs tend to flourish when presented with challenges (O'Neill & McPherson, 2002), and to be more resilient in the face of setbacks. An individual may hold different beliefs in different spheres (O'Neill, 2002), and beliefs can be influenced by significant others such as parents, teachers and peers.

Within the broad area of self-concept, two aspects which relate closely to Dweck's theory are self-efficacy and self-regulation. Self-efficacy refers to one's belief in one's ability to carry out a task successfully, while self-regulation refers to the processes or strategies which one uses to ensure success at the task. As put forward in Bandura's social-cognitive model of behaviour (Bandura, 1986; Maehr,

Pintrich & Linnenbrink, 2002) self-efficacy beliefs have a strong impact on aspects of human behaviour, including learning. A comparison of the likely outcomes based on efficacy beliefs as outlined by Bandura (1997) is shown in Table 1 (see Appendix). This comparison highlights the potential impact of efficacy beliefs on outcomes, with compelling implications for education.

Research by Hargreaves, Miell and MacDonald (2002) outlines the central role of language, and increasingly music, in the process of self-concept or identity development. Hargreaves et al. (2002) suggest that 'music can be used increasingly as a means by which we formulate and express our individual identities ... [and] it provides a means by which people can share emotions, intentions and meanings even though their spoken languages may be mutually incomprehensible' (p. 1). Tarrant, North and Hargreaves (2002) suggest that 'a major appeal of music to adolescents lies in its ability to help them form positive social identities' (p. 139), and these identities are continuously compared with other people as they grow into adulthood (Hargreaves et al. 2002).

Academic Achievement

Research suggests that there is a two-way or reciprocal interaction between academic self-concept and academic achievement, so that increased self-concept is not only an outcome of achievement but that academic self-concept also influences future achievement and other desirable educational aspects (Self-Concept Enhancement and Learning Facilitation Research Centre, 2001). It is recognized that music education may contribute positively to student learning across a range of curriculum areas, with research suggesting that learning in music may contribute to academic achievement in mathematics, reading and language skills, as well as to the development of spatial ability, and personal and social development (Australian Society for Music Education, 1999).

There have been numerous research studies investigating any transfer effects of music learning to other academic achievement (e.g., Costa-Giomi, 1999;

Deasy, 2002; Rauscher, Shaw & Ky, 1993; Rauscher, Shaw, Levine, Wrights, Dennis & Newcomb, 1997). Whilst there is recognition that there is some correlation between participation in music and the other arts and higher academic achievement, such participation does not necessarily cause higher academic results (Demorest & Morrison, 2000; Harland et al., 2000; Rosevear, 2007). It seems likely that academic success is a common characteristic of music students (rather than necessarily being caused by studying music), perhaps because music students require persistence and concentration if they are to develop musical skills, and because there may be transfer (whether cognitive or affective) to other learning areas. Anecdotal reports suggest that students who are good at music are often successful in other subjects, whilst for some students who may be academically challenged, music may be the only subject in which they are able to participate effectively. Mills (2005) suggested that:

> we teach music primarily because we want children ... to grow as musicians. But music, also, improves the mind. While it is hard to catch the results of this in a scientific experiment ... no-one who has had the privilege of observing really good music teaching ... can doubt that this is the case. It may be the raising of children's self-esteem through success in music making that helps them towards achievement more generally. It may be that enjoying music helps children to enjoy school more. It may be that chemical changes induced in the brain by music facilitate learning more generally. (pp. 5–6)

Musical Participation

Music teachers have a direct and influential effect on the development of students' self-concepts in music. Students are not likely to develop a positive musical self-concept if they have an entity (i.e., fixed) view of their musical ability rather than an incremental view (Dweck, 2000). Teachers can encourage their students to have an incremental view of their musical ability which is essential in encouraging students to 'have a go' in music. Students with an incremental view are likely to 'display "mastery-oriented" rather than "helpless" behaviour, because they believe that the work they do *can* influence their abilities' (Hargreaves & Marshall, 2003, p. 265), that is, students with an incremental view are likely to develop an effort attribution.

> In essence, this means that whether or not children *think* they are any good at maths, languages, sport or indeed music may be just as, if not more important than their actual level of ability. This may be particularly important for pupils who have the idea that they are 'unmusical', perhaps because of an unwitting remark by a teacher, parent or another pupil: this perception could lead on to a downward spiral of not trying, therefore becoming less able, therefore trying even less, and so on. In other words, children actively *construct* their own musical identities, and these can determine skill, confidence and achievement. (Hargreaves & Marshall, 2003, p. 265)

Within music education, students should have every opportunity to develop a positive musical self-concept or musical identity. The development of a positive musical self-concept is largely dependent on experiences, whether at school or outside of school. It is important to encourage students from the earliest stages to have positive beliefs about their musical ability, and to develop effort attributions. O'Neill (2002) reported on research findings in which children's self-beliefs were found to play a key role in their subsequent demonstrated ability which was over and above their actual ability. According to Hargreaves and Marshall (2003),

> it is in everyone's interest for educators to capitalise on the massive importance that music can have in young people's lives, and our analysis suggests that this is best accomplished by encouraging them to think of music as something within

reach of all, rather than as a specialised activity: that everyone can be a 'musician' at some level. (p. 272)

Music is inherently interesting, especially for younger children, and, by adolescence, listening to music is widely recognised as an extremely popular activity (Ivaldi & O'Neill, 2002; North, Hargreaves & O'Neill, 2000; Zillman & Gan, 1997), if not *the* most preferred leisure activity for many adolescents (Fitzgerald et al. 1995; Hargreaves & Marshall, 2003). Music educators can therefore capitalise on music's intrinsic interest in order to provide suitably challenging learning experiences for their students, thereby promoting students' feelings of competence in music. Music education offers plenty of scope for self-expression and creativity through activities such as performing, improvising and composing which have the potential to give students a certain sense of autonomy. There is recognition of 'the performing experience as the most engaging teaching activity in music' (Rosenshine, Froehlich & Fakhouri, 2002, p. 302). The 'globe' model of the opportunities available in music education (Hargreaves, Marshall & North, 2003) marks a growing recognition of the diverse ways that music learning can occur, and in particular the acknowledgement of the importance of informal music learning opportunities outside of schools and other educational institutions. Whether experiencing music at school or outside of school, the main appeal for students is that they 'develop the skills and confidence to "do it for themselves": to gain ownership of and autonomy in their own music-making' (Hargreaves & Marshall, 2003, p. 269).

Green (2002) has investigated the learning practices of popular musicians, which are largely informal, and compared these to common classroom music practices and traditional formal approaches to learning a musical instrument. Green found that, within popular music traditions, individuals 'largely teach themselves or "pick up" skills and knowledge, usually with the help or encouragement of their family or peers, by watching and imitating musicians around them and by making reference to recordings or performances or other live events involving their chosen music' (Green, 2002, p. 5).

With regard to the formal arena, Green (2002) suggests that 'for a large portion of the twentieth century music education was almost exclusively concerned with classical instrumental tuition outside the classroom and classical music appreciation and singing inside the classroom' (p. 4) whilst since the 1960s, there has been the growing inclusion of popular music and jazz, and more recently, world music. Even though popular music has become common in music classrooms, Green (2006) suggests that the learning practices of popular musicians have not been similarly adopted, that is, 'the changes we have made in our curriculum content lacked any corresponding change in our teaching *strategies*' (p. 107). This is reflected by Green's (2006) example that '*analysis* of popular music is not likely to engage school pupils in the classroom; and in any case, analysis bears no resemblance to how popular musicians actually learn to produce the music themselves' (p. 106).

There are five main characteristics of informal music learning practices, identified by Green (2006) in her research into how popular musicians learn, namely: informal learners choose the music themselves; the main informal learning practice involves copying recordings by ear; the informal learner is self-taught and learning takes place in groups; informal learning involves the assimilation of skills and knowledge in personal, often haphazard ways according to preferences; and, there is an integration of listening, performing, improvising and composing, with an emphasis on creativity. These learning practices can also be categorised according to whether they are solitary or group practices, 'both of which take place largely without adult supervision or guidance' (Green, 2005, p. 27).

Green (2006) advocates 'the adaptation of some informal popular music learning experiences for classroom use [as these] can positively affect pupils' musical meanings and experiences' (p. 101). There appears to be an inherent contradiction in introducing informal learning practices into formal learning, in that 'informal' implies 'without adult supervision' (Department for Education and

Skills, 2005, p. 7), whereas 'formal' learning suggests a teacher. Folkestad suggests that whilst learning can be both formal and informal, teaching is always formal. 'As soon as someone teaches, as soon as somebody takes on the role of being a teacher, then it is a formal learning situation' (Folkestad, 2006, p. 142). However, Green (2002, 2005, 2006) is suggesting that teachers could encourage, and provide opportunities for, students to make use of strategies that are used in the learning practices of popular musicians, such as, students to have some choice in the music selected, and the use of recordings for aural learning through copying. Within classroom music, Green (2002) advises that there is much that can be done with preparatory rhythmic work so that students can play simple riffs, melodies or chords accurately in time with each other. She suggests that such a foundation in keeping a basic beat is helpful before attempting to work in small groups and copying a recording.

The application of informal learning practices to classroom music is seen in the Paul Hamlyn Foundation's *Musical Futures* project which, according to the Music Manifesto Report No. 2 (DfES, 2006) is one of a range of innovative music-making programmes in England. The Musical Futures publication *Classroom Music Resources for Informal Music Learning at Key Stage 3*, written by Lucy Green with Abigail Walmsley, has adopted informal learning as a key strategy for classroom music, thus putting into practice the ideas put forward by Green (2002) based on her research into how popular musicians learn. Green and Walmsley (n.d., p. 2) put forward the five key principles of informal learning which are at the centre of the approach, which are:

Principle 1: Learning music that pupils choose, like and identify with
Principle 2: Learning by listening and copying recordings
Principle 3: Learning with friends
Principle 4: Personal, often haphazard learning without structured guidance

Principle 5:   Integration of listening, performing, improvising and composing. (Green & Walmsley, n.d., p. 2)

Such informal music learning in the classroom makes use of the typical processes used by popular musicians, and aims to increase pupil motivation to learn, enjoyment and the acquisition of skills (Green & Walmsley, n.d.). As well as the priority of motivating pupils, Green and Walmsley (n.d.) suggest that 'teachers also want to make their lessons connect with the huge enjoyment that pupils get from music in their lives beyond the school' (p. 2).

Conclusions

When considering the aspects of self-concept development, academic achievement and musical participation, there are outcomes which have relevance to learning in general and personal development, as well as musical consequences. Because music plays a key role in identity development, especially during adolescence, it is therefore an important element in general development. Incorporating the informal learning processes of popular musicians into classroom music has the potential to increase participation in music by adolescents. Developing a positive self-concept, both in and through music, has the potential to impact upon other areas, such as overall well being, general self-concept development and attitudes to learning including the development of effort attributions.

Appendix

Table 1: Comparison of likely outcomes based on efficacy beliefs (adapted from Bandura, 1997, p. 39).

Low efficacy beliefs – in particular domains of activity	High efficacy beliefs – in particular domains of activity
• shy away from (avoid) difficult tasks	• approach difficult tasks as challenges to be mastered
• hard to motivate oneself	• affirmative orientation fosters interest and engrossing involvement in activities
• low aspirations and weak commitment	• set challenging goals and maintain strong commitment to these
• slacken efforts or give up quickly in the face of obstacles	• invest a high level of effort
• slow to recover their sense of efficacy following failure or setbacks	• heighten effort in the face of failures or setbacks
• dwell on personal deficiencies	• task-focused and think strategically in the face of difficulties
• efforts undermined by formidableness of the task and the adverse consequences of failure	
• lose faith in one's capabilities	
• attribute insufficient performance as deficient aptitude	• attribute failure to insufficient effort
• easy victim to stress and depression	• efficacious outlook enhances performance accomplishments, reduces stress, and lowers vulnerability to depression

References

Australian Society for Music Education [ASME]. (1999). *Principles, policy and guidelines for music education*. Parkville, Victoria: ASME.

Bandura, A. (1986). *Social foundations of thought and action: a social cognitive theory*. Englewood Cliffs, N. J : Prentice-Hall.

Bandura, A. (1997). *Self-efficacy: the exercise of control*. New York: Freeman.

Bridges, D. (1994). *Music, young children and you*. Alexandria, NSW: Hale & Iremonger.

Costa-Giomi, E. (1999). The effects of three years of piano instruction on children's cognitive development. *Journal of Research in Music Education, 47(3)*, 198–212.

Deasy, R. J. (Ed.). (2002). *Critical links: learning in the arts and student academic and social development*. Washington, DC: Arts Education Partnership.

Demorest, S. M. & Morrison, S. J. (2000). Does music make you smarter? *Music Educators Journal, 87(2)*, 33–39, 58.

Department for Education and Skills [DfES], (2005). *Music manifesto report no. 1*. Nottingham: DfES.

Department for Education and Skills [DfES], (2006). *Music manifesto report no. 2*. Nottingham: DfES.

Dweck, C. S. (1986). Motivational processes affecting motivation. *American Psychologist, 41*, 1040–1048.

Dweck, C. S. (2000). *Self-theories: their role in motivation, personality and development*. Philadelphia, PA: Psychology Press.

Dweck, C. S. & Molden, D. C. (2005). Self-theories: their impact on competence motivation and acquisition. In A. J. Elliott & C. S. Dweck (Eds.), *Handbook of competence and motivation* (pp. 122–140). New York: Guilford Press.

Fitzgerald, M., Joseph, A. P., Hayes, M. & O'Regan, M. (1995). Leisure activities of adolescent school children. *Journal of Adolescence, 18*, 349–358.

Folkestad, G. (2006). Formal and informal learning situations or practices vs formal and informal ways of learning. *British Journal of Music Education, 23(2)*, 135–145.

Green, L. (2002). *How popular musicians learn*. Hants, England: Ashgate.

Green, L. (2005). The music curriculum as lived experience: children's "natural" music-learning processes. *Music Educators Journal, 91(4)*, 27–32.

Green, L. (2006). Popular music education in and for itself, and for 'other' music: current research in the classroom. *International Journal of Music Education, 24(2)*, 101–118.

Green, L. & Walmsley, A. (n.d.). *Classroom music resources for informal music learning at Key Stage 3*. Open access: Musical Futures Paul Hamlyn Foundation Special Project (www.musicalfutures.org.uk).

Hargreaves, D. J. & Marshall, N. (2003). Developing identities in music education. *Music Education Research, 5(3)*, 263–274.

Hargreaves, D. J., Marshall, N. & North, A. (2003). Music education in the 21st century: a psychological perspective. *British Journal of Music Education, 20(2)*, 147–164.

Hargreaves, D. J., Miell, D. & MacDonald, R. A. R. (2002). What are musical identities and why are they important? In R. A. R. MacDonald, D. J. Hargreaves & D. Miell (Eds.), *Musical identities* (pp. 1–20). Oxford: Oxford University Press.

Harland, J., Kinder, K., Lord, P., Stott, A., Schagen, I., & Haynes, J. (2000). *Arts education in secondary schools: effects and effectiveness*. Slough: NFER.

Ivaldi, A., & O'Neill, S. (2002). The influence of role models for adolescents' involvement and aspirations in music. In C. Stevens, D. Burnham, G. McPherson, E. Schubert, J. Renwick (Eds.). *Proceedings of the 7th international conference of music perception and cognition, Sydney, 2002* (pp. 59–62). Adelaide: Causal Productions.

Kalandyk, J. (1996). *Music and the self-esteem of young children*. Lanham: University Press of America.

Kazimierczak, P. (2004). *Simply music! Innovative music experiences for children under five*. Croydon, VIC: Tertiary Press.

Maehr, M. L., Pintrich, P. R., & Linnenbrink, E. A. (2002). Motivation and achievement. In R. Colwell & C. P. Richardson (Eds.), *The new handbook of research on music teaching and learning* (pp. 348–372). Oxford: Oxford University Press.

Mills, J. (2005). *Music in the school*. Oxford: Oxford University Press.

North, A. C., Hargreaves, D. J. & O'Neill, S. A. (2000). The importance of music to adolescents. *British Journal of Educational Psychology, 70,* 255–272.

O'Neill, S.A. (2002). The self-identity of young musicians. In R. MacDonald, D. Hargreaves, D. Miell (Eds.), *Musical identities* (pp. 79–96). Oxford: Oxford University Press.

O'Neill, S.A. & McPherson, G.E. (2002). Motivation. In R. Parncutt & G.E. McPherson (Eds.), *The science and psychology of music performance* (pp. 31–46). Oxford: Oxford University Press.

Rauscher, F., Shaw, G., & Ky, K. (1993). Music and spatial task performance. *Nature, 365,* 611.

Rauscher, F., Shaw, G., Levine, L., Wright, E., Dennis, W., & Newcomb, R. (1997). Music training causes long-term enhancement of preschool children's spatial-temporal reasoning. *Neurological Research, 19*(1), 2–8.

Rosenshine, B., Froehlich, H. & Fakhouri, I. (2002). In R. Colwell & C. P. Richardson (Eds.), *The new handbook of research on music teaching and learning* (pp. 299–314). Oxford: Oxford University Press.

Rosevear, J. (2007). Academic achievement and music: What's the connection? In A. Stanberg, J. McIntosh & R. Faulkner (Eds.), *ASME XVI Conference Proceedings* (pp. 178–181). ASME: Perth.

Self-Concept Enhancement and Learning Facilitation [SELF] Research Centre. (2001). *Director's annual report*. (Director: Professor Herbert W. Marsh). Sydney: SELF Research Centre, University of Western Sydney.

Tarrant, M., North, A., & Hargreaves, D. (2002). Youth identity and music. In R. MacDonald, D. Hargreaves, & D. Miell (Eds.), *Musical identities* (pp. 134–150). Oxford: Oxford University Press.

Zillman, D. & Gan, S. (1997). Music taste in adolescence. In D. J. Hargreaves & A. C. North (Eds.), *The social psychology of music* (pp. 161–187). Oxford: Oxford University Press.

14: Singing Locally; Thinking Globally: Why Community Choirs Matter

Tom Bridges

'To *make* music is the essential thing — to listen to it is accessory'

Charles Seeger[1]

Singing Locally

As a community choir director of nearly twenty years experience I frequently and inevitably come into contact with attitudes and beliefs about music as it is practised, experienced and observed in this culture held by people who regard themselves as non-musicians. If I were to paraphrase most people's considered description of music and its place in society, it would go something like this:

> Music is a commodity or service that is produced and sold by experts, to be consumed by the population when they buy concert tickets, purchase recordings, or turn on the radio or TV. These experts are skilled artisans whose craft or trade is that of a performing and/or recording musician. They are credentialed as such from a combination – in proportions that vary enormously and idiosyncratically – of a genetically bestowed 'gift' or 'talent', and specialist training, both formal and informal.

Thus seen as one of many goods-and-services panels in the social and economic quilt, any notion of music and music-making having an alternative contemporary social definition and function is rarely adumbrated. When one is suggested, invariably it comes as a surprise.

In 1915 in an article in the first issue of *The Musical Quarterly* Percy Grainger pointed to just such an alternative:

> With regard to music, our modern Western civilization produces, broadly speaking, two main types of educated men [*sic*]. On the one hand the professional musician or leisured amateur-enthusiast who spends the bulk of his waking hours making music, and on the other hand all those many millions of men and women whose lives are far too overworked and arduous, or too completely immersed in the ambitions and labyrinths of our material civilization, to be able to devote any reasonable proportion of their time to music or artistic expression of any kind at all. *How different from either of these types is the bulk of uneducated and 'uncivilized' humanity of every race and color, with whom natural musical expression may be said to be a universal, highly prized habit* that seldom, if ever, degenerates into the drudgery of a mere means of livelihood. [TB's emphasis][2]

Had Grainger been able to observe his own Western culture one hundred years on, many things – obviously – would have astonished him. He would have been confronted by massive changes in the 'ambitions and labyrinths of our material civilization'. Because they were directly connected to his observations in 1915, particularly conspicuous might have been firstly, the commodification and mass consumption of music to previously unimaginable levels; secondly, the almost universal unpreparedness of the population to use uninhibitedly their natural singing voices, if at all; and thirdly, in the popular ideology the discounting of tradition and reproduction in favour of the new in the general estimation of musical value.

Today, the vast bulk of the population consumes an unprecedented volume of music as a commodity. Electronic reproduction of music lends it universal accessibility. We today recognise electronically reproduced commercial music as a multifaceted cardinal pillar of popular culture. In approximate historical sequence its technological development might be itemised thus: wax cylinders, radio, 78rpm records, long-playing vinyl records, television, cassette tapes (and their outgrowth, Walkman-type portability), CDs, DVDs, and now in the early 21st century MP3 devices and file exchange on the internet. Finally, there is one that needs special mention because it is easily overlooked – amplification. Amplification, by spatially and aurally quarantining performers from their audience, musters them ineluctably into physically separate camps – and never the twain shall be the other. In enabling performers to be heard farther and farther away by a larger and larger audience, a plethora of microphones, speakers and attendant paraphernalia erects a wall between the two groups. Moreover, as it becomes necessary to compete with and defeat ever louder other sounds – like conversation – louder and louder amplification becomes gratuitous noise, antisocial in both essence and effect. How many long-term patrons have been permanently driven out of their local pub – and the social hub it has long provided – by the unnecessarily loud jukebox that has been installed without consultation and played without the offer or availability of an alternative?

Interestingly, the list begins more or less contemporaneously with the date of Grainger's article quoted above. The 'many millions of men and women ... [un]able' in 1915 'to devote any reasonable proportion of their time to music or artistic expression of any kind at all' would now, with more disposable income and leisure time and an unlimited availability of recorded music, probably identify their musical selves as *listeners*. With the development of a unique set of personal preferences – taste – comes listening expertise. So today, the typical self-concept around music is that of an educated consumer. Rarely if ever does anyone conceive of him or her self seriously as a practitioner, or of music having a primary social function other than *something to be listened to*.[3]

And music is now everywhere, whether we like it or not. It is even the case that music is used – that is, carefully selected and broadcast – to serve a dedicated purpose unrelated to its creation or appeal as art, and we have become unwitting subscribers to these usually covert agendas.[4] But an unintended effect is that we have learned to switch off our listening. Music is heard everywhere, but listened to ever less and less. It is no longer special or cherished, but part of the background white noise of our routines. One result is that our powers of discrimination have been weakened, and our critical faculties conditioned everywhere to applaud mediocrity dressed up as excellence. 'Recorded sound, which artificially preserves the unpreservable, increases the likelihood of hearing without listening, since it can be listened to at home, in cars, or in aeroplanes, thus allowing us to reduce music to background activity and eliminate the possibility of total concentration – i.e., thought.'[5]

When people arrive at a community choir of mine for the first time I will nearly always be told by the recruit that he or she 'can't sing'. And when I talk with others about my work, away from it, 'I can't sing' is likewise heard again and again as the first response. From numerous conversations I've had with fellow community choir directors, this experience is common to them too. The personal narratives that usually follow are bleakly similar, and draw on a standard catalogue of put-downs and discouragement in formative years by authority figures, often by those who should know better, like school music teachers. 'I was kicked out of the school choir' and 'If I sang at home my parents would get angry, and tell me to shut up' are typical anecdotes and they are repeated ad infinitum. Cruel or fickle circumstance may also play a part, but invariably in the stories the damage is done early. The uniformly silencing effect is commonly accompanied by the view that it is also irreversible. This is reinforced by the subject's self-credentialed status as an expert listener (to music): 'you wouldn't want to listen to me – I wouldn't'. But this judgement, expressed as jocose self-deprecation, is based on a more serious analysis: 'I can't sing, in comparison with, or in a similar fashion to, those who are authorised to sing – that is, professional singers'. American folklorist Alan Lomax noted with dismay that when people turned on the radio and heard a popular singer, whatever the genre they would assume that that was what singing was – what the human singing voice is supposed to sound like[6]. So of course they (the listener) 'couldn't sing'. It would do little good to point out that probably all they really meant was, they couldn't sing like that. After all, what else – what other singing – is there?

The answer – that singing is as universal a human ability as speaking, and has only relatively recently, and in highly technologised locations, faded from view as such – comes as a shock to many. As Frankie Armstrong puts it:

> In pre-industrial communities, singing and chanting are/were an integral part of every tribal and village person's life. Many activities from the cradle to the grave were accompanied by the melodic voice – lullabies; collective rhythmic working chants; hollas [sic] to bring in the cows and soothing onomatopoeic croons to milk them by; spinning and weaving songs; ritual and devotional chants; songs to dance to, to walk to the next village to, to while away the hours behind the plough, to amuse and move family and friends of an evening, to tell the stories of the gods and the ancestors, to wail and grieve by the body of a loved one – people sang thus over thousands and thousands of years. … Throughout most of human history, each child was born into a community that assumed they would sing, as we assume each child will learn to talk.[7]

The Zimbaweans say it neatly with their proverb, 'If you can walk you can dance; if you can talk you can sing'.

Now, the 'I can't sing' story can be countermanded quickly and decisively by asking the subject to sing *Happy Birthday*. It can be guaranteed that this is the *one song* in this culture that *everyone knows*. (In some locations, *Auld Lang Syne* might qualify as another). In other cultures the list would be uncountably long, and in earlier times in this (Western) culture most individuals would possess a large inventory of songs. It was a natural outgrowth of singing being regarded as a natural activity that one was born into.

This was well known to Percy Grainger a hundred years ago. To watch it rapidly vanishing in his own culture caused him great dismay, undoubtedly compounded by the vantage afforded by his own musically educated milieu. It was logical, then, that one of his lifelong enthusiasms as a musician and scholar should be the pursuit and study of folksong. After all, not very far back in the history of his society, there existed a musically active general populace engaged in creating and reproducing their own lively musical culture. Unlike the idealised and artificial expression of human experience typically found in art music, or the glamorised and packaged representations of 'life' usually delivered by pop music, this 'folk' culture was protean, authentic and accessible. Using song as a natural medium, the things that were on people's minds in their everyday lives were given musical form and shared, not primarily or necessarily for an audience, but for their own reward as an activity. Whether to ameliorate the harshness of life, to understand as well as generate relief from their circumstances, or to make bearable and more efficient strenuous work (as in sailors' shanties), this was in essence a community survival resource. The so-called 'folk' tradition with its canon of songs about work, love, sex, play, family, history, songs that told stories true and tall, songs disseminating either the latest news or a web of fantasy and fiction, songs and music to dance to, is a tradition that bespeaks resistance and survival.[8] And repeating, it was a musically *participatory* tradition: any listening, with perhaps one conspicuous exception, was secondary. That exception is of course the lullaby. Since pre-history sung by mothers to coax their infants to sleep, lullabies are the original and still the most compelling example of music used as propaganda – that is, music performed explicitly to change the attitudes and/or behaviour of its audience.

Thinking Globally
A fundamental premise of the foregoing is that the world as we know it is in grave peril and that human civilization is peering into the abyss of extinction by its own hand. Whether the result of conflagration, pestilence, climate change, or any causally

linked permutation of the three, this is not extreme or undue pessimistic fatalism; merely an honest assessment of abundant evidence. It is one shared by many people around the globe, from many different backgrounds and locations. The consensus is striking however among those of scientific métier.[9]

The importance of music in such critical circumstances is suggested eloquently by ethnomusicologist John Blacking in the words that conclude his influential *How Musical is Man?*

> In a world in which authoritarian power is maintained by means of superior technology, and the superior technology is supposed to indicate a monopoly of intellect, it is necessary to show that the real sources of technology, of all culture, are to be found in the human body and in cooperative interaction between human bodies. ... In a world such as ours, in this world of cruelty and exploitation in which the tawdry and the mediocre are proliferated endlessly for the sake of financial profit, it is necessary to understand why a madrigal by Gesualdo or a Bach Passion, a sitar melody from India or a song from Africa, Berg's Wozzeck or Britten's War Requiem, a Balinese gamelan or a Cantonese opera, or a symphony by Mozart, Beethoven, or Mahler, may be profoundly necessary for human survival, quite apart from any merit they may have as examples of creativity and technical progress. It is also necessary to explain why, under certain circumstances, a 'simple' 'folk' song may have more human value than a 'complex' symphony.[10]

Working musically can reveal in dramatically new and enlightening ways that 'everything is connected'. This fact is seminal to the peace-mongering work of eminent pianist and maestro, Daniel Barenboim[11]:

> In music, there are no independent elements. How often we think, on a personal, social, or political level, that there are certain independent things and that, upon doing them, they will not influence others or that this interconnection will remain

hidden. This does not occur in music, because in music everything is interconnected. The character and intention of the simplest melody change drastically with a complex harmony. That is learned through music, not through political life. Thus emerges the impossibility of separating elements, the perception that everything is connected, the need always to unite logical thought and intuitive emotion.[12]

Although expressed here by Barenboim more as a metaphysical than a practical reality, it is not difficult – indeed it is common – for people through their own experience of group music-making to draw direct lessons from and find direct applications of these very insights. This, I have found from working with adults who have never before been a member of a seriously constituted musical ensemble, is particularly true when that experience is new to them.

If music-making is indeed necessary for human survival, it seems reasonable to suppose that what lies at the core of this function is its binding properties, and its ability to be transformative, even in small ways. These properties do not become fully apparent until music is *made*, actively and with others: they are by definition, subjective. It is when the sum of these individual subjectivities aggregate into a single shared phenomenon that alchemy can happen, and a previously unimagined, exquisite community consciousness arises. Pete Seeger, that exemplary and possibly the twentieth-century's most effective cultural activist,[13] always maintained that this process – which he carefully studied and in his concerts deliberately generated – is unique to music:

> The most important thing is to get together…It's this word "share" I keep coming back to in my concerts all the time: I think it's more important than "love". Love has been so misused and so misunderstood – but "share" is a much more simple and direct word. And right now it's very easy to point out to anybody that the resources of the world are not being shared…Music in some strange, mystical way brings people together, in spite of our problems…I have the feeling that music is able to do something that prose and pictures haven't been able to do.[14]

Participation: that is what's going to save the human race. Once upon a time, wasn't singing a part of everyday life, as much as talking, physical exercise or religion? Our distant ancestors, wherever they were in this world, sang – while pounding grain, paddling canoes or making long journeys. Can we begin to make our lives once more all of a piece? Finding the right songs and singing them over and over is a way to start. And when one person taps out a beat while another leads into the melody, or when three people discover a harmony they never knew existed, or a crowd joins in on a chorus as though to raise the ceiling a few feet higher, then they also know there is hope for the world.[15]

In Western society, an unconscionable loss has attended our acquisition of unparalleled material affluence: the din of commodified music has silenced our musical selves. This comes at roughly the same historical moment that neuroscience has established beyond doubt that the ability and impetus to express human self through musical means is guaranteed by our hard-wiring.[16] Community choirs can *inter alia* provide an ideal setting for people to reclaim their birthright as musicians, to learn to use it co-operatively, and to experience its sometimes unexpected rewards. The potential extra-musical ramifications of such rewards should not be underestimated.

Notes

1. Charles Seeger, 'The Purposes of Music' in Pete Seeger, *Where Have All The Flowers Gone: A Singer's Stories Songs, Seeds, Robberies*, (Sing Out Corp: Bethlehem, 1993) p. 84.
2. Grainger, Percy, 'The Impress of Personality in Unwritten Music' in Balough, Teresa (ed), *A Musical Genius from Australia: Selected Writings by and About Percy Grainger* (CIRCME: Nedlands, 1997) p. 66.
3. Daniel J. Levitin, *This is Your Brain on Music: The Science of a Human Obsession* (Penguin, London 2007) pp. 6–10. 'Given this voracious consumption, I would say that most Americans qualify as expert music listeners.'

4   The obvious example is the music one hears in the supermarket aisles whilst shopping – carefully calculated to boost the day's turnover.
5   Daniel Barenboim, *Everything is Connected: The Power of Music* (Weidenfeld & Nicholson: London, 2008) p. 37.
6   'We now have cultural machines so powerful that one singer can reach everybody in the world, and make all the other singers feel inferior because they're not like him. Once that gets started, he gets backed by so much cash and so much power that he becomes a monstrous invader from outer space, crushing the life out of all the other human possibilities. My life has been devoted to opposing that tendency.' Quoted by Jon Pareles in his obituary for Lomax, *New York Times*, July 20, 2002.
7   Frankie Armstrong, 'Freeing our Singing Voice', in *The Vocal Vision: Views on Voice* (Applause Books: New York, 1997). Quoted from author's manuscript.
8   A. L. Lloyd, *The Singing Englishman: An Introduction to Folksong* (Workers' Music Association, London, 1944). See also Bob Copper, *A Song for every Season* (Paladin: St Albans, 1975); Roy Palmer, *The Sound of History: Songs and Social Comment* (OUP: London, 1988); Oscar Brand, *The Ballad Mongers: The Rise of the Modern Folk Song* (Funk & Wagnalls: New York, 1962).
9   Jared Diamond, *Collapse: How Societies Choose to Fail or Survive* (Allen Lane: Camberwell, 2005).
10 John Blacking, *How Musical is Man?* (Faber: London, 1976), p. 116.
11 Using music-making at the elite level of orchestral concert hall music, Barenboim's West-Eastern Divan Orchestra comprised young musicians from across the region is a project dedicated to peace-making in the Middle East. See 'Knowledge is the Beginning: Daniel Barenboim and the West-Eastern Divan Orchestra' documentary film by Paul Smaczny (Warner Classics, 2005).
12 Barenboim, *op cit*, p. 159.
13 For comprehensive appraisal of Pete Seeger's influence, see David King Dunaway, *How Can I Keep from Singing: Pete Seeger* (Harrap: London, 1985); Alan M. Winkler, *'To Everything There is a Season': Pete Seeger and the Power of Song* (OUP: New York, 2009); Alec Wilkinson, *The Protest Singer: An Intimate Portrait of Pete Seeger* (Alfred A. Knopf: New York, 2009).
14 Pete Seeger, in Jo Metcalf Schwartz (ed) *The Incomplete Folksinger* (Simon & Schuster: New York 1972) p. 484.
15 Quoted from *Pete Seeger: The Power of Song*, documentary film by Jim Brown. (The Weinstein Company, 2008).
16 Levitin, *op. cit*. Also, Robert Jourdain, *Music, the Brain, and Ecstasy: How Music Captures our Imagination* (Avon: New York, 1997) and Howard Gardner, *Frames of Mind: The Theory of Multiple Intelligences* (Fontana: London 1993).

15: Learning to be a Composer

George Palmer

It is not only a great privilege, it is a great delight to have been invited to contribute to this *Festschrift* in honour of Dr Doreen Bridges AM. Dr Bridges is one of Australia's foremost music educators and an inspiration to all who have followed in her pioneering footsteps.

A composer has no qualification to express views of any persuasive authority as to how music, and in particular, composition should be taught. History shows that many composers were utterly ineffective as teachers and that many successful teachers of composition never wrote a successful piece of music.

I am at a special disadvantage in offering any suggestion or insight as to the teaching of composition. In common with composers such as Telemann, Schumann, Mussorgsky, Elgar, Poulenc, Schoenberg, Walton, Nigel Westlake and Toru Takemitsu, to name but a very few, I am a 'self-taught composer' – which is simply to say that, rather than attending a formal course of instruction at a conservatorium or university, I chose to learn directly from the masters of composition by playing their music, listening to performances, studying scores and poring over the acknowledged texts on composition technique.

It is for that reason that the title of this contribution, 'Learning to be a composer', refers to my own journey in composition; it does not pretend to offer any recommendation as to how composition should be taught generally. Nevertheless, I hope that there may be something of interest, not only for the would-be composer but for the music educator, even if only in the nature of 'pitfalls to avoid.'

The teaching of music has changed unrecognizably since I was a student. The general ethos prevailing in my youth is well documented in Dr Bridges' doctoral thesis, *The Role of Universities in the Development of Music Education in Australia 1885–1970*. There was no music course available in my secondary school. Indeed, there was no musical activity at all – no music department let alone student orchestras, chamber groups or music tuition. Musically, it was a barren waste.

My own music education began with lessons given by the neighborhood piano teacher. Fortunately, not only was she a kind and effective teacher of piano technique but she insisted that all her pupils did the AMEB Theory exams. Thus was I equipped with the basics of writing down the music that had been coming into my head from a very early age.

By the time I left school, I had developed a passion for composition and had studied far ahead of the AMEB Theory course. I had acquired a large record collection and was totally immersed in 'classical' music, somewhat to the puzzlement of my mates. I bought music scores of the works I loved to hear and worked out how the composer achieved the effects which dazzled me. I devoured Dulcie Holland's books on theory. I got into trouble once when, in a study period, having finished my homework early, I ruled up a page from my exercise book into music manuscript and started writing down a septet for wind and strings. A clip over the ear from the supervising teacher reminded me to postpone such flights of fancy to a more appropriate time.

When I finished school in 1963 I was sixteen – these were the days when the secondary course of studies was only five years. I thought I wanted to be a composer. I investigated the content of the music degree at Sydney University, then the only tertiary course in New South Wales that seemed to offer serious study of composition. I formed the opinion that, in the words of Dr Bridges in her doctoral thesis, the curriculum was 'based on long-standing and virtually unchanged 19th century teaching (and) was musically constipating.' I decided that I would pursue my own directions in composition. To the intense relief of my parents, who envisaged me starving in a garret for the rest of my life if I pursued composition as a career, I agreed to study law.

I have long since realized that my assessment of the Sydney University music course as an education for a composer was entirely the product of youthful ignorance. There were, in fact, wonderful and inspiring teachers in the department, Peter Sculthorpe amongst them. In my defence, I can plead only the immaturity of a boy who had no musical mentor to steer him in the right direction at the right time.

I found the study of law interesting, but not absorbing. I still had time for writing music and recommenced piano lessons, this time with Frank Warbrick, who had recently retired from teaching and examining at the Sydney Conservatorium of Music. Frank had been a pre-eminent pianist between the Wars, and had often performed new music live on the ABC, particularly that of his friends and contemporaries, Lindley Evans and Frank Hutchens. Frank had studied in Europe and carried about him the gentility, grace and taste of a more refined time and place than Sydney in the 1960s. He was an endearing, gentle and highly knowledgeable man. I was never going to be a brilliant pianist, and I didn't want to be, but I loved the deep insights into music which flowed effortlessly from Frank during our lessons.

When I graduated in law and began to practice as a solicitor, I suddenly discovered the excitement and challenge of dealing with the real-life problems of people and finding solutions. I developed an enthusiasm for the practice of law to a degree which I would never have foreseen as a law student. I had the very good fortune to have 'served articles' – then a form of compulsory apprenticeship – with an excellent firm of commercial lawyers and soon found myself specializing in commercial law, particularly mining and oil exploration, which was booming in Australia in the early 1970s. In 1972, at the age of 25, married and with a newly-arrived baby, I became a partner of my law firm. They were heady and exciting times – a wonderful family of my own and a fulfilling, if demanding, career.

Yet the music was always swirling around in my head and every now and then, in a rare moment of spare time, I would get out the manuscript paper and start writing. I never dreamed of having anything performed – music was my escape into another world.

In 1974, I decided to become a barrister. Life became even busier than before. In 1975 our second child was born and in 1979 our third. The demands of work and family left little time for composition. Yet the piles of manuscript paper, covered with pencil scrawlings and scratchings, steadily grew in a bottom drawer somewhere. On the train going to and from work, I would study Persichetti's *Twentieth Century Harmony* and Walter Piston's and Rimsky-Korsakov's treatises on orchestration. I continued to accumulate and study scores.

In 1978 my musical development, which had been merely coasting along, received a sharp and invigorating jolt. I met the musician and singer/songwriter who was to become, and remains to this day, my best mate, musical conscience and sounding board – Scott Walker. Scott is a virtuoso pianist and clarinetist who could have made a career as a concert artist on either instrument. Instead, he has chosen to focus on writing and performing his own songs. From the very beginning his music has been unique and highly arresting – an idiosyncratic fusion of pop, rock and the most stringent contemporary 'serious' music. His depth of knowledge of the classical and contemporary repertoire has long surpassed my own.

Listening to Scott's compositions and discussing them as they developed made me appreciate as I had not done before that if my own compositions were to have any value I must not only have something of substance to say but I must be fearless in saying it honestly, whatever the fads and fashions of the time dictated. This may not sound like a startling revelation but in the 1960s, 1970s, 1980s and even the 1990s music of the kind I wanted to write was not only out of fashion, it was laughed to scorn by the musical establishment. That was one of the main reasons my manuscripts gathered dust in the bottom drawer: I would not risk humiliation by subjecting them to the jeers of the arbiters of taste.

I very much agree with the proposition that music owes its origin to the instinct urge in humans to dance and sing. Dance and song informs all of my music. Dancing and singing require recognizable and repeatable rhythmic and melodic patterns. I have always followed Shostakovich's advice to his friend, Benjamin Britten: 'Ben, never be afraid of a good tune.' Shostakovich practiced what he preached.

I acknowledge, of course, that the composition of music is an intellectual exercise and that some listeners derive intellectual stimulation from knowing that the composer has taken twelve notes at random and played around with them in all sorts of clever ways. But that sort of music rarely, if ever, dances and sings – at least, to my ear. Neither is that sort of music able to evoke for me the whole range of human emotions and their nuances. All it usually evokes is a sense of alienation and isolation – which I quickly find tedious and depressing.

I have listened carefully and sometimes with great pleasure to the works of Schoenberg, Berg, Webern and the host of post-War composers who have carried their banner forward. The work of the early serialists was astringently refreshing. I have paid a great deal of attention to contemporary composers such as Reich, Nyman, Adams and Glass. Much of their music is not to my taste but I do not dismiss it with a contemptuous wave of the hand. I think the insights and concepts of experimentalists such as John Cage and Pierre Boulez, for example, have been a necessary development in the exploration of what music is and what it does to us. Curiosity dictates that we will continue to experiment, in the name of music, with the outer limits of communication and expression but that does not mean that the results of every experiment have equal value and deserve repetition.

Happily, many contemporary composers are no longer afraid of writing music that, 10 years ago, would have been sneered at as 'accessible', meaning that it uses a musical language that is fairly familiar to the Western ear. Ross Edwards' recent work is a good example. If Mahler or Richard Strauss heard his Second Symphony they would not be shocked or mystified.

To return to the narrative. Inspired by Scott Walker's musical (and personal) courage, I resolved to write the way I felt, but to push my own boundaries too. More manuscript was added to the dusty pile. I was too busy with my career and family – and still too much of a coward – to attempt to get my music performed.

In 1986 I was appointed a Queen's Counsel. Life at the Bar became even more pressured. In 2001 I was appointed as a Judge of the Supreme Court and the pressure eased a little. At least I had a more structured working day and could, for the first time in 30 years, count on some free time most weekends.

I probably would never have attempted to have my music performed had it not been that, in 2002, it became obvious that my father did not have long to live. I very much wanted him to hear something of the music which he knew I had been scribbling for many years. He was not well enough to attend a performance. I decided to have some works recorded privately so that he could hear them on CD. I still was not brave enough for a public performance.

By a series of accidents and co-incidences I could neither have foreseen or planned, the recording of these few pieces came to the attention of the ABC. In 2004 ABC TV did an *Australian Story* about the judge turned composer and ABC Classic FM broadcast live to air a whole concert of my music. Since then I have received many commissions for new pieces and ABC Classics has issued two CDs of my works, 'The Attraction of Opposites', featuring works mostly for string orchestra, and 'Exaltate Dominum', featuring choral works performed by Cantillation and Sinfonia Australis.

I am now very busy with composition. I compose early in the morning before going to work, in the evening and at weekends. There is always a deadline for the delivery of a commission.

I am, at last, comfortable writing the music I want to write. I do not tremble at the thought that the arbiters of taste will sneer at the 'accessibility' of the music. I do tremble at the thought that I may not have succeeded in capturing on the page the pure music I have heard in my head.

People often ask about my musical influences. I have my own ideas but others are sometimes surprisingly more perceptive than I am.

To have studied the piano has been an immense benefit in learning the art of composition and it has also produced lasting influences in compositional technique and style. Bach, Mozart and Beethoven are the central pillars of any musical education. I am sure that my affection for the classical forms in my own music is the result of my piano study of these masters.

The twentieth century composers of whom I am especially fond are Ravel, Debussy, Poulenc, Bartok, Prokofiev, Shostakovich, Vaughan Williams, Britten and Tippett. Of course there are many other composers too – but lists can be tedious. In opera my favourites are Mozart, Puccini and Janacek. Britten protested to Shostakovich that Puccini's music was terrible. Shostakovich replied: 'he wrote terrible music but great opera.' That's a very perceptive observation: opera is an art form unto itself.

I try to write in a style that is clear, transparent and uncluttered. Engraved in my heart is Stravinsky's advice: a composer's most useful tool is the eraser.

I cannot say that I have now learnt to be a composer. I am still learning and I will continue to learn with each new piece. I keep listening to the new work of other composers. I find Ross Edwards particularly dangerous – he is so good that it is hard to resist mere imitation.

I often wonder what course my life – not just as a composer – would have taken had I been wise enough, at the age of sixteen, to embark on the formal study of composition in the music department of Sydney University. Many years later, when I told Peter Sculthorpe why I had baulked, he looked almost hurt. 'Why didn't you come and talk to me first,' he said. 'We would have worked out something for you.'

In the end, I have learnt to compose in my own way. Probably every composer does.

16: Two Spells

for Doreen Bridges

Ross Edwards

Spell 1 (HEALING)

opposite Spell 1 (HEALING)

Repeat as many times as you like, adding instruments, clapping, varying the dynamics. A gradual crescendo over many repetitions, from very soft to very loud could be effective. If any of the parts are sung, please find words that sound magical and have some association with healing - for example the names of medicinal herbs.

Spell 2 (WISHING)

Start softly and repeat many times until very loud. The final chord should be explosive! This spell could be used to help make a wish come true. If you'd like to add voices, please choose words that have special significance. For example, if someone's pet is sick or missing you could repeat its name over and over. be freely inventive in fitting words to rhythm – they dont have to make sense!

Spell 2 (WISHING)

17: Music for Children and Young People

David Forrest

The title of this contribution comes from the extensive collection of music by the Russian composer and educator Dmitri Kabalevsky (1904–1987) entitled *Piano Music for Children and Young People*. It directly relates to the work of Doreen Bridges who has devoted so much of her energies and intellect to the enlightened cause of music for children as willing performers and participants, discerning and discriminating listeners and audience members. Throughout her life she has maintained her active passion regarding the place of the piano within the musical experience.

I aim to provide an exploration of music for children and young people from a framework proposed by I. B. Aliev (1970). My intention is to illustrate this through the music and writings of Kabalevsky and particularly the works he wrote for children. For this purpose I will take Aliev's relatively stark definition of children's music as 'music intended for children to listen to and perform. The best children's music is distinguished by a concrete subject, lively poetic content, picturesque imagery, and simple and clear form' (1970, p. 35).

Aliev (1970) in the *Great Soviet Encyclopedia* identified a series of categories of music for children. He limited his discussion to: works written to be performed by children; songs and instrumental works written for children's broadcasts, for plays performed in children's theatres, and for children's films; works based on subjects drawn from the life of children but performed by professional musicians, and not specifically designed for an audience of children; and music for educational purposes. Kabalevsky undoubtedly contributed to each of these categories.

In many ways Kabalevsky's writings were determined by his place and time, and the political and social structures in which he lived and worked. From a present day perspective however, it is clear that his ideas have a universal application.

Background

Music for children as performers and listeners has been richly served by Russian composers throughout the nineteenth and twentieth centuries. Amongst the nineteenth century composers who contributed to the body of works for children are Glinka, Grechaninov, Ippolitov-Ivanov, Liadov, Myaskovsky, Tcherepnin, Reboikov, and Tchaikovsky. Some of the twentieth century Soviet composers who have written for children include Dunayevsky, Gedike, Gliere, Gnesina, Krasev, Khatchaturian, Prokofiev, Shchedrin, Shebalin, and Shostakovich. Russian composers from the nineteenth and twentieth centuries have made significant contributions to the literature on music that uses the subject of children or childhood from both a pedagogical and performance perspective.

Over his life, Kabalevsky published more than 250 works including large-scale compositions (principally the operas, cantatas, symphonies and concertos) as well as the sets of songs and piano pieces. Of his total output approximately half of the works were written for children or use the resources of children. The majority of Kabalevsky's works for children fall into two main groups: 80 song collections and 153 separate compositions for solo piano. The following sections provide a consideration of the categories provided by Aliev in relation to Kabalevsky and his response to children's music.

Music to be performed by children and young people

The music Kabalevsky composed to be performed by children (and young people) is divided into two sections: the instrumental music and the piano music. Table 1 presents the instrumental music written for children.

Table 1: Instrumental music for children and young people

Year of comp.	Name of work
1948	Violin Concerto 'Youth' in C major Op. 48
1949	Cello Concerto No. 1 'Youth' in G minor Op. 49
1952	Piano Concerto No. 3 'Youth' in D major Op. 50
1961	Major-Minor Studies for cello solo Op. 68
1963	Rhapsody for Piano and Orchestra, 'School Years' Op. 75
1965	Twenty Easy Pieces for violin and piano Op. 80
1977–78	Prague Concerto for Piano and String Orchestra Op. 99

The three 'youth' concertos (Opp. 48, 49 and 50) provide a major contribution to the concerto literature. They were written immediately following the 1948 Decree by the Central Committee on Music, and were seen as his response to the edict. The decree had a significant impact on the direction, work and output of Soviet composers for the next decade. The Rhapsody Op. 75 and Prague Concerto Op. 99 are small yet effusively brilliant works written for piano competitions. These works sit comfortably alongside the other works in this genre. Kabalevsky (1975) in his note on the Piano Concerto Op. 50 stated that 'by introducing the 'Our Native Land' song into my concerto I wanted the young musicians and listeners to realise that the music deals with their own lives – with the Soviet Land, its people, its children and youth' (p. 2).

Kabalevsky wrote piano music for children throughout his life. His first piano works for children were published in 1927. Between 1972 and 1987 he assembled the twelve volume collection of *Piano Music for Children and Young People* from his total published output. The collection was published in Moscow by Sovetsky Kompozitor under the composer's supervision. Significantly for any composer each of the works has remained available in the current published catalogues under a range of imprints. The works in the collection are listed in Table 2.

Table 2: Piano Music for Children and Young People

Year of composition/revision	Name of work
1927/1968	In the Pioneer Camp Op. 3/86
1930, 1933	Two Sonatinas Op. 13
1931/68	From Pioneer Life Op. 14
1937	Thirty Children's Pieces Op. 27
1939/69	Three Rondos from the Opera 'Colas Breugnon' Op. 30
1943	Twenty-Four Easy Pieces Op. 39
1944	Easy Variations Op. 40
1952	Easy Variations on Folk Themes Op. 51
1958	Four Rondos Op. 60
1958–59	Preludes and Fugues Op. 61

1964	Spring Games and Dances Op. 81
1967	Recitative and Rondo Op. 84
1966, 1968, 1969	Variations on Folk Themes Op. 87
1971	Six Pieces Op. 88
1971	Lyric Tunes Op. 91
1972	Thirty-Five Easy Pieces Op. 89

Rita McAllister (1975) stated that 'the significance of his works for young performers, which he regards not as a hack task but as a field of primary importance, is universally acknowledged; his earlier works for the young were in many respects models for subsequent children's music by Prokofiev, Shostakovich, and others' (p. 1135). Nicholas Slonimsky (1992) stated that 'Kabalevsky's music represents a paradigm of the Russian school of composition during the Soviet period' (p. 875). Punctuated throughout his compositional life are the larger instrumental, choral and orchestral and concert works (including the symphonies, concertos, sonatas, operas and cantatas). It should be emphasised that the works for children were not written in isolation from his other compositions, but occupied an ongoing and integral place within his compositional processes.

Works for broadcasts, theatre and film
Kabalevsky wrote a large number of compositions for radio broadcast, theatre and film. All of his works were performed, recorded and broadcast. Prominent

musicians, orchestras and choirs premiered each of his works. It should be noted that he held the position of Chief of the Board of Feature Broadcasting, All-Union Radio Committee – the body that determined what works would be performed and therefore also the works that would be recorded and broadcast. Although he chaired this committee for a relatively short time, he continued to exert influence on the work of this committee. The main works that fall under the category for broadcasts, theatre and film are listed in Table 3.

Table 3: Works for broadcasts, theatre and film

Year of comp.	Name of work
1931	*Galician Zhakeria* (*The Galician Jacquerie*) Op. 15 a radio work for soloists, choir and orchestra
1935	*The Merry Tailor* (incidental music), Puppet Theatre, Moscow
1940	*Komediantï* (*Comedians*) Op. 25 (incidental music)
1940	*Golden Childhood* incidental music, radio production
1940	*Parad molodosti* (*Parade of Youth*) Op. 31 presentation for children's chorus and orchestra
1941	*The City of Masters* incidental music (Central Children's Theatre)
1946	*Her First Year at School* film music
1957	*Pesnya utra, vesnï i mira* (*Song of Morning, Spring and Peace*) Op. 57 cantata for children's chorus and orchestra

1958	Leninitsï (*Lenin's Lads and Lassies*) Op. 63 cantata for children, youth, adult choir and orchestra
1958	*V skazochnom lesu* (*In a fairytale forest*) Op. 62 musical scenes for children, narrator, choir and piano
1965	*O rodnoy zemle* (*About Native Land*) Op. 82 cantata for children's choir and orchestra
1970	*Pis'mo v XXX bek* (*Letter to the 30th Century*) Op. 93 oratorio
1975	*Friendship Songs* (Leipzig Cantata) Op. 97 for soloists and women's and children's choruses

One of the great developments of the early years of the Soviet Union was the establishment of the Central Children's Theatre. This institution, through the initiatives of Natalia Satz, saw the development of a large number of composers and their contribution of works for children. It was for this theatre that Prokofiev wrote his *Peter and the Wolf* Op. 67 (1936). Kabalevsky made some important contributions of incidental music to theatre and film. Many of these works were extracted and appeared in a range of versions. One of his most lasting compositions that remains in the concert and recorded repertoire is the *Comedians* suite for small symphony orchestra Op. 25 (1940).

Works drawn from the lives of children

The titled larger works that draw on the lives and experiences of children and young people are included in Table 4.

Table 4: Works drawn from the lives of children

Year of comp.	Name of work
1932	*Mstislav the Valiant* incidental music
1940	*Golden Childhood* incidental music and radio production
1946	*Her First Year at School* incidental music
1955	*Restless Youth* film music

To this list is added the large quantity of songs and piano music that draw on the experiences of children as the subject matter. An example is the set of Preludes and Fugues Op. 61 for piano where the six preludes and fugues are identified programmatically as A Summer Morning on the Lawn, Becoming a Young Pioneer, An Evening Song Beyond the River, At the Young Pioneer Camp, The Story of a Hero, and A Feast of Labour. Similarly, Kabalevsky (1983) stated that *In the Pioneer Camp* 'its six items are unified by a common program (a day at a Young Pioneer Camp)' (p. 2).

Larger works that require the resources of children

Kabalevsky drew on the resources of children in a wide range of his works. Table 5 lists the larger compositions (including the cantatas, oratorios, opera and Requiem) that use the resources of children.

Table 5: Larger works that require the resources of children

Year of comp.	Name of work
1931	*Galician Zhakeria* (*The Galician Jacquerie*) Op. 15 a radio work for soloists, choir and orchestra
1941	*Parad molodosti* (*Parade of Youth*) Op. 31 presentation for children's chorus and orchestra
1947	*Sem'ya Tarasa* (*Taras' Family*) Op. 47 opera
1957	*Pesnya utra, vesnï i mira* (*Song of Morning, Spring and Peace*) Op. 57 (cantata) for children's chorus and orchestra
1957	*Vesna poyot* (*Spring Sings*) Op. 58 operetta
1958	*Leninitsï* (*Lenin's Lads and Lassies*) Op. 63 cantata for children, youth, adult choir and orchestra
1958	*V skazochnom lesu* (*In a fairytale forest*) Op. 62 musical scenes for children, narrator, choir and piano
1962	*Requiem* Op. 72 'To those who fell in the battle with fascism' for soloists, mixed chorus, children's chorus and orchestra
1965	*O rodnoy zemle* (*About Native Land*) Op. 82 cantata for children's choir and orchestra
1967	*Sestrï* (*The Sisters*) Op. 83 opera

1972	*Pis'mo v XXX bek* (*Letter to the 30th Century*) Op. 93 oratorio
1974	*ISME Fanfares* (orchestra) Op. 96
1975	*Friendship Songs* (Leipzig Cantata) Op. 97 for soloists and women's and children's choruses

From this collection the only orchestral work is the *ISME Fanfares* written to be played by young performers of the country hosting the conference of the International Society for Music Education. It was first performed at the 1974 ISME conference in Perth, Australia.

Educative works for young performers

The educative works of Kabalevsky form one of the largest single groups of compositions. Principally these works come under the group of *Piano Music for Children and Young People* (12 volumes), however there are also instrumental works for violin and cello as identified in Table 1. Although Kabalevsky did not organise his works into a sequential pedagogical experience, the larger collections provide a developmental progression of technical and musical materials for the young performer.

In approaching music for children Kabalevsky adopted the model of what he called the 'three whales'. The name is taken from a legend where the world was supported on the backs of three great whales. The whales in music he said were the song, the dance, and the march. Kabalevsky's education philosophy was centred on the understanding by children of the characteristics and components of the song, the dance, and the march. He believed that if children could distinguish between these three forms or genres then they could enter the larger world of music. *About the Three Whales and Many Other Things: A book about music* explores the three genres for children and in doing so makes an important contribution to the music education literature.

It is evident the audience for *About the Three Whales* is children. It was not the teachers (who would guide the children), or academics (who might construct programs around the ideas). It is directed to children to enable them to enter and appreciate the world of music.

> This book is meant not only for those children who are studying music, play musical instruments and are therefore familiar with musical notation, but also for those who do not know it at all and who cannot read music. That is why I am not going to use any examples of musical notation in the book, even though music is its main subject. (pp. 9–10)

About the Three Whales is divided into two parts: 'About the three whales' and 'About many other things'. The first part focuses on an exposition of the song, the dance and the march. He said:

> And so it is not surprising that these simplest musical forms have reached us as repositories of genuine musical treasures, representing as many national musical languages as there can be found in the world, as many thoughts and feelings as the human mind and the human heart can hold. (p. 19)

He pursues a discussion on 'Where the song will lead us', 'Where the dance will lead us', and 'Where the march will lead us'. The first part of the book concludes with 'The three whales come together' in which he discusses various combinations of the genres in a range of music and then concludes with a discussion of opera (with his focus on Bizet's *Carmen*, Rimsky-Korsakov's *The Tale of the Invisible Town of Kitezh and the Maiden Fevronia* and Shostakovich's *Lady Macbeth of Mtsensk*). The issue that he continually returned to and reinforced throughout the book was limiting your acquaintance with music to the song, the dance and the march, is like peeping into a beautiful garden through the gate without stepping inside to explore and enjoy it and to understand why so many people wish to get into this garden and why they talk about it with such delight. (p. 19)

The 'many other things' of the second part is organised around the questions: Can music depict things? Can we see music and hear paintings? Can music and literature live without each other? Should we always imagine something when listening to music? Here he guides the students to the great artistic and literary works of Russian (and Soviet) history. He refers to writers including Tolstoy, Marshak and Mayaskovsky, and the artists Repin, Grekov, Aivazovsky and Levitan. He places the discussion against music and considers how meaning is conveyed in the art forms. He established the link between music and the other arts, as well as the link between 'music and life' (Kabalevsky, 1988, p. 22).

Composition for children

Kabalevsky's compositions for children and his writings shared a common philosophy. In many of his addresses and interviews he repeated such comments as:

When somebody asked the writer Maxim Gorki, 'How should books for children be written?' he replied, 'The same as for adults, only better!' This reply can equally well be applied to music for children. (1988, p. 120)

He later extended the much quoted statement by saying:

Maxim Gorki was right when he said that the way to write for children was as for adults, only better. In my opinion, however, it should be added that in order to write well for children one also needs to be *able* to write for adults. (1988, p. 148)

Kabalevsky (1976) reinforced that when he referred to music he was talking about 'the great art of music and not music simplified specially for children' (p. 123). He clearly acknowledged that the composer of music for children must write in a considered manner, but must also be able to write for adults. He believed that composers must be able to direct their skills to different levels of performance and understanding. Elaborating on writing for children, he argued:

> it is not enough to be a composer to write such music. You have to be at the same time a composer, an educationalist [academic] and a teacher. Only this way can good results be achieved. The composer will ensure that the music is good and lively, the educationalist will ensure that it is educationally reasonable. As for the teacher, he must not lose sight of the fact that music, like any art, helps children to see the world and nurtures their education by developing not only their artistic tastes and their creative imagination, but also their love of life, mankind, of nature and their country. (Kabalevsky, 1988, p. 120)

His insistence on the importance of basing a system of music education on what he saw as the inherent nature of music is perhaps best expressed in the following statement:

> In my many years of teaching music to school children of various ages, I have attempted to arrive at a concept of teaching arising from and relying on the music itself, a concept that would naturally and organically relate music as an art to music as a school subject, and that would just as naturally relate school music lessons to real life. I have attempted to find the sort of principles, methods and approaches that could help to attract the children, interest them in music, and bring this beautiful art, with its immeasurable potential for spiritual enrichment, close to them. (Kabalevsky, 1988, p. 21)

The song, dance and the march gave Kabalevsky a means of conveying his educational beliefs to children. The three genres became for Kabalevsky the bridge upon which he was able to access the world of children, and in turn give children access to the world of music. Kabalevsky and Aliev were in agreement about what constitutes music for children. Probably more than any other Russian Soviet composer Kabalevsky devoted a considerable amount of effort to his work for children. The music he wrote and his rationale could provide a good framework for a larger study of music that is now appropriately described as 'music for children'.

References

Aliev, I. B. (1970). Children's Music. In A. M. Prokhorov (Ed.), *Great Soviet Encyclopedia* (3rd ed.). (Vol. 8). New York: Macmillan, Inc.

Kabalevsky, D. B. (1972). *Pro treh kitov i pro mnogoe drugoe*. (*About the Three Whales and Many Other Things: A book about music*). (2nd ed.). Moscow: Detskayar Literatura.

Kabalevsky, D. B. (1974/2004). *ISME Fanfares*. Perth: ISME.

Kabalevsky, D. B. (1975). Concerto No. 3 for piano and orchestra Op. 50. *Piano Music for Children and Young People*. (Vol. 11). Moscow: Sovetsky Kompozitor.

Kabalevsky, D. (1976). Music in General Schools. In F. Callaway (Ed.), *Challenges in Music Education*. Perth: University of Western Australia.

Kabalevsky, D. B. (1983). In the Pioneer Camp Op. 3/86, From Pioneer Life Op. 14. *Piano Music for Children and Young People*. (Vol. 1). Moscow: Sovetsky Kompozitor.

Kabalevsky, D. (1988). *Music and Education: A Composer Writes About Musical Education*. London: J. Kingsley in association with UNESCO.

McAllister, R. (1980). Kabalevsky, Dmitry Borisovich. In S. Sadie (Ed.), *The New Grove Dictionary of Music and Musicians* (Vol. 9). London: Macmillan.

Slonimsky, N. (Ed.). (1992). *Baker's Biographical Dictionary of Musicians*. (8th ed.). New York: Schirmer Books.

18: Schumann and the English Critics: A study in nineteenth century musical reception

Janet Ritterman

> Haydn and Mozart, with their unfailing melody and transparent treatment, Mendelssohn uttering his poetic thoughts in most mellifluous numbers, and Schubert touching every heart with piquant simplicity or melancholy grandeur, were promptly welcomed by the English public, while Beethoven was only rejected for a time when he uttered the "dark sayings" to which, even now, few possess a key. Schumann, on the contrary, has had to fight for every step towards public favour, and the conflict is not half over yet.

This assessment by the London music critic, Joseph Bennett,[1] written in 1868, fairly summarized the position in terms of mid nineteenth-century English reactions to the music of Robert Schumann. It was a situation that Bennett, then one of the most active of the London music critics, had been in a good position to observe. It was, furthermore, a situation which divided English musical life both within, and without. Although by the time of Schumann's death in 1856 reservations about his music had in many parts of Western Europe given way to a general interest in and appreciation of his work, from this, England stood apart.

Admittedly the achievement of recognition and acceptance for Robert Schumann and his music had been not without its difficulties. During Schumann's lifetime, the nature of musical life and the life of leading European composers and performers had undergone fundamental change, occasioned in part by tumultuous political upheaval which affected much of Europe in the first half of the nineteenth century. This change took various forms, but among the developments that were to have most influence on the life of the professional musician was the expansion of the ways in which music was disseminated, in particular through the growth in public concert life. For some composers the opportunities that this provided were welcome; careers flourished in the public spotlight and with the attention of the press, to an extent that had previously been unknown. Performances that would once have taken place only in private or semi-private gatherings and been shared within closely defined social groupings, became increasingly open to a larger, more anonymous general public.[2]

For composers like Schumann whose natural tendency was to seek to communicate with a circle of intimates, and whose early compositions reflect this preference, the changing musical world of the mid-nineteenth century, with its expectation that leading professional musicians would seek to function in the public arena, created tensions which he found difficult to resolve, and which in turn affected the music he wrote and its reception. The intimacy which had been characteristic of earlier music making – the close bond between composer and listener – could no longer be assumed. By mid-century concert-giving and concert attendance had expanded enormously, and continued to do so in the years that followed. In its train, the regular publication of music criticism, in daily newspapers as well as in specialist journals, became increasingly commonplace. By mid-century leading English newspapers and periodicals employed music critics, who covered significant musical events as a matter of course. While Schumann himself had strong literary leanings and was more than ready to share his views with others, his target readership was a particular circle of intimates, and his music was, at least at first, similarly conceived.

Those contemporary writers who have directed their attention to the reception of Schumann's music tend to the view that from the 1850s onward and for quite some time thereafter, Schumann's standing and reputation as one of the outstanding composers of his age increased steadily, becoming, in the genres in which he focused his energies, essentially unchallenged.[3] It is true that by the 1850s his music had been repeatedly performed, studied, and admired in cities ranging from Vienna to St Petersburg, Paris to Prague. He was honoured by colleagues;[4] he had become the subject of biographical commentary.[5] The songs, the piano works and concerted chamber works of the earlier decades had been promoted through the concert performances of Clara, his pianist wife, and other supporters within their circle of professional colleagues; the symphonic, choral and chamber works of his later years had been performed and welcomed within Germany and then in ever-widening circles, first within mainland Europe, then beyond. It is on these grounds that the 1860s – the decade after Schumann's death – became, in the view of various commentators, both at the time and since, essentially the 'age of Schumann'.[6]

English reservations about Schumann

While this view is broadly supported by the evidence of reception within mainland Europe, this was not the case in England. Here, attempts to introduce music from what was perceived as a 'new school' met with reactions ranging from passive resistance to active opposition. The question of Schumann divided musical London into opposing camps – the Schumannites and the anti-Schumannites.[7] The ensuing controversy rivalled that provoked by composers such as Berlioz and Wagner, with whom Schumann was frequently linked by English critics, as an (unwelcome) representative of the 'Music of the Future'. For quite some time after Schumann's music had achieved general acceptance in mainland Europe, it continued to provoke trenchant criticism in the London press. The gradual change in English attitudes towards the music of Schumann provides an interesting insight into the impact of public performance and music education on musical reception. The manner in which the changes took place suggest some reasons for the continuing ambivalence about the music of Schumann which can still be discerned in certain Anglo-Saxon circles.

Many present-day music lovers find it surprising that the reception of Schumann's music had a far more troubled passage in England than elsewhere. The mid nineteenth century London was widely regarded as one of the leading musical capitals in Europe, and a centre which was attractive to visiting musicians and supportive of their ventures, sometimes (at least in the view of local artists) to the detriment of home-grown or resident talent. What was so different about Robert Schumann?

As Reinhard Kapp has pointed out, there were features of Schumann's biography, in terms of his emergence as a composer, that appear to have made it harder for him to achieve acceptance and recognition as a composer than many of his contemporaries, and thus influenced the reception of his music.[8] There are at least three complementary aspects to this, some partly social in orientation, some instrinsically musical. Firstly, there was the figure that Schumann 'cut' as a musician. For much of his career, Schumann did not match the prevailing model of the mid-nineteenth century composer: while history has dealt variously with a number of those who were then most prominent, the majority of those whose names would have sprung most readily to contemporary lips in a roll-call of leading composers of the time were musicians who actively promoted their own music, predominantly through performance (and often also through teaching) and so were centrally involved in the creation of an associated performance tradition. While Schumann's early compositions were predominantly for the piano, he was no pianist – his attempts to acquire a virtuoso technique had ended in a permanently damaged hand – and therefore he needed to rely on others to perform his works. Many of these performances, at least at first, seem to have taken place in private gatherings. Admittedly Schumann became better known after 1840, the year of his marriage to the pianist Clara Wieck, through accompanying his wife on some of her concert tours to various European cities. The family's move to Dresden in 1845, and then in 1850 to Düsseldorf where Schumann served briefly as the city's music director, also broadened his range of contacts. But in an age where composers tended to promote their own music through performance, for much of his career Schumann must have appeared to many in the musical world as a relatively shadowy figure. Even one of his most enthusiastic contemporary supporters, the London-based pianist, Ernst

Pauer, considered it a significant disadvantage that Schumann had not been 'a public player, as Mozart, Beethoven, Weber, Mendelssohn, and Chopin all were'.[9]

Secondly, there were his literary activities. Through his founding of the *Neue Zeitschrift für Musik* and his writings, Robert Schumann was seen by many principally as a writer and critic – an academic, rather than a practising musician. Furthermore, the creation of the *Davidsbündler* (the League of David), with its cast of imaginary, fantastical characters, provided a series of masks behind which Schumann often chose to conceal himself. And finally, there was the character of the music itself – often idiosyncratic in terms of harmony and structure – which initially did little to convince the skeptical that what Schumann represented should be regarded as a key influence in the shaping of the musical future. One need do little more than to contrast the musical personas of Felix Mendelssohn and Robert Schumann, almost exact contemporaries, both coming to maturity in Leipzig in the 1830s – Mendelssohn the youthful prodigy, the gifted performer, poised, outgoing and sociable, and Schumann, the introverted dreamer, interested in poetry, struggling to acquire a keyboard technique, and facing the scorn of Leipzig's leading piano teacher, Friedrich Wieck – to realize how difficult it must have been for Schumann's talents to be readily recognized.

Critics' responses to early Schumann performances

In the 1840s and early 1850s, when Schumann's music was gaining increasing attention in Germany and other parts of Europe, very little was heard in London. Apart from isolated events such as the performance in 1848 of the Piano Quartet in E flat, Op. 47, by the German-born pianist Eduard Röckel,[10] Schumann's music does not appear to have featured in the London concert scene of the 1840s. For this first English performance the description of the work in the programme book – noting that the work had already been performed with success in Leipzig and Dresden – sought to reassure a conservatively-minded audience[11] that the new work had a 'claim to great excellence in the beauty of its harmonies, the classical purity of its scoring, and orthodox development of its *motivi*. However reception did not inspire repetition: some years later, when another work by Schumann was in prospect, the quartet was recalled as a work 'in which daring collisions of chords rather startled our pre-conceived notions of purity of harmony'.[12] The next Schumann work to be attempted – in 1853, also at the Musical Union – was the Piano Quintet in E flat, Op. 44, which the visiting pianist, Wilhemina Clauss, chose to perform.[13] Further advocacy for the music of Schumann in the programme book, where it was noted instead that 'this meditative and deeply skilled musician' was 'aiming at new effects and new forms' was no more successful than before. While the performer's choice was acknowledged by Ella, director of the Musical Union, as 'courageous', the work itself was dismissed by the leading London music critic of the day, J. W. Davison, as 'hideous'.

For over three decades – from the mid 1840s until in the late 1870s when his activities were constrained by illness – it was Davison's critical preferences and prejudices that dominated the London musical scene. No only was he chief music critic for *The Times* but, as proprietor and editor of the principal music journal, *The Musical World*, which appeared weekly, he had ample scope to voice his opinions, the impact of which was felt well beyond British shores.[14] For Davison, a lover of traditional forms, and a devoted supporter of the music of Mendelssohn, Schumann represented a move away from all that he most respected in the art. For him, the music of Schumann offered only '[a]n affectation of originality, a superficial knowledge of the art, an absence of true expression, and an infelicitious disdain of form' – the dismissive comment that he penned following the poorly-received first English performance of Schumann's *Overture, Scherzo and Finale* for orchestra, Op. 52, given by the Philharmonic Society[15] a few weeks after the performance of the Piano Quintet. While the choice of work may not have served Schumann's interests well (it was certainly among the works about which German critics otherwise supportive of Schumann were least enthusiastic),[16] Davison's criticisms struck at the heart of Schumann's professional credibility. In his view, '[t]he general style [of this work] betrays the patchiness and want of fluency of a tyro; while the forced and unnatural turns of cadence and progression, declare neither more nor less than the convulsive efforts of one who has never properly studied his art to hide the deficiencies of early education under a mist of pompous swagger.' Had it not been for the interest of Prince Albert, the Prince Consort, whose European connections presumably encouraged him to request the inclusion of Schumann's Symphony No 1 in the programme of a Royal Command concert in the following year, it seems unlikely that the Philharmonic Society would have felt encouraged to assay more Schumann repertoire. The performance of the symphony – another English first performance – did nothing to modify Davison's opinion. Dismissing the occasion as a 'fiasco', he observed, with more than a hint of satisfaction, that the end of each movement had been greeted by the socially influential Philharmonic audience with 'what very much resembled a dead silence'.[17]

Clara Schumann's first visit

Although Davison's vituperative outbursts were sometimes countered by expressions of written support from Schumann supporters, it was largely through the influence of live public performance that the music of Robert Schumann eventually became a part of the core repertoire in the English concert scene. Among the first to promote his music in England was his wife Clara: from 1856, the year of her husband's death, and for the next thirty years, she made numerous visits to London,[18] becoming ultimately an artist much admired and much respected by audiences and critics alike. The inclusion of works by Schumann in her concert programmes, as well as in those of pupils whom she taught, certainly contributed to the eventual establishment of Schumann's music in English eyes as a core part of the pianistic repertoire.

Acceptance was, however, far from immediate. During her first visit in 1856, although clearly aware of English predilections, Clara took at face value the assertion that although the knowledge of Schumann's works in England was 'as yet confined to a small circle, the desire of becoming acquainted with them is very general'.[19] While ensuring that Beethoven, Mendelssohn and Chopin featured prominently in the majority of her programmes for the more high profile concerts, she also chose to perform several of her husband's compositions – works which had generally been well-received elsewhere in Europe. Among these were two of the pieces from the Op. 12 *Fantaisiestücke* – 'Des Abends' (Evening) and 'Traumes Wirren' (Tangled Dreams) – the Piano Concerto, the Andante and Variations for two pianos, Op. 46, and extracts from *Carnaval*, Op. 9. By the close of the season – during which she appeared in at least twenty-six concerts – Clara had come to recognize more clearly the extent of the difference between English musical attitudes and standards and those with which she was familiar from Germany. In the privacy of her diary, she vented her disappointment and frustration: '[t]hey are frightfully backward', she wrote, 'or, more to the point, partial; they want to accept nothing new other than Mendelssohn, who is their god! *The Times* skirts around the issue, if there is anything to say about Robert.'[20]

As Clara observed, restraint was shown by the London critics, at least initially. Davison avoided comment on the *Fantaisiestücke* by dismissing 'Des Abends' as 'belonging to a school that runs counter to our ideas of musical propriety',[21] and on the Piano Concerto (which, in a brief aside, he managed to damn with the epithet, 'laboured and ambitious') by paying homage instead to the pianist's 'enthusiasm'. 'Madame Schumann', he wrote, in a masterly piece of typical English obliqueness, 'played the music of her husband as if she had composed it herself.'[22] But the combination of a performance of extracts from *Carnaval* with the publication in the concert programme of Schumann's description of the genesis of the work, with its reference to the Davidbündler (the 'League of David') and the musical Philistines against whom they waged their imaginary artistic battles – tried the patience of fellow critic, Henry Chorley,[23] chief music critic for *The Athenaeum*, too far. 'Madame Schumann at her *Second Recital* ...', Chorley wrote,

> placed us in a position which is not to be evaded without failure of duty to those who look to us. Misled by natural predilections, and encouraged by the forbearance of her English hosts, who have shrunk from giving her pain, she seems

determined to offer Dr. Schumann's music in all the fullness of its eccentricity to the public. What is more, Madame Schumann, resolute in her faith, will not allow us to forget that Dr. Schumann's attempts – whether prosy or trivial – were put forward under pretext of a "mission," and in scorn of others who thought more modestly of their place in the world of Art than himself. …

We can find nothing of the Carnival in these fourteen little pieces; which are as insignificant in scale as a child's lesson, yet without the prettiness and the character which alone make such trifles pass. Uncouth, faded, and wanting in clearness, they seem to us; and curious as commented on, and commended by, the above little history [i.e. the description of the work]. From this it must be inferred, that "an enthusiastic aim at the highest cultivation of music," and the crusade "against pedantry and hypocrisy," were, in Germany, monopolized by the association so queerly named. Indeed, we know that such a merit has been claimed for Dr. Schumann and his associates by themselves. Nevertheless, at the time when these poor and dreary trifles were written – in criticism of contemporary German music and its direction – there was still living and labouring in, and for, Germany, with all his heart and soul and strength, a certain man called Mendelssohn; "dry and empty" (to repeat the jargon of a sect), because his compositions, being pure music, stand in need of no historical or mystical explanation; and because, having studied his art as a science, he could not be other than "correct." – Well, he has his fame, which is increasing; and these 'Davidsbündler' have made their noise. They have blotted their reams of newspaper – full of dismal jokes at others and fulsome mutual admiration. They have put forth their library of pedantic music – since what pedantry is worse than the assumption of romance where no fancy has fired the brain; and of profundity were no real thought has guided the pen? So let it be; but if these things are to be thrust on us – if no warning will be taken, no consideration understood – we must speak the plain truth, in protection of the modest and the half-instructed.[24]

Davison, married to one of London's most celebrated pianists of the day, Arabella Goddard, whose interests he robustly defended, could have had reason for damning with faint praise performances given by Clara Schumann. It was, however, other works by Schumann that tended to provoke his particular spleen. The final Philharmonic concert of the 1856 season, which took place at the conclusion of Clara's visit, was devoted, again at the request of the Prince Consort, to a performance of Schumann's work for chorus, soloists and orchestra, *Das Paradies und die Peri*, Op. 50 – a work which he had envisaged as 'a new genre for the concert hall'[25] and which, following its first performance in Leipzig in December 1843,[26] had done most to advance Schumann's reputation elsewhere in Europe.[27] It was *Das Paradies und die Peri* which, for those German commentators who had previously been critical of some of Schumann's earlier works, provided evidence that, having recognised earlier errors of artistic judgement, he was now striving for 'truth and beauty' and expressing these in a 'clear, simple generally accessible and comprehensible manner.'[28]

For the London audience in June 1856, however, this work proved yet another disappointment: according to Davison, the evening was regarded by *habitués* of the Philharmonic concerts as 'utterly thrown away upon worthless music, to the exclusion of some of those imperishable works for the perpetual reproduction of which, in conjunction with novelties of well-approved excellence, the Philharmonic Society was instituted.'[29] The occasion gave rise to one of Davison's more vituperative tirades:

Robert Schumann has had his innings, and been bowled out – like Richard Wagner. *Paradies and the Peri* has gone to the tomb of the Lohengrins.

When, to drop metaphor, is all this trifling to cease? How many times shall we have to insist that the new school – the school of "the Future" – will never do in England? If the Germans choose to muddle themselves with beer, smoke, and metaphysics, till all things appear to them through a distorted medium, or dimly suggested through a cloud of mist, there is no reason why sane and sober Britons should follow their example.

...

After the disastrous failure of Richard Wagner and his music, last season, there was no excuse for devoting a whole concert to the music of another composer of "the Future", let "the Future" enjoy the exclusive benefit of their inspirations. Why perturb and vex the present to no purpose? The Present – as the most enthusiastic partisans of Schumann and Wagner admit, nay insist – is incapable of fathoming the depths of their philosophy; all the length of line which it can throw out is insufficient to get half-way down to the bottom. To abandon it as hopeless, then, and rest satisfied with Mozart and his successors, would surely be the wiser course.

Such an experiment as that of Monday evening must not, on any account, be repeated ... Imagine – oh, uninitiated reader! – three uninterrupted hours of Schumann, three uninterrupted hours of organised sound without a single tune! We are not exaggerating, but stating a simple fact. Seriously, this passes the limits of toleration.[30]

Measured against Mendelssohn

It is impossible to understand the reception of Schumann's music in England in the 1850s and 1860s without taking account of the standing which Mendelssohn then enjoyed in English musical circles. Admired and feted as a person as well as a musician, Mendelssohn had visited England on several occasions in the decade before his death in 1847, culminating in the rapturous reception accorded to the first performance of *Elijah* in 1846. For English critics such as Davison and Chorley, and others of similar persuasion, Mendelssohn epitomized the future direction which music in England should take: in him, they had found their 'ideal'. In their eyes, Mendelssohn's music offered the model for the establishment of a British 'school' of composition – an aspiration which by the mid-nineteenth century found, in principle, widespread support.[31] The emergence of a 'pretender' whose music appeared to discount traditional classical principles and whose supporters seemed, by promoting their favourite's interests, to risk his usurping Mendelssohn's position in the musical pantheon (consolidated by the latter's early death), strengthened critical opposition, as the extract from Chorley's review of *Carnaval* suggests. In the opinion of Joseph Bennett, who served as Davison's deputy at *The Musical World* from 1868 (by which time he was also serving as music critic for the *Pall Mall Gazette*), Davison made it a personal crusade to do all in his power to oppose the advancement of Schumann's music in England.

While the identification of Schumann with a new 'aesthetic' school in Germany certainly did little to endear him to English sensibilities, it was fundamentally on compositional grounds that critics like Chorley and Davison and others of similar cast of mind found fault with Schumann's music. The element of fantasy underpinning many of the early works for piano provided grounds for some of their reservations. Chorley, who had encountered Schumann's music during visits to Germany, expressed his distaste at the 'very wildest strain of extravagant mysticism' which he detected in works such as *Kriesleriana*.[32] This tendency he regarded as an undesirable sign of 'eccentricity and singularity' and associated with their 'design of not displaying any settled effect'. Equally unappealing, in his mind, was the fact that Schumann's style displayed 'a certain thickness, freaked with frivolity – a mastery which produces no effect – a resolution to deceive the ear'.[33]

For some, this lack of readiness to adapt to prevailing opinion suggested a certain obduracy on Schumann's part. Joseph Bennett believed that the fault, 'if fault there be, lies with Schumann himself, who chose, or was impelled, to write, caring less for the beauty of his work than for its faithfully reflecting certain trains of thought of emotional conditions. He could have taken no more certain means of arousing widespread distrust, if not dislike. The sticklers for form would have nothing to do with one who made form subservient, while those who wished to be pleased without effort of their own, turned away from music the meaning of which – if it had any – required patient seeking out.'[34]

It is clear that for the leading English critics of the day, steeped in the music of the classics, Schumann's approach to musical construction proved particularly troubling: they were alienated by what seemed to their ears a 'want of continuous developing power'[35] in his larger works. Schumann's tendency to take a few brief motivic ideas and extend them throughout the course of a movement or section, by repeating or transposing themes, enabling them to appear in different lights and convey contrasting moods, was construed simply as an absence of fluency. For Davison, this technique made Schumann's longer works 'appear fragmentary, as though a number of little bits, each in itself more or less attractive, had been cleverly patched together',[36] and resulted in compositions that were, overall, 'ill-knit and unsymmetrical'.[37]

The same charge was laid against Schumann in terms of melody. For those accustomed to regular and clearly delineated melodic shapes, what appeared to be 'vagueness in the melodic outlines of the themes' proved disconcerting. The fact that there was 'less melody' than in Mendelssohn, and that there was 'a certain roughness and abruptness in his harmonies and the transitions of his composition, coupled with forced effects, which look like striving for originality, from which Mendelssohn is entirely free'[38] provided further grounds for adverse judgements. Such characteristics, interpreted by some as evidence of freshness and originality, were in the opinion of traditionally-minded critics, damning evidence of a lack of thorough musical education. And underlying all was the suspicion that through extensive use of so many unfamiliar devices – 'trickeries and piquancies' masquerading as 'originality' – Schumann was seeking to conceal fundamental weaknesses in his compositional armoury. The reference in the remarks by Chorley, quoted above, to 'a resolution to deceive the ear' is typical of this line of thinking. It is little wonder that those whose views of musical quality were so strongly orientated towards classical proportions and compositional techniques found Schumann's music wanting when measured in these terms. Infrequent encounters with the music in concert did little to accustom English listeners to the new sound world which Schumann's music encapsulated.

Clara Schumann's later visits

Despite the setbacks of her first visit to England in 1856, Clara Schumann made further visits in 1857 and 1859. It is noticeable, however, that on both these visits, she rarely performed works by her husband, particularly in the more high profile events. There is no record of works by Schumann in her 1857 London concerts; in 1859, she occasionally included works such as the Andante and Variations for two pianos and, with the violinist Joachim, extracts from the *Fantaisiestücke*, Op. 73, but avoided performing any of the solo works. In the following decade it was in large measure through the advocacy of others that the tide of opinion began to turn in Schumann's favour.

However by the time of Clara's fourth visit to England, in 1865, two new concert-giving bodies had been established, each of which was to play a vital role in changing English attitudes to the music of Schumann. The first of these was the pioneering series of Saturday orchestral concerts at the Crystal Palace – an institution which in the words of Michael Musgrave, was to provide 'the major impetus to the development of British musical life' in the second half of the nineteenth century.[39] These concerts at the Crystal Palace began in 1855 and, with the German-born August Manns as conductor, working in close partnership with George Grove (Secretary of the Crystal Palace Company), continued uninterrupted for the remainder of the century. Like the second concert series which was instrumental in changing attitudes – the series of Popular Concerts initiated by Arthur Chappell in the newly-opened St. James's Hall in central London,[40] which focused on solo and chamber music performance – this new initiative was committed to the presentation of more recent works and to representing more varied compositional and stylistic approaches, and catered for larger and more diverse audiences. By the 1860s, both had begun to make their mark on English musical life.

On returning to London in 1865 Clara quickly sensed the change. Chappell proposed that the first of the Monday Popular Concerts in which Clara performed should be devoted solely to the music of Schumann: the programme for the 'Schumann Night' comprised the first String Quartet in A minor, the Piano Quartet, the *Fantaisiestücke* (piano and violin), the Symphonic Studies, Op. 13, and two of

Schumann's songs.[41] Looking back on the success of the evening, Clara wrote in her diary, 'Would that Robert had experienced this, for never he would have thought that he would ever have achieved such recognition in England (for his was certainly the greater part of this reception).'[42] And the change which Clara observed was not confined to the audience at the Popular Concerts: she also noted in the diary that by comparison with five years earlier she felt 'an extraordinary difference in atmosphere as far as Robert in concerned. I now find to my great astonishment a large number of Schumannites – one of the most fervent is Grove ...'[43]

Grove, Manns and the Crystal Palace

Grove was certainly a fervent Schumannite and, in his collaboration with Manns at the Crystal Palace which began in 1855, and where he (Grove) provided the programme notes and was in every sense an equal partner in the artistic project,[44] the promotion of Schumann's music took the form of a crusade at least as impassioned and as consistent as that waged by Davison in the press. In Bennett's view, credit for the change in English attitudes to Schumann which had occurred by the late 1860s was largely attributable to the work of Manns and Grove[45] at the Crystal Palace:

> Much of this result is owed to the Crystal Palace Concerts, at which Schumann has been exhibited through evil as well as good report with a constancy that deserves success. Happily for the composer, Messrs. Grove and Manns – each in his way as great an enthusiast as ever was their common idol [i.e. Schumann] – possess exceptional resources, and are able to do their work in the most perfect manner.[46]

As Bennett implies, it was at the weekly Crystal Palace concerts that audiences – large by comparison with those in most other concert locations of the time – were most frequently able to hear Schumann's music. This began from the very first season (1855/56), during which Manns' newly formed orchestra tackled the Symphony No 4 in D minor, performing it not once, but twice within a month,[47] 'in order to give an opportunity of forming a better judgment as to its merits than could be gained at a first hearing', as Grove sagely observed in the programme-book.[48] It was a work to which the orchestra returned regularly: by 1867, the Fourth Symphony had been heard eight times at these concerts, during which time Crystal Palace audiences had also been introduced to the other three symphonies, several of the overtures[49] and the Piano Concerto with Clara as soloist. In the next few years Clara performed this work at the Crystal Palace almost annually, and by this stage it had already been taken up by many other pianists. Contrary to some critics' initial expectations, it was to become one of the piano concertos heard most frequently in London concerts.[50]

Grove, an assiduous letter-writer, and a colleague with whom Davison regularly corresponded, who also did battle on Schumann's behalf with the pen, was quick to react to Davison's verbal attacks. In a letter to Davison from the mid 1860s, he expressed his continued surprise and disappointment that the latter was still unconvinced of the merits of Schumann's music:

> How I wish I knew wherein the difference lies between you and me about R.S. I think I love & enjoy Beethoven … as much as you do: – you yourself can't delight more in Mendelssohn Symphonies & overtures & trios than I – then why this sudden, this most profound jab [?] before Schumann. For the life of me I can't see the force of the words you use – "pretentious", "laboured", "unconnected rhapsody", "gloomy heaps" – "uninteresting" etc… . To say that his music is not so bright & cheerful and <u>out-of-doorish</u> as Mendelssohn's is simply to enunciate a truism – but what then? Is all music to be in the same style? And why compare them? Why compare their styles, anymore than compare the styles of your wife and his wife? Each are beautiful and fine in their own particular lines and there I am content to leave them. After all, science & construction apart, the <u>ultima ratio</u> in music must be its power of affecting one and this Schumann does to me in a very great degree and certainly in a <u>peculiar</u> one. I can't help recognizing a flavour or quality,

independent and in addition to anything in Beethoven or M[endelssohn] which quality touches a new chord in my nature – you are wrong about my enthusiasm being mere sentiment for his widow. His things touched & moved me long before I heard her play. But of course it's natural that she should play them with more apprehension [?] than anyone else.[51]

Davison remained unpersuaded to the end. But the momentum created by the sheer volume of performances of Schumann's music – at the Crystal Palace, at the Monday Popular Concerts, and in the chamber recitals given by increasing numbers of artists – helped even more than words had done to turn the tide of popular opinion. During the 1870s earlier resistance began to give way to acceptance and understanding. Performance classes (based on piano transcriptions) introduced at the Crystal Palace gave further impetus to the study of previously unfamiliar works and the development of a cadre of music lovers ready to make judgements of their own.[52] With the establishment of the new Royal College of Music under Grove's directorship in 1882, the music of Schumann was central to the curriculum from the outset and helped further to consolidate the standing of his music in English circles. For Davison the discovery that his deputy at *The Musical World*, Joseph Bennett, formerly loyal acolyte, had defected from the cause, and now identified himself as a Schumannite[53] must have come as a particular blow. The control of taste which Davison and his allies had autocratically exercised began to slip away: his campaign to obstruct the new ultimately a failure.

The article in which Bennett confessed his change of heart,[54] which Grove celebrated as making 'an epoch in English musical criticism', argued with force that '[t]he domain of music is a wide one, and affords ample room for Robert Schumann. Even if this were not so, room should be made for one who comes with such independent thought and original expression.' Schumann, he urged, 'should be welcomed as one who speaks, because having something new to say.' In the fullness of time, thanks to the impact of live performance and music education, he was.

Notes

1. Joseph Bennett (1831–1911) was active as a music critic for forty years, and contributed to numerous publications. His autobiography, *Forty Years of Music, 1865–1905* (London: Methuen & Co., 1908), includes a list of the publications he served.
2. For comment on changing patterns of concert audiences, see William Weber, *Music and the Middle Class* (London: Croom Helm, 1975).
3. See, for example, Reinhard Kapp, 'Schumann in his time and since', *The Cambridge Companion to Schumann*, ed. Beate Perrey (Cambridge: Cambridge University Press, 2007), 228; Arnfried Edler, *Robert Schumann und seine Zeit* ([Laaber bei Hernau]: Laaber-Verlag, [1982]), 307.
4. In 1840 the University of Jena conferred on Schumann an honorary doctorate. In 1843, having already been honoured in Germany, Schumann was made an honorary member of the *Verein zur Beförderung der Tonkunst* in the Netherlands.
5. For example, by Liszt (1856) and von Wasielewski (1858).
6. Kapp, 'Schumann in his time and since', 236.
7. Similar factions existed in Germany, where supporters of Schumann were known as the 'Schumannier'.
8. Kapp, 'Schumann in his time and since', 224.
9. Programme-book, Monday Popular Concert, 1 December, 1862.
10. Eduard Röckel (1816–1899), composer of much piano music, who studied with Hummel (his uncle), was among a number of foreign musicians who settled in England in 1848. The Piano Quartet, written in 1842, was first published in 1845. For details of the programme, see *Programmes of the Musical Union*, vol. 4 (1848), March 28. For information on the Musical Union, a society established by John Ella in 1845 for the performance of chamber music, see Christina Bashford, 'John Ella and the Making of the Musical Union' in *Music and British Culture, 1785–1914: Essays in Honour of Cyril Ehrlich*, ed. C. Bashford and L. Langley (Oxford and New York: Oxford University Press, 2000).
11. Apart from occasional works by Spohr and Onslow, chamber music works by Mozart, Beethoven and Mendelssohn dominated concert programmes in the first decade of the Musical Union's existence (1845–1855).
12. *Programmes of the Musical Union*, vol. 9 (1853), March 17. This comment may well have referred to the dramatic use of diminished seventh chords in the first movement. Accounts of the positive reception of both works in Leipzig can be found in the *Leipziger Allgemeine musikalische Zeitung*, 45 (1843), 47.
13. *The Musical World*, 31/12, 10 March, 1853, 172.
14. *The Musical World* appeared from 1836 to 1891. During the period covered in this article, its influence extended widely throughout the English-speaking world. For accounts of Davison as critic, see Charles Reid, *The Music Monster* (London: Quartet Books Ltd., 1984) and Joseph Bennett, 'Some Recollections. IX. Critics I Have Known,' in *The Musical Times*, 40/676 (1899), 381–84.

15 Concert of 17 March 1853. For programme details, see Myles Birket Foster, *The History of the Philharmonic Society of London 1813–1912* (London: John Lane, 1912). For review, see *The Musical World* 31/15, 9 April, 1853, 226.
16 See, for example, *Leipziger Allgemeine musikalische Zeitung*, 50 (1848), 928.
17 *Times*, 7 June 1854, 7.
18 For details of these visits, see Janet Ritterman, „Gegensätze, Ecken und scharfe Kanten" – Clara Schumanns Besuche in England, 1856–1888, *Clara Schumann 1819–1896*, ed. I. Bodsch und G. Nauhaus (Bonn: Stadtmuseum Bonn, 1996), 235–63. Most visits lasted several months.
19 New Philharmonic Society programme, 14 May, 1856, 4.
20 Berthold Litzmann, *Clara Schumann. Ein Künstlerleben* (Leipzig: Breitkopf und Härtel, 1910–18). 3 Bde, 3. Auflage, Bd 2, 409.
21 *Times*, 17 April 1856, 9.
22 Ibid.
23 Henry Chorley (1808–1872) wrote for *The Athenaeum* from 1833 to 1868. This journal was regarded as one of the most influential of English arts periodicals.
24 *Athenaeum*, No 1495, 21 June, 1856, 786.
25 Letter to Carl Kossmaly, 5 May 1843, quoted in *The New Grove Dictionary of Music and Musicians* (London: Macmillan Publishers Ltd., 2001), vol. 22, 777.
26 *Leipziger Allgemeine musikalische Zeitung*, 45 (1843), 952–55.
27 Within the next five years *Das Paradies und die Peri* had been performed, to general acclaim, in over half a dozen other German cities, as well as in the Netherlands.
28 *Leipziger Allgemeine musikalische Zeitung*, 49 (1847), 143.
29 *Times*, 24 June 1856, 12.
30 *The Musical World*, 28 June, 1856, 408.
31 See Janet Ritterman, 'The Royal College of Music, 1883–1899: pianists and their contribution to the forming of a national conservatory', *Musical Education in Europe (1770–1914)*, (Berlin: Berliner Wissenschafts-Verlag, 2005), vol. 2, 352.
32 *Papillons* and *Carnaval* presumably also fell into the category of works that Chorley considered similarly tainted.
33 Henry Chorley, *Modern German Music: Recollections and Criticisms* (London: Smith Elder, 1854), 51–53.
34 *Pall Mall Gazette*, 30 November, 1868, 11.
35 *Times*, 4 December 1865, 5.
36 *Times*, 21 November, 1864, 9.
37 *Times*, 20 January, 1863, 9.
38 Crystal Palace programme note (written by George Grove), 15 March, 1856, quoted in *The Musical Times*, 1 November, 1905, 717.
39 Michael Musgrave, *The Musical Life of the Crystal Palace* (Cambridge: Cambridge University Press, 1995), 67.
40 This began with a relatively-shortlived Saturday series (1859–1876). In 1865 a Monday series was introduced, which continued till 1904.
41 *Times,* 16 May, 1865, 14.
42 Litzmann, *Clara Schumann*, Bd 3, 180.

43 Ibid.
44 For a tribute to their achievements see *Times,* 15 October, 1877, 11.
45 For a series of articles on Grove's various activities, see *George Grove, Music and Victorian Culture*, ed. M. Musgrave (Basingstoke and New York: Palgrave Macmillan, 2003).
46 *Pall Mall Gazette*, 30 November, 1868, 11.
47 These performances took place on 16 February and 15 March, 1856. This was prior to Clara Schumann's arrival in London, where her first concert took place on 14 April.
48 Quoted in *The Musical Times*, 1 November, 1905, 717.
49 Overtures to *Genoveva, Manfred, Julius Caesar, Hermann and Dorothea.*
50 By the turn of the century it had been performed twenty-four times at the Philharmonic Society, and also repeatedly at the Crystal Palace.
51 British Library, Add. MS 70921, ff.149v–151r. Letter of 20 June (probably 1865). Word transcribed as 'apprehension' is unclear in the original letter.
52 See Musgrave, *Crystal Palace,* 168–70.
53 Bennett, *Forty Years of Music,* 109–10.
54 *Pall Mall Gazette*, 30 November, 1868, 11.

19: Georg Benda's Keyboard Sonatas

Warren Bourne

Although he was best known for his church music in his own lifetime, and is generally associated with the theatre by modern scholars, Georg Benda composed a small but interesting collection of keyboard sonatas that make up a significant contribution to the repertoire of the clavichord.

As the fourth member of the Bohemian Benda family to find employment at the court of Frederick the Great, Georg Benda was in some respects an outsider in relation to the traditions of clavichord playing pre-eminently represented by the Bach family and their various colleagues and successors. Born in 1722 in Bohemia and receiving his early musical training in his homeland, Georg was twenty years old when he moved to Berlin and joined the court orchestra as a violinist. Once there he appears to have gravitated into the circle of Carl Philip Emmanuel Bach and developed his skills as a composer and keyboard player. Both men may have been members of the Berlin Club that formed part of the circle of friends, colleagues and fellow artists that are recalled in Bach's character pieces (Berg, 1988, pp. 28–30). Their relationship apparently continued after Benda had gained employment away from Berlin and one has only to study the sonatas to recognise that, as Jan Racek (1978, p. x) writes, 'this contact with C. Ph. Em Bach was very important and fruitful for Benda's further artistic development and the shaping of his musical thought'.

It is not entirely clear how many sonatas Benda may have composed. Newman (1972, p. 436) lists eighteen such sonatas in his brief entry on Benda in his study of the sonata and seventeen are reprinted in Volumes 24 and 37 of *Musica Antiqua Bohemica* (Racek 1978). However, an additional sonata was printed by Haffner in his *Oeuvres mêlées contenant vi sonates pour le clavecin* around 1760 (Drake et al., 2001, p. 229) and another sonata reported to be in manuscript is said to be an early version of a sonata later printed by the composer between 1780 and 1787 (Drake et al., 2001, p. 229). A group of six sonatas was first published in 1757: *Sei sonate per il cembalo solo da Giorgio Benda: Stampate da Giorgio Ludovico Winter a Berlino 1757*. These comprise the first six sonatas in Volume 24 of *Musica Antiqua Bohemica* (hereinafter MAB 24), whilst other modern editions are edited by Hugo Ruf (1997) and Christopher Hogwood (1997). The sonatas included by the composer in his series *Sammlung vermischter Clavierstücke für geübte und ungeübte Spieler* published between 1780 and 1787 make up Sonatas 7 to 16 of MAB 24, whilst the same series includes in Vol. 37 one additional multi-movement sonata (No. 9) and 32 additional pieces called 'sonatinas'. This study focuses on the sixteen sonatas in three movements that make up the core of this repertoire. Although these clearly divide into two groups, the first six published in 1757 and the remaining ten published between 1780 and 1787, it is likely that the various sonatas were in fact composed over a much longer period of time than the years indicated by those dates.

Secondary literature on Benda is scattered in three languages: German, Czech and English. The only substantial comments in English on the sonatas are the preface by Jan Racek (1978) and Newman's introductory remarks in his study of the sonata (1972, pp. 435–8) and in his own modern edition of the first sonata from the 1757 set (Newman, 1947). He is rarely even mentioned in English language texts about the keyboard repertoire, although two German studies make more than passing mention (Stilz, 1932, pp. 45–54; Walters, 1994, p. 230). None of these writers address the question of which keyboard instrument may have been the primary vehicle for the sonatas, and the flexibility of eighteenth century performance practices precludes any hard and fast determination. Nevertheless, it is worth noting Benda's own remarks in the preface to Volume 1 of the *Sammlung vermischther Clavierstücke* in 1780.

Firstly, he singled out the Sonata in c minor (MAB 24, p. 7) as being 'set for the clavichord, or for those few players who know the superiority of expression that this instrument has over the harpsichord' (as quoted in translation in Hogwood, 1993, p. 187). Then he commented on the availability of good clavichords in Germany at the time: 'unfortunately, in the larger cities where music flourishes, for every six good harpsichords, scarcely one good clavichord can be obtained, nevertheless the latter can be found in Braunschweig, Göttingen, Gera and here in Gotha, where the instrument maker Paul is becoming a very good builder' (as quoted in Vermeij 1996, p. 111). These comments might suggest a decided preference for the clavichord, and it should be further recalled the collegial relationships between Benda and C. P. E. Bach and the latter's strong preference for the clavichord. Many of Benda's sonatas, and not just the Sonata in c minor, are ideally suited to performance on the clavichord.

As has already been mentioned, the sixteen sonatas comprise three movement cycles, with the movements invariably in the tempo order of fast, slow, fast. The tonal schemes tend to be fairly conservative, with the outer movements in the same key and only the middle movement modulating elsewhere. In these second movements there is greater variety of key selection: relative major or minor in seven sonatas, subdominant in five, opposite tonic major or minor in two, dominant in one, and submediant in one minor key sonata. Collectively, the forty-eight movements represent an exploration of only seven major keys (no more than three sharps or flats) and six minor keys (no more than two sharps or four flats). However, one of the slow movements reveals a much more adventurous use of tonality. In the 'Un poco largo' of Sonata 12 (1780/7) the middle movement in E flat major includes an episode with the separately signed key signature of four sharps. Neither key implied by this signature eventuates. Instead the music must be understood enharmonically as implying G flat major, as the music that prepares this extraordinary episode has already moved from the home key to its tonic minor of e flat minor, whilst the episode in four sharps in fact cadences most firmly with a perfect cadence, repeated several times, into F sharp major, enharmonically G flat major, the relative of e flat minor.

There are six sonatas out of the sixteen in minor keys. This is a high proportion compared with most late eighteenth century repertoires, with the exception of Benda's friend and colleague, C. P. E. Bach, who used minor keys far more frequently than any other composer of the period. Of Benda's minor key sonatas, one retains the minor mode through all three movements: No. 3 in d minor, with a slow movement in the dominant minor. As to the affective character of the minor key sonatas, there does seem to be a more impassioned rhetoric in some of the movements, particularly those from 1757 in d minor and g minor. The latter sonata (No. 5), with a first movement displaying strong dotted rhythm figures and an abrupt main motive that reiterates a single semitone, might be thought to anticipate something of Daniel Schubart's opinions about the key of g minor. He wrote that g minor reflected 'discontent, malaise, stretched into a disproportionate plane, untiring, gnawing, rancour and disgust' (as quoted in translation by Paul Marks 1972, p. 93). The later movements do not sustain this intensity, however. In the two sonatas using the key of a minor (No. 3, slow movements only; and No. 9, the two outer movements), the expression would also be compatible with Schubart's declaration of 'femininity and softness of character'. It is perhaps significant too that Benda chose to cast the one sonata that he explicitly named for the clavichord, in the key of c minor (No. 7) and that a later sonata (No. 12) uses the same key to contextualise some of his most complex tonal explorations.

The first movements are all either binary structures, or display more or less developed sonata principles. As might be expected, the six sonatas of 1757, with one exception, are straightforward binary movements. Only Sonata 4 in F suggests strong tonal and thematic contrasts between a tonic and dominant group in the first half, together with an extended development before the return of the earlier music reconciled in the tonic, in short, a move towards the sonata principle. In the later ten compositions, sonata structures occur more frequently, although as will be observed subsequently, Benda's approach to the form is by no means stereotyped. In the middle movements there is a consistent preference for the various binary schemes, some simple and direct, others more developed. Two of the movements reveal a ternary (ABA) form. Benda prefers a fairly steadily paced slow movement, with thirteen out of the sixteen sonatas headed up with what Türk (1982, pp. 105–7) considers to be directions for moderate tempos, such as *Andante, Andantino* or *Larghetto*. No use is made of the direction *Adagio*, but in three sonatas the music is headed with *Largo* (Sonata 4 with a slow movement in f minor and Sonata 10) or *Un poco Largo* (Sonata 12). Only in these three sonatas does Benda turn away from the easily flowing grace that characterises most of the sonatas which allows for the generous application of keyboard melismas and ornamental figures, in favour of a more homophonic breadth of uncluttered melody. For the faster final movements, Benda uses simple binary in the first four sonatas of 1757, and ternary in Sonatas 5 and 6 (with incipient sonata features in Sonata 6). In the later sonatas there is much variety of form, ranging from simple binary to the full working out of sonata principles. In Sonata 8 there is, exceptionally, an 'Andantino con variazioni', the only example of a set of variations in the collection. There is an occasional use of dance genres: a Siciliana in Sonata 3, 'Tempo di Minuetto' in Sonata 5, and uncomplicated Italianate gigues in Sonatas 9, 10, 15.

In a small number of sonatas there is a tendency to bind the separate movements more closely together. In Sonatas 6, 9, 10 and 15 the middle movements close with a half cadence on the dominant of the key of the subsequent finale and in Sonata 14 similarly, but the close is on the dominant of the movement, which coincides with the home tonality of the finale. Apart from the broad use of tonality, these appear to be the only attempts to create links between movements, there being no evidence of thematic relationships or use of incipits to create a sense of unity between movements of the sonatas.

In common with almost all later eighteenth century keyboard repertoire, none of the sonatas demand a high level of mechanical virtuosity, but they reveal a fluent and imaginative awareness of keyboard idioms. Writing in two parts dominates the textures, which tend to favour the middle range of the keyboard. The 1757 sonatas exploit a compass from C below the bass clef to E flat above the treble clef, whilst the later sonatas from No. 9 (1780/7) will occasionally extend to the full five octaves of the late eighteenth century clavichord. The variegated textures, often rhetorical and unaccompanied melodic gestures, use of prescribed dynamic contrast, frequent appoggiatura figures and parallel harmonization of melodies in thirds and sixths, all point to a touch-sensitive instrument for the performance of these sonatas. These traits have been especially identified as being associated with the clavichord by Joel Speerstra in a study of C. P. E. Bach's keyboard sonatas (1996, p. 43). His observations, together with the comments from Benda reported earlier in this study, would encourage the hypothesis that Benda's sonatas were written for the clavichord.

The 1757 set of sonatas reveals the composer fully at home with the sonata idioms as practised pre-eminently by the two oldest Bach sons, W. F. and C. P. E. Both sons had completed or published significant sets of keyboard sonatas in the 1740s and 1750s that could have served as models for Benda's sonatas. The use of the keyboard shows the same patterns and gestures to be found in their sonatas and the use of ornamentation lies well within the range discussed in C. P. E. Bach's *Essay on the True Art of Playing Keyboard Instruments* (1974). Three ornamental figures particularly associated with C. P. E. Bach are absent from the notation of Benda's 1757 set: the trilled turn, the *bebung* and the *portato*, although the first two ornaments might well be used at appropriate points in performance. Although the individual sonatas conform precisely to the outer characteristics of his models, the actual musical style is more free flowing and consistent in its rhythmic and textural usage. Benda largely avoids any tendency towards the involved contrapuntal writing and intricate keyboard textures of W.F. Bach, as well as the rhetorical pauses, sudden changes of tempo and other disruptive devices so familiar even in the earlier sonata sets by C. P. E. Bach. Whilst Benda's music rarely falls into the easy *galant* style of his many Italianate contemporaries, several movements recall the evenly patterned motivic regularity of earlier eighteenth century baroque keyboard pieces. Most of the sonatas exploit a straightforward binary structure for each movement, only the Minuet from Sonata 5 adopts a simple ternary form for its modest dimensions. In the first movement of Sonata 4 there is an incipient expansion of the music towards the sonata principle.

Some of these points may be more closely examined in Sonata 4 in F major. The first movement, *Allegretto assai moderato*, opens with a very leisurely and expansive eight bar melody that closes on the dominant. The keyboard writing is essentially in two parts, with the opening motive harmonized in parallel thirds. The second idea picks up the outline of the bass in bars 6 – 8 (e – f – a – b flat – c) and repeats it under semi-quaver scale passages that quickly lead the music into the secondary dominant that would in later sonatas announce the shift of the music to the dominant. Following this eight bar transition a contrasting melody implying an expressive *rubato* in the performance of the syncopated triplets is presented three times with varying figuration, before the first section closes with the expected repeat of the music. The second half of the movement proceeds with the return of the melody, now transposed to the dominant, but shifting to a minor (III of the home key) in its eight bar period. This is again answered by a development of the semiquavers from the first section before the music closes with several pauses and an allusion to the secondary melody, still in a minor. There immediately follows a full recapitulation of all the material heard earlier in the movement, now transposed to appear in the tonic. By exploiting long range thematic and tonal contrast rather than the short breathed, constant fluctuations of motive and figuration typical of most movements in the 1757 set, this movement comes much closer to sonata ideas than others.

There follows an expressive *Largo* in the tonic minor, with two short phrases replete with *appoggiatura* figures. The music makes effective use of monophonic melodic gestures contrasting with three and four part textures in suave thirds and sixths. As in many of his slow movements, Benda makes good use of melodic chromaticism, including a hint of Neapolitan sixths to intensify the closing cadence phrases. The sonata is rounded off with a lively binary movement in which running semiquaver figures dance their way to an uncomplicated finish in two part counterpoint.

More typical perhaps of the restless, constantly shifting motivic patterns of Benda's pieces is the first movement of the previously mentioned Sonata 5 in g minor. In the space of 45 bars, representing the first half of a binary movement, the music exposes eight distinct motivic gestures, each one resolved into its own cadence: a musical style that lacks both the continuous unfolding of a baroque piece and the large scale dynamic flow of the later eighteenth century sonata. What keeps the music coherent, apart from the obvious use of the functional harmonic relationships, is the way in which each new motive seizes upon an element in the preceding passage, as a springboard for the continuation of the musical syntax. Hence the surface variety, the most evident aspect of the music as it unfolds, maintains its focus by a process of renewal from one moment to another without recourse to motivic recurrence or, as was to become clearer in high classic sonatas, resorting to an underlying unity of motivic material.

It is more difficult to generalize about the sonatas published serially between 1780 and 1787, if only because they were not issued as a set, but rather represent Benda's musical development over perhaps thirty years. Much had happened in that time, including publication of all C. P. E. Bach's later sets of sonatas and other keyboard pieces, and the first sonata compositions of Haydn and Mozart, not to mention a whole host of *Kleinmeister*. One trend that Benda has in common with other late eighteenth century keyboard composers is for the latest sonatas to suggest a falling away of such difficulties of technique and expression that had occurred in earlier sonatas, in favour of a general simplification of style. It is likely that this change was in response to publishers and amateur performers wanting a more straightforward repertoire, rather than any failure on the part of the composer. Benda's last four sonatas, published in Volumes 5 and 6 of the 1780/7 series, may be quite unchallenging and contain mostly short and uncomplicated movements, but they also possess in full measure the charm and grace of the earlier pieces.

Of the ten sonatas published between 1780 and 1787, three will be singled out for closer study, in that they suggest the richness and imagination of Benda's sonata writing.

Sonata 7 in c minor has already been noted as the composition referred to by Benda as being particularly suited to the clavichord. The opening *Allegro moderato* is an extended binary movement with incipient sonata characteristics. The first theme exploits the dynamic contrasts inherent in the clavichord in an eight bar phrase in the 'singing *Allegro*' style typical of the period, albeit allowing the line to include idiomatic keyboard flourishes. The flexible nature of the writing is exemplified by a cadence on the dominant (in which the dotted rhythms would be softened in performance to retain the flow of the surrounding triplets) which is immediately followed by arpeggiated figures on VI, the relative major key. The fluctuations between *cantabile* melody and triplet scale and arpeggio figures are maintained throughout, so that there is no clear differentiation of thematic material between the opening tonic and the E flat major of the subsequent music. Neither this feature nor the abrupt and unprepared move to the relative major suggest any of the dynamic tension associated with the later sonata, rather, the movement is true to the methods and proportions of a mid-century binary structure. At the mid-cadence the music is quickly turned to the home key dominant, whilst for the continuation of the movement after the repeat the key shifts rapidly continue through the dominant minor into a return of the opening phrase, now in f minor. No new material is presented, but previously heard music is cast into the new key with corresponding changes of texture. Despite a cadence back to V and a rhetorical pause, there is no strong recapitulation. Although some figuration and melodies recur in the home key the prevailing impression is of a balanced complement to the first half of the piece, centred on f minor and A flat major, before the final cadence mirrors the abrupt twists of the mid-cadence phrases, to end the music back in c minor.

The following *Andante sostenuto* begins with an expansive melody in the warm tenor register of the clavichord, with opportunities for such expressive devices as dynamic inflection and *portato* effects. A second group of motives on V of the movement's principal key (E flat major) adds to these expressive means some effective contrasts of tessitura, before closing on V at the half way point. A hint of the initial melody in a tonally unstable context provides a few lines of transition back to the return of the entire first section, now fully presented in the tonic. In later decades this structure would qualify as a modified sonata form without development, as commonly practised in slower movements by Haydn and Mozart. Throughout this not very slow movement the melodic line, apart from the initial four bar statement and its repetitions, juxtaposes one and two bar motives and more ornamental gestures in a constantly evolving, flexible sensibility. The finale does not reach the same levels as the preceding music, being the briefest of ternary structures in which the 'A' section is a modest eight bar melody simply repeated at the lower octave. Like the middle movement, the contrasting 'B' section reveals the short breathed, slightly tremulous succession of tiny gestures into which this modestly scaled late eighteenth century music so often falls.

The first movement of Sonata 8 in G is the longest in all the sonatas and represents a fully worked out sonata scheme, although even here Benda's structure lacks the dynamic integration so typical of the Viennese masters. The underlying key dualism and working out of related thematic groups is consistently carried through. An opening flourish that foreshadows Schubert's A flat major impromptu Opus 142 sets the music in motion, and lively figuration continues to be an important aspect of this music. A clearly defined first period of twelve bars closes in the tonic and a transitional episode of twenty bars with a carefully graded crescendo of surface rhythmic activity drives the music into a strong cadence on the secondary dominant. A pause and marked change of pace to *Adagio non tanto* presents a new melody in V, the customary second group of the late eighteenth century sonata which by 1785 was well entrenched in the musical literature of the period. It culminates with a cadential opportunity for a cadenza and return to the opening tempo for a scintillating closing theme for the first part of the movement.

What later generations would describe as a development begins with a motive derived from the second bar of the piece. The motive contrasts with semiquaver figuration worked from similar textures in the exposition. Some interesting tonal progressions are explored, beginning with d minor and moving through b minor before reverting to V in preparation for a full recapitulation. The subtlety of the return of the initial flourish reminds one of the similarly unobtrusive management of this significant moment in a sonata structure as often practised by Mozart. In fact Benda usually prefers this quiet and unassuming return to earlier material, which Newman (1947, p. x) aptly characterises as 'not as a long lost friend but as an everyday acquaintance who happens to drop in quite in the course of things'. Unusually for Benda in this latter part of the movement there are no elisions and the music provides a fully balanced resolution of the earlier tonal and melodic materials, even to providing another opportunity for a cadenza.

The *Andante quasi allegretto* is a miniature rondo of easy grace and unpretentious ambition, AABACAA in structure. The finale is another movement unique amongst Benda's sonatas, an *Andantino con variazioni*. The theme is pure clavichord writing in euphonious thirds and dying falls, a perfect, utterly transparent example of the *Empfindsam* style at its most ingratiating. Both movements are short and concise.

A rather more satisfying balance between movements is achieved in Sonata 12, another work in c minor, a key which seems to have brought out the most expressive qualities in Benda's music. The two part writing that is never far from the surface in Benda's compositional thought is more explicit in the first movement, from the opening falling fifths in counterpoint between the hands that make up the initial period. The strongly affective appoggiaturas of the second and third bars seem once again to invite the special touch available to the clavichord, to enhance the expressive intensity of the phrase. A clearly defined transition leads to a second subject group in the relative major, wherein, again somewhat unusually for Benda, the underlying motive of the falling fifth binds the two principle melodic ideas into a unity. The remainder of the movement reverts to the binary plan of earlier sonatas as the same motives are played out in a similar temporal order to the first section, but now cast into the relative major before the home minor key returns towards the end. The left hand version of the falling fifth motive from the first bar is used most effectively to further bind this movement into a coherent whole.

The slow movement is one of Benda's most intense creations, a movement that has already been noted because of its wide ranging exploration of enharmonic key relationships. Harmonic complexity is matched by melodic and textural richness, with the whole operating with three-part linear writing that occasionally expands to seven voices. The harmonic scheme may be laid out as follows:

Bars 1 – 8: opening melody in E flat, cadencing on V of e flat minor
Bars 9 – 19: second period in F sharp major (enharmonically flattened III of E flat)
Bars 19 – 22: extension of previous phrase leading to g sharp minor
Bars 22 – 29: variation and further extension of the preceding phrases leading to F minor, by way of an intermediate cadence on b flat minor (bar 25)
Bars 29 – 33: brief allusion to opening theme, now in f minor, cadencing on V
Bars 34 – end: recapitulation of second period, back in the home key

The modulations are carried through with the utmost gravity and smoothness, the move from tonic minor to its relative major (e flat to G flat) being especially convincing. The key structure disguises by these extended modulations, the usual binary ground plan that in fact lies behind the music.

The finale maintains the high level of this sonata. The interplay of singing melodies and semiquaver figuration provides for a lively movement that once again suggests elements of sonata form. An exposition shapes two contrasting groups on c minor and its dominant minor, although motivic analysis reveals that the second theme in bars 21–25 is an ingeniously elaborated version of the opening four bars, in a manner not unlike Haydn's treatment of similar thematic references. The second half of the binary repeated scheme proceeds with the principle melody in the relative major, developing the phrases and introducing a new, broadly shaped melody constituted in two six-bar phrases ending with an interrupted cadence on to the supertonic (D flat major: bar 54). Thereafter the opening music returns in f minor and the music is recapitulated substantially as before: a tonal gambit reminiscent of Mozart's little C major sonata K. 545 or some of Schubert's sonata schemes.

One may regret that circumstances or opportunity did not allow Benda to build on the imaginative intensity of this sonata to create further, similar masterpieces. But the composer's reputation as a composer of keyboard sonatas was sufficiently sustained in the eyes of his contemporaries to warrant widespread admiration. He is mentioned by Türk in his great clavichord tutor (1982, p. 499), and by Charles Burney in both his account of his travels through eighteenth century Germany (Burney, 1959, p. 237) and in his *General History*. In the latter Burney wrote approvingly, '[Benda] published in 1757 a very elegant set of sonatas for the harpsichord, in the style of Emmanuel Bach, and in 1780 and 1781 two collections of harpsichord pieces full of taste and pleasing passages' (Burney, 1957 ii, p. 956). An anonymous reviewer for the *Magazin der Musik* of 7th December 1783 also commended the sonatas as revealing 'Benda's charming, novel melody, which is unmistakably his' and pointed to 'a striking modulation to c minor' on the first page of Sonata 9 in a minor (as quoted in translation Morrow, 1997, p. 116). Newman quotes Daniel Schubart, writing about 1785, as declaring 'the keyboard works of this master are admirably conceived, and show that his superior genius can cope happily with varied idioms' (Newman, 1947, p. x). Nor was Benda forgotten in the nineteenth century. The six sonatas of the 1757 set were included by Aristide and Louis Farrenc in Volume VII of their landmark collection *Le Trésor des pianists*, published in Paris between 1861 and 1872. This unassuming repertoire of keyboard works, especially apt for the intimate sensibilities of the clavichord player, deserve to be recovered and made better known as attractive and admirably wrought examples of the early classical sonata.

Summary Table Of Georg Benda's Multi-Movement Sonatas
The 1757 set published by Winter, Berlin, 1757

Sonata 1 – B flat major
Allegretto (C: B flat – binary)
Larghetto (3/4: d minor – binary)
Allegro (2/4: B flat – binary)

Sonata 2 – G major
Un poco Allegro (¢: G – binary)
Andante assai (3/4: e minor – binary)
Allegro (3/4: G – binary)

Sonata 3 – d minor
Allegro ma non troppo (2/4: d minor – binary)
Andantino (6/8: a minor – ternary [Siciliana])
Allegro (3/4: d minor – binary)

Sonata 4 – F major
Allegretto assai moderato (3/2: F – binary, incipient sonata)
Largo (C: f minor – binary)
Presto (12/8: F – binary)

Sonata 5 – g minor
Allegro moderato (2/4: g minor – binary
Andante (3/4: E flat – binary)
Tempo di Minuetto (3/4: g minor – ternary

Sonata 6 – D major
Allegro (3/8: D – binary)
Un poco lento (C: b minor – binary)
Allegro assai (6/8: D – binary, incipient sonata [perpetuum mobile])

MUSICAL DIMENSIONS

The Sonatas published 1780 – 1787 by subscription
Sonata 7 (Vol. 1) – c minor
Allegro moderato (3/4: c minor – binary, incipient sonata)
Andante sostenuto (3/4: E flay – binary, incipient sonata)
Allegro (2/4: c minor – ternary)
Sonata 8 (Vol. 1) – G major
Allegro moderato (C: G – sonata form)
Andante quasi allegretto (3/4: C – binary)
Andantino con variazioni (C: G – theme and three variations)
Sonata 9 (Vol. 2) – a minor
Allegro (3/4: a minor – binary, incipient sonata)
Andante con moto (3/4: A major – binary)
Presto (6/8: a minor – ternary [gigue])
Sonata 10 (Vol. 3) – C major
Mezzo allegro (C: C – sonata form)
Largo (3/4: F – binary)
Allegro assai (6/8: C – binary, incipient sonata [gigue])
Sonata 11 (Vol. 4) – F major*
Allegretto assai moderato (C: F – binary, incipient sonata)
Andantino un poco larghetto (3/4: B flat – repeated ABA with coda)
Allegro (2/4 – binary)
Sonata 12 (Vol. 4) – c minor
Allegro non troppo (¢: c minor – binary, incipient sonata)
Un poco largo (3/4: E flat/g sharp minor – extended binary)
Allegro (6/8: c minor – binary, incipient sonata)
Sonata 13 (Vol. 5) – E flat major*
Allegro non troppo (3/4: E flat – sonata form)
Andantino (2/4: c minor – binary)
Allegro (6/8: E flat – binary)

Sonata 14 (Vol. 5) – F major*
Allegro moderato (¢: F – binary)
Andante con tenerezza (2/4: B flat – binary)
Allegro (3/4: F – binary)
Sonata 15 (Vol. 6) – c minor*
Allegro ma non troppo (¢: c minor – binary, incipient sonata)
Andante (2/4: E flat – binary)
Allegro (12/8: c minor – binary)
Sonata 16 (Vol. 6) – C major*
Moderato (C: C – binary, incipient sonata)
Andante un poco vivace (2/4: F – binary)
Allegro vivace (6/8: C – binary)

*These sonatas are in a simpler and more straightforward style, both technically and musically.

References

Bach, C. P. E. (1974). *Essay on the true Art of Playing Keyboard Instruments.* (W. J. Mitchell Trans. & Ed.). London: Eulenburg.
Berg, D. M. (1988). C. P. E. Bach's Character Pieces and his Friendship Circle. In S. L. Clark (Ed.), *C. P. E. Bach Studies.* Oxford: Clarendon Press.
Burney, C. (1957). *A General History of Music* [1789]. New York: Dover.
Burney, C. (1959). *An Eighteenth-Century Musical Tour in Central Europe and the Netherlands* [1773], (P. Scholes, Ed.). London: Oxford.
Drake, J. D. et al. (2001). Georg (Anton) Benda. In S. Sadie (Ed.), *The New Grove Dictionary of Music and Musicians,* (2nd ed.). London: MacMillan.
Hogwood, C. (1993). A Case for the Clavichord. *De Clavicordio 1.* In B. Brauchli (Ed.), Proceedings of the International Clavichord Symposium, Magnano 1993. Piemonte: Istituto per I beni musicali in Piemonte.
Hogwood, C. (1997). *Georg Benda: 17 Sonatas for Keyboard.* Oxford: Oxford University Press.
Marks, P. (1972). The Rhetorical Element in Musical *Sturm und Drang. Music Review* 33: 93.

Morrow, M. S. (1997). *German Music Criticism in the Late Eighteenth Century.* Cambridge: Cambridge University Press.
Newman, W. S. (1947). *Thirteen Keyboard Sonatas of the 18th and 19th Centuries.* Chapel Hill: University of North Carolina.
Newman, W. S. (1972). *The Sonata in the Classic Era* (2nd ed.). New York: Norton.
Racek, J. (1978). Preface. *Jiri Antonin Benda: Sonate I – XVI.* In J. Racek & V. J. Sykora, (Eds.). *Musica Antiqua Bohemica.* Vol. 10. Prague: Editio Supraphon.
Ruf, H. (1997). *Georg Benda: 6 Sonaten.* (Edition ED 9018). Mainz: Schott.
Speerstra, J. (1996). Towards an Identification of the Clavichord Repertoire among C. P. E. Bach's solo keyboard music: some preliminary conclusions. In B. Brauchli (Ed.), *De Clavicordio 2.* Proceedings of the International Clavichord Symposium, Magnano 1995. Magano: Musica Antica a Magnano.
Stilz, E. (1930). *Die Berliner Klaviersonate zu Zeit Friedrichs der Grossen.* Saarbrücken. Ph.D. Dissertation, Friedrich-Wilhelms Universität, Berlin.
Türk, D. G. (1982). *School of Clavier Playing.* [1789]. (Translated, introduction and notes by R. H. Haggh). Lincoln: University of Nebraska Press.
Vermeij, K. (1996). Eighteenth-Century Lovers of the Clavichord. In B. Brauchli (Ed.), *De Clavicordio 2.* Proceedings of the International Clavichord Symposium, Magnano 1995. Magano: Musica Antica a Magnano.
Wolters, K. (1994). *Handbuch der Klavierliteratur.* Mainz: Schott.

20: Musicianarchy[1]

Michael Kieran Harvey

What do you think of music exams?
There is little scope for imagination, creativity or interpretation for the examinee, otherwise penalties are incurred. (I have sat on tertiary jazz assessment panels where players have been penalized heavily for not playing 'in style' even though the skill levels were astonishing – this to me is insane.) This major fault lies at the heart of any competitive music situation, whether it be eisteddfods, music exams, tertiary degrees or international competitions. It encourages a conservative musical outlook in the student and teacher, otherwise lack of 'success' will ensue. This results in a very unsatisfying experience for the student in most cases. They remain mystified as to what the essence of the artform is or why it should be important to them, and are encouraged to approach the musical act as a routine, spending months or years 'perfecting' small pieces without any idea why, apart from the reputation of their teacher (and perhaps their parents) being at stake. Imaginative and independent musical thinkers are penalized heavily in such systems ... And what sort of thinkers are we desperately short of as a species (he asks rhetorically)? Some musicians who achieve well in these systems think that they are somehow musically superior to their colleagues, when in reality they are simply good at upsetting fewer people. This can have a detrimental effect on their self-assessment. I do not think the objective of any artform is to create a 'good student' whatever that is (perhaps someone who doesn't make waves?) – surely it should be about opening up people's minds to experimentation, curiosity and imagination, and to generally

enriching their pathetically finite existence? I am not against training and the accruing of technique and knowledge – indeed this is crucial – but there must be a strong reason for this other than some competitive carrot. What about the goal-setting aspect of exams I hear some *defatigable* teachers and parents ask? I'm not sure it's wise forcing such tests on kids who really don't want to do them as we risk turning them off the whole thing. But then, having been in this situation myself and still surviving as a musician, for those really determined, or unable to do otherwise, perhaps it doesn't hurt. But my point is that it does seem to turn other people off music for life, and could be contributing to the antipathy towards music that requires more than a superficial engagement. The satisfaction of making and enjoying music as a 'normal' lifestyle component is crucial to a child loving the musical process. This teaches more about life as a process than anything else I know. It de-emphasises the 'getting and having' mentality which is so destructive. Up to a point a music exam system or competition can slake the parent's/teacher's/university's/government's thirst for 'results' or 'progress' but such old-fashioned thinking achieves little in providing the student with a lifelong artistic or philosophical outlet. How on earth such systems are supposed to turn out musicians anyone would be interested in hearing is beyond me, as the emphasis is necessarily on regurgitating known approaches. I do not know of any alternative to this, and so I think systems like this should not be applied to music (nor other artforms either). Most amusingly this conservative competitive mentality has even infected more 'rebellious' music forms which now hold their own versions of exams and competitions, ultimately leading to performances in places that are the antithesis of this music, that is, concert halls – sometimes even with the collaboration of symphony orchestras!

How should we approach the teaching of an instrument to young children? What are the imperatives?

There's only one imperative – don't turn them off music. Music is capable of staying with human beings for their entire lifetime, and so far I have not noticed any studies of deleterious effects from acoustic music, apart from hearing loss from unwise proximity (generally from sitting directly in front of the brass section). The child's experience of music should be the same as for language, that is, music is happening all the time, and any particular instrument is simply part of the weft and warp of their lives. The Venezuelan youth orchestra experiment has proved that even the poorest child's life can be enriched immeasurably by playing a musical instrument, so I do not think it is a luxury only for private school kids. After all, is language only spoken and studied in private schools? Language is used to understand history – why not music? Language is used to explore Maths and Science – why not explore these subjects via music and vice versa? Philosophy? Mythologies and Religions? Atheism? When music can communicate so much more than language why limit the teaching of our young? What is language anyway but music? How is it taught? Through parents and teachers singing and repeating musical rhymes, at least initially. Music makes connections in the brain in ways which are still mystifying to brain surgeons, and the benefits of playing a challenging musical instrument in a way that develops through one's life results in extraordinary growth of the white-matter myelin sheathing – the decision-making part of the brain which continues to regenerate. Autopsies reveal musicians' brains are heavily endowed with this white matter (when not affected by excess alcohol consumption of course).

How should we go about training musicians after they have finished their primary and secondary schooling?
The worst thing you can do to young aspiring musicians I think is saddle them with an education debt before they've even had a chance to test themselves in the music scene. At the age of 17 or 18 it is too late to start effective music training, which is what the greater percentage of the undergraduate intake currently reflects. By implication then, it is the early stage of life, especially before age 11, that is critical for music education. My advice is to encourage school leavers who are contemplating a music career to immediately attempt to earn a living by engaging with music in the 'real world'. This is a rude shock to the system, and enables maturity and reality to effect their

judgement about a career. In my experience, the most mature and interested tertiary music students are those involved in the more commercial areas of music, who are working, or who have returned to education somewhat older and wiser. They are able to see that those teaching music at the tertiary level have no idea about the music scene, and are clinging to these fast-disappearing jobs in futile desperation rather than any altruistic educational responsibility. But these students also know that the tertiary music institution contains valuable information they can access. When I left school the last thing I wanted to do was further study, so I spent 2 years lugging a Fender Rhodes 88 around the club circuit in Sydney doing mind-numbing pub gigs. When finally at the pinnacle of this light-entertainment career a drunk footy official threw up in the piano I was playing at the then Regent Hotel ballroom in Sydney I decided I had to get out of Australia and renew my love of music someplace where it was respected. This was a character-building experience (amongst many in Australia ... Andrew Ollie once put the rhetorical question to me on air when I was interviewed about my debut recital at the Sydney Opera House in 1988, 'You're not just going to sit in front of the piano and play it are you?'). I am obsessed with the idea that young musicians need a crash course in philosophy, politics, history, finance and the sciences and humanities generally to give them some hope of dealing with the world. Expert skill in music is simply a given. If they can't earn a living by music then they must find some way of sustaining themselves through other work. If they have energy left over for music, then great – this is a fantastic test of resolve.

From what you know of the type of tertiary studies (BMus for example) that are offered in music in Australia, is the training adequate?
The training is woeful because it is predicated on the past. There is some dumb notion that music is some neat consecutive progression. The history of music is sustained anarchy, and this is the core of what youngsters should be investigating in my opinion. Then we might have some resistance to the triumph of the commercial business 'industry' model.

Further, what has not been looked at enough is the issue of living a life as a musician. Personally I think it is important for young musicians to feel that they can contribute to Australian life if they want to, and not feel that there is so little culture and work for them here that they must necessarily look elsewhere. I think we have largely failed in bringing fine music into the larger society as a perceived benefit to people – it is looked upon as an elite pursuit, but unlike Formula 1, which is also elite and effete, we have not argued for the trickle-down effect of this artform ('the technological achievements of Formula 1 eventually end up in the family car blahblahblah'), and so no-one understands it, or thinks it is important enough to need funding.

Is there any country where you think they are training their musicians better than Australia?
No. Not any more. Hungary was, but having joined the EU in the early 1990s all resistance to market economics (which influences education) has been lost. The importance of culture in occupying and distracting people from the realities of their miserable lives was an artform in itself in the former USSR. Hungary was especially fortunate (or unfortunate depending on your perspective) in having been the Carpathian corridor of war and pillage for centuries – when things and lives can be so easily taken or destroyed art means so much more. Hungary has been extremely well-represented in the arts and sciences on the world stage (for a population smaller than Australia's), but I wonder if this will survive the new order.

Do you care to comment on the importance of children having access to contemporary music.
'Contemporary' music is a pretty vague term – it's used mainly by the pop/rock industry now. I presume you mean difficult contemporary classical music. In my experience of my own two kids, they were very excited when young by the surface of contemporary classical music, especially at live concerts, and it was only the acculturation of prejudices and trends which deformed this openness. I think this has

a lot to do with the mindset of the parents and to a lesser extent the teacher (if there is one) – the child's prejudices will be formed unconsciously by these influences. An attitude of curious skepticism is a priceless gift that parents can give their kids.

I'm wondering if your delving into 'Doreen Bridges: Music Educator' has prompted you to say anything else about any issue that she has raised ...
I agree with her completely. There's so much ground that she covers, it's quite humbling. I do feel that unless we have political and business leaders who can lead on education from the *front*, then tinkering at the bottom of the food chain is going to remain a thankless task. It gets down to the individual teacher being able to make a difference despite the system. In league with the interested and involved parent(s) this is the only way to provide adequate stimulation for a child's musical development irrespective of what method is used.

Note

[1] Michael was invited to respond to a number of questions that were presented to him. Ed.

21: A Case for Multiculturalism in the General Music Classroom

Marvelene C. Moore

Music educators generally agree on the importance and value of a multicultural approach to music instruction in the general music classroom. However, there is a tendency to support this approach to curriculum and instruction by giving merely 'lip service' to its inclusion. All too often music curricula reflect a dominance of Western classical music and a small percentage of music that proports to represent other cultures. In many instances, this music is composed in the style of the music culture and upon close examination is found not to be authentic to the culture. The degree to which Western classical music occupies a place in the music curriculum, of course, depends on the country and the community in which the school resides, determined by the activism of parents and community leaders who may exert some influence on curriculum design. When ultimately faced with the challenge of altering or designing a music curriculum that is truly multicultural in philosophy and practice, teachers may approach the process by asking the following questions: 1) What is multicultural music education? 2) Why should I make time for teaching music of ethnic cultures when students lack exposure and experience with Western classical music? And 3) How does one construct curricula that maintain high standards of performance, instruction and learning?[1] In this article, the writer will attempt to address these concerns, provide responses to the queries and offer suggestions for creating a curriculum that embodies a multicultural approach to teaching music.

What is Multicultural Music Education?

Multicultural music education in its broadest sense refers to an approach to teaching and learning that incorporates the music of various cultures and ethnic groups along with the study of the history, customs, and social issues. Patricia Shehan Campbell, in an article published in the *American Music Teacher* defines multicultural music education as 'the study of music from groups distinguished by race or ethnic origin, age, class, gender, religion, life style and exceptionality.'[2] Terese Volk goes a step further in defining multiculturalism in music as 'the ability to function competently in several cultures…and includes the possibility of reforming an educational system to embrace students from a variety of cultures.'[3] Indeed Mary Reed goes even further and takes the position that diversity (inclusive of multicultural music instruction) is 'an 'obligation' to teach music in a variety of ways, in a variety of settings, to a variety of students.'[4]

In the United States, the move towards teaching from a multicultural perspective can be traced back to John Dewey, professor of philosophy at Columbia University in 1916. In a paper presented at the National Education Association, Dewey declared that 'No matter how loudly anyone proclaims his Americanism, if he assumes that any one strain, any one component culture, no matter how early settled it was in our territory, or how effective it has proven in its own land, is to furnish a pattern to which all other strains and cultures are to conform, he is a traitor to an American Nationalism … Our unity cannot lie a homogeneous thing … it must be a unity created by drawing out and compassing into a harmonious whole the best, the most characteristic, which each contributing race and people has to offer.'[5] This spotlight on unity through diversity in every facet of the American society, including education, was continued through the Civil Rights movement of the 1950s and 1960s. In music education within the United States, the focus moved closer to becoming a reality at the Tanglewood Symposium where music educators included in their Declaration the importance of including current music and avant-garde music, American folk music, and the music of ethnic cultures. The result was emphasis on representation of diverse cultures in music education in instructional materials and in practice. The most recent pronouncement in the United States on the importance of multicultural music appeared in the MENC National Standards for Arts Education. In Standard #9: 'Understanding music in relation to history and culture' and in the achievement competencies that relate to this standard, students are expected to a) identify by genre or style aural examples of music from various historical periods and cultures; b) describe in simple terms how elements of music are used in music examples from various cultures of the world; c) identify various uses of music in their daily experiences and describe characteristics that make certain music suitable for each use; d) identify and describe roles of musicians in various music settings and cultures; e) demonstrate audience behavior appropriate for the context and style of music performed.[6] It can be concluded then that multicultural music education is an approach to instruction that incorporates diverse music cultures as an **integral** part of music learning and performance that is not driven by focus on a particular culture or period, but promotes inclusion of music from many cultures along with that of the Western classical art music.

Why Multicultural Music?

As we consider why multicultural music is important in education/music education, perhaps a look back at the role of the arts (music) in society would be beneficial. Harold Williams, former president and chief executive officer of the J. Paul Getty Trust in the United States, believed that the arts are basic and central to human communication and understanding. He advanced the ideas that the arts are how we talk to each other and that they are unquestionably the language of civilization, past and present, through which we express our anxieties, our hungers, our hopes and our discoveries.[7] Former United States assembly woman Maureen Ogden of New Jersey supported Williams' position and held to the conviction that when comparing two similar schools, one with a strong arts (music) curriculum and one without, you will soon discover that there are non-artistic benefits that make the school arts curricula a higher performance environment.[8] Since music and the related arts have been documented as having profound effects on student learning, it seems logical that a curriculum rich in music from diverse cultures would yield greater benefits. It can be central to experiencing a range of music styles and genres and contribute to understanding cultural heritage. Consequently, when considering a plausible reason for creating a multicultural music curriculum, two categories of benefits emerge: musical benefits and social gains. Musical benefits may include: 1) broadening students' exposure to musical sounds; 2) providing opportunities for different types of musical performances; 3) offering experiences in creating music representing various cultural styles; 4) learning about a variety of musical types from one's own culture; 5) providing opportunities for examining music through traditional and non-traditional analytical techniques; and 6) learning music in the manner in which it is taught in a culture. The social and personal gains may encompass: 1) acquiring a greater understanding of one's self and culture; 2) reaffirming one's self-worth; 3) confirming that experiences in one's culture are of value in a multicultural society; 4) learning about culture through a multidisciplinary approach; 5) expanding one's knowledge of languages through the study of texts; 6) aiding in eradication of biases of cultural groups; and 7) developing skills for successful living in a diverse society.[9]

It is possible that students may not respond initially in a positive way to music that is unfamiliar to them. However, with repeated exposure and active participation in the music, they will gradually acquire a greater appreciation and possibly a preference for the once unfamiliar music. In a study on children's preferences, Demorest and Schultz found that students' proclivity for World Music increased with greater exposure, experience, and manipulation with the music.[10] The challenge for the music teacher is to present the music in the most positive way, regardless of personal preferences or biases of the music and individuals from the cultural groups.

How Can Multicultural Music be Taught?

In preparation for teaching multicultural music the teacher must approach instruction with respect for the music and sensitivity to the people of the culture. Music instruction must be accompanied by accuracy, integrity, authenticity, and attention to issues related to the group. Before and during instruction, the teacher should conduct an in-depth 1) examination of the culture and 2) analysis of the music.

An examination of the culture will require a study of customs, traditions, religion and cultural values of the people. A study of the history, geographical location, foods, dress, children's games, stories, and celebrations will enhance the examination. If the teacher feels uncomfortable in addressing some of these areas it may become necessary to locate and invite native people from the community into the classroom to provide first hand information about the culture. The teachers should be aware of the tendency to expose students to too many cultures within a limited period of time. Focusing on a few cultures at a time is the most preferred procedure for successful instruction. The cultures may be selected from those represented in the school and the community or minority groups within the country and/or world music cultures that are completely foreign to the students.

A thorough analysis of the music from the cultures to be studied is a 'must' for successful music teaching. Rhythmic and melodic features, form and harmonies (if they exist), should be examined for their uniqueness as well as similarities to all music. An investigation of authentic, real, true melodies should be a priority. Often this is a difficult task to achieve because of the limitation of Western notation in representing pitch, rhythm and timbre of non-Western music. It becomes necessary then to listen extensively! In addition to CDs and DVDs, the internet has made music of all genres and cultures more accessible to people of all nations. Therefore, authentic versions of music have been made easier to acquire. Instruments that characterize the culture should also be authentically represented in the music classroom. It is understandable that teachers may not possess the instruments, but should make an effort to acquire visuals of instruments and listening examples that will support music learning. Here again, the internet can be a useful tool for exposing students to many types of instruments through YouTube and other websites.

In summary, the importance of inclusion of multicultural music in the general music classroom cannot be overstated. Through exposure to music from cultural groups students will 1) acquire new musical experiences, 2) actively participate in different ways of making music, 3) develop understanding of indigenous music groups, 4) acquire an appreciation for diversity, and 5) develop a tolerance and respect for people of other cultures. If we are successful in achieving these goals, we will convey to our students, the school and the community that our society is not merely a 'melting pot.' Rather, it is a mosaic that requires the music, representative of many, to make the picture complete.

Notes

1. Marvelene Moore, 'Multicultural Music: The Connection to Music Learning and Performance,' *Tennessee Musician* 58, no.2, Winter 2005: 42–44.
2. Patricia Shehan Campbell, 'Music Instruction: Marked and Molded by Multiculturalism,' *American Music Teacher*, June/July 1993: 15.
3. Terese M. Volk, *Music, Education, and Multiculturalism: Foundations and Principles* New York: Oxford University Press, 1998, 196.
4. Mary Theresa Reed, 'Some thoughts on Diversity in Music Education...It Is More than Multiculturalism,' *Illinois Music Educator* 65, no. 1 Fall 2004: 70–71.
5. John Dewey, 'Nationalizing Education,' *Addresses and Proceedings of the National Education Association* 54, 1916: 184–185.
6. Moore, p. 43.
7. Harold Williams, The Language of Civilization: The Vital Role of the Arts in Education, *National Conference of State Legislators*, 1992: 1–7.
8. Ibid, p. 5.
9. Moore, p. 42.
10. Steven M. Demorest, and Sara J.M. Schultz, Children's Preference for Authentic versus Arranged Versions of World Music Recordings, *Journal of Research in Music Education* 52, no. 4 Winter 2004: 310.

22: Western musical identity and practice in contemporary South Africa? Lessons from Doreen Bridges

Caroline van Niekerk

Introduction

One of my current research interests is the field of musical identity, specifically within the South African context, and it has proved interesting to see how, in that regard, one of the people from whom I have been able to learn is an Australian, and no less than Doreen Bridges.

I first had the privilege of meeting Doreen in 1988, at the very first ISME conference I attended, plus two preceding commission seminars, one of which was the Early Childhood gathering in Brisbane. She and Katalin Forrai and Olive McMahon immediately stood out for me as highly respected seniors in a field in which I was still a novice: Doreen had both a commanding presence and a warmth and openness towards younger academics like myself. What a privilege to be in the company of such a lady, who set for me an example both of rigorous scholarship and of caring and concern and practical, hands-on involvement. The example of such people, that seminar and ISME involvement generally changed my life from that point on, and I have never since missed an ISME conference.

In 1988, with South Africa close to the death throes of the apartheid regime, as a White South African abroad I was very definitely *persona non grata*. In fact, I even endured the experience of being spat upon at an ISME social function, by an Australian woman who claimed: 'They should never even have allowed you to come!' The interesting thing is that I had virtually forgotten that unpleasant event, until reminded as I sat now to write this article, and yet I have at no time over the more than 20 intervening years forgotten the impact made on me by meeting a doyenne such as Doreen.

In 'A Life in Music and Education' Martin Comte writes: 'Looking back on her student days, Dee expresses both appreciation and criticism of her teachers, and reflects on how her experiences during this period shaped her future ... her student experiences laid the foundation for her subsequent determination to explore principles and ideas to make music teaching and learning more effective and more relevant – a quest which has dominated her professional life' (Comte, 1992, pp. 3–4). In the Abstract from Dr Bridges's own unpublished PhD thesis, she wrote: 'The intention of this historical study is to show how universities have exercised a controlling influence on music education in Australia at a number of levels, to analyse the conservative nature of this influence, and to trace to their sources some of the problems and contradictions which beset music education in the last decades of the 20th century' (Comte, 1992, p. 11).

From these quotations and the wide variety of topics addressed in her publications, it seems clear that Doreen has not been unsure of her personal musical identity[1], however critical she may have been about aspects of her own music education and the 'problems and contradictions which beset music education' generally. So why should so many South Africans, and even established South African music educators, be currently so uncertain of their musical identities?

South African music practice and education[2]
Needless to say, much currently happening in South Africa is as a result of political developments over the last two decades. These political developments have resulted *inter alia*, and in no specific priority order, in a) expression of previously often unarticulated resentment against missionary/colonial influence; b) wide-ranging

policy changes, including policies of affirmative action and Black Economic Empowerment (BEE) and c) new focuses in the education system, including a move to an Outcomes-Based Education system with seven years of compulsory Arts and Culture Education. These three aspects all have a bearing on music education: resentment against missionary/colonial influence especially can result in derogation of Western music; BEE has elevated individuals into positions of power where they have the influence to promote and grant funding for certain cultural and music practices and not others, and the 'new' education dispensation has also created many 'new' problems[3]. These include teachers un- and under-trained for integrated arts teaching, as well as for the new elective Music curriculum for the last three years of secondary school. I contend that much in the current South African identity crisis is politically related – certainly, even within the field of music, more so than musically related.

Already in 1997, three years after South Africa's first democratic elections, I wrote, 'In music ... diversity relates not just to new diversity in terms of classroom populations, as we no longer have racially-based education, but diversity in the musics demanding to be taught, when many teachers feel that they don't even have the requisite skills to cope with teaching one musical practice' (Van Niekerk, 1997, p. 267). This is only a single facet of the challenges teachers face: the different musics, many previously unknown to them, which they are now required to teach. They also have to teach Arts and Culture from grade 4–9, encompassing Art, Dance, Drama and Music, without possibly even having a solid foundation in a single one of those art forms. In the Foundation Phase (grade R – standing for the reception year – plus grade 1 to 3) only three areas are identified in the curriculum: Numeracy, Literacy and Lifeskills, and the Arts, including Music, are supposed to be integrated in this curriculum, but with very sketchy guidelines given as to how this should be done. Especially older teachers of all population groups are concerned about the music technology aspects previously unknown to them; teachers of all ages and races are concerned about the African music aspects in the curriculum. I state this advisedly, and include Black African teachers themselves in my contention. This is largely because, for them, often any formal music education that they have enjoyed has been entirely Western based and oriented.

Shining through the above and other problems is nevertheless often a deep love for Western music among Black South Africans, and this provides a clear *raison d'etre* for several musical outreach projects, mentioned below, with which I am involved, in various degrees, but whose rationale is certainly no form of cultural imperialism. DeNora (2000, p. ix) writes: 'He told me he was originally from Nigeria, where, he said with emphasis, they "really knew" how to use music ... By contrast, in the cold and over-cognitive climate of pre-millennium Britain, people were considerably less reflexive about music as a "force" in social life ... It is certainly true that music's social effects have been underestimated in Western societies.' Many Black South Africans truly *use* Western classical music[4] in their lives, entirely of their own volition, and often spending considerable personal financial resources, especially in the field of choral singing. This choice of Western music is not because of a desire to aspire to a Eurocentric identity; the love for this music is based on the feeling that it is music of good quality.

Projects in which outstanding work is being done include those about to be listed. They all offer the sort of quality music education so dear to the heart of Doreen Bridges. And they do so to disadvantaged children and youth in a situation where such education is hardly on offer in the majority of schools throughout the country.

- the STTEP Music School[5] and its symphony orchestras, run by Julie Clifford on the campus of the University of Pretoria. I have written a great deal about this project (see two articles quoted in the references), including its genesis from the ISME '98 conference, and its purpose – not mainly to produce professional black instrument players and thus to help the continuation of Western art music culture in South Africa, but improving the lives of often disadvantaged children and developing their love for music. Numerous other, similar orchestral projects exist throughout the country, most notable and well-known among which is possibly Buskaid under the inspirational Rosemary Nalden. Buskaid's stated vision is 'that all township[6] children will be given the opportunity to channel their creative energies and talents through learning and playing classical music to the highest international standards' (http://www.buskaid.org.za).

- Dr Zenda Nel's active listening programme based on Classical music education for learners, mostly in pre-primary and primary schools, using dramatization and instrumental play and thus introducing them to the music in a fun-filled way. This has taken place, when money has been available, all over the country, in addition to a successful pilot project in Mauritius. The main research which she did on the success of this work, for the purposes of her doctorate at the University of Pretoria, was done at 240 schools in underprivileged areas in South Africa and especially in places like squatter camps.[7] Focus has also been on training teachers, so that they are then enabled to continue with this type of work. Continuity and replication are two important aspects, if work is not to be limited to what single individuals can do personally.

- the Black Tie Ensemble, often known for short as the Blackties, now a leading South African opera company which has already successfully staged numerous opera seasons, in collaboration with a number of generous sponsors. As with several other opera-based projects which also exist throughout the country, some of South Africa's most beautiful voices can be found amongst its ranks. In addition, an Incubator Scheme was established to train young singers who have the potential of making a career out of opera, but who may not otherwise have the resources necessary to pursue a formal musical education. All singers' talents are nurtured by a group of some of the country's leading vocal teachers, music tutors, and acting and movement lecturers. These efforts are supported by the training of a group of technical incubators, providing them with the necessary skills to conceptualize, design, stage and manage a full-scale opera production. More recently, The Black Tie Opera Chorus came into existence – a large chorus of trained singers who serve the function of a professional opera chorus in all

Black Tie productions requiring a chorus, although it also functions as a separate performing entity. As part of ongoing opera education and outreach initiative, and although itself an outreach project, the Black Ties do numerous schools tours to introduce children to the magical world of opera, alternatively inviting schools to join them at the theatre.

These projects may be viewed as unusual, and by some people questionable, with their focus on Western classical music, in an African country, and yet their wider focus is simultaneously empowerment and offering both education and constructive enjoyment to the disadvantaged – certainly not manipulating anyone's musical identity against their will. The reaction of the largely Black African beneficiaries clearly demonstrates that they are not being coerced into a cultural practice against their inclinations. In interviews for research purposes many STTEP pupils, for example, have stressed that their orchestral instruments are now their best friends and if they did not play instruments they would probably spend their time 'on the streets doing crime'. Also, and not only with STTEP students, interesting musical fusions have already taken place: they have started to play together some traditional songs and kwela[8] music with their Western instruments.

Playing instruments provides the young with new equipment for dealing with their feelings, clearly having a therapeutic effect. Singing, and utilising their rich African voices in the integrated art form of opera is an empowering experience for many Black South African singers, who also participate in integrated African musical arts[9], with their voices as one of the best and most natural vehicles. Opera also involves the valuable aspects of dramatization and fantasy, as does the work done by Dr Nel, with children as young as three years of age.

MIAGI, which stands for Music Is A Great Investment, has as its mission 'To unite the power of classical, indigenous and jazz and thus offer a key to positive social development and to deep understanding between people across all borders'. It thus encompasses more than Western classical music, although originally it was called the International Classical Music Festival or ICMF. But it was found that this name did not achieve the desired results – perhaps precisely because of associated negative perceptions of Eurocentrism. Having been renamed, however, this dynamic not-for-profit organization continues to aim at empowering musicians throughout South Africa. Furthermore it is also about promoting music education as an effective tool for positive social development. In a sense, therefore, MIAGI is an umbrella for projects such as those mentioned above, and in fact this is the case, as by supporting numerous existing initiatives, MIAGI makes music education available to a growing number of young people, especially in historically disadvantaged areas. In addition to providing ongoing financial and technical support for such projects, MIAGI arranges workshops and the MIAGI Orchestra Course, and also provides mentorship with renowned artists. Collaborations with organisations and festivals abroad offer many young South African musicians opportunities to present their talents internationally. MIAGI's annual Festival sees world-acclaimed musicians perform to extensive media coverage with many of our finest aspiring young artists.

By 'offering a platform for intercultural creative dialogue, MIAGI brings young people, artists and audiences together that would otherwise never meet'. MIAGI's Aims and Objectives also include inspiring composers to explore African traditional music and lesser-known indigenous music styles and thus enhance the appreciation, and the value and integrity, of indigenous music; promoting indigenous and traditional African musical idiom in South Africa and abroad by introducing African music to audiences, musicians and music educators world-wide; creating career opportunities for local musicians; contributing to poverty reduction through social upliftment and international exchange, encouraging investor confidence and tourism and structuring and adding to a national network of music initiatives with the aim of strengthening music education in South Africa.

MIAGI introduces South African music to audiences worldwide, inspiring dialogue among people of different cultures through an intense process of artistic exchange that includes commissioning new intercultural compositions. This underlines the objective to educate in the broadest sense of the word. MIAGI has support from local government, the corporate sector and the international community: since 2001 sponsorship worth R35,000,000 (approximately US$350,000) has been generated for the music education and performance sectors in South Africa.

MIAGI has also commissioned eleven major intercultural works, many now frequently performed both locally and during international tours, and facilitated numerous international opportunities and tours for South African soloists, ensembles and music students. Robert Brooks, the founder of MIAGI, and his colleagues spend most of their time working on and supporting music education initiatives. 'Unfortunately the very nature of education means these projects will never be self-sustaining – they will always require funding – but we can make these projects sustainable by investing in humans so that they can have the know-how to set up the infrastructure and impart their knowledge, enabling them to link to other sustainable funding structures. MIAGI also gives budding artists, increased opportunities to build their careers locally, rather than feeling a need to leave South Africa. MIAGI offers scholarships and has also set up a mentor protégé programme. We have already had many successful protégés go through the programme. One in particular, Pretty Yende, recently won an international singing competition in Verona which we are very excited about' (http://www.miagi.co.za).

Brooks is convinced that music can play a fundamental role in present-day South Africa, in the process of overcoming the negative repercussions of discrimination. And so am I, without in any way prescribing what should be regarded as "acceptable" cultural and musical identities.

Conclusion

In much of the sterling work being done in outreach projects in music in South Africa, the following two quotations remain in the forefront of my mind: that attributed to the anthropologist Margaret Mead: 'Never doubt that a small group of thoughtful, committed citizens can change the world. Indeed, it is the only thing that ever has', and Harry Truman who reportedly said: 'It's possible to achieve almost anything as long as you are not worried about who gets the credit'. Both of these quotations are also eminently applicable to Doreen Bridges, whose life and work have also clearly demonstrated that 'Music Is A Great Investment'.

Notes

1   "Of course it is notable that to date very few people have expressed themselves on their own musical identities – musicians and researchers mostly consider and write about the musical identities of others" (Van Niekerk, 2008, p. 1).
2   Music Practice and Education is the title colleagues and I chose, at the University of Pretoria, for the subject Music Education which we teach. The reason for this is that we believe that in this subject we encompass a wider ambit than merely "Music Education".
3   The "newer", as opposed to the frequently named 'new', South Africa is a term coined by the internationally renowned music therapist, Mercedes Pavlicevic, and used in the title of a 2004 article of hers. This well reflects reality in South Africa, where not surprisingly, everything is not necessarily suddenly 'new' (Joseph & Van Niekerk, 2008, p. 487).
4   In this article I do not enter into the debate as to the acceptability of this term or not, whether Western art music is a better term, with its acronym WAM, or not. I trust that readers will generally understand what type of music is under discussion.
5   The acronym was devised to acknowledge the South African Music Education Trust (S), the Tshwane district, under which Pretoria falls, and the then Transvaal Philharmonic Orchestra, no longer in existence. STTEP is referred to as a school, but the different aspects of music taught to participants constitute more of a hobby than a formal, school-type subject.
6   According to Wikipedia (accessed 18.06.08), "In South Africa, the term township usually refers to the (often underdeveloped) urban living areas that, under Apartheid, were reserved for non-whites."
7   After her very first visit to work with children in a squatter camp/informal settlement, Zenda said: "This proved again to me that classical music does not need an audience with bow ties and loads of money to be appreciated, but it could be appreciated by anybody, even by people from the poorest of poor areas. The recipe to achieve this is to expose them in such a way to this music style, that it will come alive and be exciting and fun for them" (2005, p. 30).
8   Kwela is a happy, often pennywhistle based, street music with jazzy underpinnings.
9   The term 'musical arts' was emphasised by the African music scholar Meki Nzewi in 2001 in his keynote address at the conference of the Pan African Society for Music Education (PASME) in Lusaka, Zambia. As a result of his address, the name of the society was changed to the Pan African Society for Musical Arts Education (PASMAE) to reflect the integrated

nature of music, dance, drama and the visual arts in indigenous Africa (Herbst et al. 2005, p. 276).

References

Adhikari, M. (2005). *Not White Enough, Not Black Enough: Racial Identity in the South African Coloured Community.* Ohio University Research in International Studies Africa Series No. 83. Athens: Ohio University Press.
Comte, M. (1992). *Doreen Bridges: Music Educator.* Parkville, Victoria: ASME.
DeNora, T. (2000). *Music in Everyday Life.* Cambridge: Cambridge University Press.
Erasmus, J. (2005). Crossing Barriers with Music. *Classicfeel Magazine*, September 2005, Johannesburg, South Africa, 30–31.
Herbst, A., De Wet, J. & Rijsdijk, S. (2005). A Survey of Music Education in the Primary Schools of South Africa's Cape Peninsula. *Journal of Research in Music Education,* 53(3): 260–283.
http://www.buskaid.org.za. Accessed 02-04-09.
http://www.miagi.co.za. Accessed 03-04-09.
http://upetd.up.ac.za/thesis/available/etd-07312007-081226/ (Zenda Nel's full doctoral thesis, in which her work is described)
Joseph, D. & Van Niekerk, C. (2007). Music Education and minority groups' cultural and musical identities in the Newer South Africa: white Afrikaners and Indians. *Journal of Intercultural Education* 18(5): 487–500.
Pavlicevic, M. (2004) Taking Music Seriously: Sound Thoughts in the Newer South Africa in *Muziki, Journal of Music Research in Africa,* 1(1), 3–19.
Van Niekerk, C. (1997). Recent Curriculum Development in South Africa. *Music in Schools and Teacher Education: A Global Perspective,* ed. Sam Leong. ISME Commission for Music in Schools & Teacher Education and CIRCME), Perth, Australia. pp 267–269.
Van Niekerk, C. (2008). Fathoming the musical identity/identities of James Phillips aka Bernoldus Niemand. *South African Journal of Cultural History* 22(1): 1–28.
Van Niekerk, C. & Salminen, S. (2008). Sttepping in the right direction? Western classical music in an orchestral programme for disadvantaged African youth. *Journal of Intercultural Education* 19 (3): 191–202.
Van Niekerk, C. & Typpö, M. 2009. Sttep by Sttep in the spirit of *Umuntu ungumuntu ngabantu.* Article in progress.
www.blackties.co.za. Accessed 05-04-09.

23: We Sing Now: A Rirratjingu Song Session

Jill Stubington

In the mid 1970s I made three trips to north-east Arnhem Land to make recordings of clan songs *(manikay)* which I could use in preparing a PhD thesis. My aim was to investigate the musical structures within their social and ceremonial contexts. Musical performances consisted of a number of discrete short items sung one after the other. A session, as I called them, might include anything from 20 or 30 items to hundreds. Individual items proved to be highly structured, with voice, sticks and didjeridu combining in well-coordinated self-referencing patterns. It seemed to me, however, that besides the careful and attractive forms of individual items, the whole session could be seen as one musical structure with a compelling over-arching thrust. The aim of this paper is to demonstrate how an analysis of a whole song session might proceed, and the kind of conclusions that may be drawn from such an analysis.

On 14th November 1973, Roy Dadaynga Marika invited me to record an evening song session outside his house at Yirrkala. When I arrived, the singer and members of his family were seated on a blanket outside the house, and I was asked to set up my recording equipment there. A number of women were present, and one of them was also going to record the session on a cassette recorder. At first a young man called Don Guyuwuyu played the didjeridu, but after some time Dadaynga sent for another didjeridu player, and in the meantime his ten-year-old son Phillip played the didjeridu (*yidaki*). Dadaynga indicated to me that this part of the performance was only a practice session, but he agreed to my request to record it anyway. Later, Micky

Munungurr arrived to play the didjeridu. D̲adaynga accompanied himself with one proper stick *(bil̲ma)*, and one longer stick which the children called a 'fighting stick.' The end of the didjeridu was placed in a large aluminium cooking pot. Traditionally, a baler shell would have been used. Its effect is to modify the sound of the didjeridu and to reflect it back to the player so that he can hear what he is doing more clearly. During the session it started to rain, and the performing and recording group moved to the verandah of the house. Rain and the additional resonances of wall and roof change the sound qualities of the recording. Later in the session we were disturbed by the arrival of two men who had been drinking and I was asked to turn the tape-recorder off until they moved on.

    The recording includes two items, 43 and 58, which consist only of mouth sounds and one, 50, of voice and sticks only. Mouth sounds are vocal imitations or vocal expositions of didjeridu patterns which musicians use to communicate with each other about didjeridu parts. D̲adaynga executed these three items during the part of the session where he was instructing his young son who was attempting the didjeridu part. In item 50, D̲adayanga sang quietly to himself a melody quite unrelated to the other items. Its musical importance in the session rests on the change of vocal pitch between items before and after it. Item 69 had only just commenced when a group of alcohol-affected men interrupted and it was discontinued. In all, 82 items were performed and they are to be heard on field tapes S1973/2 and S1973/3. These recordings will not be publicly available until the Marika family decides to release them.

    Spoken versions of the song texts were given in June 1975 by a Ngayimil speaking man, Larrtjanga. We used the method employed by Alice Moyle in which two tape recorders are used. The already-recorded sung performance was played back on one tape recorder, phrase by phrase, and the words sung in each phrase were spoken by Larrtjanga into a microphone recording on the second recorder. Over a period of 3 weeks, Larrtjanga gave spoken versions of songs recorded on 35 of my field tapes, 6 of Trevor Jones's and 19 of Richard Waterman's. Usually without prompting but sometimes in answer to the question "What is this one about?" Larrtjanga would give a song subject in Yolngu *mata* (language) and English. We did not discuss the meanings of the sung texts.

My purpose in recording spoken versions was to enable accurate notations of the vocal line. In order to see how successful these spoken versions would be in illuminating the sung versions, I roughly and quickly notated all the spoken texts Larrtjanga provided. To my delight it proved very easy to match the rough notations of spoken versions with the sung material, and I used them to notate the 114 items included in my PhD thesis. The spoken versions given by Larrtjanga await careful examination, notation, translation and exegesis by a linguist, preferably a Yolngu linguist.

In the course of my doctoral studies I examined the musical relationship between the three sound components, voice, sticks and didjeridu in north-east Arnhem Land clan songs and found such accord between them that it seemed that each item had been thoughtfully constructed according to a tight overall plan, with each component referencing, balancing and reinforcing the others. More than that, it seemed to me that the whole song session had a remarkable unity of sound and structure which extended beyond that provided by the consistent ambience of the recording and the use of one singer and one didjeridu throughout.

Each sung item may include three sections. In the first section, labelled Introduction, the singer prepares. He may hum or sing quietly on the notes to be used and begin the stick-beating pattern. The text of this part of the item in this session often provides a comment addressed to the didjeridu player or the audience. The second section, labelled the Song Proper, is the only non-optional part of a sung item. For Yolngu, this is the real song. Here the three sound components work together to produce finely coordinated musical structures. In the third section, labelled Unaccompanied Vocal Termination, sticks and didjeridu are silent, and the voice continues in a somewhat freer pattern until the end of the item. This section is also optional, and Yolngu regard this, like the Introduction, as peripheral. In Dadaynga's performance however, the words in this section are very clearly and emphatically enunciated, and his musical manipulation of melody and rhythm are characteristically deliberate. In his performance, the Unaccompanied Vocal Termination does not tail away as it does with some singers.

Musical phrases are easily distinguished because short notes occur at their beginnings and long notes occur at their ends. In the notations, a bar line indicates the end of a phrase. Where there are consistent rhythmic patterns in bars, a time signature is given simply for ease in reading. In some cases, where bars are of uneven length, no time signature is given. The description of melodic contour is given by means of the concept of pitch areas. A pitch area consists of one or two notes which are used together and discretely in vocal phrases. Their significance for melodic contour is that only one pitch area is used in each musical phrase. The following phrase might use the pitch area of the previous phrase, or might move on to the next, usually lower, pitch area. Notes belonging to different pitch areas would not usually be used together in one phrase. When a pitch area includes two notes, melodic movement between these notes is determined by musical and textual considerations. The higher of the two notes is used for accenting and emphasis when the musical or textual shape of the line requires it. When the descent through the pitch areas is complete, a process occupying several vocal phrases, the singer leaps to the highest pitch area again. The common form of vocal lines is for the voice to begin at the highest pitch area and move down through the other areas. This is referred to as one descent. In the notations, the pitch areas are identified in the boxes which act as key signatures for the vocal line. In notation 2, for example, two pitch areas are identified in the key signature box. The Introduction uses pitch area two. The Song Proper begins at bar two with pitch area one, moving to pitch area two in bar four. At bar six, he moves up to pitch area one again and at bar seven, back to pitch area two which he maintains until the end of the Song Proper. The Unaccompanied Vocal Termination uses both pitch areas, beginning with the higher one, pitch area one, and then falling to pitch area two. There are therefore two descents in the Song Proper and another in the Unaccompanied Vocal Termination. In notation 12, the singer takes the unusual step of beginning on pitch area two, and then moving to the higher pitch area at bar six. Here the lower pitch areas, three and four, are used in the Unaccompanied Vocal Termination. These pitch areas, three and four, echo pitch areas one and two at the lower octave. It is not suggested that this concept of pitch areas is anything other than a useful analytical tool. It is not an inflexible rule, and moving from one pitch area to another is often less stark than this account proposes. Nor is it suggested that singers think of the musical structures in this way. It is merely a pattern observed during analysis.

Twelve of these items have been notated and copies of these notations are given as Appendix A. The music notations include two staves, the upper one for the voice and the lower one for the didjeridu part. Stick beats are indicated on the line between the staves. The song text arrived at by the method just described is noted underneath the vocal line. Two boxes indicating pitches used in the item, one for the voice and one for the didjeridu, are given at the beginning of each item. This takes the place of a key signature. Within the box referring to the vocal part the pitches are divided and numbered according to the pitch areas used in the item. Refrain is the label given to a stick-beating pattern different from that used in the rest of the item. It occurs usually twice, once in the middle of the Song Proper and once at the end. Distinctive didjeridu patterns and vocal texts may also occur in the refrain. A few special signs are used in the didjeridu part to indicate particular didjeridu techniques.

Looking at the session as a whole, it is possible to trace the use of various musical structural elements through, and the following is an abbreviated account, using those items notated as reference points. Contiguous items are listed and group together according to musical style. Usually a notation of one of these items is available. A brief verbal description follows each listed group.

Description of the Session

One didjeridu is used throughout. It has a fundamental at a flat D. The first harmonic is also used and in this instrument it is about a major tenth above the fundamental, at about a flat f sharp. Neither of these pitches is particularly important in the vocal parts.

Group 1:
1   S1973/2: 1 *dhuwinyin* (water snake) 30" Notation 1
2   S1973/2: 2 *dhuwinyin* (water snake) 38"
3   S1972/2: 3 *dhuwinyin* (water snake) 49"
4   S1973/2: 4 *dhuwinyin* (water snake) 46"
5   S1973/2: 5 *wangubini* (cloud) 48"

Two pitch areas are used, first g, and second f and e. The stick pattern consists of slow single beats. The didjeridu uses a pulsating pattern with the upper note only in the terminal pattern. Item 1 is not vocally taxing: it is sung quietly in a slow meditative way appropriate for a vocal warm-up. Subsequent items extend these patterns. In item 2, the two pitch areas are used twice in the Song Proper. The second and third items are each longer as the momentum builds. Item 5 introduces a new song subject, although the musical characteristics remain the same.

Group 2:
6   S1973/2: 6 *wangubini* (cloud) 49"
7   S1973/2:7 *wangubini* (cloud) 56"
8   S1973/2: 8 *wangubini* (cloud) 56"
9   S1973/2: 9 *wangubini* (cloud) 1'6" Notation 2

Items six to nine are similar and are illustrated in notation 2 which is of item 9. The same two pitch areas are used in three descents, but there are new rhythmic patterns in all three parts. The sticks have a pattern leaving every third beat silent. The didjeridu has a pattern using the upper note and a new formal structure with a refrain appearing twice, once in bar seven and once in bar eleven. The enlivened effect is generated by the stronger voice, the new patterns, especially the use of the upper note of the didjeridu. As the longest and liveliest item so far it has the effect of a climax.

Group 3:
10   S1973/2:10 *bara* (cloud) 47" Notation 3
11   S1973/2:11 *bara* (cloud) 45"
12   S1973/2:12 *bara* (cloud) 1'

In item ten, notation 3, a radical change in musical style coincides with a change in song subject. The new musical style has been labelled non-metric, since the lack of both regular rhythmic patterns and of rhythmic coordination between three parts is an outstanding characteristic. The previously used pitch area number one is abandoned, and a new one is added below the previous pitch area two, giving two new pitch areas. The sticks beat fast singles, notated as regular quavers, and the didjeridu plays a pulsating pattern with the upper note used only in the terminating pattern. Item 10, notation 3 presents a great contrast with item number 9, notation 2. The tight rhythmic patterns achieved in item 10 are now completely loosened and the difference is perceived as a relaxation in the musical style

Group 4:
13   S1973/2:13 *bara* (cloud) 52"
14   S1973/2:14 *bara* (cloud) 30"
15   S1973/2:15 *bara* (cloud) 33"
16   S1973/2:16 *bara* (cloud) 46"

After the loosening in items 10 to 12, these four items gradually gather the musical elements together again. The voice takes up the original pitch areas again, and the three parts adopt coordinated rhythmic patterns in groups of four. The stick and didjeridu patterns are drawn in to the accents of the vocal line. Two short 30" items may be seen to indicate musical beginnings.

Group 5:
17   S1973/2: 17 *bara* (cloud) 47"
18   S1973/2: 18 *bara* (cloud) 42" Notation 4
19   S 1973/2: 19 *bara* (cloud) 52"

The next three items, 17 to 19, use the same pitch areas, but triple metres and an extended formal structure. The refrain, in bars 12–13 and 20–21, is marked in the stick part by beating two of the three beats in quavers instead of crotchets, and in the didjeridu part by the use of the upper note. The rhythm of the vocal line is underlined in the didjeridu part. From bar 6, the didjeridu often uses the same rhythm as the vocal line, while the sticks mark the three beats with deliberation. In the stick refrain, the two quavers at the beginning of the bar repeat the familiar vocal rhythm. Once again a longer item of 52 seconds concludes the section.

Group 6:
20   S1973/2: 20 *murunda* (bird) 36"
21   S1973/2: 21 *murunda* (bird) 31"
22   S1973/2: 22 *murunda* (bird) 35"
23   S1973/2: 23 *murunda* (bird) 40"

A new song style and song subject follow in items 20 to 23. These are similar to previous items but extend the phrases and stick patterns into groups of four rather than groups of three.

Group 7:
24   S1973/2:24 *murunda* (bird) 36"
25   S1973/2: 25 *murunda* (bird) 34" Notation 5

An immediate relaxation of musical style is found here. The tightly controlled rhythm of the items in groups 5 and 6 gives way here to a more lackadaisical approach. Phrases and stick patterns are loosely extended into patterns of six, but the three sound components are not exactly together. The rhythmic pulses in the didjeridu part stay more or less within the pattern of the sticks and voice, not tightening up until the last three bars of the Song Proper where a more tightly controlled pattern of four is established. There is no refrain.

Group 8:

26   S1973/2:26 *many'tjarri* (leaves) 29"
27   S1973/2:27 *many'tjarri* (leaves) 29"
28   S1973/2:28 *many'tjarri* (leaves) 39"
29   S1973/2: 29 *gulwiriwi* (cabbage tree palm) 36"
30   S1973/2: 30 *gulwiriwi* (cabbage tree palm) 43"
31   S1973/2: 31 *gulwiriwi* (cabbage tree palm) 31" Notation 6
32   S1973/2: 32 *gulwiriwi* (cabbage tree palm) 38"
33   S1973/2: 33 *gulwiriwi* (cabbage tree palm) 39"
34   S1973/2: 34 *gulwiriwi* and *munoy munoy* (cabbage tree palm and paper bark tree) 36"
35   S1973/2: 35 *gulwiriwi* and *munoy munoy* (cabbage tree palm and paper bark tree) 45"

Ten items, three about *many'tjarri*, five about *gulwiriwi* and two about *gulwiriwi* and *munoy munoy* follow, using similar patterns to those represented in notation 6. These are short, straightforward items using the same two pitch areas, with sticks beating in fast even beats. A refrain is hinted at where the didjeridu uses the upper note, and stick beats conclude with an alternative pattern. The ensemble is gradually tightened, and brought out of the freedom shown in notation 5. Notation 6 shows the regular quaver pattern of the sticks and didjeridu, and the voice also has a great deal of quaver movement.

Group 9:
36   S1973/2: 36 *munoy munoy* (paper bark tree) 30"
37   S1973/2: 37 *munoy munoy* (paper bark tree) 28"
38   S1973/2: 38 *munoy munoy* (paper bark tree) 34"

A change in rhythmic patters with a move to triple metres at item 36 is maintained until item 38.

Group 10:
39   S1973/2: 39 *biwiyik* (bird) 26" Notation 7
40   S1973/2: 40 *biwiyik* (bird) 28"
41   S1973/3: 1 *biwiyik* (bird) 31"
42   S1973/3: 2 *biwiyijk* (bird) 31"

Another rhythmic change occurs at item 39, notation 7. Here the very distinctive text with repetition of the word *didurang* or *didura* is given a particular rhythmic pattern. The sticks beat three crotchets and leave the fourth silent. The didjeridu part is unornamented by the upper note until the last bar of the Song Proper. It is useful to compare notation 7 with notation 8, which is a more developed item about *bewiyik*. Perhaps notation 7 represents an unambiguous statement from the singer about the items which are to follow. It has the air of an announcement.

Group 11:
43   S1973/3: 3 didjeridu mouth sounds only
44   S1973/3:4 *biwiyik* (bird) 33"
45   S1973/3: 5 *biwiyik* (bird) 35" Notation 8

There is a new didjeridu player from item 41, the singer's young son Phillip Marika. The singer's mouth sounds in item 43 are an instruction to his son about how to play the didjeridu for the next items. Notation 8 shows the very steady three beats of the sticks, leaving the fourth beat silent. The didjeridu player attempts a complex pattern using the upper note throughout. After items 44 and 45, the singer says "*yo, manymak*" (yes, good) to the didjeridu player. The song text is an extended version of the skeletal one in notation 7.

Group 12:
46   S1973/3: 6 *biwiyik* (bird) 48"
47   S1973/3: 7 *biwiyik* (bird) 31"
48   S1973/3: 8 *biwiyik* (bird) 34"
49   S1973/3: 9 *biwiyik* (bird) 46"

The next four items, 46 to 49 are still about *bewiyik*, but the rhythmic patterns have changed to groups of three,

Group 13:
50   S1973/3: 10 voice only
51   S1973/3: 11 *gurrumattji* (goose) 50"
52   S1973/3: 12 *gurrumattji* (goose) 40"
53   S1973/3: 13 *gurrumattji* (goose) 50"
54   S1973/3: 14 *djarrak* (seagull) 41"
55   S1973/3: 15 *djarrak* (seagull) 32"
56   S1973/3: 16 *djarrak* (seagull) without didjeridu 30"
57   S1973/3: 17 *djarrak* (seagull) 37"
58   S1973/3: 18 mouth sounds only
59   S1973/3: 19 *djarrak* (seagull) 41" Notation 9
60   S1973/3:20 *djarrak* (seagull) 28"
61   S1973/3: 21 *djarrak* (seagull) 28"

This group continues the teaching part of the session. At item 50, the singer, during a break in the session, sings quietly to himself a diatonic tune covering an octave. The word *yidaki* can be heard, possibly indicating that the young didjeridu player's efforts are still the centre of attention. Item 56 has the singer, without the didjeridu player, going over the vocal line to assist the didjeridu player. In item 51, the pitch levels have dropped a tone. Pitch area one, formerly g, is now f and pitch area 2, formerly f and e is now e and d. Over the next items, until 61, these pitch areas are gradually pushed up. Intervallic relationships are not always exactly maintained as notation 9 demonstrates. At item 60 there is a change in the stick pattern which now uses groups of four.

In item 59, notation 9, where the young didjeridu player was being given some practice, the words of the Introduction were translated by Larrtjanga as "If I change that *manikay* singing then you stop your *yidaki*." Notation 9 illustrates the very straightforward early part of the item where voice, stick and didjeridu all have four crotchets per bar, and in the later part, the young didjeridu player's valiant attempts at the more difficult didjeridu part.

Group 14:
62   S1973/3: 22 *djarrak* (seagull) 39" Notation 10
63   S1973/3: 23 *djarrak* (seagull) 35"
64   S1973/3: 24 *djarrak* (seagull) 57"
65   S1973/3: 25 *djarrak* (seagull) 49"
66   S1973/3: 26 *djarrak* (seagull) 52"
67   S1973/3: 27 *djarrak* (seagull) 52"
68   S1973/3: 28 *gudurrku* (brolga) 39"
69   S1973/3: 29 voice only – interrupted
70   S1973/3: 30 *gudurrku* (brolga) 30"
71   S1973/3: 31 *gudurrku* (brolga) 31"
72   S1973/3: 32 *gudurrku* (brolga) 31" Notation 11

WE SING NOW: A RIRRATJINGU SONG SESSION

Micky Mununggur takes over the didjeridu here, and his experience is immediately audible in the more confident handling of the didjeridu. The croaked note associated with brolga items is heard in the second last bar of item 62, notation 10, and the initial hummed note is apparent in item 72 notation 11. Faster tempo and more complex parts are evident in this group. Three entirely new pitch areas are used, the whole covering a range of nearly an octave. The sticks have a completely new pattern. Vocal refrains of trilled notes, imitating birdcalls, are heard in items 64, 65, 66 and 67.

Group 15:
73   S1973/3:33 *gudurrku* (brolga) 28"
74   S1973/3: 34 *gudurrku* (brolga) 32"
75   S1973/3: 35 *gapu* (water) 29"
76   S1973/3: 36 *gapu* (water) 25"
77   S1973/3: 37 *gapu* (water) 35"
78   S1973/3: 38 *gapu* (water) 34"
79   S1973/3: 39 *gapu* (water) 36"
80   S1973/3: 40 *gapu* (water) 38"
81   S1973/3:41 *gapu* (water) 38" Notation 12
82   S1973/3: 42 *gapu* (water) 36"

Four pitch areas, the two lower ones providing a lower octave echo of the upper two are used through this series of items. This has two effects. It rests the singer's voice by allowing him to vary the pitch considerably, and it adds musical interest as the session is coming to an end. These concluding items provide a heightened tension which suggests a climax at the end of the session. The musicians knew where the end of the session would be since they and other singers recorded during those years watched the reel-to-reel tape on the recorder and kept a check on when the end of the tape was coming up. The song texts for *gapu* (water) contain a great deal more repetition than earlier items. From item 78, there are fast stick beating patterns, and the overall tempo pushes up. The didjeridu is energetic and forceful, with liberal use of the upper note in fast intricate patterns. In bar 6 of notation 12, the single crotchet stick beats, and the stressing of the regular beat in the didjeridu part throw the more complicated stick patterns and syncopated didjeridu parts of other bars into strong relief. The brilliance of this didjeridu part can be shown by comparing this item with notation 2. There, the upper note is used throughout in a bright regular pattern, but here in notation 12, the accent provided by the upper note is continually shifted in the bar, giving the very characteristic energy of north-east Arnhem Land didjeridu parts.

An encompassing view

The session begins with a slow reflective item, the voice soft and sticks and didjeridu in gentle undemanding patterns. The session concludes with fast energetic and flamboyant patterns. There are sub-climaxes such as at item 9, where the duration of items has gradually built up from 30" to 1'6". After item 9 a new beginning is made with quite different patterns. The music ebbs and flows as the session continues and this movement from short slow items to long fast complex patterns suggests that the musicians recognised and manipulated the impact of the overall structure.

Text and tune

If it is legitimate to ask whether the words or the musical forms take precedence in north-east Arnhem Land *manikay* style, and if the final forms can be expected to provide some clues to this question, then it seems to me that items 10 (notation 3) on the one hand and items 45 (notation 8) and 59 (notation 9) on the other hand sketch two extremes. In notation 3 there is no tight correlation between voice, stick and didjeridu parts, and no consistent metrical divisions in the vocal part. This particular musical form is very adaptable and could accommodate syllable strings of almost any length. Notation 8, on the other hand, shows a very strong correlation between the three sound components, not only metrically, in that each part falls in bars consisting of four beats, but there is considerable rhythmic imitation between the parts, in that the fourth stick beat is often silent and the upper note of the didjeridu is heard only during the first two beats of each phrase. In notation 9 the correlation is even stronger with four plain crotchets in each part for the three bars of the Song Proper. The detailing that is then introduced in stick and didjeridu parts is typical of the elaboration so musically employed by these musicians. These two patterns of relationship between words and musical form demonstrate two opposing possibilities, and indicate the range of possible structural mechanisms available.

Song subject and musical form
In several items, the singer begins with the word *wangganya* which Larrtjanga translated as 'one more'. In some cases for example in item 19, it comes at the beginning of the last item about *bara* (cloud), the following item moving on to deal with *murunda* (bird). Item 13, another where Dadaynga sings *wangganya* at the beginning of the Introduction, is also about *bara* and so is item 14, so the reference here is not to song subject.

Items 1 to 5 and 6 to 9 present another challenge. Items 1 to 5 are very similar and significantly different from the following ones. The song subject changes at item 5. The first 4 are about *duwinyin* (snake) and the following five are about *wangubini* (cloud). The change in song subject does not coincide with the change in musical style.

Conclusions
The analysis and conclusions clearly suggest the improvisatory nature of this performance, and emphasize the difference between these performances and those of north-central and north-west Arnhem Land which seem to be much more fixed. On looking at this material, Ronald Berndt commented that these songs would not usually be sung together. Perhaps the singer here was playing with the material, improvising, and treating it creatively. In that case, the session might show a fluidity which allowed the creativity of the musicians an unusually full scope.

The structure of north-east Arnhem Land clan songs and the relationship between musical structure and social structure have been the subjects of considerable and long standing academic argument. Ronald Berndt (1966: 196) for example, whose studies were mainly concerned with texts, says that the tunes are more stable than the words. Alice Moyle (1967: 27) reports the opposite – that the words are more stable than the tunes. Recent studies by Knopoff (1998), Toner (2003) and Corn (2007) make interesting contributions. In 1974 a Yolngu musician gave me a list of names and explanations for stick beating patterns, including one whose translation repeated word for word a definition I learnt as a child for *andante* – easy walking pace. However as we discussed the differences between the patterns and attempted to reconcile them with recorded song items, the musician became uncomfortable with the lack of congruity we were exposing and eventually excused himself. I still hold to the position taken in 1978, that all these studies have something of relevance to contribute to an understanding of Arnhem Land *manikay* style, and that there will probably not be a satisfactory conclusion to the arguments until we have a thoroughgoing study of Yolngu musical theory which can be shown to illuminate the wide variety of musical forms of Yolngu *manikay*. My discussions with Yolngu musicians in the 1970s lead me to believe that such a theory would take account of not just melodic contour, but also vocal timbre, tempo, song text, stick beating patterns, didjeridu patterns, duration and the context of performance.

Notation 1 item 1
dhuwinyin (water snake) S1973/2:1

*Where two notes appear side by side with an accent on the first tied by a broken slur to the second, the second note is lightly pulsated but not tongued.

Notation 2 item 9
wangubini (cloud) S1973/2:9

The figure in the vocal part sometimes written as two semi-quavers and a quaver (bars 2, 3, 4 etc.), and sometimes as a triplet of three quavers (bars 6 and 13) is something between the two.

Notation 3 item 10
bara (cloud) S1973/2:10

v
sts
dj
ma-wi e
bi-djan dha-wu-nhan
ma-ta - wir
ma-pa-yin
may - ngum - ba
buy buy buy buy buy buy buy buy buy
Unaccompanied vocal termnation
gunhdhu-ri - wanh gunhdhu-ri - wanh nyaku - ra may - ngu may - ngum - ba dhum - bi - lir

Notation 4 item 18
bara (cloud) S1973/2:18

Notation 5 item 24
murunda (bird) S1973/2:24

In bars 2-6 the sticks slightly anticipate the beat.

Notation 6 item 31
gulwiri (cabbage tree palm) S1973/2:31

Notation 7 item 39
bewiyik (bird) S1973/2:39

Notation 8 item 45
hewiyik (bird) S1973/3:5

Notation 9 item 59
djarrak (seagull) S1973/3:19

Notation 10 item 62
djarrak (seagull) S1973/3:22

*The x signifies a croaked note.

Notation 11 item 72
gudurrku (brolga) S1973/3:32

*The note enclosed in a circle is hummed.

Notation 12 item 80
gapu (water) S1973/3:41

Unaccompanied
vocal termination
12
v
sts
dj
gi - ri - ring gi - ri - ring gi - ri - ring gi - ri - ring
gi - ri - ri - ring gi - ri - ri - ring
ga la - ra nya - ku ga - pu
v
sts
dj
bar wu la ri - ya - la ni ning gur
ma da wal ma da wal gi - ri ring gi - ri ring lu ru na - nyin dju ku lu - lu

References

Anderson, Gregory. 1992 *Murlarra: a clan song series from Central ArnhemLand*. (PhD thesis) The University of Sydney.
Anderson, Gregory D. 1995 "Striking a balance: limited variability in performances of a clan song series from Central Arnhem Land." In *The essence of singing and the substance of song: recent responses to the Aboriginal performing and arts and other essays in honour of Catherine Ellis*. Ed. Linda Barwick, Allan Marett, Guy Tunstill. Sydney: University of Sydney 12–25.
Berndt, Ronald M. 1966 "The Wuradilagu song cycle of north-eastern Arnhem Land." In *The anthropologist looks at myth* Ed. J. Greenway. Austin: University of Texas Press, 195–243.
Clunies Ross, Margaret and Stephen A. Wild. 1982. *Djambidj: an Aboriginal song series from northern Australia*. Canberra: Australian Institute of Aboriginal Studies.
Corn, Aaron. 2007 "*Buḏutthun ratja wiyinmirri*: formal flexibility in Yolngu *manikay* tradition and the challenge of recording a complete repertoire," *Australian Aboriginal Studies* 2: 116-127.
Knopoff, Steven. 1992 "Yuta manikay: juxtaposition of ancestral and contemporary elements in the performance of Yolngu clan songs," *Yearbook for Traditional Music* 24: 138–153.
Knopoff, Steven. 1997 "Accompanying the Dreaming." In *The Didjeridu: From Arnhen Land to Internet* Ed. Karl Neuenfeldt. Sydney: John Libbey and Perfect BeatPublications 39–67.
Knopoff, Steven. 1998 "Yolngu clansong scalar structures." In *The Garland Encyclopedia of World Music Volume 9 Australia and the Pacific Islands* Ed. Adrienne L. Kaeppler and J.W. Love. New York and London: Garland Publishing, Inc. 301–302.
Marett, Allan. 2005 *Songs, Dreamings, and Ghosts: The Wangga of North Australia*. Middletown, Connecticut: Wesleyan University Press.
Moyle, Alice M. 1967. *Songs from the Northern Territory Companion Booklet*. Canberra: Australian Institute of Aboriginal Studies.
Stubington, Jill. 1978 *Yolngu manikay: Modern Performances of Australian Aboriginal Clan Songs*. (PhD thesis) Monash University.
Stubington, Jill. 1984 "Extended review of Djambidj: an Aboriginal song series from Northern Australia." *Australian Aboriginal Studies* 1: 68–76.
Stubington, Jill. 2007 *Singing the Land: The Power of Performance in Aboriginal Life*. Sydney: Currency House.
Toner, Peter. 2003 "Melody and the musical articulation of Yolngu identities," *Yearbook for Traditional Music* 35: 69–95.

24: What does it mean to be a good teacher?

Stephen Hough

What does it mean to be a good teacher – of anything? Especially of music, when nothing can really be taught that can't then have a doubt cast upon it. The pianist, Sviatoslav Richter, when asked if he taught, apparently replied, 'No. What if I were wrong?' But the French novelist, Julien Green, teaching English literature in America during the Second World War, wrote, more helpfully, that if a student left his class after graduation and still wanted to read books then he felt that his teaching has been a success.

We can cast the pearls of facts, dogmas, suggestions or experiences at the feet of our students, but only nurturing can make them want to form a necklace out of them, and then wear it for life. The teachers who I remember as being the greatest influence on me were not those who presented me with folios of facts to pick through, but rather the ones whom I first respected and loved as human beings. I learned more from Gordon Green's roaring laugh as he removed his pipe from his mouth than I did from the smoky words which followed. I learned more from Douglas Steele's rapt face as he played Debussy's *Hommage* à *Rameau* (week after week – he would forget he had played it for me seven days earlier) than I did from his examination of, and comments on, my compositions. I learned more from Robert Mann's intense concentration as he tried to match a phrase I'd just played in a Beethoven violin sonata than any comment he might have made after the run-through.

Example and encouragement … and a big heart. If we tighten people's hearts they may keep beating, but they will do so with less freedom, less joy, less productivity, less responsibility, less creativity. To let someone loose to make mistakes and not to care is the first step to a perfect performance – if not always in notes, then certainly in spirit. To welcome warmly a student into the room who came last in a competition the previous week is to begin the process through which he or she might come first the following year. Every stone tripped upon creates the possibility of unearthing a truffle underneath.